SPELLBINDING

SPELLBINDING

MICHELE HAUF

NINA CROFT
ELLE JAMES
SERESSIA GLASS
LAUREN HAWKEYE

MILLS & BOON

Published in Great Britain 2014
by Mills & Boon, an imprint of Harlequin (UK) Limited,
Eton House, 18-24 Paradise Road, Richmond, Surrey, TW9 1SR

SPELLBINDING © 2014 Harlequin Books S.A.

This Soul Magic © 2013 Michele Hauf
The Darkness © 2010 Nicola Cleasby
The Witch's Seduction © 2013 Mary Jernigan
Seducing the Jackal © 2013 Seressia Glass
Some Like It Wicked © 2013 Lauren Hawkeye

ISBN: 978 0 263 91389 7

89-0314

THIS SOUL MAGIC

MICHELE HAUF

A Minnesota native, **Michele Hauf** lives in a Minneapolis suburb with her family. She enjoys being a stay-at-home mum with a son and a daughter. Michele writes the kind of stories she loves to read, filled with romance, fantasy, adventure and always set in France. Though she has yet to leave the US, since her family knows that, once gone, she might set up house in a little French village and never return! Always a storyteller, she began to write in the early nineties and hasn't stopped since. Playing guitar, hunting backyard butterflies and colouring (yes, colouring) keep her creativity honed. For more information on Michele's books visit michelehauf.com. You can also contact Michele at: PO Box 23, Anoka, MN 55303, USA.

Chapter One

I am a mortal man.

I'm not sure how I feel about losing my immortality. I gave it up freely.

For a woman.

Did I make the right decision? It's too soon to know. It has only been a week since I changed from an all-powerful soul bringer to mere mortal. Yet the woman does seem like a good trade-off. To be a part of Libertie St. Charles's world is a wonder and a learning experience....

I, Reichardt Fallowgleam, watched through the kitchen window from Libby's hexagon house as the bold redheaded witch wandered through the backyard garden, here and there plucking a petal to nestle in her basket of spell supplies.

The sun shone in her candied hair like the clear coat on a Maserati. (I find that car the only thing capable of distracting me from Libby.) Her hips rocked to a rhythm I couldn't hear. She wore the earbuds often, listening to music from the tiny metal box clipped at her hip. There were so many kinds of music, and I was just dipping my toes into Libby's favorite genre, country. I had to take it slow, though. So much to overload my new senses in this world—like shiny red cars.

Generously curved hips shifted side to side, swaying her gorgeous bottom and the flirty hem of her purple skirt. Libby's ample curves filled my hands whenever I put them on her. Everywhere I touched her she was soft and so warm.

Yet I had a lot to learn about touching a woman.

I'd tallied over two thousand years in my lifetime, yet thanks to recent events, I now felt as new and lacking in experience as a newborn. Once I'd been a soul bringer, an angel forced to Fall from Above and assigned to collect souls from this realm immediately following the death of the mortal body. Constantly—24/7, as Libby referred to it—I'd delivered souls to Above and Beneath without regard or judgment for the destination. I had known nothing else.

Save for the woman now smiling at me from over her shoulder.

I waved to Libby and received a wink in return. Her long lashes, which she lengthened with some fancy black stuff from a stick, drew me to her green eyes. Green like thick moss coating a lush forest floor. Mesmerizing. Made my heart shudder in a good way.

My heart hadn't beaten until a week ago.

Apparently, as the soul bringer, I had taken Libby's soul, and her sister Vika's soul, as well, because I felt I'd been owed after Vika had inadvertently stolen souls from my usual daily rounds. The theft hadn't been purposeful on Vika's part; she was a witch possessed of a sticky soul who attracted lingering souls, those myself and other soul bringers couldn't get to quickly enough.

According to Libby's report, I'd been unemotional and hadn't cared less to strip the sisters of their most prized possession. Vika's boyfriend, a dark witch named Certainly Jones, had offered up his soul in trade. I had refused the offer.

When the dark witch had found the halo that contained my earthbound soul—lost after my fall to the mortal realm millennia ago—and had offered it in trade for the sisters' souls, apparently I had also refused. To have a soul would strip me of my powers and condemn me to mortality. It would also strip away memory of my angelic life.

What I knew now was only what Libby had told me after the transformation. Yet I could remember why I had finally decided to take that deal. I had looked into Libby's eyes, and she had promised she would be there for me. And I'd remembered all the times she'd offered me chocolate-chip cookies when I'd come to scrub her sister of souls. Something about the feisty red-haired woman had rapped against my glass heart.

Placing a hand over my heart now, I was glad I'd made that choice. Yet I regretted the lost power. Libby had detailed the few times she'd seen me move objects or command people to act against their will. I had shaken entire buildings and brought the rain and lightning to this realm. Fierce stuff, that.

Now, to look at my hands, I felt…less. As if I was missing something. The air also felt wrong. Heavy upon my shoulders. Intrusive.

Beyond that ineffable longing, I did look forward to learning emotions, something I'd never utilized while immortal. But had the sacrifice of power been worth this new step as a mortal?

I needed to find out.

He was watching me again. The attention made my ears grow warm and my core tingle. And yet I guessed Reichardt wasn't sure *why* he was watching me. The man was like a babe venturing through the big bright world. Certainly he knew the world and all its trappings—he'd retained that knowledge after gaining his earthbound soul—but he didn't know how to use his newly beating heart.

I intended to help him learn.

Because I, Libby St. Charles, was all about indulging one's pleasures. And if the sexy new mortal fell in love with me, then who was I to protest?

Plucking a few sprigs of potent dill for a cleaning spell I wanted to try the next time Vika and I were called to do a job,

I placed it in my basket, along with various flowers and herbs. Turning, I sashayed down the stone garden path toward the French doors at the back of the kitchen. A tune hummed in my brain. I loved to listen to music while concocting spells and hoped to turn Reichardt on to music, as well.

Baby steps, I said to myself, reminding of my big plans. I didn't want to overwhelm the man and push him away.

Yet this was the first time I'd known—deep down in the depths of my soul—that a man was for me. Even when he'd been the emotionless soul bringer and had almost stolen my soul, I had loved him.

I believed in soul mates, because the universe could be sneaky like that.

Reichardt is my soul mate. Now I just need to make him believe it.

The house I had shared with my sister since we were children was a white hexagon tucked in a cozy neighborhood of Paris's fourth quarter. According to the nineteenth-century builder's notes, each of the six outer walls had been positioned to face a celestial body and was aligned with the planets. An excellent place to practice magic, and, while warded against vampires and werewolves, my sister and I had decided against warding it for soul bringers and angels. We didn't want it to repel Reichardt should he retain any latent angel mojo.

Which, I suspected, did linger. Because the man glowed. More like an aura of all colors permeated off his being. I had seen auras on people. They came and went, sometimes very obvious, other times elusive. Reichardt's aura was bold, yet sometimes it blinked at me as if it were a lightbulb losing its juice.

Remnants from his previous existence? If so, I would love to get my magical hands into that and stir it up a bit. I'd always preferred the paranormal types over a plain mortal, so adjusting to Reichardt's new status would take some doing.

My big, handsome former soul bringer opened the glass-paned door for me. So tall and built like a Spartan warrior,

I mused, though his features were forged from all nations. Though his name sounded German, angelic in origin, the man must represent all walks of life.

When he held his arms out to receive me I wasn't sure it was because he wanted to hug me, or because I'd explained to him a hug was something friends did, and even people who were more than friends.

But resist his powerful embrace? Never. The man's muscles had been forged by angelic means.

I intended to keep the cookies available, but not in such great quantities that he became a softy. That was my department. I might wear a double-digit size, but I was proud of my curves, and especially liked the way his hands slid over those curves as if exploring uncharted territory.

"The air is better now," he whispered in that stalwart tone that always tightened my nipples in anticipation.

I had no idea what he meant by *better air*, but he'd said it a few times before. The heat of his iron-hard body lulled me into a swoon and I laid my head against his biceps. Happy to be there. *Let this fantasy never end.*

When a few flowers fell from the basket hooked at my elbow, I reluctantly pulled from the hug and twisted to pick them up.

Reichardt commented, "Now *that* I could look at all day."

"What? My ass?" I straightened and wiggled my hips. "You can touch."

"Really?"

Such innocent devilishness in the man's tone. Monsieur Sex on a Stick had it all, yet was naively unaware of what that *all* did to a woman.

He slid his hands down my hips and cupped my derriere, growling a satisfied purr, and whispered at my ear. "Teach me about kissing."

"Oh, lover, I adore your curiosity."

We'd kissed once, before he'd gotten a soul. It had been a means for me to distract him from harming Vika—and it had worked. At the time I had almost thought Reichardt had been all in with the emotions and fresh love thing, until he'd then taken my soul.

But now was different. He'd hadn't the power, let alone the heart, to enact such an evil scheme.

"Or will this stop me from getting too close?" he asked, tapping the object strung around my neck on a thin leather cord.

I touched my grandmother's nail, coiled about the leather. All three St. Charles sisters wore one of the nails that had been pounded into our grandmother's jaw by a witch hunter in order to keep her down during the burial process, following a vicious dunking that had ended in her death. The nail possessed power and acted as a sort of protector.

"Grandma would approve, I'm sure, lover."

"Why do you call me lover?" he asked. "We aren't lovers, as far as I know."

"It's just a pet name," I said, batting my lashes coyly. "You don't like it?"

"I do like it. It would be more fitting if it were true."

The man was big on truths and morality, which clashed only a little with my energy. I hated lies and tried to be as moral as a witch possibly could. Did chocolate binges and crushes on celebrities count against my moral compass?

I trailed a finger along his chin, tapping the black goatee that called attention to his rugged square jaw and gave him some rock-star appeal. "Soon enough, lover boy, soon enough. Much as I'd love to push you onto the floor and ravage your sexy body, I think it best we take things slow."

"Is ravaging good?"

"Ravaging is the bomb. But let's do something about the kisses first. You want to learn?"

"Such a lesson would prove more interesting than how to mow the lawn or sweep the floor."

So I'd been teaching him a few domestic skills. *Every man should know the routine, am I right?*

"Come here." I grabbed his shirt and pulled him close enough to feel his breath against my chin.

The man's eyes had retained the kaleidoscopic colors innate to angels. Every time I looked into them I saw a different color, from blue or gold to violet and even emerald. I could stare into them for hours.

"What do you see?" he asked with a concern that gave me a tickle.

"Curiosity."

And that flickering multicolored aura that I had no intention of telling him about, because to do so would distract from my goal of a kiss.

"That's because I am curious." He squeezed my derriere. "I like this part of you. It's soft and fills my hand."

"Oh, lover, what did I do to deserve you?"

"From what you've told me, you gave me back my soul."

Indeed, I had held his halo—which contained his earthbound soul—above his head but a week ago. That had caused Reichardt to rise from the ground, the halo affixed above his head. Briefly, Vika and I had witnessed the blue smoke wings Reichardt had never worn as a soul bringer, and had watched them shatter into so much angel dust, leaving the man lying unconscious in the garden before us. It had been a beautiful yet frightening experience.

"Come here," I coaxed. "A little closer so our mouths almost touch, but not quite."

He smelled like the homemade bay rum soap I'd slipped into his shower a few days ago to stock his barren apartment. I loved a spicy man, and it was all I could do not to hook a foot behind his knee and throw him to the black-and-white harlequin-tiled kitchen floor.

Patience, Libby.

But not too patient. This woman had needs and desires that demanded attention. How long could a girl be happy with a fumbling beginner when what she really needed was a skilled lover to master her mind, body and soul?

"Your breath on my skin feels good," he said. "I know your lips are soft because they are the color of the rose petals in the garden."

Mercy, but the man was a romantic without even trying.

"You don't remember, but we've kissed before," I said. "When I was trying to distract you from taking Vika's soul."

"I wish I could remember. I've lost so much."

"I'll refresh your memory."

"Should I tilt my head?"

"No, I'll do that. You just let it happen."

I pressed my mouth to his and spread my hands across his rock-hard pectorals. I had to stand on my tiptoes, which gave me a thrill because—hell, it just did. The connection—no movement, just touching—activated all my nerve endings to scream *pleasure* and *feed me*.

I gripped him by the back of the head, running my fingertips through his short dark hair, and deepened the kiss. The man's mouth was receptive and so hot. Spice teased my senses. I could have stayed right there all day. *Oh, to bespell his heart and make him mine!*

The guy was mine. *Let no woman dare to take him from me. Wait. Really? Claiming the guy?* I was being too forward.

Breaking the kiss, I stepped away, smoothing my hands down my dress. "Whew! Sorry about that."

He touched his lips and shrugged. "Sorry for what? I liked it. Did I do it wrong?"

"Not at all."

His brows fell and his mouth pouted. The puppy dog had been denied a treat.

Shame on me. Libby St. Charles was not the denial sort. Be damned this too-forward business. I tended to take what I desired, and if it made me feel good, I'd overindulge.

"All righty then, here goes nothing, lover boy."

This time I dashed my tongue across his, coaxing him to a sensual dance that teased at my inhibitions like a feather tracing me from head to toe. Every part of my skin craved contact with his. Clothing felt bothersome. And when I wanted him to dip me backward and make me his, the man simply took what I gave.

So I would become the teacher. He would learn, and then take the control I wanted him to own.

Sliding my hands down over his, I moved them lower on my hips. Reichardt squeezed and I moaned into his mouth. "You squeeze all you like, lover."

"So much of you to enjoy," he murmured, and this time he initiated the kiss.

He pressed my body against the counter and probably wasn't aware how hard he leaned into me. I didn't care. I wanted to be controlled by a man, needed it. His mouth, firm and seeking, tasted my lips and a murmur of satisfaction was my reward for this teaching session. I loved every moment of this connection, even his awkward movements as he tilted his head one way and then the other.

And when I felt his erection harden and lengthen against my mons—oh, baby. Did I mention I was a master of overindulgence?

"Uh…" Breaking the kiss, Reichardt looked down at his groin. "I'm not sure…"

"That's supposed to happen," I said sweetly and traced his moist lower lip with my finger. "That means you're doing things right."

"It's so…hard. I feel as if I want to…"

I lifted a brow, waiting for him to list his fantasies about me. I could ramble off a salacious litany for him. But one step at a time. It was going to be difficult to control my urges around this man.

"I need a moment to myself." Reichardt dashed out of the kitchen and through the swinging French doors.

Turning to the flower petals in the sink, I whistled a tune about two lovers finding one another. The former soul bringer had never had sex. I had myself a two-thousand-year-old virgin.

And I had so many great plans for him.

Chapter Two

While I dressed, Libby waited out in my starkly furnished living room. She was an early bird, or so I'd heard that expression in the market the other morning as we'd shopped for milk and bread and the apricot jam I enjoyed.

I liked to linger in bed, tucked between the sheets that smelled like cedar. If I wasn't so compelled to become a useful, working part of society, I could entirely imagine becoming a bum who slept and ate his way through life.

I noticed the blue feather lying on the floor before the bed and picked it up. When I moved my fingers over the vanes, they shivered as if liquid yet felt cold and hard like iron. It was my feather. Libby said she'd found it in the pile of crystal ash that had remained after my wings had shattered and fallen away.

"Wings," I murmured. "Could I get them back?"

I flexed my shoulders and spread out my arms, wondering what wings must have felt like. How large had they been? What purpose might they have served in the mortal realm? Had they been blue like this feather?

I overheard Libby out in the living room, on the phone with her sister, chatting about everything from cleaning solutions and getting blood stains out of vinyl couches to the latest music and—me.

My ears perked, my arms dropping the imaginary wings.

"He's doing well. Still pretty weak. I wonder if he'll always be so? He's the muscles of a workhorse, but he can barely lift the vacuum."

I clasped my hands across my chest, inadvertently squeezing a bicep. The muscle was hard, and it seemed I should be stronger. It bothered Libby that I couldn't do some things? Hell, I'd needed her to help me move around the sofa. Shouldn't a man be able to do that himself?

"Yes, he's adjusting. CJ did that? I couldn't imagine Reichardt lifting a washing machine to let me get to the dust beneath."

I winced. Indeed, I needed to become stronger to gain Libby's admiration. I'd seen the commercials on the television that featured muscle-bound men lifting heavy weights. Women swooned over them.

A man of my stature and with all these muscles shouldn't be so weak. It had to do with transforming from a soul bringer to a mortal, I felt sure. If I had once traveled from Above and Beneath, I must have had some crazy powers. And Libby had detailed how I'd once lifted CJ and Vika with no more than my mind and had speared them with an invisible bolt that had left them bleeding.

I'd been a cruel man. But I'd also been strong.

I wanted to win Libby's respect. I just had to figure out how.

After hanging up with my sister, I waited for Reichardt to finish dressing. The man shouldn't cover up those washboard abs, but okay, so it was autumn and raining, and—still. It hurt my sense of wanting to drool over man muscle, but I'd have to deal. The man preferred all black clothes because he said putting colors together hurt his brain.

Boys. Gotta love 'em.

After he'd gotten his soul—and before his memory of being

a soul bringer had been completely vanquished—Vika and I had quickly learned Reichardt kept an apartment in the fifth quarter, in the shadow of the Jardin des Plantes, and discovered it was empty: no furniture, no food, not even clothing. Just a few odd items sitting on windowsills and counters. The blue feather, a half-full bag of cat food, a yellow-cloth Jewish badge and a live sansevieria plant that looked well cared for.

We'd also learned the entire nineteenth-century building belonged to Reichardt. The building manager had explained their beneficent owner hadn't charged rent in over two decades. The elderly building residents, upon seeing Reichardt, had offered a "bonjour, Monsieur Reichardt," and one had told me that while the stoic building owner never chatted, he always ensured the residents were well through a liaison who visited them monthly to check medical stats and ensure their bills were paid, and who also sent food when needed.

I strolled my fingers along the glossy blade leaves of the sansevieria plant now. Quite the fellow, my emotionless and uncaring soul bringer.

We'd decided Reichardt should remain at his place, because when I had suggested he move in with me, he couldn't get around the idea of it being sinful if we were not married. The man's morals were old-fashioned yet sweet, and I didn't want to rush him into the twenty-first century too quickly.

That sounded good in theory, anyway.

"Ready!" He looked over my black-and-white polka-dotted dress and skimmed his fingers along the fringes that hemmed the skirt.

"It's my rock-star dress," I said, tilting out a hip and hooking a hand akimbo. I could work a fringe like nobody's sister.

"But you're not a rock star. Or are you? You're so talented—perhaps I've not seen all that you can do."

"No, lover boy, I am not a rock star. But sometimes you gotta put on the fringe and rock out, you know?"

"No." He eyed me curiously.

Poor amnesiac man. He took everything literally. It was

kind of sad and yet a little fun to know I would get to teach him everything he needed to learn.

"Stick with me, Reichardt. You'll be rocking with the best of them soon enough. Did you ever figure out the cat food?"

"No, but perhaps there is a stray that visits on occasion?"

"I hope so. I love kitties. Though Salamander might be jealous if I went home smelling like another cat." Sal was Vika's cat, but since moving in with CJ, she'd left him behind. She never had been a cat person. "Let's go."

Outside, we slid into the white hearse I drove for our cleaning business. I'd stuck a sticker that read Jiffy Clean on the trunk years ago as a joke. It annoyed Vika.

Vika and I cleaned up dead paranormals such as slain werewolves, demons and the occasional newer vampire who didn't completely ash at death. Couldn't have the mortals seeing such nightmares lying about the city. Cleaning was Vika's life. Since the rock-star thing would probably never happen and my small flower garden brought in a pitiful amount at the bazaar, I had to do something to earn a euro.

I drove down the street toward the witch's bazaar, a place I visited every other Saturday to buy and sell spellcraft items, pick up pointers, and chatter with fellow witches.

"Do you have male friends?" Reichardt asked out of the blue.

"Of course I do. A life without men is dull and a little too clean. Why do you ask?"

"I have the feeling I should talk to a man," he said. "To learn things that a woman can't teach me."

"Like what?" I asked cheerfully, excited he was asking for knowledge.

"Like how to get stronger, and how to treat a woman."

"Best way to learn that is from the source. Trust me on that one."

"What about how to sexually fulfill a woman?"

My neck grew hot yet my grin may have touched both ears.

I met Reichardt's sweetly wondering gaze in the rearview mirror. "Again, the source would be your best bet."

He crossed his arms, uncomfortable with the suggestion. Hell, the guy could have used a male friend. Just because the best information came from the source didn't mean it was easy to ask about the intimate stuff.

"You remember CJ, Vika's guy?"

"Yes, Certainly Jones, the dark witch with the curious tattoos."

"Mmm, I love a tattooed man."

"Is that so?" Reichardt considered that one a moment. "But why is he dark?"

"He practices dark magic to balance the light, which is what Vika and I practice. Yin and yang. It's a karma thing."

"Karma is the universe, yes?"

"Exactly."

"Do you think I could talk to CJ? No offense, Libby, but there are things that...come up." He looked aside and was suddenly very interested in the door lock.

I recalled our embrace in the kitchen when he'd gotten an erection. If the guy wanted to learn how to use that, then perhaps it was time to call in Team Man.

"I'll give CJ a call once we get to the bazaar. I'm sure he'd love to get together with you and talk man stuff."

"Thank you. I don't mind the cleaning tasks you've taught me, but I feel there are more manly things I should be learning. Like how to drive this vehicle. Shouldn't the man drive the woman?"

"I can teach you how to drive. But let's concentrate on getting your immediate needs met first."

Like learning how to please a woman, I thought with a sneaky curl of lip. I'd have this guy eating out of my hands soon enough.

I pulled into a parking space and Reichardt got out and rushed around to my side. He opened the door, which had never once happened in my dating history. He already knew how to please a woman. What the man really needed was confidence and a sense of place in this realm.

The bazaar was indeed bizarre. I wandered the aisles in the small church basement—yes, the witches gathered in a former Catholic church. How about that for irony? And I did know irony, which pleased me into a grin as I passed a table featuring Charms to Devastate and Divulge.

The room was populated with all varieties, from normal-looking women and men to those sporting outrageous clothing and hair and a few with tattooed faces. I thought the one with the tiny wings at her back was a faery, but what would she be doing here?

"You want me to show you around?" Libby asked as she handed me a paper cup of coffee.

I loved coffee—it was like mead—and I guessed I might have drunk mead if I'd come from Above. Maybe?

"I think I'll just take it all in, if that's all right with you. Go and do what you must. I like watching you walk away from me."

Blowing me a kiss, Libby sashayed down the aisle, her hips swaying and the fringes bouncing. She wiggled her torso in that sexy groove that made things on me very hard. I needed to talk to CJ soon. I wanted to get my hands all over that woman's bounce, yet when I did, things came up. Things that felt great yet, I knew, required further research.

I strolled past a table that sold various vials of blood in all gradients of crimson. Werewolf blood, vampire blood, faery ichor, kitsune blood and black demon blood. Mermaid blood was a tint of green. What were the uses for such things? Did I really want to know?

Sipping the last of the coffee, I turned abruptly and bumped into a tall, thin woman clad in frumpy black with snow-white hair that fell like silk about her shoulders. She spun, revealing pointed teeth and a pale face, and hissed at me.

That hiss disturbed me so much I flinched and stepped back.

She tracked me backward until my shoulders hit the wall and a tendril of dried garlic bobbed at my head. When she stuck a finger in the air before my face I felt as if I'd been struck by invisible magic. Hell, who could know in a room full of witches?

"You're different," she said with a craggy voice that belonged buried under tangled tree roots. "Not the same as you once were."

That summation was difficult not to question. "What do you know about me?"

"I see it. Your aura. It's all colors. Never see that unless it's an angel, don't you know."

I clamped my jaws shut before blurting out my truth. How she'd guessed such a thing was beyond me. Yet I supposed it wasn't a big secret. Could those with paranormal proclivities *see* what I had once been?

"I can feel your yearning."

"I—don't yearn." Yet, in fact, I did just that.

"You do. And for more than what men yearn for."

"Is that so?" Because I'd learned that most men did yearn for the red sports car.

"You want what was once yours."

Damned good guess. Did she also know I desired Libby? "And...just how would I get that? What was once mine."

"Ha! Knew it."

I leaned in closer, lifting the coffee cup beside my cheek to shield our conversation from anyone who might hear, though the room bustled and everyone was occupied with their own doings. "And what if I do yearn? Can you help me with that?"

"Nope."

My shoulders deflated. Just as well.

"But I know someone who can. You go see her and she'll read you and tell you if she can release the, uh...lingering power that dwells within you," she said with dramatic flair.

"I have power?"

"I can see it blasting out of you like a heat wave, handsome. Bet you attract the womenfolk like bees to honey."

I glanced around, but didn't catch sight of Libby's bright red hair. The womenfolk were attracted to me?

"You bond with your soul mate yet?" the witch asked.

"Uh...no?"

"Good. She'll be pleased I've found such a rare—er, pleased to help you. You need to go to the sixteenth quarter."

"I'm not sure where that is. I'm new to the city."

"Yes, you are, aren't you? I'll write it down for you." She hobbled over to her table, which was littered with crystal balls and vials of various potions, some marked "for the low, low price." She handed me a paper with an address, then slapped a vial of dark substance onto my palm. "Five euros."

Potions and magics were not my thing. I could get whatever I needed from Libby's arsenal of witchcraft supplies. And I'd already secretly checked for "angel cures" and "wing restorers" only to be disappointed. "I don't think I need whatever this is."

"Oh, you do, or you won't be able to see the person you need to see. You rub this ointment under your eyes to see beyond this realm and into theirs."

"You want me to look into another realm?"

She nodded and held out her hand in wait of payment.

Having a few euros that Libby had tucked into my back pants pocket to buy whatever caught my eye, I paid the woman and she shoved me away as if my presence offended her.

I turned right into Libby's smiling yet wondering green eyes and discreetly shoved the vial into my shirt pocket before pulling her into a hug. "Get everything you need?"

"Mostly. I have one more table I need to stop by that sells dragon's breath. Won't take but ten minutes."

"I'll wait for you here."

"Can't wait to be back by your side, lover." She kissed my cheek, curling the heat to my skin as quickly as my smile. "You're so cute."

When she had left, I tugged out the vial and inspected the sparkly black contents. A glance to the elderly woman who'd sold it to me found her—missing. Her table was no longer there.

Turning about, I wondered if I'd mistaken her location, but I didn't see the odd white hair anywhere. She had been *right there*.

"Witches," I muttered. "They creep me out."

Save for the ones who planted skin-warming kisses on me. I did like kissing. Much better than vacuuming.

Ten minutes later, I had been compelled to listen to an elderly witch's explanation that she could bespell the frown from me (really? I didn't frown. Maybe? Hmm…), had watched a set of blonde twins perform allotriophagy—they'd made each other spit up butterflies—and had decided that mugwort stank and I preferred frankincense as a scent.

Libby's boisterous voice carried above the hubbub of chatter. I noticed a thin dark-haired man approach her and lean in close. As he spoke, the frail and poor example of male touched her wrist.

Marching toward my red-haired goddess, my fingers curled tightly and my chest expanded. I growled. The man looked at me, gaped and stepped away from my woman.

Libby turned, and just as I swung up a fist to connect with the idiot who had touched her, she stopped me with a smack of her palm over my knuckles.

"What are you doing?" she asked forcefully. "Reichardt?"

"He touched you." *Had been close enough to kiss*!

"It was just a friendly touch. He's not—"

"I must defend your honor."

"Monsieur, no…" the man started.

Libby slid between me and the male witch—who cast me a snide look down his narrow nose. "You can't go around punching witches," she said. "He'll return with a blast of magic that'll send you across this room. Holster it, lover boy."

"But…"

Libby's stern gaze deflated my anger and made me feel as if everyone was watching my admonishment. I didn't want to look around to verify if that were true.

I stepped back and shoved my hands in my jeans pockets. "I'm going to wait in the car."

"You do that. I'm almost finished here. I'll be right out."

I wandered through the crazy din of witches, not lifting my head to look again for the white-haired hag. Nor did I care to look back for

Libby, because if I saw the thin man near her again— I sighed.

Outside, the rain chidingly smattered my head and cheeks. I'd never felt so…castigated. It wasn't a nice feeling and it ached in my new beating heart. This feeling was going soundly in the bad-emotions category. And Libby had made me feel that way.

Perhaps I had been wrong about wanting to win Libby's admiration and love? Did I even know what love was? It would certainly never make a man feel as I did right now.

Slapping a palm over my chest, I felt the vial of dark ointment. The person this stuff would help me to see could restore my power? How great would that be? Albeit I had no clue what those powers once were. But certainly they should keep a woman from chiding me in front of others as if I were a child.

I strolled past a glossy black BMW beaded with rain. *Nice ride*. Would driving a fancy car gain Libby's respect?

"*Bonjour, mon ami!*"

I spun around to find a water-soaked woman standing at the curb on the other side of Libby's hearse. Rain plastered muddy-colored hair to her round face. "Hello?"

"My name's Hester. I saw you inside."

"You're a witch?"

She nodded. Wide brown eyes blinked beneath a fall of soaked bangs. "Your girlfriend shouldn't have spoken to such a big, strong man as you like that."

"I, uh…" No, she should not have. But she wasn't my girlfriend. Libby was a friend who was a girl. "It's okay. She's uh…protective." *Of herself, not me.*

Hester sighed and walked around to my side of the car, leaning against the door and crossing her arms over a shapeless long brown dress as she looked up at me. She had to—the woman personified short and stout. "Libertie St. Charles doesn't realize how lucky she is."

"Why is that?"

"Look at you. The epitome of *l'homme*! Every witch at the bazaar couldn't keep her eyes from you."

"Why? Do I not dress correctly? Libby told me this shirt was standard for most men. I should have worn the tie. It looked so uncomfortable."

"Oh, monsieur, they couldn't stop looking at you because you are so handsome."

I straightened and lifted my chest. "Really?"

"Best looking man for kilometers."

I shrugged subtly. For kilometers? That covered quite a lot of area.

"I heard about you getting your earthbound soul," Hester said. "That is remarkable. But now you're just going to stick with Libby?"

"Well, I—"

"There's a whole world of women out there to bond with—Uh, what's your name?"

"Reichardt."

"Such a manly, powerful name."

Everything this stout woman said lifted me higher. I liked talking with her. My head wasn't so muddled as it was with Libby when all I could do was think with my—well, my cock. The darned thing wasn't even hard right now, and that was fine by me. I didn't need that distraction to have a conversation with a woman.

"I wonder if you'd like to bond with me?" Hester asked.

She touched my forearm, which initially made me flinch. I'd never been touched by a woman, save for Libby and her sister. I relaxed and resumed calm. Because I was a man, as she'd said, and a handsome one at that.

"Bond? I'm not sure I understand, little one?"

She twisted her head down and blushed, despite the chilly rain sprinkles. "Little one. You're a charmer, Reichardt. I know you'd give me whatever I asked for."

"Well, I would certainly consider it. What do you need?"

"It's a bonding love spell I've been honing. Your blood is one of the ingredients. First we need to make you compliant."

She pressed both hands to each of my shoulders, her fingers digging in, and a strange electrical shock surged through my system. My fingers stiffened at my sides. The woman was somehow controlling me, forcing agonizing pain through my system.

"Reichardt!"

I heard Libby's voice, and just as my mind teased blackness, the electrifying connection ceased, and I fell to my knees, depleted and huffing.

Hester went soaring over the hood of the car to land on her hands and knees before Libby. With a growl of warning, Libby lifted her up by the hair and slammed her against the iron street pole. "What in Herne's hair are you up to, you little troll?"

"Release me," Hester cried. "Or I'll invoke the witches' rede against causing one another harm, and you'll have the entire bazaar on your ass, Libertie St. Charles."

Libby pushed away from the stout witch and, with hands on hips, stepped back, lifted her chin and looked down over the woman. "Keep your hands off my man," she said.

Her man? I bowed my head and caught my palms on the wet tarmac. She'd claimed me as her own, but in a manner that didn't jibe with how I expected. It was such a personal claim. It felt…strange. Like I was a possession, or just another herb she'd stuff in a bottle and set on her shelf for display.

Was Hester right? Should I keep my options open and check out other women before settling with Libby? Bond with her? Whatever she'd done to me had hurt like hell.

Libby's high heels splashed through puddles and around the front of the car and she bent over beside me. Her voice softened from the stern and authoritative tone she'd used with Hester. "Oh, lover, what did she do to you?"

"Not sure. Her touch shocked through my system. Another few seconds and I would have blacked out."

"Let's get you home and take care of you." She began to help me to my feet, but I shoved her away. "What's wrong?"

"I can do this myself. I am a man, Libby. I don't need you to coddle me."

She pouted, and at sight of those luscious red lips that always felt so good against my mouth, I winced and apologized. I clasped her hand as I stood to give her the idea that she was helping. "Take me home," I said. "And…take care of me."

For now. Until I learned more about all those women who thought me handsome and who wished to bond with me.

The driver's door opened and Libby got in, infusing the interior with her light and energetic air. "I smoothed things over with Reginald," she said. "The guy you almost punched."

"Why? I wasn't in the wrong."

Libby sighed. "I know how you saw it, lover boy. You wanted to protect me from some perceived threat. But I was completely safe."

"It wasn't a perceived threat. He touched you! And you admonished me in front of him." I slammed my arms across my chest. "Made me feel less than a man."

"Oh."

I pulled from her touch, yet it hurt in my heart to pull away from Libby and her bright, bold air. "And then with Hester—"

"What about with Hester? She was hurting you. Using some kind of magnetic earth magic on you."

"She mentioned something about bonding with me. That woman's form of bonding hurts."

"Bonding? But that means— Oh. I'm glad I got here when I did."

"Yes, but you charged out and treated me like a child again."

"I'm sorry. I didn't realize. You're an amazing man, Reichardt."

"I have done nothing to earn your praise. I want to be worthy of you, Libby. I want to be strong and as powerful as I once was." I met her gaze and swallowed down a choking gasp. So beautiful yet... Did her eyes water? What had I said to make her upset? "Don't cry. I've been cruel. I shouldn't—"

"It's not sad crying," she rushed out. "It's emotion welling up and spilling over. Of course every witch in Paris will try to bespell you, one way or another. And bond with you. You're hot and sexy and—"

"Sexy?"

Sniffling, she nodded. "So sexy you take my breath away."

I liked the sound of that.

"This is going to be hard for the two of us," Libby explained. "I've already fallen madly head over heels for you, and yet I realize I know nothing about you at all. And how can I?"

Yes, how could she love me when I couldn't grasp the meaning of that word?

"You're like a newborn learning about life and emotion," she continued. "Yet you have a secret past. What did you do when you weren't collecting souls? There are things in your apartment, tiny clues to your life, like the Jewish badge. Don't you want to know what that's about?"

I shrugged. "Perhaps—"

"And you. You think you want me, but what about all the other women out there?"

Did they *all* think me handsome? A man really should look into that.

"I'm being possessive," Libby confessed.

"Maybe a little." I leaned over the seat and stroked the wet fringes that wiggled into waves high on her thigh. Her skin was warm and sprinkled with rain, and when she placed her hand over mine, I turned mine up to clasp her fingers. "Did you talk to CJ?"

She nodded. "He said you could stop by anytime."

"How about now?"

She chuckled. "You want to get into my pants that badly, eh?"

"You're not wearing pants. And I don't think a pair of your pants would fit me, Libby."

"It's a figure of speech. It means you want to do somethin' somethin' with me."

"Somethin' somethin'?"

Her mouth curved into that soft, alluring bow and she whispered, "Sex."

The word curled inside my head with a teasing finger colored hot candy-red like Libby's hair. "Yes, sex appeals to me. And to hold you close and caress your curves is all I can think about. Is that wrong?"

"It means you're a man."

"That I am," I said proudly.

She leaned over and bumped foreheads with me. "Kiss me, Reichardt."

I threaded my fingers up through her wavy sports-car hair. I was feeling more confident with the kiss, and realized the talent was in letting go. Not thinking too much. And doing what felt natural.

Libby's mouth felt like summer and warmth. Her breath mingling with mine worked an alchemy I felt sure none of the witches inside the bazaar could ever master. *But how did I know*? And when the tip of her tongue dashed out and met mine I was initially startled, and then I tried the same move. Mmm…I liked that.

Diving inside her lush, sweet mouth, I danced with her tongue, inhaling the lingering notes of coffee, and then slicked across her teeth and painted her lips. She hummed in satisfaction, and I slid a hand down to cup behind her hip. My fingers always seemed to fit there. Pulling her closer, I moved across the seat and leaned over her. She smelled like frankincense and tasted like dark coffee with a touch of softness because she liked cream in her brew.

"You're good at this," she whispered. "Makes my toes curl."

"Is that a good thing?"

"That's a very good thing, lover boy. You sure you want to go to CJ's right now? Maybe we could stop by your place first and make out on the new couch? I'm feeling frisky."

"Frisky sounds like fun."

Chapter Three

My brand-new mortal guy had mastered kissing, as far as I was concerned. We embraced on the black leather sofa before the rain-streaked window that looked over the Seine, which glittered with streetlights.

Reichardt fluttered soft kisses from my mouth to tasting licks down my neck. It was as if he were learning every inch of my skin, tasting me, recording the smell, touch and tone of me. And, oh, did I want him to take his time.

He looked up, his kaleidoscope eyes bright. "Can I…" His fingers skated along my ribs, nudging up toward my breast. "Touch you here? I feel them against my chest, so big and soft, and—"

"Yes," I gasped. "Go for it. Oh…"

His intimately curious touch arrested my heartbeats. Tentative at first, he traced the generous curve of one breast through my dress, gliding slowly to the dip between them and up the other double-D side. With a gleeful smile overtaking his normally serious expression, he caressed each one gently, then a little firmer, as if to weigh them.

His lacking experience kept me guessing at what his next move would be, and that was startlingly hot. A gentle squeeze here, and then he strolled his palm across a nipple, which was tight and hard beneath my dress. And then he tongued the cleavage where I always dabbed a touch of vanilla.

"Oh, yeah," I said on a sigh. "I like that."

"You smell like cookies here. I want to taste them like I did your lips and neck."

"Mmm-hmm." I shrugged a shoulder to slip down a sleeve. The elastic neckline allowed for easy access. "I think you should."

Reichardt slid the polka-dotted fabric down my arm, kissing my skin and exposing the tops of each breast. A buxom girl like me had to wear a bra, but the sheer fabric was thin enough to feel his heat. Stroking softly, all five fingertips moved over my skin, painting indelible designs of desire in their wake.

"You are made of softness and fire," he whispered. "Amazing to touch."

Both his hands cupped me firmly. His eyes widened, a little boy who'd finally gotten his hands into the candy jar. His mouth moved slowly over my flesh as if pinpointing each and every pore, taking my measure. Owning me in ways he could never comprehend. Alchemizing a new kind of magic that I had every desire to learn and would fall to my knees to succumb to.

And when his mouth hovered over a nipple, still covered by the sheer bra, I moaned for his achingly sweet touch. In anticipation, I squeezed my legs together, which heightened the coiling hum at my core.

"Reichardt, you should know what you're doing is just right. It makes me…Oh."

A bend of his finger pulled the bra cup away to reveal my nipple. He paused, his parted lips but a breath above the tightly ruched bud. "It makes you…?"

"Breathless," I managed. "So good. Like it. Don't stop."

His tongue twisted about the nipple, setting free my long moan and coaxing my spine into a wanting arch that hugged my stomach up against his rigid chest.

"I like this," he said around my flesh. "You are a vast variety of textures and tones. I get a new sound from you with every different way I touch you."

I couldn't help a giggle.

"You see?" he said with his own chuffing smirk.

A dash of his tongue frenzied my want. A tickle here, a slashing stroke there. Yes, the man was playing me like an instrument, producing new sounds, finding interesting scales to trace with his tongue. He wasn't near to composing a symphony, but I wanted to be his muse.

I glided my fingers down his back, wishing he'd taken off his shirt. I needed to touch hot man muscle! Yet his intent suckling at my nipple, soft and then harder, teased me to an edge I could trip over and fall off, arms out and eyes closed. All Reichardt had to do was catch me in his big, strong arms.

Then the hot, wet sensation stopped, and he switched to my other nipple, but kept his fingers tight about the wet bud. If I didn't know better, I'd guess he had done this to other women, many times. But he had not. And that he was learning on me, and so quickly, was amazing.

"Libby."

"What, lover?"

"Is this called bonding?"

"Uh, well, yes. A little. Sort of?" When certain paranormal breeds bonded, it was a soul thing. Witches did not. But soul bringers? Who could know?

He suddenly looked down his abdomen, and I figured he'd gotten a hard-on again. Did the poor guy not know what to do with it? He really did need to talk to another man, because while I was perfectly confident with telling a man how to please me, I was a little skittish about explaining the working mechanics of his own body.

So I had my weak points. A girl couldn't rock it all the time.

"It's what's supposed to happen," I reassured him.

But the man backed off, kneeling back on the sofa and leaving my breasts bare, wet and aching.

"I need to talk to CJ," he said, easing a palm over his groin. "Soon."

I nodded effusively and pulled up my bra straps.

"No," he said, tugging down my hands. "Let me look at them. You are a goddess, Libby. And your breasts are— I don't even know what to say." He actually blushed. "I like the feel of them in my mouth."

His words worked the same kind of alchemy his tongue on my skin had. Basking in his adoration, I closed my eyes and stretched out before him, thrusting back a shoulder like some kind of retro sex kitten posing for the month of August. Let him look all he liked. I'd never felt so sexy in my entire life.

As the head Archivist, CJ was working at the Council archives today but had invited me over in the evening for a guy chat. With Libby at home stirring up spells, I decided to wander out on my own, the address the witch at the bazaar had given me in hand.

I had to ask many times for directions, and one man told me to get a cell phone with GPS. I had no idea what GPS was, or why I would need a phone to find a location, so I marked it off as Mohawk-induced anger as the man had sported a yellow jut of hair down the middle of his scalp and many fierce tattoos.

Tattoos were neat. And apparently, Libby liked men with tattoos. Hmm…I had one on my chest. A bunch of blue dots. Not sure what it meant. That whole forgetting everything about my former life was not neat. I thought I'd like to get a tattoo from an ink witch that had meaning to me. But what spell did I need?

"Strength," I muttered, and wandered onward. "I will get it back."

I strolled down the street, nodding to a vendor who hawked crepes with thick, oozing chocolate syrup, and decided to purchase one on my way home. Libby's crepes were great, but she always sprinkled them with fruit and flaxseed that got stuck in my teeth. Oozing chocolate seemed the better way to go.

I didn't recognize any residence or store front yet suddenly remembered the black ointment the old witch had given me. Drawing it from a pocket, I opened the vial. The stuff smelled sweet and sparkled. For a man who was trying desperately to regain his sense of manliness, I didn't see the purpose in painting women's sparkly stuff on my eyes.

Did I want this enough to go with eye shadow?

"Yes, I want my powers back. I need them to be what Libby wants. Here goes."

I dipped in a finger and smeared a thin line under each eye. With a blink, I looked around.

And the world changed.The woman walking toward me in a pink skirt and popping her bubble gum suddenly grew wings and elongated arms. The wings fluttered as she passed me by, sweetening the air with a swish. I spun, marveling at her retreat, and she turned and sneered and called me a pervert.

I turned back around and saw two more people with wings. "Faeries?"

Yet among the winged creatures appeared to be normal mortals, going about their business, buying crepes and chatting over a newspaper. It was as if two worlds were superimposed upon one another—the mortal realm and a different realm, one of the faeries.

And then I noticed—sandwiched between two larger houses—a narrow house that hadn't been there before. The wood door was painted bright magenta and...sparkled. I bet if I hadn't been wearing the ointment I would've merely seen a space there, sky instead of the faery home.

Intrigued, I skipped up the steps and strode the long path between high hedgerows to the front door. Before I could knock, the door swung inward of its own volition. I entered a narrow hallway steeped in incense and wispy white smoke.

"Hello?"

No answer.

Compelled forward, I walked to an open archway and peered through the long strands of closely spaced hanging beads. A woman stood with her back to me, her arms posed in a crook with hands flat as if she were an Indian goddess. Cranberries entwined with glossy leaves crowned her ruby hair.

"Uh, I was sent here by a witch…" I realized I had no physical proof of invitation or the witch's name.

"Enter," the woman said in dulcet tones that seemed to dance into my chest and wiggle there, which made me smile.

She pointed to the left, and I walked in and took in the small half-circle room. Didn't seem as if it made sense that it would fit, because from the outside the hallway had seemed to take up the whole space between the two buildings.

"You are Kryatron, Angel of the Seventh Soul."

Heartbeats suddenly pausing, I almost fell to my knees. How could she know? And yet, *did* she know? Was that—had that been my angelic name?

She turned and cast her violet gaze upon me. White arabesques that looked like reverse tattoos decorated her face and bare arms. Bright silks swung across her skin, covering her intimate parts yet revealing a sleek, elongated form that glinted with faery dust.

"Why do you name me that?" I asked. It wasn't a name I had heard before. Libby had told me Reichardt Fallowgleam was my name.

The faery placed her hand over my heart, nodded decisively, then removed it. "I see. You've your earthbound soul. You've lost all memory of your past."

"Was…was that my angel name?"

She nodded. "Mustn't tell too much. And yet, you know you were once angel?"

"Yes, my— The woman who gave me back my soul told me. She knew me when I was a soul bringer."

"Soul bringer," she said on the tingly dulcet tones that seemed to ring in my chest. "We are alike."

"I don't understand."

"The sidhe are descended from the angels, as are soul bringers. Yet, stuck halfway between the two worlds, we are neither accepted by Above nor this mortal realm. Our souls are similar, as are our powers and hearts. You've latent magic clinging to you, Kryatron. You must have taken your soul recently."

"A week. So I've magic? Like a witch? I don't feel it. I've never felt so weak and ineffectual."

"You've come to get back that power." She strode to an altar of branches and vines and touched an incense stick to a flame that wasn't attached to a candle and which appeared to float upon water.

"*Can* I get back what was once mine?"

She nodded.

Exciting news! I approached her, but she lifted her head so abruptly I felt as if she'd repulsed me with that simple move, so I remained.

"I will offer you a bargain." She turned to face me, splaying out her hands as if to offer a gift. Her palms were decorated with more of the elaborate white arabesques. "I can return to you half the power you once possessed. As well, immortality. You will once again walk with a lightness upon the earth, possess power over the elements—" She paused and opened her eyes. "You are still pure, yes?"

"Pure?"

"You've not bonded with a woman, such as a soul mate, or otherwise engaged in sexual activity?"

"Uh, well…Libby and I—we've…"

"Have you loosed your seed within her womb?"

"No. Uh, we haven't done that yet." I didn't think so, anyway. I really needed to talk to CJ.

"Good. You must remain pure or I cannot take your soul."

I clasped a hand over my heart. "You'll take my soul?"

"That is how it works. You hand over your soul and become what you once were. Almost."

"But I don't want to be a soul bringer again. I've made friends. I don't want to leave—"

"You won't be a soul bringer, but instead something like

me, fixed between Above and this realm. But for that to happen you must relinquish your soul and remain pure."

"No sex?"

She nodded. "Nothing that completes the transaction, so to speak."

Which, I assumed, meant I could still kiss Libby and touch her and make her feel good. I just couldn't— The rest was a fuzzy notion I wanted to entertain.

Yet to have the power I once held, and immortality? I could be with Libby forever. And she would surely appreciate my renewed strength. I could finally be the man she needed.

"I need to think about this."

The faery lifted a brow.

"It's a big decision."

"So quickly you've succumbed to mortal indecision. Very well. You have forty-eight mortal hours to bring me that which will transfer your soul. It should be an object you have, something that binds the soul to your mortal body."

"What could that be?"

She shrugged. "Perhaps a feather?"

"I have a feather!"

"Very good. Return to me, Kryatron, Angel of the Seventh Soul, and I will grant you your greatest desire."

I nodded and headed outside, picking up speed toward the river Seine until finally I dared to look back. I saw no winged beings. Perhaps the ointment had worn away from beneath my eyes.

"Immortality," I said with wonder.

It was a prize that rang sweetly in my newly beating heart. But to sacrifice my soul again? What would be the ramifications?

Libby had loved me before, when I'd had no soul. Hell, I'd had a glass heart that hadn't even beaten when she had fallen in love with me. Surely she would continue to love me if I ransomed my soul again?

But what was love, and would I know it if I felt it—and ultimately, miss it if I lost it?

This cleaning job had taken us to an old dark abandoned mansion in the third quarter. Windows were boarded over, floorboards missing here and there, and the few pieces of furniture had been covered with dusty white sheets. The entire place smelled like demons.

"Demons stink," I said to Vika, who scrubbed a plastered wall with a spell-enhanced cleaning solution. "Like tar and old dead things."

"And you would know what old dead things smell like?" Vika asked over her shoulder.

"Well…we *do* clean them up."

"Yeah, but these are new dead things. Big difference."

She had a point. I sighed and pushed a strand of long red hair up under the white Tyvek head wrap I wore and walked carefully around a sticky black pool of demon blood. "Reichardt and I made out."

"Is that so?" Vika's Tyvek-clad hips swished side to side as she scrubbed vigorously. "Could the man find all the right places?"

"He's learning. Gotta love a beginner, though. He may not be suave but his curiosity is well worth the effort."

"I probably don't need details. But I heard he needs some extra study time with Certainly."

"Yes, I think Reichardt is talking to CJ now. I'm going to run up with you when we're finished here, okay?"

"No problem. So CJ is giving Reichardt man lessons?"

"The guy's having trouble getting a grasp on this realm. But not on me." I shimmied my hips, clad in a white hazmat jumpsuit. "That man really knows how to kiss."

"I would have never believed he had it in him," Vika commented. "He was so cold and emotionless when he was a soul bringer."

"Don't I know it. But not now. He's on fire. But he still has to learn how to use what God gave him, if you know what I mean."

"Interesting." Setting aside the scrub brush, my sister handed me a bag of remains we'd collected earlier. "CJ should be able to handle any questions he might have. He is a sexual genius."

"Yeah? So how goes it with you and the dark witch with the magic hand?"

CJ wore spellwork tattoos all over his body. His left hand, in particular, was covered with them. Vika had learned early on that hand could do some amazing things to her sexually.

"I'll never tell," Vika said with a wink.

"You know I hate it when people keep secrets."

"You really want the details?"

I thought about learning the intricacies of my sister's love life—then shook my head vehemently. "I'd rather clean up demon guts."

"Just so."

Chapter Four

CJ's loft was a marvel. Libby had explained that the dark witch had recently been infested with demons after he'd journeyed to Daemonia on a quest for a magic spell. I had no clue what Daemonia was, but it didn't sound like a party. The whole realm of paranormal creatures was fascinating. I was glad to still be a part of it, even if only by association with Libby, because it gave me some connection to what I'd once been.

Yet did some of my innate angelic powers exist within me? According to the faery, they did. And the old hag had recognized my angelic origins, as well.

I felt sure, as an angel, I'd know how to please a woman and not flinch at all the weird things that resulted while touching her. Like my penis getting rock hard—I wanted to do something with it, but I just wasn't sure what. How embarrassing was that?

And even more embarrassing? The fact I now knew what it was like to be embarrassed.

The dark witch greeted me with palms pressed together in a Namaste pose. CJ wore slouchy jeans that covered his bare feet, and a loose red shirt partially open to reveal the many spellwork tattoos he wore on his body. Long black hair, neatly braided, queued down his back. I recalled now Libby had said something about the man being a twin. I'd not met Thoroughly Jones yet.

CJ gestured with a completely tattooed hand I follow him to the living area where two big comfy gray velvet couches mastered the wide-open area, backed by floor-to-ceiling windows. I tilted my head back, taking in the chandeliers that hung overhead as if constellations.

"There used to be hundreds," CJ explained of the dozens of light fixtures, some sporting clear while others black, red and even multicolored crystal. "Kept the demons back, the prismatic light. After I vanquished all the demons from within, Vika made me get rid of most of the light fixtures, which I was very happy to do. You can't imagine trying to sleep with all those lights on. But we kept a few of the more interesting ones. So."

The man stepped closed to me and stretched out his arms as if flexing the muscles. "There's something I need to get off my chest before we begin."

"Very well." I stood there, waiting for what he had to offer.

The sting of his fist to my jaw ignited a piercing red pain through the left side of my face and clattered my teeth within my skull. I slapped a palm to the bruised skin and, mouth agape, couldn't summon a single word.

"I owed you that. You hurt Vika and Libby when you took their souls."

I nodded. Yes, he did owe me this. My cruelties must have been numerous. But—ouch!

"Now we're good," CJ stated. "Whiskey?"

I shrugged and, still clutching my jaw, nodded yes. I hadn't tried the spirit and was open to all new things. CJ poured a small amount in a tumbler and handed it to me. Smelled sharp and leathery. I drank it all in one swallow, then gasped as my throat burned. I wanted to scream but any noise my vocal chords could produce was smothered by the wicked brew. It did redirect from the pain in my jaw, though.

"You should probably take it slow for starters," CJ said with a humorous tone. "I forget you're new to everything. Should have started you on the Chartreuse."

He tilted the whiskey bottle toward my glass and this time only poured half as much.

"Why don't you sit back and close your eyes. That stuff will go straight to your head. Might have to feed you before you go home or Libby will strangle me for getting you drunk."

"How can one drink make me drunk?" I asked. I closed my eyes because the crystals overhead suddenly starting dancing.

"You're a teetotaler," CJ said. "And this whiskey is eighty proof. You'll find out soon enough what drunk means. So Libby said you had some questions?"

Right, but I had no intention of mentioning my visit to the faery this morning. That, I needed to keep under my hat. No one could help me decide whether or not it was worth sacrificing my soul for immortality.

Another swallow of whiskey burned, but this time the burn was sweet.

"I need to talk to a man about..." I stretched my aching jaw, testing. "Things."

"I understand. Living with the queen of clean can be annoying at times, eh?"

"I thought that was your woman's title? Libby is a goddess, not a queen. But she does tend to have me vacuum and clean a lot. I feel I should be learning more manly stuff. Like how to drive and fix things. The sink is leaking in Libby's bathroom, and I'm not sure what to do about it. If I was still immortal, could I stare it fixed? Could I do that before?"

"Stare things fixed?" CJ chuckled. "Probably. You used to wield catoptromancy like a pro. Used your eyes to draw souls out of Vika's body. But don't compare your life now to what you had then, because, dude, all you did was ferry souls. Boring."

I nodded in agreement, and the shake of my head wobbled my brain inside my woozy skull. "Ohh..."

"Yeah, I'm going to fix you a sandwich, man. Avocado and sprouts with fresh radish spread. You'll love it."

The witch got up and strolled into the kitchen. Always barefoot and effortlessly casual, that man, like he belonged in another age singing protest songs and smoking hashish. I didn't know why I pinned CJ that way. I wasn't even sure what hashish was. I innately knew things about the world and society and how everything worked.

All save how *I* worked.

Correction: today I'd learned my flesh and bone could feel real pain. And I did not like it. Nor did I care for the spinning brain. I remained on the couch, grabbing the seat cushions for stability. Felt like a sturdy rock anchored amid a suddenly swashing sea. Maybe one drink could make me drunk.

"You need some tools," CJ called. "There's a hardware store down the street. A twist of the wrench will tame that leaky pipe in minutes. As for driving, you can take a class, and then have someone teach you behind the wheel."

"Libby did say she could teach me driving. I need a job so I can buy a Maserati."

"Lofty goals, my man. But I'd suggest mastering more pressing skills before subjecting yourself to the hazards of Parisian drivers. What's the one thing you most want to learn?"

"How to please Libby."

"Yeah? I get that. She's a fierce, sexy woman. Doesn't hide her feelings, either. She's claimed you, man."

"She has. I'm not sure I like that."

"Really?"

"What about all the other women who think me handsome?"

CJ chuckled again, and I found the laugh annoying. Or was it the sharp triton repeatedly poking my brain and jaw?

"You think all the women are swooning in your wake, man? Well, maybe. I'm no judge of handsome, but you're not ugly. But before you go all Casanova on any woman you have to learn the basics. And just because you're with Libby now doesn't seal the two of you together forever. Although...don't say that to her. If I know my St. Charles women, that's not something you want to casually drop into conversation. Those witches retaliate with painful magic."

"I've already seen Libby's jealous side. As she has seen mine."

"Protecting your woman? Way to go, man. But don't overdo it."

"Yes, well, she chastised me in front of all at the bazaar. Made me feel awful."

"That's just Libby reacting. Let it pass. She genuinely cares for you. And try to avoid the bazaar in the future. It's a bunch of old witches hawking mugwort and love spells."

And the one witch who had directed me toward my possible fate via a faery.

"So." CJ raised a bread knife dramatically. "How to please a woman? Are you telling me in the two thousand years you have existed you've never had sex with a woman?"

"Never."

"My balls are turning blue just thinking about that. If you lost your memory how do you know you've never had sex?"

"I just…know. And apparently, I was busy ferrying souls all those millennia. I have never touched female flesh until Libby."

"Wow. We have to get you laid, buddy."

"Is that like bonding? With a soul mate?"

"Could be. You think Libby is your soul mate?"

I shrugged.

"Yeah, who knows. It's such a vague term. So the basics!"

"I think I've started to learn the basics by kissing Libby. And she let me kiss her breasts today. I do like breasts."

"They are one of life's finer pleasures. Vika's are small and so—" CJ paused, one hand in the air before him caressing what I guessed might be the figment of his woman's breast. "Uh, well, apparently you know."

"Touching breasts is great. But every time I kiss or touch Libby, I get…hard. What is that about?"

"Ah? It's called a hard-on." CJ leaned an elbow on the counter, dangling a bread bag. "I'll explain everything over sandwiches."

I accompanied my sister up to CJ's apartment because I figured I could give Reichardt a ride home. Vika had moved in with CJ right after Reichardt got his soul back. The woman was madly, deeply, truly in love with the dark witch, and the energy she put off was like fireworks. I loved being near her.

We entered the vast loft to the sound of two guys laughing. I strolled inside and found Reichardt leaning against the kitchen counter, an empty bottle of whiskey in hand.

He spied me and raised the bottle. "My goddess!"

"Oh hell, CJ. Did you get him drunk? And what's that? Does he have a bruise on his jaw?" I cast CJ the evil eye and realized the dark witch was as wasted as Reichardt because he wobbled forward and tripped, landing in Vika's arms in a sprawl. "Men."

"Sorry," CJ muttered. "I did feed him, but you shouldn't open a good bottle of whiskey and let it sit. We had to finish it. Mmm, Mistress of My Desires." He kissed Vika on the neck, and my sister nuzzled a kiss onto one of his eyelids.

"We were on a cleaning job," Vika said.

"And now I've a drunk former soul bringer to escort home to sleep it off," I remarked. "Nice, CJ. You're lucky Vika won't let me use magic against you."

"Don't worry," Vika said, "I'll make sure he suffers for this one. Let me help you get this big ole lunk down to the car."

We lifted Reichardt under his arms and managed the trip down six flights—the elevator hadn't been in order for weeks—and stuffed him into the passenger seat of the hearse alongside the cleaning equipment.

"He's got it bad," Vika commented. "Don't be too hard on him."

All the way home Reichardt sang about sexy, curvy redheads who delivered hot kisses. I couldn't help but smile. He had a nice tenor and could carry a tune. Once in his apartment, he passed out as soon as his head hit the couch. I left him a note, but felt sure he'd sleep this one off through the night.

Picking up the blue feather from the kitchen countertop, I trailed it across my lips. "Wonder if he learned what he needed to know from CJ?"

Was I asking too much of the man too soon? He'd only been mortal a little over a week. And I'd had my claws in him since before that. Did I dare ask CJ if Reichardt had wondered about other women?

I shook my head. "Not my business."

And yet, more and more I felt as though I were holding something to my heart that might be better off set free. The old adage about if you loved something then you should set it free tweaked at my conscience.

I closed my eyes. "I can't. He's my soul mate."

And while the universe might be sneaky, it was also never wrong. Reichardt was in my life because he belonged in it. I wasn't prepared to believe anything else.

I closed his front door quietly and pressed a palm to the wood, releasing a tendril of protective magic and whispering a spell that would bless all those who crossed the threshold.

Chapter Five

Orange juice was the work of the Devil Himself. I finished off the glass Libby handed me, then two minutes later raced to the bathroom. I'd never felt so awful. My head buzzed like bees had fashioned a hive inside my skull. Even Libby's cheery singing bored a hole through my cranium in search of the brain crevices.

I had to get back my immortality. Then I'd never have to face the toilet bowl like this again. Tonight, I intended to return to FaeryTown and ransom my soul to the faery.

"I've made you special cookies this morning," Libby called from the bathroom doorway.

Perched before the toilet, I muttered, "No food. Please."

"They're hangover cookies," she said. "My regular chocolate-chip recipe with a touch of magic to take the hurt away and make you feel better. Promise. I'll leave them in here." She set the plate on the bedroom vanity and left me to my misery.

From the bathroom doorway I spied the plate, which sat beside the blue feather. That feather was my key to immortality.

But more so? Just imagining the taste of Libby's delicious treats melting on my tongue made my mouth water. I turned and crawled into the bedroom.

Must. Get. Cookie.

* * *

Transprojectionary dislocation was a mouthful to say and an even bigger spell to accomplish correctly. It sounded simple enough, moving an object through the air with only the power of one's mind, but it took intense concentration, and I was slightly ADD so concentration was not my forte.

Sadly, we rock stars couldn't be masters of everything.

Vika's boyfriend made it look easy. CJ could move vehicles or animals through the air. He had once sent a train car flying through a brick wall. But he'd been practicing dark magic for over a century.

I garnered but two and a half decades to my magical arsenal, so the fact that a grain of salt floated in the air above Reichardt's new kitchen table now gave me a giddy thrill. I squealed and the salt crystal dropped.

"I did it!"

"That was amazing."

I spun to find myself in Reichardt's arms. He'd showered and smelled like bay rum soap—and was standing straight—which said a lot for my hangover cookies.

"How do you feel?"

"Like I was a fool last night. Those cookies are magic."

"That's the point. And what do we think of whiskey?"

"Devil's brew. Good stuff, but I don't like the way it attacked my better senses. So are you practicing magic?"

"Yes, trying to master moving objects around with my mind."

"Is that something I used to be able to do?"

"Yes, but don't let it get you down. You'll learn so many new skills, all your old tricks will seem boring by comparison."

"Yes, I imagine scrubbing the tub until it gleams ranks right up there with startling skills."

"Oh, sweetie." I bracketed his face with my hands and he winced so I moved them away from the bruise CJ had rightfully left there. "You're so down on yourself. What can I do to make it better?"

"You have already cured me of a hangover."

"Do you feel like breakfast now?"

"Maybe in a bit. A kiss wouldn't be unwarranted."

I kissed him and tasted the mint toothpaste on his tongue. And there, the traces of chocolate and vanilla I'd put in the cookies. His mouth was a garden of deliciousness.

"So while imbibing the wicked wiles of whiskey did you happen to learn anything useful from CJ?"

"Man stuff," he said with a wink. "He lent me some of his tools, which I forgot because I was—ahem. But I should be able to fix the leaky faucet at your place now."

"Awesome! Vika usually took care of the household repairs. I miss having her around. The house is so big without her in it."

"You and your sister are very close. I will never know what it's like to have family."

"You've a new family now, lover boy."

"I suppose."

"Oh, you're getting pouty again. I know it's going to be hard, and I think you have to go through a grief stage."

"Isn't grief for losing people?"

"It is, but you've lost a whole life."

"CJ made it sound as if I won't be missing much."

"I don't think you will, but I didn't know you for the two thousand years you lived."

Two thousand years was a long time. Surely, he had done things, explored the world and…women? Why did the man have cat food? And that Jewish badge was a curiosity.

Reichardt nodded and tapped the grains of salt on the table. "Have you always been this way? A witch?"

"I was born a witch. All three of the St. Charles sisters are natural witches. Vika's the most powerful, and Eternitie is still out adventuring in some third-world nation, learning new magics. I can't wait for you to meet her and her girlfriend."

"Girlfriend?"

"Yes, she called last week to tell us about Merrily, her significant other. It's so crazy because Merrily is CJ and TJ's sister! We're keeping it all in the family."

"So they are both women and they are...a couple?"

"Yes, they're called lesbians, and we humans tend to fall in love regardless of sex."

"I like that. But I think I prefer women. Especially the curvy kind." He cupped my breast and bent to kiss me there. *Mmm, baby.* "I know what to do now, when things get hard."

"Is that so?"

"I'm going to enjoy learning about sex with you, Libby. But CJ said to go slow. The emotion has to be there, as well. I'm not sure what love really means."

"You and all the rest of us. Love is sort of ineffable. And I don't mind taking things slow." *Mostly.*

I trailed my fingers down his chest, pausing at the waist of his jeans. My big manly man sucked in a breath as a finger strayed beneath his shirt to tickle across his belly where the dark hairs curled. I'd yet to get a good look at those incredible abs. Just looking could be considered slow, couldn't it?

"Vika is stopping by my place in a bit. Why don't I give her a call and remind her to bring along your tools?"

"Yes, I want to start doing man things." He growled at my ear, then nipped the lobe. "What would you think about me if I could get back my immortality and all the powers I once had?"

"I'm...not sure. I don't think that's possible. Though you do flicker."

"I flicker?" He tilted his head in wonder.

"It's your aura. I didn't mention it before because I didn't want to confuse you. It's bright yet it flickers."

"Like my batteries are running low?" he asked.

"Interesting way to put it. Do you feel as if you are growing weak? Why would you even want to have back immortality?"

"So I can take care of you, be the man."

"You already are a big sexy hunk of man."

"Yet sometimes you make me feel as though I am not. That I am a child."

"I didn't—" *Ah, the incident with Hester.* "I should have never spoken to you like that. I'm a bit of a—"

"Fierce woman," he offered. "I wouldn't have you any other way. I will have to learn to adjust to your overbearing manner."

I cringed at that statement. I didn't want to be that for him. I just wanted...him.

"But, Libby, I feel as though something is missing in my life."

"Like a whole freaking history? And you want it back? Oh, I should have never told you about being an angel. Then you wouldn't be so conflicted now."

"That would have been a lie to not tell me."

"I know, but I feel protective of you."

"You shouldn't be. The man is the one who protects the woman, and I would do anything to keep you safe."

"I don't need protecting, but I like that you feel that way. Hester Powler bothers me. What did she say to you the other day in the rain?"

"That I was handsome and all the women thought so, too."

"I see." I slid my eyes down his chest. Yes, any woman would want to get her hands on that. Again, and again...I shook my head to obliterate the lusty images that thought conjured. "That short little woman is after my man. Do you think she's attractive?"

"The stout one? Not at all. But..."

"But?"

"All those other women she mentioned..."

"I see." Apparently he had been thinking about *other women* a lot if we were actually having this conversation. I stood and gathered my purse and walked to the door, leaving him sitting there in a towel. "I should be going."

"Let me get dressed. I want to come along and fix the pipe."

I shrugged. "If you need to."

A dismissive reply, but I couldn't stop thinking about other women wanting Reichardt. I had to stake my claim or lose him.

But in doing so would I only push him away?

* * *

It really was as easy as taking a wrench to the pipe and giving it a twist. I gripped the heavy tool in a triumphant thrust toward the ceiling. A manly grunt felt appropriate.

Now to claim the spoils of my accomplishment.

Libby stood inside the big walk-in closet, humming as she sorted over the racks of shoes. I had no earthly idea why one woman could need so many pairs. She only had two feet. Though I liked how they made her legs look, and they lifted her up to my chin level, so I didn't have to lean down so far to kiss her.

Thinking of kisses...

I grabbed her from behind, and she squealed as I turned her against the wall, smashing a fake fur coat between her and the wall. I kissed her soundly. Her mouth opened to mine and I shivered as our soft, wet tongues touched. She slid a leg up along my thigh and hooked her heeled foot behind my knee. Man, I was sensitive back there and her aggression inspired my desires. I leaned into her, resting against her generous breasts.

"I fixed the faucet."

"I heard your grunt of triumph. You know that deserves a reward. You want a cookie?"

"Nope." I kissed her along the neck, a place I had learned made her squirm with pleasure. She moaned languorously as I touched her there, and then there. "Try something else."

"A nice hearty supper?"

"I do enjoy your cuisine, but I'm not hungry right now."

"Hmm..." Her big green eyes glittered. She could command me with a flutter of her thick lashes. And she was making things very hard.

I pressed my groin against her hip. "I won't run off this time. Promise."

"So CJ gave you all the details, eh?"

"He filled me in between shots of whiskey. Touch me here, Libby." I moved her hand down to my erection. She boldly cupped my rod and cooed. "Wow, that feels better than I expected it would. I, uh…Would you like to…" CJ had said the man should be the one in control. "I want you to stroke it."

"You really have learned some new things. What happened to slow?"

"Was that too fast for you? Hell, I'm messing it up again."

"No." She squeezed me, and I gasped at the intensity of pleasurable sensations her touch coursed through my body. "I'm very cool with this. I like touching you, Reichardt. Mmm, you're so hard."

I lifted her and carried her out into the bedroom, dimly lit by the twilight. An explosion of purple ruffles and fringes decorated the bed. I set her on the bed, then she sinuously moved into a crouch, luring me with a crook of her finger.

"Come here, big boy."

I would go to her, all right. But I wouldn't come. Couldn't do that and remain pure, which was important if I were to ransom my soul later this evening. But until then? I wanted to know as much pleasure as I could before it was too late.

My fallen angel, who had once collected souls endlessly without emotion, without regard for right or wrong, was quickly becoming a real, feeling, wanting man.

I drew him across the bed, unbuttoning his shirt and pulling it off to expose his magnificent abs and chest. So bold and hard, like iron, yet warm as a smoldering fire. I pressed a cheek to his chest and closed my eyes. By the goddess, he was as good to touch as I'd imagined.

"What are you doing?"

"I can hear your heart beat," I said. "I once laid my hand on your chest when you were the soul bringer. Not a single beat from that unfeeling old glass heart. It's amazing to hear it now."

I tongued his nipple. Reichardt sucked in a hissing breath. And then I noticed the small blue dots about three inches above his left nipple.

"Seven of them," I said, "sort of shaped like an H. Is this your angel sigil?"

"You tell me. I thought it was a tattoo but couldn't reason why a soul bringer would get such a thing."

"All angels have sigils," I said. "This is probably yours. Cool. I wonder what it means?"

I quickly decided the meaning: *this sexy, hot guy belongs to Libby St. Charles. Hands off!*

Okay, so I wouldn't mention that to him. Yet.

Mapping my tongue down his fiery skin, I journeyed over the ridged muscles, and lower, and—no belly button. That disturbed me only a moment. I knew the facts. Angels were not born but created.

Still.

His fingers worked through my hair as I kissed lower down his abdomen. He had more than a six pack—this was a good eight pack, and I'd never known the mortal body could be so hard, truly like stone. I lashed my tongue over the ridges, marking each one as my own.

Stroking a palm over his erection summoned a groan from him and he rocked his hips forward.

"Oh, yeah, you've got rhythm. I'll make you a rocker one way or another, lover boy. Speaking of which, we need music."

I clapped once and the stereo turned on, emitting Wynonna Judd's brassy form of rock 'n' roll blues into the room.

"You've some interesting magic."

"That wasn't magic—that was the Clapper. Now let's make sure this tight zipper doesn't do any damage to your main stick."

I eased down the zipper of his fly and the thick red head of him landed against my palm. I gave it a squeeze, marveling at the size of it. So hot and ready for attention. I wanted to study it, to lick it, to make it my own, but I was still completely dressed and in heels.

"Dress off," I whispered, giving him an encouraging squeeze.

"Right."

My dress flew off and landed on the floor. Beneath, a matching bra and panties—purple, of course, emphasized my curves. I'd never been self-conscious of my extra pounds when getting naked with a man, but the way Reichardt looked at me now, dragging his eyes over my breasts and down to my panties, made me slide a hand in front of my stomach.

"What's wrong?" he asked. "Don't cover yourself. You're so beautiful. I love the curve of your belly. It's so feminine."

He bent to kiss me there as I knelt before him. I slid the hand away and raked it through his short dark hair. In Reichardt's embrace, I felt like the goddess he named me. A kiss to my panties traveled a heat path up to my nipples and back down again. Sighing out a languorous moan, I grew wet for him and knew nothing could possibly go slow from this moment onward.

Overindulgence? Here I come!

"It's all or nothing now, lover boy," I whispered as his kisses moved lower and his tongue crept out to tickle my mons. "Oh, yeah." The panties dropped down my thighs and he moved up to unfasten the clasp at the back of my bra. Remarkably, he got it on the first try. "Most professionals can't even master that move, let alone a beginner."

"Maybe I've some magic, as well?"

"Oh, you do. It's right here."

I kissed him hard and desperately, because he needed to know this was going to happen now. While doing so, I kicked my panties aside and toed off the high heels. Crazy peeling-off-the-clothes-and-stumbling-because-it's-so-awkward sex is my kind of fun.

Pushing down Reichardt's jeans, I oohed and aahed as his remarkable penis sprang forth. It was worth the adulation, and it fell heavily into my grasp.

"Is it manly enough for you?"

"Reichardt, it's amazing. So thick and hard. I can't wait to play with it."

"Play?"

"Yes, sex is fun and can be playful. Now lie back," I said.

"No, the man should be the one in control. I want to play with your body." He pushed me back to land against the pillows.

I had wanted the man to take control.

The phone rang. *Oh, hell no.*

Reaching for the man stick jutting from his thicket of dark curls, I pulled Reichardt over my body. I glided a leg up along his and cooed over his cock, something I knew every man could appreciate.

The phone rang again.

"I don't care for those loud ringy things," he said between kisses to my breasts. "Can you make it stop with another clap?"

"It'll stop after the fourth ring. See?"

He nuzzled against my belly and laved his tongue over my skin. His path was heading south. I moaned appreciatively, but the bedamned phone rang again.

"Oh, drats. That's Vika."

"How do you know?"

"We have a signal. If either of us doesn't answer the first round of rings, we immediately call back if it's an emergency. I hope this isn't another job so soon. I have to get this."

Carefully and slowly, I extricated myself from the man, who was, by the minute, growing more comfortable and wanting to touch, tease and taste my skin.

This was so wrong. *Thanks a lot, Universe.*

By the time I sat upright, the phone had stopped ringing and I hesitated at the edge of the bed.

Reichardt stroked his fingers down my back, landing on the sensitive curve indenting my derriere. "Wasn't so much of an emergency after all?"

Again the phone rang. And my heart sank.

I dashed for the nightstand and flicked open the cell phone. "This had better be good."

"Testy, sister. What's up that you didn't answer? Twice!"

"Me and Reichardt are—"

"Oh. Then it's a good thing I kept calling."

"Why? What's going on, Vika?"

"I'm at the Council Archives with Certainly right now. He has work to do, and so I thought I'd explore the library."

Her boyfriend kept the dusty old grimoires and books of lore on all paranormal nations. "Vika, I really don't need to hear about your boring dates with the dark witch."

"I looked up the lore on soul bringers."

"Oh, yeah?" I glanced to Reichardt. He sat against the pillows, his focus on me. His cock was rock hard and standing at attention, and he didn't realize it but he had clasped the base of it. I licked my lips. *Let me do that for you, big boy.* "Make it quick, sis."

"Do you know Reichardt still has most of his power?"

"No, he doesn't."

"This book says that if a soul bringer is granted his earthbound soul, he maintains all powers of the angelic unless and until he ransoms his soul bond and his purity."

"His soul bond? And purity? What in Herne does that mean— Oh. Wait. Do you mean…?"

"I don't know about the soul-bond part, but you two haven't had sex yet, have you, Libby?"

"Erm…"

"That's what I interrupted," Vika guessed. "I hope I'm not too late."

"No, you're not. And I'm not sure how I feel about that."

I knew exactly how I felt, but I'd never actually murder my sister. My posture deflated and I turned away from my lover's wondering gaze, granting him my backside, which elicited a growling moan from the bed.

"Seriously?" I whispered into the receiver. "But he hasn't shown any abilities to do…whatever it was he could once do."

"Remember when he rattled CJ's apartment trying to get to me? He could have torn that building down had we not warded it to the nines. He's strong, Libby. I don't know why he hasn't used his skills since becoming mortal. Maybe they're trapped somehow?"

"Then how to get them out? Vika, this would mean the world to him." I tucked my head down against the phone, glad Wynonna was still singing loud enough to muffle my voice. "He's felt so ineffective. No strength whatsoever. He needs to feel like a man again."

"And you were just helping him with that."

"I was. Oh, Vika, that means we could never…"

Vika's sigh over the line matched the fall of my heart. "I'm sorry, Libby. It's a choice the two of you will have to make. I'll let you get back to him. Sorry to have spoiled the evening."

"No, I'm glad you discovered what you did. Soul bond," I muttered, wondering what the heck that could possibly mean. "Thanks, Vika. Night."

I turned, crossed my arms over my chest and let out a sigh that had been lingering in my heart.

"What is it?" Reichardt asked. "You don't look happy."

"We need to talk."

"No more kisses?"

I shook my head. Could I ever kiss the man again without wanting to rip off his clothes and have sex with him? And if I did, would I strip away his powers?

Chapter Six

"I don't have any powers." Reichardt zipped up his pants, wincing because he still had an erection. He sat at the edge of the bed, looking at his hands as if he expected lightning to streak out of the fingertips. "Not yet."

I remained by the nightstand, not trusting myself to get too close to him. I was still riding a sexual high after our intense make-out session and needed to flutter down before I could bring myself to sit beside him.

I rubbed my palms down my bare arms and paced before him, aiming for my abandoned dress to cover my ultra-sensitive skin. "Vika said you should have all your powers until…"

"Until?"

I pulled the dress over my head. Reichardt toyed with my lacy purple bra. "Until you ransom your purity."

"What the hell does that—" He dropped the bra. "Oh."

"Exactly." That simple, understanding *oh* brought me down and I crashed into frustration and plopped onto the bed beside Reichardt. "She also mentioned something about a soul bond. Do you have any idea what that is?"

He slapped a hand over the front pocket on his jeans. "Uh, no?"

That sounded suspiciously like a lie, but I wouldn't press.

My thoughts were too scattered to focus. "It's not fair. Just when we were both so ready for sex."

He leaned in to kiss me, yet I couldn't bring myself to kiss him back with any passion.

"Libby? Has this information changed the way you feel about me?"

"No." But against my better judgment, I stood and strode to the window and pushed aside the curtain. The moon has half-full, the streets below dark. My bedroom looked over half the garden.

"I don't want to do something that could take away any hidden powers you might have." I shrugged a shoulder. "I remember you could move things and people with but a sweep of your hand. Sort of like the transprojectionary dislocation we witches practice, but you did it without a second thought. And your eyes would turn silver when you scrubbed Vika of the souls without even touching her."

I hooked the sleeves up over my shoulders. The mood had been lost.

"I wish you wouldn't cover those beautiful breasts."

I sighed. "Not like I'm the only naked woman you've ever seen."

"What?"

"You have seen Vika naked."

"I have?"

With another sigh, I shook my head. "Sorry. I forgot you don't remember that. She had to get naked for you to scrub her of souls."

He looked aside, gaping with the new knowledge of that explicit information. I'd said the wrong thing. The man didn't need my doubts charging to the surface right now—he needed my support.

Reichardt's hands caressed my arms. I hadn't heard him stand and approach me. I let my head fall back against his chest and closed my eyes. The only place I wanted to stand was in his arms.

So why must it change?

"I already love you, Reichardt," I whispered. "And I know you don't understand love so that might be hard for you to grasp, but this changes things between us. We can't have sex."

"Why should that change things?"

"It'll take away your powers."

"I know that. And you want to have sex with me because that will mean we are in love."

"Oh, no, sweetie. Sex is not love. Sex is a great part of love, but it's not the be-all and end-all." Even I wasn't that sexually depraved. I knew the difference between booty-call sex and the real, emotional kind of making love.

"So you would be okay with us never having sex? So long as I had my powers?"

He sounded so hopeful. As if he were on board with the idea of it already. How could I speak the truth? That I didn't care about any stupid powers. All I wanted was to have him in my life, sex or not. Though who was I kidding? I wanted the man's sexy cock between my legs. As often as I could get it.

"You haven't tried to use these supposed powers. Maybe all you need is to purposely try? If you could access your powers, then *voilà*! Strong man. And we could make love."

"Perhaps. Maybe it requires powerful magic to bring them up? Libby, what if I knew someone who could bring up my powers?"

"I don't understand."

"You want me to be the man I once was and not this new mortal person I'm trying to figure out, so I feel like I need to get back my powers."

"I like you just fine mortal, Reichardt. I just don't want to be the woman who denies you your full potential."

"But you don't want to sacrifice sex for me getting back my strength."

A wince betrayed what I could not speak.

"So sex is that important to you?"

"It shouldn't be. It's not. A little. Oh. I need to think about this. I'm going out to the garden to be alone and maybe pluck some chamomile blossoms to calm me. Why don't you…try to move something with your mind? Please don't be angry with me?"

"I'm not angry, Libby. I just can't figure you out."

I offered him a small grin. There were days even I didn't have my funky ole self figured out. "I'm a woman. You're not supposed to figure me out."

I kissed him on the cheek, then left him alone in the bedroom while I sought sanctity amid the fragrant night blossoms in the garden.

I peered out the window. Below, the garden frothed with every flower in the world, or at least, a small part of the world. Libby always smelled like a treat after coming in from the garden. She brought that air with her and swirled it into my psyche.

Now she knelt before a ruffled white flower and as she put out her fingers, I witnessed the flower head bend to meet her touch.

I felt like that flower. I wanted to bend to meet every touch she would give me. Yet right now I felt as though she'd rejected me. All because of a phone call.

She wanted me to have powers, yet she wanted me in the carnal sense, as well. That should sound perfect, but she couldn't have both.

I looked at my hands. They looked normal, kind of long, thick fingers, and the fist I clenched could put down any man. But what could I do with them beyond touch a woman and knock out a man?

Spreading my fingers, I gestured toward the bed. Nothing. Another flick of my fingers—and this time I thought about pulling back the covers—but still nothing. I pointed to the chrome floor lamp. Not even a wobble. Looking out the window, I directed stiff fingers toward Libby.

"Look at me," I murmured. Bending my fingers and curling them up as if to command her attention, I waited.

Libby turned away from me to study a yellow rose.

Shoulders falling, I shook my head. "If I could control things with but a gesture, that would be amazing. But is it worth gaining that power to sacrifice what I want from Libby? To sacrifice my soul?"

I tugged out the blue feather from a pocket and stroked the liquid vanes. I should have told her when she'd asked about the soul bond, yet this was the only part of the former me I still owned. *The thing that tied my earthbound soul to this mortal body.*

I had intended to return to the faery this evening to ransom my soul by handing over this feather. I had one more day before the forty-eight-hour deadline expired.

Was sex all that I expected it to be? Sex wasn't love? Then what was the purpose beyond pleasure? Albeit amazing pleasure, or so I guessed from the few times we'd gotten close to making love. When Libby touched my erection it had felt amazing. All my senses had focused there, in my core and at my cock. The woman could control me with that touch, and I had not minded that control.

Or perhaps I should sacrifice for some greater skills and good I could utilize? Could I do good in this world? My immediate goals were learning about love and buying a sports car. Didn't sound very selfless. Did I need to be selfless?

From below, the beautiful redhead looked up. With a white flower pressed to the corner of her lips, she smiled at me. And my heart beat soundly in favor of loving Libby.

I studied the feather. Could I do it?

Chapter Seven

With this new information about Reichardt and his latent powers, I wasn't sure how to feel. Talk about the universe throwing a whammy at me. Actually, the universe had aimed at Reichardt, but he was just too naive to notice. No, that was wrong. He did notice, and apparently he wanted back those powers. So much so that the idea of never making love to a woman didn't bother him terribly much.

Oh, Libby, how you've failed to teach the man!

I'd stopped by his apartment, using the excuse that I wanted to see his new chair that sat in the corner by the window. Because it felt wrong to say, "Hey, I want to crush you up against me and inhale you!"

That would only make his decision all the harder, I felt sure.

As I swept a palm over the brown velvet I held back a sigh. I could imagine us curled up on this oversize chair, wrapped in each other's arms, kissing, touching, giggling over conversation—making love.

But if he wanted to get back his powers it seemed he could never have sex. How to know if any soul bringer–like power existed within him?

I wandered through his apartment while he was in the shower. The man had greeted me with tousled hair and a sleepy smile. His bedroom was coming together nicely. The king-size platform bed was low and the black velvet spread was also another of my picks. As was the black marble vanity and the black leather ottoman.

Perhaps I should allow him some freedom of choice? Did I coddle him too much? Had I claimed him as my own and now he was resisting that claim by inadvertently suggesting we never have sex?

Could be a subtle way of rebelling against my control. But what man could live without sex?

Only a man who had never experienced it to know what he was missing.

Oh, Libby, what to do?

I strolled my fingers over the glossy marble vanity top, touching the silk tie I'd picked out to go with his black shirts. The price tag dangled over my hand. That purchase may have been pushing it. Reichardt was more muscleman than business suit and a tie. The heavy biker boots he wore were *très* sexy.

Beside the tie lay the blue feather I'd given him after his transformation from soul bringer to mortal. When an angel died or became human, their wings shattered to dust—CJ had collected Reichardt's angel dust and now kept that with his magical supplies—and what remained had been a feather. An angel's real wings were not composed of feathers, but rather, fashioned from their talent or skill. Steel, wire, vapor, wheat, even binary code were the stuff of angelic wings. I recalled Reichardt's wings had been bold blue and like smoke. I wasn't sure what substance they had been made from, so I couldn't be sure what his skill had been.

To judge from the seven-dot sigil on his chest, I'd got no clue to his origins.

My heart stuttered now to recall seeing him in all his glory those brief moments before he had grasped mortality, wings spread and halo glowing atop his head. The ultimate form of male, a warrior with a higher purpose who had been exiled to endlessly ferry souls.

Did I want that in my life? Or would I be happier with a mortal who could fulfill me sexually?

Don't answer that, Libby.

Beside the feather sat a tiny vial, half-filled with a sparkly black substance. I pulled out the cork stopper and the sweet aroma tickled my nose with a familiar tang. Vika had once shown me the same and explained its use.

"Goddess, this is faery ointment. Why does he have this stuff?"

As I spoke, Reichardt strolled into the bedroom, a black towel wrapped about his wide hips. The tight Adonis arcs that formed a V down his torso and toward his main shaft drew my eye.

He saw me holding the vial and his mouth dropped open. "You weren't supposed to know about that."

So quickly he had learned to conceal truths. I couldn't decide if that was a good thing—because the art of lying made him merely human—or sad.

"Why do you have an ointment that allows you to see faeries? Wait. This is none of my business. This is one secret I'll have to let stand. I have to stop being so controlling, so insistent I know everything you do. That's what is pushing you away from me."

"Libby, you're not pushing me away."

"Then why would you not want to make love with me?" Yikes, that had come out a bit more shrieky than I'd intended. "Just for some stupid powers?" I asked, softening my tone. "What do you think you'll do with them?"

"I don't know. Maybe I can…help others?"

I nodded, reluctantly agreeing. "That would be noble of you. Although the few powers I saw you wield were rather dangerous and dark, I'm sure you can use them for good. But a superhero can never have a girlfriend. Conflicts, don't you know."

"I don't want to be a superhero. Don't they wear capes? I don't think I could work a cape."

"Oh, sweetie, I love you so much. But you're a big boy. You know what you want, and it's not me."

"Libby." He swept me into his arms and kissed me so soundly I felt sure he'd been practicing on other women, but I knew he had not been because he was honorable like that. Truly, a superhero to a woman's heart.

"I do want you," he said, smoothing the hair from my lashes. "And no other woman."

"Really? But you don't know what's out there. There could be an amazing—"

He pressed a finger to my mouth, silencing foolish protests. "You are the amazing woman. No other woman changes my air as you do."

"What does that mean?"

"Since I've been mortal the air is…not right upon my skin. It feels cumbersome and stale. Like when I move it's slower and unnatural. But you…"

"Me?"

"When you are near me, Libby, the air around me changes. You bring sunshine to my life. The air lightens and I can breathe freely." He hugged me against his big, powerful chest. "I need you to lighten my air."

"Wow." I closed my eyes and listened to his steady heart-beats. "I didn't think I possessed such magic."

He traced a finger along my décolletage. "I want to swim in the magic of Libby St. Charles."

"But what about your powers?" I looked up into his gaze. "Immortality? I know you crave it. It's that something missing you want to get back. I don't want to be the one to deny you that desire."

"I do want what I once had. But if it means never having sex with you…?"

"That shouldn't be the reason for you to deny your birth-right. We can manage without sex." *Really, Libby?*

Yes. Really.

"Maybe. The faery said I had to ransom my soul to get back

my powers. And I know what the soul bond is." He picked up the feather from the vanity and drew it along my cheek.

I closed my eyes to focus on the sensation. It was as though he touched me with warm liquid that permeated my very being. Indeed, it touched my soul. How to make him understand we were soul mates?

"You would do that?" I whispered. "After you just got your soul restored to you? That would make you a soul bringer again, wouldn't it?"

"No, I wouldn't have the duties, only the angelic immortality and skills."

"Hmm...Yet Vika's research tells it differently. Maybe if you held off from sex until you got your powers. But after, could you?"

"I'm not sure. The faery was specific about needing this soul bond to make it happen."

"That sounds suspicious. I can see your aura. It's not like any mortal aura. I think maybe your powers are latent, and if we could just find a way to bring them up...Oh, there I go again, telling you what to do."

He wiped a teardrop from my cheek and studied it. "I don't like it when you cry. Do I do this to you?"

"Yes. No, it's me struggling with my own bad self. You really went to see a faery about this? What was the faery's name?"

"Didn't get it. But she knew my angel name."

"What is it?"

"Kryatron, Angel of the Seventh Soul."

"Wow. That sounds—" *Ominous. Important. And*— Oh, but the man needed to get all that back. "The seventh soul?" I tugged open the buttons on his shirt to reveal the blue dots. "Seven dots in your sigil. Interesting." I kissed the sigil and he hugged me closer.

And yet the visit with the faery sounded suspicious. The sidhe and angels were similar, yet not. They kept to their own territories, usually.

"So you're going to dive in to all this without any references, any real proof?" I asked. "Just hand over your soul and hope it all works out?"

"I think you're trying to tell me what to do again."

Shoulders sinking, I nodded that yes I was. "Sorry."

"Don't be. I like it. I never asked the questions you're asking right now. It's a good thing I told you about this. I have a lot of thinking to do before I return to the faery."

"When are you going?"

"Soon." He kissed me. "Can we kiss for a while?"

Despite the heavy subject, I liked the ease with which the man's mind turned onto a new course. I took the feather from him and stroked it down his chest. "Maybe I can distract you so much you'll stay here with me and forget all about some silly old immortality."

"There is that possibility." He lifted a brow in challenge.

The lights flickered, and thunder followed. Outside the window a flash of lightning brightened the dark sky briefly.

"A rain storm," I said. "I adore making love while it rains. Well, we don't have to make love. I know how important it is to you to remain a virgin. I respect your choice, no matter what you decide. We can fool around. Do everything but." I sighed. *Strength, Libby. You stand behind your man. No matter what.* "There are ways for a man and a woman to please each other without the actual act of intercourse."

"I have a few hours," he reassured, "before I forfeit the faery's offer. Let's think about it while we're kissing."

Reichardt kissed along my neck, tonguing the pulsing vein and giving my skin a few testing nips. I moaned, but I was distracted by the flashes of blue light outside the window. Strangest lightning I'd ever seen. It looked more like—

Glass shattered, and the blue streak of light hissed through the open window and struck me on the shoulder. I cried out in pain.

"Libby? What is that?"

"It's magic," I gasped, then dropped my head in a faint.

* * *

Standing outside, framed by the broken glass, the short, stout woman who had spoken to me at the bazaar held an orb of blue light and wielded a wicked grin. She flew through the window. I slid off the bed and dashed toward Libby, but a slash of lightning kept me from getting close to her.

I was no match for a witch who could fling blue streaks of lightning. But I wouldn't let her hurt Libby. Grabbing the stem of the ugly floor lamp, I swung the iron stick at Hester.

"I'm not here to hurt you," Hester shouted. She dodged my swings with a surprising ease for one so stout. "I just need your blood!"

"You're a vampire? I thought you were a witch?"

"It's for a spell, pretty virgin boy."

I narrowed my brows. She was after me because I was a virgin? I glanced at Libby, who was still unconscious on the floor. "No one is taking any part of me!"

Using the lamp like a spear, I aimed at Hester and gave it a thrust. The witch waved her hand, turning the lamp around. The lamp shade flew off and the lightbulb broke, exposing the inner wires and sharp parts. The lamp arrowed toward me.

With a gesture she redirected the lamp to land in the wall but a foot from my head. It stuck in and the long stem wavered up and down.

"Witches," I muttered. "How to fight them?"

"Don't fight it," Hester said. "I need your blood for an angel-summoning spell. I want my own angel lover. So give me what I want, and I won't hurt Libertie."

A female groan preceded "What's that about hurting me? There isn't enough magic in your big toe to take me down, you ugly old hag."

Now on her feet, with a gesture Libby swept the mattress up from the bed. It slammed into Hester, crushing her body against the brick wall.

"Are you okay?" I rushed to wrap Libby in my arms and kiss her.

"No time for tenderness now, sweet lips. I'm fine. But she's not down for the count. What does she want?"

"My blood," I said. "Because I'm a virgin. It's for a love spell to summon an angel."

Libby nodded and shoved me toward the door. "Faeries and witches want you. What next? Demons? You need to get away from here, and I'll hold her off as best I can. Go to the faery while you've still time!"

"I'm not leaving you!"

"Yeah? Do you know what a witch can do with an ancient virgin's blood? It's not pretty. And it's not like she'll take a few drops. You won't survive, Reichardt."

"I won't let that stout, angry witch push me around."

The mattress flew toward us. I saw it coming and spun in front of Libby, putting my back to the soaring object. It hit me hard, but I managed to protect Libby by caging her against the wall with my arms.

"Let me do what I can," she said, then kissed me quickly. "One witch is a better match than a mortal, no matter how many muscles you have."

"You see what me having my powers could do?"

The mattress fell to the floor. Hester's blue lightning streaked past my head and surrounded Libby's shoulders. Angered, I turned and put up a palm to block the lightning. Then a remarkable thing occurred. My palm actually cut off the stream of lightning and released Libby.

"How did you do that?" Hester asked.

"This home is protected against foul magic," Libby called. "You are not welcome here!"

"I'm not leaving without the virgin!"

Charging forward, I plowed into Hester, jamming my elbow into her gut and slamming her against the wall. The witch put her hands over my skull and it felt as if thousands of stinging insects were crawling over my skin and chewing at my bones. I fell to my knees.

She would kill this feeble mortal body to get what she

wanted. And that meant I'd never see Libby again. Never kiss her gorgeous red lips. Never again eat one of her chocolate-chip cookies. Never hold her. Never make love to her.

Never again stand in her air.

That was *not* going to happen.

Head-butting the witch in the stomach put her back for but a moment. Drawing up from my core, I willed all the unknown power I contained out through my hands and sent a storm toward her. The energy waves were purple and green and wavered like tentacles about the woman. The witch flew out through the window and landed in the cobblestone courtyard below.

I pulled back my hands. They tingled and shot off tiny sparks of green, electric and bold.

"What in great Herne was that?" Libby asked from the floor.

"I'm not sure. My powers? Stay here. If I've got some magic, I need to use it before I lose it."

Stepping through the broken window, I leaped to the ground two stories below and landed with ease. Didn't hurt—it felt as though I'd the grace of a cat. I stood over the fallen witch. With one hand I reached out and twisted, which lifted Hester up to her feet and then to her toes, where she hung before me a pitiful, defeated wreck.

"Apparently no one ever taught you manners," I said. "If you hurt Libby in any way, I will come after you."

"Big talk for a mortal." Hester spat at me.

"Silence!" A sweep of my hand closed her mouth, sealing it so I could not see a crease between her lips.

Startled at that, I maintained the authoritative manner so she wouldn't see me sweat. However I was utilizing this power, I didn't want to lose it until I'd made this witch fear me.

"You will leave this property never to return," I said. "Or I will retaliate." A twist of my hand turned her head, and when Hester's lips broke open in a scream, I released the hold before her neck could break.

The witch dropped to the ground and scrambled upright.

"You're powerful," Hester said in shaky tones. "I thought you were mortal. Are you neither a virgin? So Libertie has already gotten her claws into you. This was a foolish endeavor."

She turned and ran off. I let her go. I didn't want to end her life and suspected she'd stay away from Libby and me now.

I got startled when I felt a hand on my back and turned, raising a palm to fend off— "Libby."

"Whoa. Holster that hand, lover. How did you do that?"

"I'm not sure. But I know one thing." I swept her into my arms and leaped back up and through the broken window. "I can do that. And I can do this."

With a grand gesture that squared my hands in the shape of the window, I put back the glass and then returned the mattress to the bed frame. And then with a powerful breath, I blew toward the window and it glowed yellow.

"That's a ward," Libby said in awe. "You've your angel powers back? Reichardt, what are you?"

"I'm not sure. What time is it?"

"You still think you need to go to the faery?"

I sighed. It was an opportunity I couldn't pass up. The powers I'd just utilized— Hell, I couldn't know if they would last. Handing over my soul to the faery would guarantee they stayed with me.

I kissed Libby on the crown of her head.

She nodded and stepped away from me, looking aside to the havoc around the room. "Right, then. You should get going."

And so I left. Because I didn't know what to say, and if I had looked into Libby's eyes one more time I wouldn't have been able to leave.

Chapter Eight

Once back at home, I flopped onto my bed and caught my head in my hands. Tears wobbled in my eyes but I was too proud to let them fall. He'd left. Just like that! After defeating Hester's dark magic with such ease—and some magic of his own—Reichardt still believed he needed to ransom his soul again to have what he desired.

Immortality. Strength. Power.

I could understand how that might mean something to him, to any man, but that didn't mean I had to like it.

By ransoming his soul, he was changing our relationship forever. Damn it, but I'd held on too tightly. I had forced him away from me.

"Should have used a love spell on him," I muttered.

I shook my head. No. I'd tried my best. The man needed to spread his wings and be free to learn the world.

And other women?

A teardrop plopped onto my hand. And then I couldn't hold them back anymore and burst into a fit of tears.

It was the only right thing for Reichardt Fallowgleam.

I'd just lost my soul mate.

The walk to the sixteenth arrondissement was a long one, but I inhaled the fresh night air. I needed the breather after the battle with the stout witch. And after walking away from Libby.

Had I actually done that? Walked away from the one perfect thing in my life? And for what reason? A stupid, selfish desire to have something I probably wouldn't utilize too often anyway.

Libby had been so selfless toward me. In everything she did, I could feel her kindness, her warmth and her genuine care for me. Always on her kitchen counter, that cookie jar was filled to the brim. Even if I took out a cookie or two (or three or five) when I returned, the jar had been replenished. And seeing that made me smile.

Was that love? If so, it was an amazing feeling.

So why now did I intend to ransom that love for the unknown?

Handing over this feather and my soul would give me power. But did I already possess power? I knew I did. I just wasn't certain if it had been a one-time, in-the-moment reaction to someone threatening Libby. And how long would this new strength last?

It shouldn't matter. Libby had made my heart beat by giving me my earthbound soul.

I stopped and tugged out the blue feather. It wavered in the breeze. This was the symbol of what I had once been. Something I couldn't even remember let alone grasp the enormity of once possessing such power.

I closed my eyes and imagined the feather leaving my grasp and circling skyward, and when I opened my eyes, I watched the delicate thing spiraling upward and away.

"Adieu," I whispered. "There's something that means more to me."

I knocked on the pink door of the white hexagon house. The yellow flowers planted beside the door swayed and I spied Salamander creeping along the foundation, stalking a mouse. The door opened and Libby's eyes flashed wide.

"Reichardt?"

"I didn't go to the faery," I said.

"But...?"

"I'd give up immortality to hold you, Libby. I don't know if the power I used earlier is here to stay, but I don't want to risk losing you in an attempt to keep it. Will you accept me back?"

"Will I?"

She lunged into my arms and kissed me soundly. Every gorgeous curve of her melded to my skin and I sighed into her mouth, relieved and elated to have won the only thing that mattered to me. No matter what the future handed me, I knew that she would be at my side.

"I bet that faery just wanted to get her hands on your soul," she said. "It could be a powerful tool in her hands."

"Perhaps." I studied my hand that curved against her hip. "I feel as though it is mine, this power. But if not, at least I had a moment to utilize it when it was most needed." I smiled at her, triumphant in the new knowledge. "There's so much I've yet to learn, so silly powers would have been a nuisance."

"What about sex?" Libby pressed both hands over her mouth, shaking her head. "I shouldn't have said that."

"Sex is important to you."

"Yes, but, well—yes. I love you, Reichardt."

In her bright green eyes I did not see fear but a stunning respect. It was the first time she had really looked into my eyes and said not a thing yet spoke volumes with her eyes.

"What I am," I said, "is madly in love with the most beautiful witch in the world. And I know that because my heart hurt when I thought Hester had hurt you. And it ached a little more with every step I took away from you to go to the faery. I had to turn back." I stroked her cheek. "Whatever I am now, can you love me, Libby?"

"Oh, yes. But don't you want to know what's up with the power? Reichardt, what if you're not completely mortal? What does that mean?"

"Who to ask?"

"I'm not sure. Maybe Vika will know."

I brushed a thumb over her lips. "You are a smart and bold woman. I love you for that. And I believe I know the meaning of that word when I speak it."

"Love can be many different things."

"Can it make my heart feel strong and warm?"

She nodded.

"Can it make me want to always be with you, powers or not?"

Another nod.

"And it can change my air." I kissed her, then said, "I love you, Libertie St. Charles."

"I love you, too, Reichardt," she said on a sigh.

Her kiss captured my breath and as the air about me lightened, my heart swelled with the immense feeling of newfound love. I didn't ever want to lose this witch who challenged my every reason for existence. And I had a good idea exactly how to seal our bond forever.

"And love is also cookies," I added.

"Cookies?"

"Whenever I look in the cookie jar you keep on the counter, it's filled to the top. No matter how many I eat, you replace them. And I realized it's because you like to do good things for me, to make me happy."

"Cookies *are* love," she said, beaming. "Should I get one for you?"

"I had something even more pleasurable in mind. But I suppose the mood has been lost," I murmured.

She smiled and bowed her head. "I never lose the mood around you, big boy."

"I do have this sudden urge to take care of this virginity issue before the next crazed, blood-hungry witch arrives at my windowsill."

"Then let's do it."

I mapped out the freckles that littered Libby's hips and lower back to the indents above her derriere that I could fit my thumb into, and I followed with my tongue. She cooed and wiggled her derriere. Mmm, she tasted like all the rich desserts she had ever baked for me, but even better.

She lay stretched along the bed, her body like the garden out back, arrayed for me to wander over and touch, smell and admire. I tongued that sexy curve at the base of her derriere and she lifted her hips. I took that moment to slide a hand under her stomach and lower. The heat of her at the apex of her thighs was astounding.

I flipped her over, and she wrapped her legs about my neck. Perspiration bejeweled her skin. My body has hot, too, and I didn't think my erection could get any harder, but prolonging the outcome was more appealing than having been done with it too quickly.

"What are you thinking about?" she asked, coming up to her elbows to meet my gaze.

I hovered above her mons, where more freckles dotted about the thatch of red hair. "I'm thinking how good you taste. And how I want to taste right here." I licked her folds.

"Oh, lover, you do what you want."

"CJ said it takes time to learn a woman."

"As it does a man. But that's the fun part. All the time spent learning and exploring. You don't have to master me right now, Reichardt. You've already won my heart."

"Have I?"

She took my hand and dragged it up to place over her heart and breast. "It beats for you."

That sounded better than any powers I may have gained. A woman's heart was a delicate and wondrous place. That I'd ventured into Libby's heart humbled me, and at the same time empowered me.

I dashed my tongue across her slick wetness again. Her hips tilted toward me and her soft moans increased, growing throaty and wanting. Here was her center, the place of mastery that I was determined to learn. But she was right; it didn't have to happen all at once. The learning would be sweet, and I intended to stretch it over many mortal years.

Was I immortal now? I suspected I'd have to ransom my soul for that. But I was fine with the trade-off, for some power and strength. And an intimate place in Libby's heart.

I glided my fingers inside her and used her moans and motions as a guide to how fast or slow to stroke her. A few times she reached down to guide me, which I appreciated, and then...

I let loose my voice like a rock 'n' roll crooner. My shoulders pushed into the bed, and my fingers clenched the sheets as Reichardt's ministrations burst me free from the impending coil in my core and set me off in that giddy, goofy kind of wondrous joy called orgasm.

Thank you, Universe! It just had to toy with me a while. I understood that.

My cry of happiness settled into a breast-jiggling giggle. I always laughed after orgasm, and it tended to freak men out, so I tried to cut it off abruptly.

"I love your laughter," Reichardt said. "It was that good that you couldn't control your joy?"

He understood me. How cool was that?

Pulling him to lie on top of me, I kissed him deeply and murmured "Yes, yes, and yes" against his mouth. His panting chest heaved against mine. "You make me laugh, and that's the best feeling ever. But now it's my turn to let you feel what orgasm is like."

"I'm ready to learn."

"I do love an eager student."

I pushed him to the bed and straddled his hips, fitting myself snugly against his erection. Pleased to be on top where I belonged, I kissed down his throat and chest and to each of his nipples. I tapped his sigil, knowing we'd never learn what being an angel of the Seventh Soul meant, but thinking maybe someday the universe would let us in on the truth.

"Am I expected to laugh?" he asked, his fingers running through my loose hair and stroking down my shoulders.

"You do whatever the mood demands of you, lover boy. Just don't hold back. Wow. I can't believe I'm going to take your virginity."

"Is it that big an event?"

"For some it is. For you it must be monumental. It's been two thousand years. Are you sure you want to do this? If we're wrong about you retaining the powers you just gained, losing your virginity may keep you from ever obtaining immortality."

"In your arms, Libby, every day is forever and filled with joy and laughter. I'm not going to turn back now. Oh." I gripped his erection. "Why any man would refuse to have sex is beyond me. I want to feel myself inside you. Ohyesthat'sjustrightdon'tstop."

Dipping my fingers into the wetness between my legs, I then slicked it over Reichardt's firm shaft and found a rhythm that quickly silenced him, save for gasping breaths and some wanting moans. I knelt, positioning the thick head of him at my entrance so he could feel my heat while my hand did not cease coaxing him to a gasping, panting pinnacle.

His hands caressed my breasts, not purposely, but more like he'd placed them in the best spot in the house and was ready to hold on for the ride.

I loved my big, hunky man. Now it was time to win one for Team Reichardt.

Shimmying my hips, I lowered myself over his shaft to the satisfied baritone groans of one very happy man.

"You like that? Let's try this rhythm."

Rocking my hips, easing up and down, I worked him to a shuddering mass of muscles, moans and gasps. A squeeze to the base of his cock would hold him off for a bit, but I didn't want to torture him his first time up to bat. Besides, he shuddered and his arms had stiffened, bracketing my breasts. His jaw tight, he squeezed his eyes shut.

A few more slides up and down his erection and I rewarded

my lover with an orgasm that burst out in a triumphant shout. He shuddered and pumped his hips against mine, driving deep into me, and I took it all, giving what I had wanted to give since that first moment I'd laid eyes on the stoic soul bringer with the glass heart.

He was mine now. His heart was real and his soul had just bonded with mine. Soul mates. I would allow nothing to break us apart.

So why did I suddenly feel as if I'd stolen him from something better? Was the man still part angel? To judge from the powers he'd used against Hester, he was something. By making love to the man—literally stealing his virginity—had I taken that away?

I felt...everything. I saw it all. My past soared through my thoughts.

The wars that had kept me busy delivering souls to Above and Beneath.

The births that had ended tragically and the human tears that had not caused me to waver in my steadfast reaping of souls.

The foul murders.

The suicides.

The boy standing beside his dead father in the concentration camp who had handed me the Jewish star. I'd had to return for his soul two hours later.

The plant, currently in my apartment, given to me by the old woman downstairs in my building. I'd taken her soul following a peaceful death a year later.

The cat, named Thomas, who was a familiar, and a friend, when he was in human form. I'd have to look him up first thing.

Seeing Libby for the first time and taking the cookie she'd offered me. Made with so much love. She had loved me before I could comprehend the emotion.

I loved her now.

And the orgasm faded, as did the images. I collapsed on the bed beneath the witch, knowing all yet also knowing I was now free of the servitude of a soul bringer. Yet I still retained power and immortality because I had just bonded with my soul mate.

The shower stream pattered over our shoulders and Libby slicked soap over my rigid abdomen. I turned my face to the stream and let the water beat down upon me. Felt great. But nothing felt better than sex.

Nothing. Not even knowing my past.

I truly had learned the secret to life, and I wanted to do it every day, all day, from now on.

Libby stroked my hard-again cock with soap, and I studied the logistics of the shower. I could lift her and fit her onto my cock, but the floor was slick and I didn't want to risk a tumble and injuring her. On the other hand, I did have some crazy skills at moving people about with but a gesture....

But before I could suggest we cut the shower short and head for drier ground, she dropped to her knees and took me in her mouth.

"Angels above and demons beneath," I growled. I'd not imagined a woman could do something like this for a man, but oh, that Libby did. She sucked me in and nibbled gently with her teeth and I was going to come very quickly. "Libby, be warned..."

She took in my seed and swallowed it. An amazing woman. I lifted her to hug against my body, still racked with orgasmic shudders, snuggled into her wet flesh.

"Later, I'll let you do the same for me," she said and kissed me.

I wrapped a silk robe about my body and posed before the floor-length mirror, never shy of my reflection. My bright red hair clashed with the purple and it did not. Long ago, I'd stopped worrying what colors went with each other. I felt like a million colors right now as Reichardt snuck up from behind and embraced me, slipping his hands around my stomach and nuzzling his nose into my wet hair.

"Is the mortal realm always this good?" he asked.

"It is when you're in love. I imagine what you're feeling is satisfaction from some damn good lovemaking."

"Yet you claim to love me, when I know you've only reason to hate me for the awful things I did to you and your sister."

I turned and opened my robe, pressing my breasts against his bare chest. Mmm, his heartbeats were sound and strong. And oh, there was that ever-ready erection. "I love the potential I see in you, lover boy. And I love your handsome face and strong muscles. I love the way you wrap me in your arms. And I love that you accept me exactly as I am."

"That's a lot of ways to love."

"I could list many more, but I'll save them for tomorrow and the next day and ever after."

"We should tell each other things we love about the other every day. I love your hair—it's bold and bright—as well as your eyes. I love the way you make me feel when we are naked and close like this. I love that you feed me and take care of me. But is that enough?"

"Does it feel like enough for you?"

"Yes. I feel very rich in your arms, Libby. And yet…"

He'd explained to me in the shower that he'd seen a sort of movie of his life during orgasm, and he was good with not having what he once had now.

But he was still missing something, and I didn't know what to give him to fill that hole. It was a place in the universe, I suspected. Reichardt needed ground to stand on and know himself, and the only way he could get that was through experience.

I was comfortable in this world. I had family, a good life and a new lover. Nothing could be better.

Nothing, except knowing Reichardt also felt at peace.

"You want to know about your powers," I guessed. "Me, too. I hope…"

"You hope what?"

"What if I took them away by having sex with you?"

He twisted his finger in the air and pointed at the bed. The pillows flew to the floor and the sheets peeled back to expose the rumpled undersheet. "Still got it."

"Simple tricks. But do you feel strong? I know you wanted to get back your strength."

He lifted me about the waist with one arm. "If there was another of you, I could balance you with both arms."

"So this is good?" I asked with hope. "But you're still unsure."

"I'll have many questions, Libby. And I know you can't answer them all, nor will it ever be as it once was. I intend to move forward. I just don't want to stumble."

"Wherever you are, you're just…there. You own where you stand. You still do. You need to believe that. Can you believe that?"

"With you to remind me of it, I will. I'd like to have a job. Something to make me feel worthy."

"We'll find something for you. You need to figure out what your passion is."

"That's easy. My passion is Libertie St. Charles."

"Yes, but I don't think you can make a job out of me."

"Pleasing you—"

"Don't say it's work."

"Oh, no. That's not what I mean."

"I know what you mean, lover boy. It's a labor of love, yes?"

"It is."

"Then let the labor begin, because you've some woman-pleasing to learn. It may have been all fun and games for you earlier, and believe me it was awesome for me. But you're the only one who came in the shower. My turn now."

"I'm eager to please."

"You know all the right answers."

Chapter Nine

"Good thing you didn't return to the faery," Vika said to Reichardt.

CJ had gone to make tea in the main office of the Archives, while Reichardt pulled a chair up to the table beside me.

"I found an interesting fact about the sidhe. They have a thing for angel feathers," Vika said. "Can create great magic with them. I doubt the faery could have given you back your immortality, but she certainly would have kept the feather."

"You'll have to keep that in a safe place now," I said to him, kissing his cheek.

"And this is the other information. The reason I called you two over here today."

Vika turned the huge ancient book bound in green leather on the table toward Reichardt and me. After I had told my sister everything, I wondered if the book from which Vika had learned about soul bringers might answer the lingering question: How did Reichardt now have his powers if he hadn't again ransomed his soul?

"It's an angelic grimoire," Vika explained. She leaned forward across the table on her elbows, her thick red braid falling with a plunk onto the wood surface.

My sister always wore long dresses tightened around the waist with a corset. Me and Vika; the retro rocker and the goth chick. Add in Eternitie, the hippie chick, and you had better be prepared for what the St. Charles sisters packed in their magical arsenal.

"You're looking rather happy today, Reichardt," she said.

The man splayed out a hand and met gazes with me. The grin hadn't left his face since we'd had sex. Again. And again. And yet again.

Hey, Queen of Overindulgence, here. And I'd just crowned my king.

"Your sister makes me happy," he said.

"I can see that."

I did not miss the teasing tone in Vika's voice.

"And she makes me cookies."

"Is that so?" Vika caught my gaze. "Well, cookies are important to a relationship."

"Most definitely," Reichardt said, my sister's snark soaring high over his head.

I wanted to shout to the world that I was in love with the most handsome and kind man to walk this earth, but my eyes landed on an interesting paragraph.

"'Love is the object that binds the angel soul to the man,'" I read out loud.

"What does that mean?" Reichardt asked.

That was all the text said, but with some thought, I decided it was a monumental fact. "It wasn't your feather after all. For you to have loved and given love must have bound your angel powers to you. No matter what occurred, not even taking your soul and gaining mortality could take away those powers."

"But I didn't know I had the powers until—"

"Until you were forced to fight to protect me from Hester." I met his violet and emerald gaze. "Love made them emerge."

"So...I had them all along? But what love bound them to me before that?"

"My love," I said on a gasp. I stroked a finger along his

hairline and traced the soft stubble forming along his jaw. "Reichardt, I loved you before you got your soul."

"Yes, I know that because I saw it when I, uh—" He glanced to Vika, blushing.

"When you had an orgasm." I finished what he couldn't say in front of another woman. "I've always known we were soul mates, but this means it's for real."

"Wow," Vika said. "That's so freakin' cool. You two really were meant for one another." She tapped the nail wrapped around the leather cord at her neck. "Did grandma know?"

I nodded. "I think she did."

"Soul mates," he said and pulled me onto his lap to kiss me. "You've changed my air, Libby. That's some powerful magic."

"It wasn't witch magic," I said. "It was soul magic."

* * * * *

THE DARKNESS

NINA CROFT

Nina Croft grew up in the north of England. After training as an accountant, she spent four years working as a volunteer in Zambia, which left her with a love of the sun and a dislike of nine to five work. She then spent a number of years mixing travel (whenever possible) with work (whenever necessary) but has now settled down to a life of writing and picking almonds on a remote farm in the mountains of southern Spain.

Nina shares the farm with a husband, three dogs, four cats, a horse, two goats and a handful of chickens. It's a perfect place to indulge her two great passions, reading and writing.

Chapter One

Thunder crashed overhead, and flashes of crimson lit up the night sky, bathing the city of London in a bloodred glow. Darius Cole breathed in deeply, his nostrils flaring as he caught the acrid stench of fear drifting up from the alley ahead.

He'd been stalking his prey for an hour, but he was growing bored with the chase. Besides, this close to mid-summer, the nights were short and dawn was approaching. He needed to finish this soon. With that thought, he loosened his control on the blood-thirst. It rose hard and fast, flooding his body, and beneath the blood-thirst, the Darkness struggled to break free. He'd sensed it often in the past week, lurking in the recesses of his mind, and for the first time in his long existence, he welcomed its presence.

Darius.

A voice whispered through his head, soft and low. He recognized her instantly and rage surged through him. Then he shook his head. It was nothing but his imagination playing tricks on him. Again.

Gina wasn't here. Why would she be?

She'd left him twice now, the last time only a week ago. If she'd wanted to talk to him, she could have done so then, face-to-face. Instead, she'd fought beside him, and when the fighting was over, she'd walked away without a backward glance.

The lightning flared again, and he caught sight of his prey cowering in the shadow of a parked truck. Darius stalked forward, no longer troubling to keep under cover. The young man's face was slack with fear, his eyes glazed, but it aroused no pity. Instead, the Darkness clawed its way a little closer to the surface.

Reaching out, Darius clasped one hand in the greasy blond hair, jerked back the head and exposed the line of the throat. He breathed in the rank scent of terror oozing from the skin, and then he lunged. His fangs sank into the flesh and he fed convulsively, gaining no pleasure from the act, but unable to stop as the Darkness gripped him.

Darius, no! You cannot take the lives of innocents.

Her voice was clearer now. This time he couldn't deny it. He raised his head, inhaling, as though he would scent her perfume on the warm night air.

Nothing.

Still, his fangs retracted, and the Darkness receded. He relaxed his tight hold, and the man slumped to the ground. Darius glanced down at him. "He deserves death," he said. "He's a pimp and a drug pusher."

But not at your hand.

He nudged the still form with the toe of his boot. The man stirred, his eyes fluttering open. Crouching down beside him, Darius stared into the terror-filled gaze. "Forget," he murmured, his power flowing out to bind his victim's will. "Now, go."

For a moment, the blond man peered up at Darius, his eyes unfocused, then he staggered to his feet and lurched away.

"There," Darius said, "still alive. Happy, now?"

No, not happy.

Then she was gone.

He whirled around, searching the surrounding buildings, not quite believing she had left him, again. But she was close.

He sensed it with every beat of his heart. She was here, in the city somewhere, and he would find her.

He raised his head and screamed up at the night sky. "Where are you?"

Chapter Two

"Just two more days," Gina whispered into the phone. "Give me two days, then I'll come back on my own. I swear."

She held her breath as she waited for her sister's reply. In the background, she could hear the howling of dogs, and her whole body tensed.

"We don't have two days," Regan said. "I've tried, but I can't stop this. You used the earth magic and blacked out the sun. Only you can restore the balance."

Regan was the oldest and most powerful of her sisters, and Gina had prayed that somehow Regan could put things right. Now the last of her hope died. "I had no choice."

"That changes nothing." Regan's tone was harsh, but beneath that, Gina could sense a deep well of anguish. "The magic is out of control, and it will get worse until you pay the price."

"I will pay," Gina said. "But first, I need…"

"There's no time," Regan interrupted. "I'm releasing Diablo and Satan. Expect us soon."

The connection was cut. Gina stared at the cell phone clutched in her hand, then hurled it across the room. She raised her head and listened, as though she would already hear the baying of the hounds as they raced across the night sky, hunting her down.

Regan had set the hellhounds after her.

How could she? Her own sister. But Gina knew how. She crossed the hotel room and drew back the heavy curtain. Outside, darkness had fallen and flashes of crimson fire lit up the night sky. She bit her lip. Regan was right—time was running out.

Gina dropped the curtain and sank down to the floor, hugging her knees.

She would never be sorry for what she'd done. There was always a price to pay for wielding the earth magic, and she had known the consequences would be severe when she'd used it to save Raven's life. She'd done it anyway—no price was too high to save her daughter, and Gina was willing to pay. Just not yet. First, she needed to be certain Darius was safe.

She knew she could never see him again. She'd accepted that when she'd walked away a week ago. She'd wanted to stay, desperately, but how could she after what she had done? Knowing what she must soon do?

Twenty-two years ago, Darius had abducted her, seduced her and taken her blood. In doing so, he had forged a bond between them, a bond so strong they felt each other's thoughts and emotions. That bond had faded with time, until now only a tenuous thread connected them. Then last night she had felt his bitterness, and realized how close he was to embracing the Darkness. Dread filled her at the thought; it would be the end of him. He would be an outcast, hunted down by his own kind.

She'd reached out to him. He had heard her and stepped back from the edge. Now she needed to be sure he would not give in.

A light tap sounded on the door.

Her eyes flew open; her muscles tightened. The hounds couldn't have found her yet. Then she breathed out, forcing herself to relax. After all, a hellhound wouldn't knock. Scrambling to her feet, she crossed the room and opened the door.

Her breath caught in her throat, and a fierce wave of delight washed over her.

Darius was leaning against the wall, arms crossed over his broad chest. He appeared outwardly relaxed, but the air around him throbbed with tension. A slight smile lifted the corners of his lips, but his eyes remained cold as black ice, and Gina's delight oozed away. She knew she should slam the door in his face, but was unable to move.

When she'd first laid eyes on him, she'd thought him the most beautiful thing she'd ever seen in her entire life. She'd lived for over two hundred years, and in all that time she'd never seen anything quite so perfect. His looks hadn't changed—he was still perfect—but now there was a cold, bitter edge of cruelty to his beauty, and she knew the change was due to her.

Black hair fell in an unkempt, wild tangle to his shoulders, stubble lined his strong jaw and a vicious scar ran down his right cheek. Her finger trembled with the need to reach out and smooth away the angry line. His faded jeans hung low on his lean hips, and a faded T-shirt stretched taut over his wide shoulders and muscular chest.

"Are you going to invite me in?" he asked, and the coldness in his voice matched the ice in his eyes. If she'd had any notion he still harbored feelings for her, it disappeared in that moment.

But if he didn't have feelings, then what did he want from her? A flash of fear hit her hard, and Gina fought it down. She tried to tell herself she trusted Darius with her life, but that had been long ago. She knew in her heart this wasn't the same man.

His eyes roamed over her. They lingered on her throat, and her fear instantly vanished, replaced by something far more dangerous. She could almost feel the scrape of his fangs, and prickles of excitement shivered across her skin. Her body quivered with the memory of the pleasure she knew he could bring. The muscles of her belly cramped, and her insides turned molten. She could scent her own arousal on the night air and

knew he could, too. He leaned closer and breat
as though trying to inhale her.

"Pleased to see me?" he murmured.

Her eyes flashed to his face. He was makin̲g̲ ̲n̲o̲ ̲a̲t̲t̲e̲m̲p̲t̲
to hide his response, his eyes darkening to black, gleaming
under heavy lids. He looked like a hunter who had scented
his prey, and he was starving for her. The breath caught in her
throat once more, and her blood thickened until she could feel
it pulsing through her veins.

She'd forgotten the way he made her feel. Although that
wasn't entirely true. The truth was she'd known she would
be unable to get through the long years alone, with his memory haunting her at every step, so she'd built defensive walls
around those memories. Now the walls were crumbling. She
shook her head, forced herself to ignore the feelings, gather
her self-control around her like a cloak.

She licked her lips. Opened her mouth. Closed it again.

A frown formed on his face as he watched her. He lifted his
head to scan the room behind her, and her hand tightened on
the door, ready to slam it in his face if he made a move to enter.

"Invite me in," he said.

She shook her head again.

He raised an eyebrow. "Can't you speak? Somebody cut
out your tongue?"

She swallowed, trying to ease the tightness in her throat.
"What do you want, Darius?"

"At this moment, to come in and…" He paused, his eyes
running over her body again. This time she was ready, and
steeled herself against any response. "…talk to you about old
times."

"I don't remember the old times."

"Really?" He sounded as though he didn't believe her.
"Well, we'll talk about new times then."

"I don't want to talk about new times."

"You might not, but I do."

The sound of voices drifted down the corridor, and Gina

jumped. She peered around Darius to see a couple of girls walking toward them, young, pretty and vivacious. Their steps slowed as they caught sight of Darius. They whispered to each other as they stopped by the door of the next room along, taking too long fiddling with the key card, and casting sideways glances at his tall, indolent figure.

Gina glanced at his face. He was watching them, a speculative look in his eyes, and something hardened inside her. The two girls finally managed to open the door and disappeared inside with a last longing look in his direction.

He turned back to Gina. "Perhaps they would invite me in."

"No doubt."

He looked after them thoughtfully, eyeing the closed door. He licked his lips, and her eyes narrowed. "Do you really want me to eat the neighbors?" he asked.

"You wouldn't."

"Try me." He smiled, showing the tips of his fangs. "You know what I'm capable of. I could drain them dry and still come back to you for more."

She shook her head. "What is it you want, Darius?" she asked again.

"Invite me in."

She remembered then that he couldn't enter without her invitation, couldn't cross her threshold. If she closed the door on him, he could do nothing about it. Except go to the next room. She glanced at the closed door where the girls had disappeared. Did she believe he would coldly slaughter them?

She rejected the idea with her whole heart. If he hadn't been able to kill a drug dealer and a pimp, he wasn't going to kill two young girls, just to teach her a lesson. However, he might very well go next door and have his way with them, and she wasn't any happier about that. Less so, she realized, with an unpleasant jolt. She knew he was quite capable of taking their blood, sating himself in their bodies and wiping their minds of the whole thing. A vision of him flashed in her mind, his golden limbs tangled with theirs, and the thought of that happening made her want to go drain them herself. Or turn them into toads.

"You're thinking too hard," he said. "Just invite me in, sweetheart."

Her eyes flicked to his face at the endearment, but she could read nothing from his expression. She gave him one last, long look, then shifted to the side. "Come in," she muttered.

He smiled and stepped past her into the room.

Chapter Three

Gina closed the door and stood for a minute, her forehead pressed against the cool, smooth wood. When she turned, Darius was prowling the hotel room, examining everything, picking up her belongings, holding them to his face, putting them down again.

It was actually a suite of rooms, consisting of a comfortable sitting area and a large bedroom. It didn't take him long to circle the entire sitting room, for she didn't have many possessions. He came back to stand in front of her.

"What are you doing here?" he asked, almost gently.

She frowned. "Shouldn't that be my question? This is my room."

"That wasn't quite what I meant." He sank down onto the sofa and patted the seat beside him. "Come and sit with me."

"I'd rather stand."

He looked thoughtful, but didn't argue. Instead, he relaxed against the cushions, his arms stretched out along the back of the sofa, and watched her through half-closed eyes. "I presumed, when you disappeared so quickly, that you'd gone back to your sisters."

"No."

"Well, obviously not. I think I'd notice if the old harridans were hidden away here." He sniffed the air. "I'd smell them."

She almost smiled at his words. He'd never liked her sisters, and to be fair, they hadn't done anything to make him like them. Quite the opposite, in fact. Now, Gina turned away to hide the wave of anguish washing over her at the memory of all her sisters had done.

Her eldest sister, Regan, had always been like a mother to Gina, and Gina was quite aware that Regan would have happily killed Darius twenty-two years ago. Gina had stood in her way back then, but Regan's bitterness had festered, until she was willing to use anything, including Gina's daughter, to settle the score.

It had taken a long time for Gina to forgive her, but in the end, she'd come to accept that Regan had only done what she believed was needed to protect her.

Now Gina was beyond even her sister's protection.

She turned back. Darius still watched her, and she shifted under his gaze, uncomfortable. She looked around the room, searching for something to say. "Would you like a drink?"

His eyes darkened even more. "Are you offering?"

His gazed flicked back to her throat, and she realized what she had said. Heat rose in her cheeks, and her mouth went dry. "I've got beers in the fridge."

"Spoilsport," he murmured. Then he shrugged. "A beer would be good."

She got him a bottle from the minibar, and then took one for herself; it would give her something to do with her hands, something to hide behind. She handed him the opened bottle, then stood in front of him, not sure what to do. Though there was one thing she desperately needed to know. Did he have news of Raven? Her heart softened as she thought of their beautiful daughter. It would make it all worthwhile if only Raven were safe and happy.

"Tell me about Raven," she said. "How is she?"

He raised an eyebrow. "You expect me to believe you care?"

"Just tell me."

He shrugged. "She's fine. Better than fine. She and Kael were married five days ago. As you would have known if you'd stayed around after the fight, instead of taking off."

Gina ignored the comment. She couldn't have stayed; it was impossible. She would have only caused more hurt to her daughter if she had. But something relaxed inside her at the news of Raven's marriage. Kael was a good man, a shape-shifter and head of the Council. He had risked everything to save Raven. Now Gina would trust him to keep her safe.

She opened her mouth to speak, but at that moment, a dog barked in the distance, and her gaze flew to the window. She knew it was a dog, not a hellhound, but it reminded her that her time was running out. She didn't want Darius anywhere near her when they caught up. Even a vampire as old as Darius was no match for a pair of hellhounds.

She had to get him away from her and soon.

"For God's sake, relax," Darius muttered. "I'm not going to leap on you." He gave her a long look out of those dark eyes. "Well, not unless you ask me very, very nicely."

Darius watched her reaction to his words. She was nervous, her eyes flickering to the window, her whole body jumping at every sound.

Gina was afraid of something, and if she feared him, then she was only being sensible. However, he was aware that fear was not the only reaction she was feeling to his presence. She was also aroused, and that was as far from sensible as it was possible to get. He could scent the perfume of her arousal on the warm night air, and his hunger was rising.

That combined with the anger that had simmered beneath the surface for the past week made a dangerous mix.

His cock was already hard, and sex had been at the forefront of his mind since he'd first seen her. Now his gums prickled with the need to feed. He longed to do both. Only force of will kept him sitting here when what he wanted to do was pin her down and take her in every way possible.

But he didn't dare touch her, not while the Darkness still ate at his mind. He could feel its lingering pull, waiting for something to set it free.

He took a sip of his beer and let his gaze wander over her face and body. What had she done to herself? She'd always been slender, but now she was almost gaunt. Her skin was pale, and she had cut off her hair. That was recent; a week ago, it had hung down to her waist. The short style suited her, though, showing off her high cheekbones and emphasizing her enormous eyes. She could have passed for human, if not for those. They were witch's eyes, silver rimmed with black, gazing at him, unblinking, until he was sure he could sink into them, lose himself in her soul.

No doubt she'd kick him out fast enough if he did.

She hadn't wanted him before, and she didn't want him now. She had made that very clear. What had he thought when he'd seen her last week? That she had come for him? He was a fool.

The old pain gripped him again, but he wouldn't give in to it. Instead, he allowed his anger to rise, because anger was easier to bear.

"How did you find me?" she asked.

He glanced up at her question. "What?"

"How did you know to come here?"

"When you spoke in my head, I knew you must be somewhere close, so close I could almost smell the sweetness of your blood." He leaned toward her and breathed in again.

Gina flinched, but stood her ground. "You're not supposed to be here," she said.

His eyes narrowed, and the anger crept a little higher. "Where exactly am I 'supposed to be'?"

"Anywhere. Not here. You have to go."

He could hear the panic in her voice, and he looked at her curiously. "Are you going to make me?" he asked, allowing a small part of his anger to leak into his voice.

He knew she'd heard it. The little color in her face fled, and a savage wave of satisfaction washed through him.

She wrapped her arms around herself, searching his face. "I'm going to ask you," she replied.

He laughed, genuinely amused. It occurred to him then that his little witch had no idea what he was feeling. Perhaps he'd become too good at masking his emotions. Maybe she needed to know something of the rage seething inside him. "You can read my mind?" he asked.

She shook her head. "Just an impression of what you're feeling if I concentrate very hard."

"Then try, little witch."

Her eyes widened in surprise, but a moment later, he sensed the gentle brush of her mind against his, and opened to her.

She paled even further and took an involuntary step back. "You hate me." The words were ripped from her, a statement, not a question. She stared at him, her eyes wide and bright with unshed tears.

It was a trick. He knew it was a trick. Why would she expect anything else from him after what she had done?

"What did you expect?" he said. "That I would still love you?" He rose to his feet and took a step toward her. She backed away until she was up against the wall and could go no farther. Something in her face warned him to get a grip, leash his anger before it overwhelmed him, but it was too late.

He flew at her then, his hands gripped her shoulders and the force of his attack slammed them both into the wall. He pinned her there with one hand at her throat, and stared down.

"I could forgive you for not loving me," he snarled. "I could forgive you for leaving me without a word, but I will never, never forgive you for what you did to our daughter."

Her eyes widened at his words. She opened her mouth as if to speak, but then closed it again. Some expression passed across her face, acceptance maybe. She relaxed in his hold, quiescent.

Do what you will.

The words reverberated in his mind. Briefly, his fingers tightened until he felt the blood throbbing in her throat. Her silver eyes glowed with power, but she made no effort to release herself, and something snapped inside him. Darius stared down into the face that had haunted his dreams since his first sight of her. He knew, in that moment, she would never come to harm at his hands. He forced his hunger down, and after a minute, he loosened his grip. Let his hands fall to his sides.

He'd wanted Gina from the first moment he saw her. He'd worked for the Council back then, fighting in the war against the fire-demons. The war had not been going well. Everyone knew witches possessed the power to see the future, and Darius had wanted to go to them for guidance. Kael, as head of the Council, warned him the witches were not to be trusted, but as usual, Darius had gone his own way, and there he'd seen Gina.

He could clearly remember the shock ripping through him as he'd stood before her; speechless, unable to do anything but stare. He'd never wanted anything as much in his entire existence, and he'd been so used to taking what he wanted that he hadn't thought twice about snatching her away.

They'd had three glorious months together, and she had come to love him. He was sure of it. Right up to the day she walked out without a word. He'd been angry, then hurt and finally bitter, but those feelings were nothing compared to how he'd felt when her sisters turned up nine months later and presented him with his daughter, Raven.

They'd refused to speak of Gina, just handed the baby to Darius, and then told the Council of the prophecy made at Raven's birth. It foretold that if either the Council or the fire-demons sacrificed his daughter on her twenty-first birthday, then they would gain a great victory over the other side. Kael had been furious, and he'd acted in anger, passing a sentence of death over the baby.

Darius had believed Gina knew all this, and his bitterness turned to rage, but still he'd wanted her.

He had taken his daughter and run, then spent the next fourteen years hiding from both sides. But after the fire-demons captured Raven, he had returned to the Council, knowing they were his only hope of finding his daughter. Kael had agreed to help, and for years they'd searched, but it was only through Gina that they'd finally managed to find and save Raven. That was a week ago, and afterward Gina had disappeared. Again.

But this time, he had found her.

Her tongue came out to lick her lips, and he almost reached for her again as heat coiled in his belly. He saw her swallow, his eyes riveted to her throat, where he could see her blood pulse so close to the surface, smell the sweetness of it.

"Would it make you feel better?" she asked, and her voice was soft and low.

His gaze flew to her face. "What?"

"If you kill me, will it lift the Darkness from you? Will you be as you were before we ever met?"

He imagined her dead, and pain ripped through him. She couldn't die. He wouldn't let her. She was his. "No!"

Shock flashed across her features, and she reached out a hand. Darius stepped back and turned away.

"Darius?"

He forced himself to turn back to her. There was some expression on her face. Pity. He didn't want her pity.

"What?" he growled.

She flinched at his tone, but didn't back down. "I can do a spell," she said.

"A spell? What sort of spell?"

"I can make it as though we never met. You will forget I ever existed."

"No!" The word was torn from him.

"I would not want to forget you, either." They were both silent for a minute before she spoke again. "I didn't know."

"What didn't you know?"

"About Raven and the prophecy. I didn't even know she was alive. My sisters told me our daughter died at birth. They lied to me." He could hear the pain of betrayal in her voice and knew she spoke the truth.

"Where were you?" he asked. "I searched for you, but I couldn't feel you anywhere."

"I was banished to the Shadowlands."

Shock washed over him. "I thought they were a myth."

"No, the land where the souls of the dead gather before their final journey definitely exists."

"Sounds like a fun place."

"Oh yes," she said. "I had fun there." She shook her head. "At first it didn't matter. After I left you, I was..." She shrugged. "It wasn't so bad there. Before you came, I'd lived my whole life in isolation, with just my sisters, and the occasional visitor who came to seek a vision of the future. It wasn't much different."

"Have I mentioned that I hate your sisters?"

"Once or twice," she said, "but you don't understand. They have a great responsibility. No, *we* have a great responsibility. Anyway, Regan released me about five weeks ago."

Darius frowned. "Why would she do that?"

"I don't think she ever believed things would go so far. She couldn't risk the fire-demons sacrificing Raven, but no one could find her. Regan hoped we would have a bond, and once free of the Shadowlands, I did sense our daughter. I felt her pain and knew she was alive."

Chapter Four

Gina glanced at him. He was deep in thought, but the rage had left his face.

No wonder he hated her. All this time he had blamed her for what happened to Raven. He'd also said he could forgive her for leaving him, but suddenly she needed him to know she hadn't abandoned him lightly.

"I didn't want to leave you," she said. "That first time. I had no choice."

"No?"

"It was daytime when Regan came. We were in your room, deep underground. You were sleeping." He'd been naked, beautiful, gilded in the light from the lamp she kept on so she could watch him.

Darius scowled. "And it didn't occur to you to wake me?"

She almost smiled at the disgust in his voice. "You didn't think I could keep you safe?"

He still didn't understand. "You didn't have to keep me safe. Regan is my sister. She would never hurt me. It was never me who was in danger."

His eyes narrowed into dark slits as he processed the information. "You went with her to protect me?"

She nodded.

"I can protect myself," he growled.

Gina wondered how much she should tell him, how much she should reveal of their powers, but he had already seen what she could do. "Regan threatened to destroy you."

"How?"

"She was going to open a gateway to the outside, the sun would have entered, you would have been destroyed utterly, gone forever, and it would have been my fault." Gina remembered the panic clawing at her insides as Regan had issued the threat. "We have a saying in my family—take what you want and pay for it—and I would have been willing to pay, but not with your life."

"You still should have woken me." He looked at her. "There's more, isn't there?"

She nodded. "Regan told me she'd seen a vision of the future. That one day you would take my life."

"And you believed her?"

"Of course. The visions do not lie." But her sister did. Had Regan lied about that, as well?

"I would never hurt you," Darius said.

Gina took a step toward him, reached out a hand and ran her finger over the scar bisecting his cheek, as she'd been longing to do since she'd first seen it.

"How did you get this?" she asked.

"After the Council called for Raven's death—"

A jolt of shock hit Gina. "The Council wanted Raven dead? But Kael was head of the Council. Why would he order her death?"

"He was furious with me for taking you, and he thought it was the only way to ensure the prophecy could not come to pass. He told me later he'd regretted the decision almost immediately, but it was too late, I'd taken Raven and run."

"How can you defend him!"

"I'm not, but I understand why he acted as he did. Nevertheless, if we'd had the Council's protection the fire-demons would never have found us. As it was, they did, and I got this—" he gestured to the scar "—in the attack when they captured Raven. They left me for dead out in the open, where the sun would find me. Luckily, I woke before dawn."

She laid her hand against his cheek. His skin was cool to the touch, or maybe she was hot. He turned his head so her palm brushed his lips. His tongue snaked out, licked the tips of her fingers, and pleasure ran through her, settling low in her belly.

The intensity shocked her. She went to take a step back, but his hand reached out and clasped hers. He brought it back to his mouth and kissed the sensitive skin of her palm, then the inside of her wrist, tracing the blue veins where her blood throbbed close to the surface. The action was so tender, tears pricked at the back of her eyes.

Vampires couldn't love. She tried to hold on to the idea, but it was slipping away.

His other hand wrapped around the back of her neck, and he tugged her toward him. His fingers spread in her hair, cradling her skull, ruffling the short silky strands. "I miss your hair."

"You do?" she asked, and a moment later, long silver tresses reached down to her waist.

"Clever," he said. "Is it real?"

She sighed. "No, it's a glamour. A cheap trick."

"Not like blacking out the sun."

"No, not like that. That had to be real." She shuddered as she remembered the terrifying moment when the sun had risen, and she'd thought they were too late to save the daughter she'd never met. Raven was half vampire—the sun's rays would have burned her to ashes— so Gina had extinguished the sun for the time it took them to save her. It was powerful magic and came with a high price, but Gina knew she would do the same again. Now, she pushed the memory away. If this was all she was going to have with Darius, she didn't want to spoil it.

His hands held her still as he lowered his head. She made no move to evade him, her whole body rigid with expectation.

Their lips met.

She'd forgotten what it was like, one more of those things

she had buried deep in her consciousness as too painful to remember. His lips were soft. His tongue licked at her lower lip, then his teeth nipped until her mouth opened beneath his, and his tongue filled her, slick, wet, velvet. The taste of him flooded her, driving everything else from her brain as his mouth hardened against hers.

She was so incredibly soft, and the taste of her was driving Darius wild. His fangs throbbed with the urge to feed, and the hunger rose in his belly. His cock was already rock hard, and his balls ached viciously. He shifted, trying to ease the pain, but he knew there was only one thing that would do that. He needed to be inside her, deep inside her. He slid his hands down her back, cupped the globes of her backside and pulled her against him, pressed her softness against the hardness of his shaft, and she groaned into his mouth. He drank the sound down.

He picked her up without breaking the kiss, strode across the room with her in his arms and lowered her to the sofa. She was so beautiful. His gaze ran over her body, over her nipples pressed against the soft material of her T-shirt.

"Take off your top." His voice sounded hoarse in his own ears.

She looked up at him, her eyes glowing silver. She held his gaze as her hands clasped the hem of her T-shirt and she wriggled out of it, tossed it to the floor. She was naked underneath, and he feasted on the sight of her.

Her breasts were small, with dark red nipples already swollen with need. He reached down and trailed his fingers over the engorged peaks, watched them pucker and tighten. He pinched one between his finger and thumb, and her hips rose from the cushions.

He came down beside her then, needing to feel her against the length of him. He shifted lower down her body, and his face nuzzled her tender breasts, his tongue flicking over one tight nipple until it glistened with moisture. He drew it into his mouth and suckled, careful that his fangs didn't cut into her flesh, but desperate for the taste of her blood.

Gina was boneless, a mass of sensitized nerve endings. His mouth tugged at her nipple, slowly melting her insides. She could feel him hard against her, and her own sex was hot and swollen with need. Her hands slid under the worn material of his T-shirt to the satin skin beneath, her nails raking his back. She lifted her hips, rubbing herself against him, and he went still above her.

He released her breast and raised himself so she could look up into his eyes, so dark now they were almost black, glittering, burning with a hunger she knew matched her own and beyond. His gaze shifted to her throat, and he reared up above her. His lips drew back, his fangs gleaming white against the darkness of his skin. She realized what he meant to do, knew she had to stop him, and the need broke through the fog of desire holding her captive. If he fed, the bond between them would be renewed. He would feel her thoughts, know the truth, and would never let her go. Not without a fight. A fight she could not let him win.

"No!"

For a moment, she was sure she'd left it too late, that he was beyond control. She could see the force of his will, his powerful shoulders rigid with tension as he held himself poised above her. He looked savage and wild, his lips drawn back in a snarl.

His fangs retracted, and he closed his eyes. When he opened them, they were back to normal, though tension throbbed in the air. He moved slowly, first onto his knees, then rising to his feet to stand beside the sofa, staring down at her. He raked a hand through his long hair, and finally, the tension drained from him. "Why?" he asked.

She pulled herself up and hugged her knees to her chest, hiding her naked breasts. "You feed and the bond between us will strengthen."

"And that's a bad thing?"

"When we part I can't…" She paused, gathering her thoughts, careful of what she revealed to him. "When we part, I can't exist if I feel you all the time."

His eyes narrowed on her. "When we part?"

"You don't understand."

"Then explain it to me."

"Regan is coming for me."

Gina didn't mention the hellhounds, though she didn't know why; maybe she didn't want to scare him off completely.

"When will she be here?"

Gina shrugged. "Tomorrow, maybe tonight, I don't know, but she's searching for me, and she will find me. Besides, I was always going back. I just wanted to see something of life before—" She broke off and swallowed. "I have to go back. This was only ever a break from reality for me."

"Reality? Well, change reality. You don't have to go back. I can keep you safe from your sister. She can manage without you."

Anger rose in Gina then. "You understand nothing of what we do. Do you think we were brought into existence merely to perform party tricks at your command, to give you pretty visions of the future? That is nothing. We have duties to perform, without which the world would descend into chaos."

"What duties?"

"We lead the souls of the dead away from the land of the living. Without us the world would sink under their weight. Besides…"

"Besides?"

She got to her feet, crossed the floor and drew back the curtain. The room was instantly lit with the crimson flashes. "This is because of me."

"I don't understand."

"Magic has to be paid for," she said. "Oh, not the glamours and tricks…" She gestured to her long hair, and it vanished. "They cost nothing. But proper earth magic has a price. I had to use it to black out the sun—that was the only way I could save Raven. But now the world is out of balance. This—" she gestured at the night sky "—will get worse, until I have paid."

"Paid how?"

"I don't know the details," she lied. "Perhaps I will have to return to the Shadowlands." Well, at least that was the truth; she had no doubts she would be visiting the Shadowlands very soon.

"Do you want some company?"

Panic flared inside her. "You cannot follow. It is forbidden."

His eyes narrowed. "One day you will come back?"

"Perhaps." She forced a smile.

He was regarding her curiously. "Have you seen our future?"

Gina frowned at the question, then shook her head. "No, I haven't had a vision of the future since before Raven was born. I think my gift may have passed to her."

"Yes, Kael mentioned she has the sight."

"Then I pity her."

"There's no need. She's happy now with Kael, and besides, she's strong."

"I hope so. She'll have to be."

"So," Darius said. "Where does this leave us?"

She turned away from him, schooled her expression to grimness. He needed to understand this. "There *is* no us," she said, turning back. "There can never be any us. Tonight is all we have."

He stared at her for a minute longer, his expression blank. "Then I think I'll forgo the evening's entertainment. If I just wanted sex, there are plenty of willing partners without the problems. Maybe they're still up next door."

He turned from her and walked out. The door slammed shut behind him. Gina stared at it without seeing, a desperate urge to call him back rising within her. She bit her lip to stop the words from tumbling out.

Running to the door, she opened it and caught sight of his figure disappearing down the stairs. Something relaxed inside her. She didn't know what she would have done if he'd gone next door.

She started shaking then. Sinking to the floor, she curled into a ball and wept.

Chapter Five

It took Darius all of about one second to realize he'd behaved like a complete shit.

He hadn't meant it. He could no more go to another's bed than he could physically hurt Gina. No, he'd said it to cause her pain, and he'd succeeded. The shock had been clear in her face, and he'd wished immediately that he could take back his words. Instead, he'd walked away.

If he'd believed causing her pain would lessen the anguish that ripped through him, he'd been way off course.

The truth was, he'd seen the love in her face, knew she wanted him, and he could still feel her, soft and willing beneath him. For a brief moment, he'd allowed himself to believe there could be a happy ending, and because of that, her rejection had been the bitterest of blows.

Still, the knowledge that she hadn't betrayed him, hadn't betrayed their daughter, was like a huge pressure lifting from his mind. He realized the Darkness had retreated; he no longer felt as though he was balancing on the edge of a precipice. The hatred had drained from him, leaving him empty.

He wanted to go back, say he was sorry for hurting her, but the hunger still clawed at his stomach. He couldn't confront her again until he had himself under control, but time was running out. How long had she said she had? A day? A few hours?

He walked through the city streets, the crimson lightning flashing overhead, mocking him, reminding him at every step of all he had lost.

Finally, he entered an all-night bar and sat down, oblivious to the stares of the humans. The bartender placed a whiskey in front of him and Darius sipped the drink, wondering where to go next. What to do. He wanted Gina with every part of him, and he knew she wanted him. But if she could be strong enough to do her duty, then perhaps he should learn from her.

For a long time he sat drinking, staring into space, working out how to pick up the pieces of his life and move on.

Maybe it was time to stop wallowing in self-pity, as Kael had told him, and get back to work. There were always fire-demons to kill, if the Council would take him back. Darius would fill his time waiting for her return.

First, he had to see her one more time.

When the knock came, Gina almost didn't open the door. She didn't believe for one minute that Darius would be back. He'd made his feelings clear. Only after the third round of knocking, when it turned into hammering, did she rise to her feet.

She opened the door slowly, her eyes widening as she took in the tall figure on the other side. He'd changed his clothes, and her eyes widened further at the sight of him. She'd never seen him in anything other than casual dress. Now he was wearing a dark gray suit that fit his tall frame to perfection, and a white silk shirt open at the neck, contrasting with his golden skin. His hair was pulled back into a ponytail, emphasizing the high cheekbones. His sensual lips curled into a slight smile.

He looked alert and shifty, as though he was hiding something, and he kept his hands behind his back. As she stared at him, openmouthed, he brought them forward and offered her a single red rose.

She blinked in bewilderment, then shifted her gaze from the flower to the man holding it, unable to look away.

"May I come in?" he asked when she continued to stare.

"Can I stop you?"

"All you have to do is say no."

She considered it for a millisecond. She glanced again at the flower. No one had ever brought her flowers before. She opened her mouth again, but couldn't think of a thing to say, so stepped to the side and gestured for him to enter.

He nodded once, then stepped past her. She shut the door behind them and turned to face him. He held out the rose. "This is to say I'm sorry."

"You are?" She blinked again, in confusion. "For what?"

He shrugged. "Take your pick, but mostly for the way I left earlier. I was..." he paused as if searching for the right word "...disappointed. You can blame my oafish behavior on that."

She looked at him suspiciously. "I won't change my mind."

"I don't expect you to. I'll take whatever you're willing to give, for however long you're willing to give it."

A thrill of excitement ran through her at his words. She'd believed it was over. That she would never see him again, and the thought had very nearly torn her apart. Now she had a chance to be with him one last time.

She reached out and took the rose, raised it and breathed in the rich perfume. When she looked back up, Darius was watching her.

"I want to make love to you," he said. "You know that?"

She nodded.

"Good. Now put the flower down. I need to hold you."

She laid it on the coffee table and moved into his arms. She buried her head in his chest, pressing her face against the silk of his shirt, wrapping her arms around his waist as though she would hold him forever and never let him go. His arms went around her, pulled her closer, and for long minutes they stood entwined. After nowhere near long enough, he kissed the top of her head, and she released him and stepped back.

She glanced down at her jeans and T-shirt; which didn't seem right when he looked so stunning and sophisticated. But she was a witch, wasn't she? She whispered a spell , and a moment later stood before him in a slinky crimson dress the color of fresh blood. It skimmed her slender body, clinging to her small breasts and reaching midway down her thighs. Her feet were in crimson stilettos with straps that wrapped around her ankles. She imagined her hair down to her waist, and instantly the heavy weight tipped her head back. Darius was staring at her, and she could see the hunger in his eyes. Her own hunger rose, tightening the muscles in her belly, turning her nipples to hard little peaks pressing against the thin silk of her dress.

She looked up to find him gazing at her breasts. He cleared his throat. "Do you have anything on under that?" he asked, his voice hoarse.

"Wait and see," she teased.

His eyes glittered, dark and hot, and his hands clenched at his sides as he obviously fought for control. After a minute, the tension drained from him. He smiled. "I'll wait, little witch, but not for long."

He took off his jacket and laid it on the back of the black leather sofa, then released the band holding his hair. He ran his hands through it, so it fell to his shoulders, dark as night. She watched the play of muscles under the thin white shirt. She could see the dark body hair on his chest, and her fingers itched to feel it.

He sank down onto the sofa and once again patted the seat next to him. This time she came and sat in the crook of his arm, and he pulled her tight against him.

She felt no hurry now. Held safe in his arms as she was, it seemed inevitable they would be together. She snuggled closer, and his fingers stroked the skin of her shoulder.

Tomorrow she would have to face her fate, but for tonight, Darius was hers.

Chapter Six

How did you make love to someone when it might be the last time, and you wanted to show her what she meant to you?

Darius stared down at the woman in his arms.

She had been an innocent the first time. He remembered his shock. A two-hundred-year-old virgin—who would have believed it? He'd known she'd led an isolated existence; witches tended to keep to themselves. But it had been a surprise. She'd learned quickly, but still, he'd been careful of scaring her. He'd always held something of himself back. Tonight he wasn't going to hold back anything.

Except no feeding.

He could do it. However much he wanted to taste the sweetness of her blood, he would not. He suspected she didn't trust him, and why should she? Perhaps she believed if the link was strengthened, he would come looking for her. She was right.

They were wasting time. "Let's go to bed," he said.

She looked into his face and nodded. Rising to her feet, she held out her hand to him as though she was the one leading the way. He took it and stood up. Then lifted her effortlessly in his arms and carried her into the bedroom. He put her on her feet and tugged at the thin straps holding up her dress. "I love this gown," he said, "but it's coming off."

"It is?"

He nodded. He was about to remove it when a moment later the dress vanished, leaving her naked but for a crimson thong. She was perfection. Long and slender, but her body honed, with graceful lines of muscle showing beneath the pale skin. He reached out a hand, stroked her shoulder, cupped one small, sweet breast in his palm and ran his thumb over her nipple, watching as it darkened under his touch. She swayed, and he moved his hand lower, tracing a finger along the mark above her left hip bone. It was black, stark against the paleness of her skin, and shaped like a bird, wings outstretched. He remembered the first time he had seen it. He'd known immediately what it was, what it signified. It was the mark of the Morrigan. Still, he'd had to ask.

"Your mother is the Morrigan?"

Gina had nodded, and shock had ripped through him—her mother was a goddess. And not just any goddess, but the goddess of war and pestilence.

Now he rubbed his thumb over the mark and wondered what other blood ran in her veins. "You never told me," he said. "Who's your father?"

"I don't know, but according to Regan our mother has terrible taste in men." Gina smiled. "Regan reckons that's where I get it from."

Darius snorted. "Yeah, and I love your sister, too." He looked at her. "What's she like? The Morrigan, I mean."

"I don't know. I've never met her. I told you, she left me with my sisters when I was a baby. I used to wonder what she was like, and I used to pray to her. She never answered, and I gave up praying years ago."

Her words were a lie, but Gina had no wish to tell Darius that she had spent much of the last week praying. What was the point? There had been no answers; her mother had remained silent, as always. Gina reached down and took his hand in hers, pressed his open palm against the mark. "This is all I have from my mother."

She was sure he meant to pull away, and panic flared inside her. She wanted this so much it was like a live thing clawing at her insides, ravenous, demanding to be fed. Her hips pushed against him, and his hand relaxed beneath hers. His fingers flexed, then pressed into the flesh of her stomach, sliding over her skin to slip beneath the tiny scrap of satin that was all that covered her. They ruffled through the soft hair, then moved lower, curling upward, probing, searching.

She knew the moment he realized how much she wanted him. His breath caught as his long fingers slipped between the folds of her sex and sank into the hot, slick heat. He went still for a moment, and then leaned forward and kissed her. A slow drugging kiss, his tongue filling her mouth, while his fingers stroked the swollen, sensitized flesh, massaging the hard little nub until her legs gave way, and she clung to him for support. She closed her eyes tight, concentrated on the feel of his fingers moving against her. The pleasure intensified, radiated outward and then exploded in a shower of lights that flashed behind her closed lids.

"Oh!"

He laughed softly against her mouth, then drew back, picked her up and dropped her onto the huge bed behind her.

She opened her eyes. He was standing over her, staring at her nearly naked body while he stripped off his own clothes. He didn't bother unbuttoning the shirt, just ripped it open, tore it off and dropped it on the floor. He was beautiful, his chest broad, with a covering of dark silky hair that ran over the muscular ridges of his lean belly and disappeared into the waistband of his pants. He was already hard; she could see the outline of his erection beneath the material. Her mouth went dry, and she held her breath as his hand moved to the fastener. He flicked it open and slowly drew the zipper down. She started to breathe again as he slid his pants down over his thighs and stood before her naked.

His skin was golden, his legs strong columns, his cock long and heavy, springing up from a nest of midnight curls. It twitched and pulsated with life under her hot gaze, and she came up on one elbow, reached out and curled her fingers around it. He gasped, and she tightened her hand, loving the feel of his burning-hot, silky soft skin over the rock-hard shaft.

"Easy, sweetheart," he murmured, and she loosened her grip, her fingers fluttering up over the long length of him, then down to cup the heavy weight of his balls.

He groaned again, and then dropped down onto the bed beside her. She released her hold, her hands moving to his shoulders to drag him closer. Darius pulled her against him, cupping her buttocks in his palms, then rolling her so she lay beneath him. He bent down, his lips taking hers in a savage kiss of possession, and she opened her mouth, welcomed the scalding thrust of his tongue.

He ripped the thong from her body, and for a moment stayed poised above her. He inhaled, his nostrils flaring as they drew in air heavy with the musky scent of sex. His hands tangled in her hair, and he held her still beneath him.

"I've wanted you for so long," he said. "In my dreams, in my waking moments."

She stared up into his face. He was fierce, predatory, his lips drawn back, exposing the sharp whiteness of his fangs, but she knew no fear.

One of his hands moved between them. He parted the folds of her sex with sure, skillful fingers, and her body tightened in anticipation. Then the head of his cock was nudging, seeking entrance to her body, finding it. She could feel herself softening, opening for him. Even so, when he plunged inside her, sheathing himself in one hard lunge, she gasped in shock. He went still above her.

"Okay?"

She nodded. He filled her completely, but after a moment, her body adjusted to him. She twitched her hips, and he pulsated inside her, growing even larger, and she moved again. He closed his eyes. When he opened them, they glittered, filled with a hunger he made no effort to hide.

He moved then. The first thrust was a long slow curl of his hips, and she lifted up to meet him. She knew the exact moment when he released the hold he had on his control. Felt it snap. He plunged into her hard and fast, so all she could do was hold on. Her nails dug into his shoulders, and she wrapped her legs around his waist, pulling him closer.

He rode her hard, driving them both toward their climax, ruthlessly taking everything she had to give. With each lunge, the exquisite pleasure rose, until the whole world was reduced to nothing more than the feel of him moving on her, in her.

Already sensitized from her orgasm, each thrust of his cock, each roll of his hips brought an exquisite, dragging pleasure that finally spilled her over the edge.

She shuddered beneath him. Darius went still, staring down into her silver eyes, which glowed with power.

Mine.

The word echoed through his mind as she claimed him. He gave one final thrust and spilled himself inside her, holding her tight as they both rode the wave of pleasure.

He stroked her, soothing her as the tremors racked her body. When she finally lay still beneath him, he raised himself and kissed her, long and slow.

Still lodged deep inside her body, he rolled onto his side, pulling her with him, tucking her close so he could watch as she lay limp and boneless against him.

While his body was sated, his gums ached with the need to feed, but he had sworn he would not make the future harder for her. If it was easier to forget him, then forget him she must.

She opened her eyes.

"All right?" he murmured.

"I don't remember it being quite so overwhelming," she said, pulling away from him. For a moment he held on to her, then let her slip away. She didn't go far, just backed up a little and lay watching him.

"What?" he asked.

"Nothing. I just want to look at you."

Darius rolled onto his back. "Then look," he said.

She inched closer, rose up on her elbow and let her eyes wander over him. Pulling herself up, she knelt beside him and reached out to touch him on the shoulder.

"You're so hard," she said, her fingers sliding down to tease the fur on his chest, scraping across his nipples. Darius closed his eyes as her hand trailed over his belly and ripples of pleasure ran through him. Her fingers stilled, and he opened his eyes again to find Gina staring at him.

He held his breath as her hand hovered over his cock. She leaned over, blew gently, and he had a sudden blood rush to the groin. He could feel himself stirring beneath her gaze, and lay back and enjoyed the feeling.

"It's like magic," she whispered.

"Witch's magic."

Her fingers touched him, lightly at first, grazing along the hardening length, fluttering over the head, then down to stroke him. It was heaven.

He was hard again now. She leaned over again, her warm breath washing across him. Then she kissed him. He jerked beneath her, and she sat back.

He looked up to find her staring at him in speculation. She leaned down and took him in her mouth. His hips reared up off the bed as she suckled the head. He was almost bursting when she sat back again.

Darius forced himself to remain still, but it was an effort, when every fiber of his being yearned to toss her onto her back and plunge into her again.

After a moment, she moved toward him. He waited, his breath caught in his throat, as she decided her next move. In the end, she flung one long leg across his hips and straddled him. He reached out for her, but she shook her head.

"It's my turn," she said. "I want to do this."

He lay back and put his hands behind his head. "I'm all yours, honey."

She sat back on her heels, placed the tip of his cock at the hot, slippery entrance to her body, and then sank down onto him.

Darius held her steady with his hands spanning her waist while he shunted up the bed, until he was leaning against the headboard. She was wrapped around him, so hot, so tight that he had to fight for control. His arms slid around her to cup one full buttock in each palm, massaging the globes, widening her stance and pressing her down so he was burrowed deep inside her. He rocked her gently against him.

"Oh," she murmured, her eyes widening as her most sensitive point rubbed against him. She placed her palms on his shoulders and started to move on him, lifting herself, then sliding down, and with each stroke he held her closer, his hips rotating in tiny circles against her. Her eyes drifted closed, and he watched the play of emotions crossing her face.

This time, it was a slow, exquisite buildup of pleasure. Shivers rippled through her body as he ground her hips down onto his. He held himself in check, wanting to give her pleasure. Finally, when he was sure he could control the need no longer, her inner muscles contracted around him and tremors shuddered through her body.

She flung back her head and screamed as the pleasure tore through her. He pulled her hard into him again. She spasmed against him, and he let himself go, his own pleasure ripping through his body, and he burrowed his face in the softness of her breasts and filled her with his seed.

Gina kissed him, tasted the salty tang of sweat gilding his skin, and nuzzled her face into the silky body hair. She could feel the slow, steady thud of his heart beneath her. It soothed her, and she almost started to doze off.

She shook herself awake, not wanting to waste this time

they had together. She realized she knew almost nothing about Darius. After he'd abducted her, they'd had three months together, but during that time they'd lived for the present, too busy making love to talk about their past or their future.

She rested her chin on one hand and looked at him. "Tell me about yourself," she said.

He stroked a hand through her hair. "What do you want to know?"

"Everything." She thought for a minute. "Where were you born? When were you born?"

"I was born in Greece, not far from Athens. Around two thousand years ago."

She sat up. "You're that old? That makes you almost as old as Regan!" Gina stared at him for long moments, then opened her mouth to ask how he had become a vampire, and closed it again.

She cocked her head to one side, listening, trying to convince herself she'd imagined the sound, but then it came again. The howl of a hound. They had picked up her trail. Despair gripped her.

"What is it?" Darius asked.

He couldn't hear the hounds, but that didn't make them less real. It was over.

"I thought we had longer," she whispered. "I'm sorry."

Chapter Seven

"What is it?" Darius asked again.

She lifted her head. They were so close now. "Can't you hear them?" she asked.

Across the room, the air shimmered and wavered. She held her breath as a portal formed, and a pair of hounds leaped through, snapping and snarling.

Darius shot upright. "What the hell are they?" he said, staring at the creatures standing poised, red eyes glowing, low growls trickling from gaping jaws. They were so close she could smell the fetid stench of their breath.

"Hellhounds," she said.

They were huge creatures. Bearing only a vague resemblance to dogs, they stood almost shoulder high, with rough russet coats, and a thick black stripe down their backs. Powerful legs ended in long, savage claws. Their heads were misshapen, with pointed ears and razor-sharp teeth.

Darius rolled off the bed in one fluid move. Keeping his eyes on the hounds, he reached down picked up his pants and pulled them on, then placed himself between the hounds and Gina.

"No, Darius!" She stumbled to her feet, clumsy in her

need to protect him. He carried no weapons. Even a vampire couldn't last long against the hounds under those conditions.

"Get back," he snarled.

"They won't hurt me, Darius."

He ignored her, pushing her behind him. "Can you get me a weapon?"

A moment later, a long silver dagger appeared in his hand. He nodded his thanks, but didn't turn. "Just stay out of the way."

She frowned, but stepped back. She whispered another spell, and she was dressed, a knife in her own hand. She would intervene if she was needed. The hounds wouldn't harm her; at least she was pretty sure they wouldn't. They belonged to her sister Regan, and they knew Gina.

She bit back a gasp as the first of the hounds leaped for Darius. Its talons raked his shoulder, and the sharp metallic scent of blood filled the room. He growled, his own fangs showing as he reached out and gripped the rough fur of the beast's head. He raised the knife high as the second hound pounced, and he crashed to the floor under the combined weight.

"Stop!"

Gina whirled around. Her sister Regan stood at the portal. Gina shot her a furious glare, then turned back to the fight. Neither the hounds nor Darius had taken the slightest notice of the command. The knife flashed crimson now, and one of the hounds was hurled across the room. It lay quiet, but Gina could see the heaving of its flanks. The other was still rolling on the floor with Darius.

"Regan, call your hound off," she said sharply. "If you want it to live, that is."

"Diablo!" Regan snapped.

One minute the hound was fighting for its life, the next it went still. Darius lifted the knife, but something held him back. The animal stared at him, and then whined softly. Darius met its red eyes, and their gazes locked as it backed slowly away. He lowered the weapon.

He rose to his feet, the knife dangling from his hand, but ready if he needed it. He glanced across at Gina, needing to know she was still safe.

A woman stood beside her—tall, beautiful, with Gina's silver witch's eyes and long, dark red hair that hung like a cloak to her waist. Darius recognized her immediately, and a flash of hatred gripped him, only to be washed away by a wave of despair. This was the end. She was here to take Gina away, and Gina would go with her.

He glanced down at himself. He was covered in blood. Some of it was the hound's, but more of it was his own, and he couldn't seem to care. The knife dropped from his fingers and clattered to the floor. What was he supposed to fight?

He caught Gina's gaze and saw the same anguish reflected in her eyes. For a brief second, a savage wave of satisfaction washed through him, but it passed quickly, and he knew he would do anything to take that sadness from her.

He turned away. Picking up his shirt, he used it to wipe the blood from his shoulder. The cuts were deep and stung viciously, but he relished the pain.

"Darius," Gina said softly. She reached out a hand to him, then dropped it, as though she, too, knew the futility of any gesture at this point. "This is my sister Regan."

"Oh, we've met," he said, keeping his voice clear of emotion.

"You have?"

She wrinkled her brow, and he realized she didn't know of his visits to her sisters. "I went to find you, after you'd disappeared the first time. She..." he nodded at the redhead, who was bent over the fallen hound "...threatened to set the dogs on me."

Gina frowned. Her sister hadn't told her that Darius had come looking for her all those years ago, but then, why would she? Regan was crouched beside the hound, her hand stroking its huge head. The hounds were the only creatures she had ever known Regan to show affection to. Now she turned to stare at Gina, accusation clear in her face.

"He's hurt."

"Well, it's your fault," Gina muttered. "You shouldn't have sent them."

"You gave the vampire a knife."

She glared at her sister. "What did you expect me to do, stand by and watch while they ripped him to pieces?"

"Yes," Regan hissed. She stood up and whirled toward Darius. She raised her hand, and Gina knew she was going to release magic that would destroy him forever. Gina stepped between them.

"Stop it," she said.

Regan looked at her, but her hand remained poised to strike. "We should have finished this years ago."

A soft growl came from behind her, and Gina knew it was Darius. She glanced at him. With his whole body radiating tension, he stood poised to leap. Maybe he would make it. Maybe he could get to Regan before she released the magic.

Then what?

There was no good way for this to end. Gina didn't want either of them to die, and she had accepted her own fate long ago.

She put up both hands, palms out, one facing Darius, one Regan.

"Stand down. Both of you."

Regan stared at her through narrowed eyes, but lowered her arm. Gina turned to Darius. He nodded once and stepped back. The tension drained from his body and acceptance dulled his dark eyes. She reached out and touched him gently.

"I'm sorry," she said. She wasn't sure what she was apologizing for—the hounds, her sister, for coming into his life and ruining it forever.

He looked at her, his eyes bleak. "So am I," he replied. He

walked away from her and sank down on the edge of the bed, the blood-soaked shirt clenched in his fist.

Gina stared at him, trying to imprint his face on her mind. Then she turned back to her sister and drew herself up tall. She knew Regan loved her. She had cared for Gina her whole life, brought her up when their own mother had abandoned her as a baby, but it was time her older sister learned that Gina could be pushed only so far.

"I'm coming back with you, because I know my duty, not because you are forcing me." Her voice rang cold in her ears. "I'm willing to pay the price for what I did, but know this. If you lay so much as one finger on him, I will disappear."

Regan watched her carefully. Her eyes flicked from Gina to Darius, as if weighing the risk. "It wasn't hard to find you this time," she said.

Gina shrugged. "You can send the hounds after me, they can drag me back and you can do what you must. But remember, a payment given freely is of far more worth than one taken."

"You would force me to do that?"

"Yes." Gina knew, in that moment, that she spoke the truth. After all, she was the daughter of the Morrigan, goddess of war and pestilence, and a part of her knew that if Darius died she would let the whole world burn, and not care about the consequences.

She allowed the truth to show in her eyes.

Darius looked at her and despair flooded him. A moment ago he'd stood poised, knowing he could take her sister before she could speak the spell. Then there would have been nothing and nobody to stand in their way.

Gina's words had stopped him. He realized now that he had always thought of her as vulnerable. He'd clung to the idea that she needed protection. His protection. In the deep recesses of his mind he'd believed she was going back only because her evil sister was forcing her. She'd spoken of duty, but he hadn't believed it.

Now he saw her clearly. She was strong, powerful. She was going back because she knew it was the right thing to do. She would take on the world to protect him, but she wouldn't be his.

His gaze flicked to her sister. Their eyes met, and he saw the same knowledge reflected in her face, and knew he was safe from her attack. The thought brought him no pleasure.

"I won't touch him," Regan said. She turned to Gina. "Come now, we must go." She clicked her fingers, and the hounds came to her, whining softly, nudging at her hands.

Darius forced himself to sit unmoving, not to call out to Gina. He was so used to taking what he wanted, but now he must let her go. He had to be strong for her. At the last moment, as they stood at the portal, Gina hesitated.

"Wait," she said to her sister. "I need to say goodbye."

Regan nodded once, then backed away to stand by the portal, the hounds at her side.

He watched as Gina walked toward him. Her beauty tore at his heart.

"What?" he asked. "Tell me what I can do for you."

She swallowed, then reached out and touched his cheek. "Forget me," she said.

He shook his head. "I wouldn't even if I could."

He took her hand, kissed her palm. It wasn't enough, and he tugged her toward him. When she didn't resist, he dragged her closer so she tumbled across his lap. He held her against him, feeling her heart beating against his. Then he lifted her chin, baring the long line of her throat.

He could see her pulse thundering beneath her skin. He kissed it softly. She stiffened in his arms and then relaxed, going boneless and languid. His fangs ached, and he knew she wouldn't stop him, but instead, he kissed up her throat, along her jaw, his lips settling on hers, his tongue slipping inside to taste her. His body hardened against her as hers grew softer.

Finally, he forced himself to pull back and look into her strange eyes one last time. They were soft with longing.

"I will never forget," he said, and released her.

She rose to her feet, swayed slightly. He reached out a hand to help, and then let it fall. She turned and walked away, glancing back over her shoulder once.

Mine.

The word echoed through his mind, and then she was gone.

Her sister stood staring at him, hatred stamped on her face. She turned to follow Gina, but Darius needed to make one thing clear. "She's mine, not yours," he said. Regan paused. She glanced back over her shoulder, and he continued. "When she comes back, we will be together. However long, I'll wait."

Regan's eyes narrowed on him. He'd always believed her cold, entirely without feelings. Now she allowed him a glimpse of the pain that lay behind the coldness. "You don't understand, do you?"

A wave of foreboding washed over him. "Understand what?"

"Gina is never coming back."

"You can't banish her forever."

"Banish her? If she told you that was the payment due, then she lied." Regan looked at him, and something close to pity crossed her features. "No, Gina's life is forfeit. She dies tomorrow night."

Shock ripped through him. He stared, unable to speak.

"That is what you have brought her to, Darius Cole. This is your fault." Regan turned back to the portal.

Darius stumbled to his feet. "Wait," he said. "There must be some way. Take my life as payment."

She ignored his words and took the final step.

"Come back," he screamed. "Tell me what I can do."

A single word echoed back as the portal closed.

"Pray."

Chapter Eight

Darius stared at the spot where Gina and Regan had disappeared. The portal had vanished, leaving only the lingering scent of ozone hanging in the air.

He wanted to believe Regan had lied, but he'd seen the truth in her eyes. He forced the panic down and went over everything Gina had told him. She'd cleverly hidden the truth, speaking in half lies, and he had believed her. Now it was too late. A scream of pain tore through him. It couldn't be over. She couldn't die. He wouldn't allow it!

He crossed the room to the window. Opening it, he climbed out onto the fire escape. It took him up to the roof of the building. The air was hot and crimson lightning still flashed across the sky.

He'd never been one to pray, even before he had lost his soul. He'd always taken whatever he wanted and to hell with the consequences. Now he would pray. He would make the gods listen. He sank to his knees.

A shadow passed across the moon, and he glanced up as a huge crow swooped down and landed on the wall beside him. Darius rose to his feet as it watched him, head cocked on one side, yellow eyes bright. It hopped down to the floor, and a moment later, a woman stood before him.

She was tall, slender, with long black hair threaded with crow's feathers, and yellow eyes rimmed with charcoal. Her skin was smooth and olive toned, her face marked with curling runes, radiating out from the corners of her eyes, and she wore a band studied with rubies around her upper arm.

She was beautiful, yet something about her made him step back and widen the distance between them.

She smiled. "Darius Cole, I presume?"

He nodded, watching her warily, and her smile widened. "Do you know who I am?"

"I can guess." He looked her over carefully. "Am I supposed to kneel or something?"

"No, but perhaps a little humility would not be amiss."

He thought about it for all of two seconds. "I'm not very good at humility," he said.

"No, I'd heard that about you."

He stared at her. Had she come to answer his prayers or had Gina's family decided to finish him off, after all? He remained silent, waiting.

She was still studying him in return, head cocked on one side like the bird she'd appeared as. "You know," she said, "I have often been accused of being an unnatural mother, of not caring for my children. I suppose there is some truth in that, but while I have never involved myself in their upbringing and their lives, I have not cut my ties with them entirely."

"Are you going to help us?" he snarled.

"Such impatience. I can see why you wind up Regan so much. Then again, I can also see the attraction." She ran her eyes over the length of his body, and his skin prickled. "I've never had a vampire," she mused. "I always thought they'd be too much trouble, but maybe I should give it a go. Maybe I would like you to kneel for me, after all."

He growled low in his throat.

"Oh, don't worry," she said, "you're already spoken for."

"I am?"

Her eyes narrowed at that. "Aren't you?" she asked. "I was under the impression my youngest daughter had claimed you."

Something close to hope flickered to life inside him. Darius pushed it aside. Hope was a wasted emotion. What he needed was action. "Tell me what I can do," he said. "Tell me how to save her life."

"You cannot. Her life is forfeit. She must die to return the world to balance."

Rage surged through him. "Then why are you here? To taunt me? To tell me I am to blame?" He turned away, fists clenched at his side. "I don't need to be told—I already blame myself." The Darkness was rising inside him. He forced it down and turned back to face her. "Why did you come?"

"Because you asked me." She considered him, her eyes boring into his soul. "What are you willing to do to be with my daughter?"

He answered without thinking. "Anything."

"And what do you think Gina is willing to do, to be with you?"

He frowned at the question. "She will not risk the world."

"Well, that's good. But beyond that?"

"Beyond that, I believe she would risk anything." He shrugged, then gritted his teeth. "Goddamn it, tell me what to do."

She sighed, as if impatient with his slowness. "You are a vampire?"

His eyes narrowed in frustration. "You know that."

"And what must one do to become a vampire?"

He closed his eyes. At last, he understood. "You have to die."

Darius stood on the clifftop, high above the sea. The tang of salt filled his nostrils; the crash of the waves sounded in his ears. The stone circle loomed stark before him. It lay in ruins, many of the great stones fallen and overgrown, but the hum of magic still radiated from the place. The Morrigan had told him Gina would come here tonight. She'd take her own life here, among the stones, in payment for saving their daughter.

He leaned against one of the rough stones, shoved his hands in his pockets. All he could do now was wait, but panic clawed at his insides. What if she wouldn't agree? What if he was wrong and she didn't love him enough to risk her soul? What if she would rather die than become a vampire?

Then again, what if she agreed, and he failed? The transition didn't always go smoothly. Many died and were not reborn. If the vampire's blood was not strong, or the recipient was too weak. Darius gritted his teeth. He would make it work.

He caught a glimpse of movement beyond the rim of the stones. He straightened. Gina was here.

The night was warm, but Gina shivered as she followed the narrow track up the steep hillside. Fear gripped her mind, and only force of will kept her feet moving forward, one step at a time.

The stones came into view, and she paused. She was nearly there now. It was almost time. She closed her eyes and tried to picture Darius, but fear clouded her mind. Some part of her wished he had fed from her one last time and strengthened the bond between them. It would have been good to feel him now, as the end drew near, but that wouldn't have been fair. This way, he would eventually forget, move on with his life.

She took a deep breath and opened her eyes. The lightning was almost constant now, illuminating the ring of stones that stood on the crest of the hill.

She walked on, finally stepping between two huge fallen rocks to stand within the circle. The flat altar stone lay before her, and the air throbbed with magic. Gina's hand slipped down, her fingers stroking over the ceremonial dagger at her waist. She would use it to open her wrists. The blade was sharp, it would be painless and her life would simply drain away.

And she would never see Darius again.

Her whole being screamed against that thought, and in her mind she sensed a faint flicker of response. She whirled around.

Darius?

A tall figure separated from the dark shadows of the standing stones. He walked toward her. She could sense his fear and, beneath the fear, an eagerness she did not understand. Had he come to try and stop her? He couldn't know what she was about to do.

He halted a foot away, so close she could reach out and touch him. Her hands clenched at her sides. "What are you doing here?" He looked at her for long moments, and she saw the pain in his eyes. "Oh God," she said. "You know?"

"Regan told me."

"She had no right."

He shrugged. "I asked her what I could do. She told me to pray." Gina frowned, but he continued. "I didn't believe I would be heard, but your mother came."

Gina started in shock. "I…"

He put up a hand. "Hear me out," he said. "She told me there was nothing I could do to prevent it. You must die. But…" He paused, ran his fingers through his hair. He appeared unsure about how to go on.

"Tell me," Gina urged.

"There is a way for us to be together."

She searched his face. He'd said she had to die. Did he mean to die with her, then? Her whole being rejected the idea. "I will not allow you to take your own life."

He stared at her intently, searching her face. "Then will you allow me to take yours?" He looked deep into her eyes. "Are you willing to become a vampire to stay with me?"

Gina's brain stopped. Then she was flooded with thoughts, all clamoring in her head. To be a vampire. She would lose her soul, but gain Darius for all eternity. Was it possible?

Something struck her then. "Regan told me you would one day take my life. Could this be what she saw?" Gina was finding it hard to take in. "My mother suggested this?"

He nodded.

"Will it be enough? Will the price be paid?"

"She said so, but you must know the risks. You will lose your soul, never see the sun again."

It didn't matter. A wild surge of hope was building inside Gina, and she knew then that she would rather have the night with Darius than the daytime alone. "I'm willing."

He closed his eyes. When he opened them, she saw the same hope reflected in his face. He reached out for her, and she slipped her hand in his. He led her to the altar.

"What must I do?" she asked.

"Your body must die. I'll drink from you until your heart stops beating, then you must take my blood to be reborn. Will you accept my blood?"

She nodded once.

He pulled her into his arms and sank down onto the soft grass, leaning his back against the altar stone. She lay across his lap, and for a minute, he held her close. She'd thought she would never be in his arms again, and it was almost enough, but not quite.

She raised her head, baring her throat, and heard his sharp intake of breath. Then his mouth was on her, his fangs piercing her skin, sinking deep into the vein.

He drank. There was no pain, only pleasure and a relentless tugging that drew on places deep within her body. As he drank, she could feel his thoughts and emotions growing stronger. His fear that he would not succeed, and she would truly die. His love.

Her life was ebbing away, and she needed to tell him something before it was too late.

I love you. I've always loved you.

He paused as he heard her words in his head. She clutched

his shoulders, squeezing to urge him on, and he continued drinking. Her mind was clouding, his thoughts fading, then blackness.

Retracting his fangs, Darius pressed his lips to her throat. He could detect no pulse. She was dead, her heartbeat silent. Standing up, still holding her in his arms, he laid her gently on the altar. He looked up, and found the lightning was gone, and the sky was at peace. It was done.

Gina's hair was silver in the moonlight, her face serene. He leaned over and kissed her cold lips.

Drawing the dagger from the sheath at her waist, he tore open his shirt and sliced the blade across his chest, above his heart. As the crimson blood welled up, he prayed it would revive her. He scooped Gina up against him and pressed her mouth across the open wound.

For endless minutes, she lay still in his arms, and his panic flared. He pressed her tighter still. "Come back to me, Gina," he whispered. "I love you."

She convulsed against him. She swallowed, weakly at first, then more strongly, as each beat of his heart forced his blood from the wound.

I love you.

The words whispered through his mind, and suddenly he needed to hear them for real. He tilted her head with the hand in her hair. "Say it out loud," he growled.

She licked the crimson blood from her lips. Her mouth opened, and he saw the flash of small, white fangs.

"I love you," she said.

Elation filled him, and the Darkness was gone forever, banished by her words.

* * * * *

THE WITCH'S SEDUCTION

ELLE JAMES

Award-winning author **Elle James** grew up as an air force military brat. She received her work ethic from her rock-solid father, her creative streak from her artistic mother and inspiration from her writing partner and sister, Delilah Devlin.

As a former member of the army reserves and a current member of the air force reserves, she's travelled across the United States and to Germany, managed a full-time job, and raised three wonderful children. She and her husband have even tried their hands at ranching exotic birds (ostriches, emus and rheas) in the Texas hill country. Ask her, and she'll tell you what it's like to go toe-to-toe with an angry three-hundred-and-fifty-pound bird and live to tell about it!

Her adventures in the army and air force reserves, and the wild antics of her life on a small ranch in Texas, give her fodder for mystery, suspense and humour in her writing. A former manager of computer programming and project management professionals, Elle is happy she now has the opportunity to pursue her writing full time. Elle's paranormal romantic comedy, *To Kiss a Frog*, won the Romance Writers of America's 2004 Golden Heart for Best Paranormal Romance.

You can reach Elle by e-mail at ellejames@ellejames.com.

Chapter One

"Look! There she is!"

Deme Chattox smiled as she stepped off the escalator into the baggage claim area of Chicago O'Hare Airport. All four of her siblings stood in a group. Each one of the Chattox sisters were so different in looks and personality, no one would guess they were related.

But Deme knew. Even when they weren't nearby, she felt their presence, sensed when one of them was in trouble and shared their emotions from happiness to sorrow, more intensely than normal humans.

Truth was, the Chattox sisters and all the sisters on the Chattox side before them weren't normal. They were witches. Once Deme had railed against the differences. Now she embraced their uniqueness. Not everyone was as in tune to the world around them, nor could others wield magic like herself and her siblings.

"We missed you so much." Aurai, the youngest, engulfed her in a bear hug so tight Deme could barely breathe. A wisp of wind swirled around her, a sure sign of Aurai's emotions. The young woman had so much power at her fingertips, sometimes it scared Deme.

"Hey, loosen up a bit. I was only gone a month." Deme

laughed and hugged her little sister, smoothing her hand over her long, silky hair. "I missed you too. How's college?"

Aurai laughed. "Much better without a monster in the cellar."

Deme frowned. "Any other weirdness going on at Colyer-Fenton?"

Aurai shook her white-blond head. "Not since the initiation. I've kept busy studying and flirting with the hot guys."

Deme sighed. "As it should be for any college student."

"Hi, Deme." Selene shook back her thick, chocolate brown hair. She wore one of her signature flowing broomstick skirts and peasant-style blouses, all soft and feminine compared to Deme. Selene wrapped her arms around Aurai and Deme, smiling softly. "I'm so glad you're moving back to Chicago. We're not the same when you're gone."

"Let me have some of that love." Gina grinned, her sea-green eyes sparkling as she slid into the group hug.

"Hey, Sis. About time you came home." Brigid crossed her arms over her chest, her black leather jacket swooshing softly. She looked like a badass biker chick, but Deme knew it was a front to protect her big heart from being broken.

Deme held out a hand. "Get over here."

Brigid's cheeks reddened, but she complied, completing the clutch of woman, all hugging.

Deep inside, Deme could feel the rightness of having all of them together. They were meant to be close, to live in the same city and be a part of each other's lives. Her time in St. Croix had only added to that conviction. With so many miles between them she'd been a shell of herself, running a business she had no passion for.

"Okay, okay, let her have some air." Brigid was the first to back away.

Deme caught her hand and Aurai's. The women formed a circle of joined hands. Then whispering quietly so that others wouldn't hear, Deme lead a prayer to the goddess.

"With the strength of the earth
With the rising of the wind
With the calm of the water
With the intensity of fire
With the freedom of spirit
The goddess is within us
She is power
We are her
We are one
Blessed Be."

Her sisters repeated, "Blessed Be."

Aurai let go first, heading toward the luggage carousel. "Let's collect your bags and get you home."

Deme followed more slowly, walking in step with Brigid. "How's everything been in Chicago? Anything I should know about?"

Brigid worked in a motorcycle shop in the heart of the city and moonlighted for the Chicago Police Department. If something was happening, she'd know. "Guess you heard they captured Vladimir Romanov?"

Deme nodded. Cal had filled her in during their last telephone conversation, several days ago. "Cal said it took some doing. Did they get enough evidence for the Tribunal to put him away?"

Her sister nodded. "The knife he used to kill Franco Ledet and an eyewitness to the murder."

"It's hard to believe anyone would come forward and testify against Vladimir. He's about the worst of the worst paranorm mafia there is."

"Lucky us to have him in Chicago." Brigid shrugged. "If it had been me, I'd have dusted him on sight. This waiting for the Tribunal to punish him leaves too much time for him to plot his escape."

Deme shot a sideways glance at her sister. "Think he'll get out of the paranormal holding cell?"

"There've been rumors." Probably from Brigid's sources at the bike shop. "Most say he won't make it to the Tribunal. He'll either get out, or all the evidence will disappear. Or both."

"Can't let that happen." Deme stared across the baggage claim area, noting the people gathered close to watch for their bags. Old, young, mothers, fathers, grandparents and children. Having a badass demon thug like Vladimir off the streets would be a blessing. "I'll check with the chief when I get to the station."

"Huh?" Deme's youngest sister spun, nearly tripping over her own feet. "You're going by your apartment first, aren't you?"

Deme smiled at the expectant look Aurai gave her. "Sorry, sweetie, I need to check in with my new boss first. I was supposed to be on the job two weeks ago."

"Then it can wait another twenty-four hours." Gina hooked Deme's arm. "We just got you back. And we're not letting you go, yet."

Deme's heart swelled with the amount of love she had for her sisters. "I promise I'll spend time with you soon. But I really need to get to the station."

"Well, phooey." Gina's lips twisted. "I'd hoped you would come out with us for dinner. We were going to have Chinese."

Her mouth watering, Deme's stomach rumbled. It had been more than a month since Deme had indulged in her favorite. St. Croix was small and quaint and didn't have even a tenth the choices afforded in a city the size of Chicago. Given she'd had only the cold sandwich on the plane, along with several tiny bags of peanuts, Deme was hungry and Chinese sounded really good.

Her willpower wavered, but an image of Calais Black, the hot Chicago police officer and her partner on the force, floated across her mind. Her insides ignited with a white-hot flame. A month without Cal in her bed had felt like an eternity. "Sorry, I need to go to the station first."

"Leave her alone." Selene lifted a hand to Deme's face and

smiled. "She wants to see Cal." Trust the sister of spirit to read Deme's thoughts. In this case she was glad for it. Selene took the edge off the others' disappointment.

Deme waved at her suitcase as it passed by on the carousel. "That's mine."

"Got it." Aurai dove for the black bag with the bright green ribbon tied to the handle.

Gina grinned. "None of us told Cal you were on your way back."

Selene led the way out of the airport terminal to the parking garage. "He'll be so happy to see you. We took him out to dinner one night a couple weeks back, but he's been tied up with work since."

Deme shivered as the cool Chicago air hit her. She wished she'd had the foresight to wear a jacket. For a moment she missed the warmth of St. Croix in the sunshine. Still, Chicago was home, and she was glad to be back. Especially to see her sisters and her lover.

She wrapped her arms around her middle, anxious to be on her way. Eager to see if things were still the same between her and Cal. Deme adored that he was her flame. He was strong, handsome and made her feel so good when he lay naked beside her.

He'd pushed past her defenses, claiming her, as he'd put it. He'd even spoken the "M" word, but Deme had put the kibosh on that. If she married anyone, it would be Cal, but she wasn't certain she could trust anyone, even Cal, enough to commit to him. Not yet, anyway. Because of her and her sisters' unusual talents, she'd grown up suspicious and wary.

Cal had called Deme every other night since she'd been gone, except for the past week. He'd checked in only once. Deme had counted it off as him being too focused on the job. Her attention retured to her sisters. "He said it's been crazy. The special task force has been burning up the overtime with one fire after another to put out."

"I heard that a stranger nabbed Vladimir, drugged him,

tied him up and delivered him to the station. No one saw who. Even Vladimir was clueless and madder than a stirred-up hornet when he came out of his drug-induced stupor." Brigid laughed. "Must have been one of his own, to run off without claiming the credit."

"Either that or he didn't want the retribution." Deme shuddered. "I'll bet everyone is on alert at the station and the holding cell."

Brigid stopped in front of Gina's SUV. "You don't know the half of it. Everyone's punchy, waiting for Vladimir to make his move."

Deme sank into the leather bucket seat and buckled her belt.

"You could ask Cal to come out to dinner with us, you know." Aurai wasn't giving up on the idea of having dinner with Deme.

Gina climbed into the driver's seat. "She wants to get naked with Cal, not eat Chinese with all of us. We'll have plenty of time to go to dinner."

Deme's face burned, but she grinned. "Right on all counts."

"Especially the getting naked part." Selene squeezed her shoulder over the top of the seat. "Right?"

The teasing continued all the way to the police station where her sisters dropped her off at the door, promising to deliver her suitcase to her apartment for her.

"Don't do anything I wouldn't," Gina called out.

"That leaves the options wide open, doesn't it?" Deme stepped out on the sidewalk. "I'll see you all tomorrow. Dinner?"

"No excuses. We want time with you too." Aurai jumped out, hugged Deme and slid into the front seat with Gina. "Kiss Cal for me. He's so yummy. If you decide to dump him, I call dibs."

"You sure you don't need a ride to your apartment?" Gina asked.

"No." Deme glanced at headquarters, anxious to get inside and hoping Cal wasn't on a call. "I'll get Cal to take me home."

The SUV slid away from the curb and disappeared around the corner.

Deme squared her shoulders, ran her hands through her long red hair, cursing the fiery color. Why couldn't she have been blond like Aurai, and where had all the tangles come from? Then she strode toward the entrance, her heart fluttering and her belly tightening with each passing step. She couldn't wait to have Cal's strong arms around her.

Much as she promised herself she wouldn't get involved to the point of obsession with any man, she couldn't resist Cal.

Inside the station she checked in at the desk, asking for her boss. No use looking too eager to see her lover. Based on the reports of rising incidents involving the paranorms of Chicago, lead investigator Chief Martin Warner would be glad to see her back and ready to go to work.

She just hoped he'd give her a night to unwind from her trip. Not that she'd relax that night. Deme had other plans for her evening. They included one tall dark and ruggedly handsome police officer, a bed and the can of whipped cream she planned to purchase on her way to Cal's apartment.

A smile spread across her face as she stepped off the elevator into the Chicago Police Special Investigations Division.

Detectives and other members of the Paranorm Task Force hurried around desks, some escorting detainees, others leaning into telephones, intent on information gathering or ordering a pizza delivery because most were too busy to take time out to get a meal.

"Deme Chattox." A booming voice made her jump. Chief Warner swooped out of his office, a grin on his face. "I'd almost given up on you. Thought you'd changed your mind about coming to work on the force, what with the weather in St. Croix being so much nicer than winters here." He clapped a hand on her back, sending her stumbling forward.

Deme's lips twisted in a wry grin. "Going back to St. Croix had me wondering if I'd lost a marble or two."

"Not too late to change your mind." Warner tipped his head,

his brows rising. "We haven't officially put you on the pay-roll, yet."

"Thanks for the out, but I don't need it. I'm back in Chicago to stay and could use a paying job."

The chief stuck out a hand and shook Deme's, squeezing so tightly she could swear her bones crunched. "When do you want me to start?"

"Yesterday," he replied without hesitation. "No, really. But I'm sure you have a lot to do to get settled in. Tomorrow would be soon enough. Have you touched base with Black, yet?"

Her pulse leaped. "No, sir." Foolishly she'd been counting the days, hours and minutes until she could touch bases and a lot more with the man. Now she was only seconds away from him, if he was on duty.

The chief craned his neck. "He's around here somewhere. I saw him five minutes ago. Check in the conference room. I think he's in there."

"Sir." A plainclothes officer stood beside his desk, waving the chief over, a phone pressed to one ear. "We got a call from the Third District. Got a situation going down."

"Excuse me." Chief Warner ducked around Deme. "Look in the conference room," he repeated over his shoulder.

Adrenaline hopping, Deme stood in the middle of the room, wondering which way the conference room was.

"It's in the far corner." A man with shaggy sandy-blond hair pushed past her, carrying a jumble of wires and USB cables. He tipped his head to the rear of the room.

"Thanks." Deme turned in that direction and wove her way through a maze of desks and people.

New to the department, she held her head high and pretended she belonged, although that was as far from what she felt as it could be. Starting over was hard. Running her own private investigations business in St. Croix had proven easy. Rich businessmen and desperate wives came to *her*. Deme had mastered the art of being low profile. To be a good investigator, you had to blend in. She'd done that well, pretending to be a tourist or local depending on the need.

Now, with nothing assigned, she stood out as the only person in the room without a pressing task. That would come soon enough. First she wanted to see Cal.

The conference room door stood open only enough for her to poke her head around.

A man and a woman stood in front of a large white board with pictures stuck to the surface with magnets and markings linking some of them to dates.

The man had longish dark hair and his back was to Deme. The woman's arms laced around his neck, pressing his head down toward hers. From their stance Deme could only conclude that they were engaged in a lip-lock.

Deme ducked back out, heat rushing into her cheeks. Oops. Someone had taken an opportunity to sneak a little nookie on the job. She'd witnessed enough clandestine assignations during her stint as a private investigator. The amount of lying and cheating had hardened her to the idea of opening her heart to a man. Until Cal had come back into her life.

She moved on, hoping to find another conference room with Cal in it. There were other rooms, but they were smaller and empty. As she turned back to the large conference room where the couple was making out, a niggle of doubt pushed into her mind.

A beautiful raven-haired woman with ice-blue eyes emerged from the room.

Wow. She was gorgeous. She was almost too pretty, with her porcelain skin, deep red lips and a mass of long loose curls framing her face. Her gaze scanned the room, lighting briefly on Deme. With a dismissive rise of her brows she turned and headed for the elevator, moving like sex in motion.

Every male and some female gazes followed the woman until she disappeared around a corner.

Deme frowned. "Good grief." She retraced her steps to the conference room, intent on asking the man the dark-haired woman had been kissing if he knew where Cal Black could be found.

When she stepped into the room, her heart skidded to a halt, her blood freezing in her veins. The man who'd been standing with his back to her the last time she'd entered the room turned to face her, his eyes glazed, a slight frown marring his handsome brow.

Calais Black. Her partner and her lover. Make that former lover.

"Deme?" He blinked and blinked again. A smile spread across his face and his feet ate the distance between them. "When did you get in? Why didn't you tell me you were flying in today?"

"I wanted it to be a surprise." She forced the words out around constricted vocal cords.

Hell, the surprise had been on her.

Chapter Two

Back at her apartment Deme climbed out of Cal's SUV and slammed the door before he had a chance to shift into Park. "Don't bother coming up. I'm sure you have better things to do."

She'd insisted on calling a cab to take her home, but Cal had refused to let her. Now he sighed, got out of his vehicle and hurried to catch up to her. He grabbed her arm, forcing her to face him. "What's the matter?"

"Seriously? You have to ask?" She shook off his hand and entered the building without looking back.

The short burst of happiness Cal had felt at seeing Deme had been effectively wiped away by the angry glare and brusque sentences. "Are you having second thoughts about us, again?"

"I would have had to have first thoughts. Just leave it. And leave me." She fitted her key into the doorknob and twisted.

The door swung open. Deme stepped inside and turned to face him, blocking the entryway with her body. "You're not welcome here."

"Like hell." He shoved the door open so hard it banged the wall. "I'm not going anywhere until you tell me what the hell has your panties in a wad." He closed the door behind him and leaned on it, crossing his arms over his chest. "Start talking."

Deme threw her purse on the sofa and walked away. "And to think I'd been looking forward to seeing you."

His heart flipped and raced on. He'd been looking forward to her return since the day she'd left. "And what changed your mind?"

"That woman, the conference room, the kiss." Deme faced him, her hands on her hips. "Did you think I'd be happy to see you making out with another woman?"

His brows knitted together. "I don't know what you're talking about."

"You and the black-haired bitch in the conference room." Deme shook her head. "Don't play stupid with me. I saw you kissing her. You know...black hair...blue eyes...a body that doesn't quit..."

Cal pushed his hand through his hair, trying to grasp what Deme was saying and not getting it. "The cop who transferred here from New York City? Medea?"

"Is that her name? I liked *bitch* better." Deme pointed toward the door. "You can leave now."

"I wasn't kissing her." Cal stalked across the floor, his gaze pinning Deme's.

She didn't back down, her head tipping back in order to maintain unwavering eye contact the closer he came. "Could have fooled me."

When he stood in front of her, he took her hand, raising it to his lips. "You're the only woman I care about."

"Then why the kiss?" Deme's body remained rigid.

"I don't know what you saw, but we were discussing a murder case. That's all." He tipped up Deme's chin, every ounce of his being yearning to take her into his arms and crush the anger out of her.

Her full, peach-colored lips softened, though her eyes remained narrowed. "I wasn't imagining it."

"Let's start over." He brushed her lips and sighed. "I've been waiting a month to do that."

Deme swayed. The starch seemed to go out of her and she leaned against his chest. "I swear I saw you kissing her."

"Jet lag, sweetheart. You were seeing things that wouldn't happen. I only want to kiss *you*." She felt so good in his arms. As soon as she'd pressed her breasts against his body, heat flooded his system, speeding toward his groin.

"Don't play with me, Calais Black," she whispered against his lips. "I don't like games."

"No games. But I would like to play with you." His hands slid down her arms to the hem of her rib-knit blouse. In one long and lazy glide he hauled it up over her head and tossed it into the corner.

"Fine. But I'm only in this for the sex." She poked a finger into his chest. "I don't know if I can trust you."

"Uh-huh." He captured that finger between his lips and sucked on it, releasing it with deliberate slowness. Then he pressed his mouth to the pounding pulse at the base of her throat. "I've got news for you." He flicked the catch on her bra and slid it down her arms, her naked breasts springing free. "You might only be in this relationship for the sex. But I'm in it for the long haul."

"Whatever." He figured she was trying for nonchalant, but the catch in her voice with that one word belied her attempt to remain unaffected. "I really don't care why you hang around. I've got an itch and since you're here, you might as well scratch it." She shoved his leather jacket off his shoulders and it dropped to the floor with a soft thump.

The more naked he got, the harder his cock. God, he couldn't wait to plunge deep inside her. Her anger only made him that much more determined to bed her. And where she'd gotten the crazy idea he'd been kissing the cop on the Paranormal Task Force…well, hell…he could only guess.

Medea didn't do it for him. Not like Deme. The red-haired Wiccan had had him bewitched from the first time he'd met her, and being assigned to help her find her missing sister had only brought his desires to a head. She was the toughest, smartest, softest-in-all-the-right-places woman he'd ever met and he couldn't imagine being satisfied with anyone else.

After stripping him of his shirt, Deme unbuttoned her jeans.

Cal pushed her fingers aside and slid his hands inside the waistband of her panties, cupping her warm bottom. Then he eased the denim jeans and her silken underwear over the curve of her hips and down her long, sexy legs. "Lose the shoes," he breathed against her ear.

Without hesitation Deme toed the back of one shoe and kicked it off. The other followed, giving Cal a clear path to slide the jeans off her legs. Once she'd stepped clear of the fabric, Cal ran his hands back up the insides of her thighs to the soft fur of her sex.

"Oh, baby, I've dreamed of you like this." His fingers cupped her, one sliding into her warm wetness, his thumb pushing through to her folds, finding and stroking her clit. His other hand smoothed over her breasts, tweaking first one, then the other.

Deme clutched his arms, her nails digging into Cal's skin, sending a delightful edge of pain through him, heightening the sexual tension between them.

His cock strained against his fly, eager to be set free from the confines of his trousers.

Deme's gaze captured and held his, her eyes glazed, her breathing coming in short gasps. "Promise me you'll tell me if you're tired of us, before I find you screwing around."

"What?" His mind on his cock, Cal had to drag himself back to reality to address her comment. He sucked in a deep breath, his finger still buried in her pussy, his heart racing at the stall. "Baby, I'd tell you. I promise. But it isn't gonna happen. I want you in my life and I wouldn't do anything to jeopardize that." One hand squeezed her shoulder, his fingers sliding down her arm to her waist. He dragged her close, nudging her with the hardened ridge beneath his pants.

"Good, because if I catch you cheating on me again..." She

reached for the button on his jeans, pushing it free, then slid his zipper down.

"You'll what?" His cock jutted out into her palm and he hissed, his skin sensitive to her every touch.

"I'm make you sorry." Deme wrapped her fingers around him and slid down the length of him, all the way to the base where she fondled his balls, squeezing gently.

Done with talk, and past the point of no return, Cal swept Deme into his arms, strode across the room and through her bedroom door. He sat her on the edge of the bed and stripped off the rest of his clothing. Then he dropped to his knees and parted her thighs, draping them over his shoulders. He kissed a path from the inside of her knee all the way up to where her channel glistened with the moisture of her desire.

His tongue lapped at the musky juices, swirling into her, tasting and teasing as he worked his way up to the tiny stretch of skin cradled between her folds. A hidden treasure to be teased and coaxed until she screamed out her frustration and need.

Cal flicked her clit with the tip of his tongue.

Deme lay back against the comforter, her back arching, a moan rising from her chest.

"More?" he asked.

"By the goddess, yesss." Her fingers threaded through his hair and dug into his scalp, urging him closer.

He tapped her again, this time sliding his tongue over the length of her opening and then sucking her clit into his mouth, tugging on it gently. Cal let go and blew a cool stream of air over her heated flesh, knowing she loved it and hated it all at once. He liked that he could bring her to orgasm so quickly and liked even more to prolong the torture until she lost herself completely.

She drew in a deep breath, her body going rigid. "Oh, please. Don't stop now," she wailed.

Taking pity on her frustration, he lapped, nibbled and

stroked her until she cried out, her heels digging into the muscles of his back, a spasm shaking her body.

As she shot over the edge of her climax, Cal rose quickly, rolled a condom over his cock and thrust deep inside her in one fluid movement. He rammed home, burying himself up to his balls before he slid back out to the very tip.

Her legs wrapped around his waist and tightened, forcing him back in. "You're killing me. Don't tease."

Cal laughed and entered her again, settling into a fast and furious rhythm, pumping in and out like a racecar piston. As he neared his climax, he scooted her fully onto the mattress and lay down over her, his arms around her, crushing her to him as he drove in one last time.

Then his body tensed and his cock twitched shooting his seed into the safety of the prophylactic.

For a long moment he lay atop her, skin to skin, reveling in her beauty and the scent of peaches and roses that was uniquely Deme. Then he rolled to the side, taking her with him, refusing to break their intimate connection.

Deme lay for a long moment, basking in the afterglow of making love with Cal. During the intensity of their coupling, she'd pushed aside the memory of him and the black-haired beauty. Now the image returned banishing the residual warmth, making Deme all too aware of her nakedness and the coolness of the air in her apartment.

Cal must have sensed her withdrawal. "I didn't kiss her." As if to emphasize his point, he brushed his lips across hers.

The more she thought about it, the more convinced she was of what she'd seen. "It doesn't matter. You need to leave now."

His brow furrowed and his rapidly deflating cock slipped out of her. "Are you sure? You've been gone a month..." he pressed a kiss to her eyelid. "I've missed you..." his lips slid along her cheekbone and trailed down the side of her throat.

Deme's gut tightened. She had dreamed of her homecoming,

of Cal staying in her apartment, them making love throughout the night and sleeping through the next day.

With a resigned sigh, she shook her head. "You need to go. We have to work tomorrow. It'll be my first day on the job, and I want to make a good impression on Chief Warner."

Cal captured her face between his palms and forced her to look him in the eye. "You can have your space, but know this…I don't give up easily." He kissed her, his tongue pushing past her clenched teeth to stroke the length of hers.

His hand cupped the back of her head, urging her closer, lengthening the connection.

When Cal broke away, Deme wanted to reach out and bring him back, to go for round two.

And based on the stiffness of his member, Cal was ready too. Instead he rolled off the bed and stood, staring down at her, his mouth set in a grim line. "Welcome home, Deme." Then he gathered his clothing and dressed quickly.

Deme pulled the sheets up over her breasts and feasted her eyes on his naked hard body with broad shoulders that seemed to fill any room he entered. What was she doing? What was she trying to prove? She wanted him more than anything she'd ever wanted in her life. Then why the hell was she pushing him away?

When he had his pants and shoes on, he slipped his shirt over his shoulders and grabbed his jacket from the floor. He stood in the doorway to her bedroom and glanced back at her, giving her every opportunity to change her mind.

When Deme didn't say anything, Cal left, closing the door behind him.

Deme rolled out of the bed and headed straight for the bathroom and a shower to cool the heat raging inside. The ivy plant she'd left on the counter drooped. Her sisters had checked on her apartment once a week, but the little plant seemed neglected, forgotten in the mad rush of her sisters' desire to get in, check on her stuff and leave to get on with their own lives.

Deme touched a finger to a dull green leaf. "Be happy.

I'm home for good." Energy flowed through her body and out the tip of her finger into the little ivy. Like a desert eager for water, the vines stiffened, each leaf fluttering, reaching for the light. A small measure of peace washed over Deme. "Thanks, I needed that."

Deme grabbed a towel from the linen closet and tossed it over the shower rod. The sense of peace didn't last long. As soon as she moved away from the ivy, thoughts of Cal pushed back into her mind.

She should have known better than to let a man beneath her skin, especially this man. She'd done it before with Cal and walked away–all the way to St. Croix in the Virgin Islands. Back then it had been one of the hardest things she'd ever done. This time she couldn't completely walk away.

She'd signed on with the Chicago Police Department to help them investigate the odd and interesting cases involving paranormal events. And lucky her, Chief Warner had partnered her with Calais Black. She'd been excited by the prospect when she'd left Chicago to return to St. Croix to close up shop on her business and list her beach house with a local realtor.

She'd given it up. All of it—the beach, the sand and laid-back life—to return to Chicago and give her relationship with Cal a second chance. Now as she turned the water on in the shower, she questioned her mad rush to get back to Chicago.

She stepped into the shower and water sluiced over her face and shoulders. Droplets ran off the tips of her sensitized nipples that only a few moments ago Cal had nibbled and tongued.

Deme groaned and grabbed a bar of soap, lathering her body to scrub away the sticky feeling of traveling. But no amount of scrubbing would wash away the memory of Cal's hands on her skin, his lips visiting every pressure-point on her body, of his magnificent cock sliding into her.

She turned the water colder, rinsed suds from her hair and body, then she got out of the shower, toweling herself dry quickly. Everywhere she touched, he'd touched.

The sound of her cell phone ringing brought her out of her

self-imposed sexual torment and sent her hurrying into the small apartment's kitchen where she'd deposited her purse. Her first reaction was to wish it was Cal, calling to ask her to let him in. By the time she'd stepped out of the shower, she'd worked herself up into a froth of lust. She might just let him in. As she dug into her purse, the phone stopped ringing.

She dug faster, emptying boarding passes, receipts, packages of gum onto the counter. Finally she located her phone beneath her wallet and snatched it out, reading the number on the screen. Her brows knitted as she pushed the button to redial.

"Warner here." The gruff voice of her supervisor barked in Deme's ear.

"This is Deme Chattox. Did you try to call me?" she asked, securing the towel around her body, feeling exposed and a little naughty standing there naked talking to her boss. She knew he couldn't see her, but it still felt weird.

"I need you and Black in the station ASAP."

Deme's pulse quickened. "What's happened?"

"The evidence storage facility has been compromised and the evidence we had on Vladimir Romanov was stolen. I need you two to follow up while the trail is hot."

Deme squared tired shoulders. No time like the present to start her new job. "Yes, sir. I'll be there."

"And bring Cal with you. He didn't answer my call. I left a message on his cell."

Deme started to tell the boss she didn't have a clue as to Cal's whereabouts, but thought better of it. Chief Warner had hired her knowing she and Cal were seeing each other. No use airing her dirty laundry the first night on the job. "Will do."

The chief hung up, expecting no less from her.

Deme dug into her closet and fished out black jeans and a matching black sweater. It suited her mood and if she had to do any sleuthing in the night, she would be camouflaged to blend into the shadows. A quick attack with a brush and she had her hair slicked back into a damp ponytail and secured out of her face.

After sliding into a pair of black tennis shoes with soft rubber soles, she grabbed her purse and keys and left her apartment, locking the door behind her. Her car sat in the parking lot where she'd left it a month earlier. She dodged the other vehicles and had almost made it to hers when Cal's sleek black SUV pulled in front of her.

"Get in."

"I'll take my own car, thank you." She stepped to the side and would have gone around behind Cal, but he reversed and said again. "Don't make this any harder than it already is. Just get in."

Rather than make a big stink, Deme climbed into the passenger seat and glared out the front windshield. "I told you, the sex is just recreational. I'm not looking for a relationship at this time."

"Good, because I need a partner. Not a liability."

Deme blinked at Cal's harsh words, but, given what she'd just told him, she probably deserved it. Yet his words stung more than she would like to admit.

They headed back to headquarters, arriving in less than fifteen minutes. As late as it was, there was little traffic on the streets to slow their progress.

Inside HQ, they met Chief Warner in the conference room.

Deme gritted her teeth. This was where Cal had kissed Medea. No matter how much he denied it, Deme could barely stand to be in the same room. Either Cal had told the truth and not kissed the other woman, or he had faked his sincerity so well, he'd almost convinced her that he hadn't done anything wrong. She moved to the opposite side of the large table occupying the center of the room.

"Here's the deal." Warner didn't wait for them to settle. He launched in as soon as they entered the room. "Evidence has gone missing from the storage facility." He clicked on a remote control and the large computer screen at the end of the room blinked to life. "Watch this."

The scene was from the security camera inside the storage

facility, pointing at the desk of the duty officer charged with guarding evidence linked to thousands of cases. Everything seemed normal until the duty officer rose from his desk, smiling at whomever was on the other side of the window from him.

His smile remained in place, fixed as if stuck to his face. Something black fluttered over the screen, blocking the image.

Cal leaned forward. "What happened to the video?"

Warner's mouth pressed into a line. "The best we can tell is someone threw black fabric over the camera."

The chief replayed the clip again.

Deme pointed at it when the guard stood and smiled. "Stop the video."

Chief Warner hit the pause button.

Still pointing, Deme asked, "Who entered the storage facility?"

"By the expression on his face it had to be someone the officer knew." The chief hit fast-forward. For the next five minutes of video the screen remained blank. "Pay attention."

The black lifted, like fabric fluttering away from the camera. In the same spot and wearing the exact expression as before, the duty officer stood in front of the window to the facility.

Deme frowned. "It's as if he's frozen in time."

"Five minutes passed according to the video."

"Did you get a shot of the visitor?"

"No. The camera angle only takes in the duty officer and anyone leaning close to the window."

"What about other cameras leading up to the storage facility?"

"I've checked. Nothing."

"Have you interviewed the duty officer? What does he have to say about what happened?"

"He swears he was on duty and alert at all times. No one came or left."

"No visitors? Nobody?" Cal asked.

Chief Warner shook his head. "He claims there weren't any. He even agreed to a lie detector test. I had to call in a favor for that one."

"And?" Deme prompted.

"Came back clean." The chief sighed. "The guy seems to be telling the truth."

"Or thinks he's telling the truth." Deme held out her hand to Chief Warner. "May I?"

The detective handed her the remote. "Be my guest."

Deme backed the video up to the point at which the duty officer froze. "Look at his eyes."

"What about them?"

"He's staring straight ahead, without any movement to the left or right."

"So?"

"Most people can't stare for that long without glancing in different directions or blinking."

Warner squinted, moving closer to the screen. "He looks kind of deer-in-the-headlights blank."

Her pulse leaped. "No, he looks like he's in a trance."

Cal nodded. "We need to find out who was at his window."

"It had to be someone he knew," Warner said, "or he wouldn't have smiled and looked relaxed in the first place."

"Where is the man now?" Deme asked, without taking her gaze off the screen.

"In one of our interview rooms."

Deme's mind raced. She wished her sister Selene was there. She had the knack for a little mind reading. Not so Deme. She could manipulate plants and earth to give up information, but not people. Still, the key lay with the duty officer. He'd been there the entire time, if the brief glimpses of video hadn't been compromised. "Mind if I ask him some questions?"

"Have at him." The Chief Warner waved his hand toward the conference room door. "The sooner we get that knife back, the better."

Cal hesitated. "What about the witness?"

"Talked to the witness a few hours ago." Chief Warner was careful not to reveal the sex of the individual. "The witness is not happy that the only evidence clearly identifying Vladimir as the killer has been stolen. That leaves that person as the primary target, the only thing standing in the way of the Tribunal convicting and sentencing Vladimir in this case."

"Have you beefed up security on the witness?" Cal asked.

"We have. I sent only the best and nobody outside the department knows where to look. Not even me."

A blur of movement at the doorway to the conference room caught Deme's attention.

"Sorry, Chief. I came as soon as I got your message." The dark-haired beauty Medea entered the room.

Deme's hackles rose automatically. The aura of the room changing immediately to a confusing mix of what felt like pheromones.

Chief Warner smiled and held out a hand to the latecomer. "Medea, come in. I want you to meet the newest member of our team, Deme Chattox."

The woman crossed the room like a model on a runway, one foot in front of the other, her sooty brows rising delicately on her porcelain face.

From the corner of her vision, Deme saw Cal's gaze fix on the raven-haired diva. Deme wanted to step in front of him and break that connection, shift his concentration and pummel his chest for the amount of attention he gave the female cop.

"The pleasure is mine." She held out her hand to Deme.

Deme took Medea's hand and gave it a brief, perfunctory shake. "Hi." She found no pleasure in the introduction. The woman standing in front of her had kissed Cal in this very room. It took every ounce of willpower for Deme to sheath her claws, when her entire being urged her to scratch out the other woman's eyes.

"I understand you're one of them?" Medea stated, her nose twitching as though she smelled something bad.

Deme bristled. "If you mean one of the team, yes."

"No. I meant a paranorm." Medea smiled, the effort not quite reaching her ice-blue eyes. "Just what kind of paranormal ability do you posses?"

"I'm Wiccan."

Medea's brows arched. "Concentration?"

"Earth." Deme wanted to ask if Medea was a troll, but that would have been far too catty and beneath her. She could daydream about it though for the little pleasure it gave her. One corner of Deme's mouth twitched as she imagined Medea's reaction. Deme tilted her head in a similarly haughty position as Medea's. "And you? Are you paranormal?" Deme forced herself to ask.

"Some say I read minds." She shrugged, leveling her stare at Deme. "I like to call it reading body language." The way she said body made the hairs on the back of Deme's neck stand at attention and that itch to claw reared its ugly green head.

Caught thinking bad thoughts about the dark-haired woman, Deme's cheeks burned. "Mind reading would be a handy talent."

"A body language expert is just what we needed." Chief Warner whacked Medea on the back. "That's why we hired her onto the force. She'll be a huge asset in investigations and on cases where we have to canvass the streets and question witnesses."

"Medea has shed some valuable insight on a couple of cases already." Cal grinned. "You're gonna love having her on our team."

Don't count on it. Deme thought the words as she stared into Medea's eyes. *Calais Black is mine.*

Medea's expression didn't change.

Deme snorted softly. *Mind reader my ass.*

Chapter Three

Cal wanted to laugh at the mutinous expression on Deme's face. Clearly the presence of the new gal on the team wasn't making her happy. Since Deme thought he'd kissed Medea, he couldn't blame her belligerence toward the other woman. He'd have to convince Deme that the woman meant nothing to him, other than another body to cover the bases in their war on paranormal crimes in the city.

Cal faced his boss. "I'd still like to question the guard in charge of the evidence."

Warner held his hands out, palms up. "Be my guest. He's been through a lie detector test and several other interrogators and his story remains the same. The truth according to him is that no one entered the building at the time the security camera went black. Nor did he take the evidence himself."

"I understand. While I talk to him, could we feed the video from the outside of the building into the war room? We'll want to study that as well."

"That's another thing." Warner heaved a huge sigh, looking older than his fifty-five years. "The video from the external cameras has a ten minute gap."

"Coincidence?" Medea asked.

Deme's eyes narrowed. "Personally, I don't believe in co-incidence."

"Neither do I." Chief Warner led the way toward the interview rooms. "Cal, you can interview the man. Chattox and Medea can watch from the other side of the two-way mirror." Halfway down a long hallway the chief opened a door and waved the two women in.

Cal continued on to the interrogation room and stepped inside.

The man seated at a table raised his head, his eyes hollow, his face pale. "Hey, Black. You gonna take a shot at me too?"

Having checked evidence in and out of the storage facility on multiple occasions, Cal recognized Johnny Houston. "Hey, Johnny. Got yourself in a pinch, did ya?"

The man shook his head. "I don't know what's going on, but I didn't take anything out of the facility and I didn't let anyone in."

"I believe you."

"You'd be the first." The man ran his hand through his hair, making it stand on end. "Hell, I got a wife and kids. I wouldn't do anything to jeopardize my life or job. The whole reason I took the position in the first place, was so that I wouldn't get shot at. Why would I screw that up?"

Cal pulled up the other chair and sat across the table from the man. "Did you see anything unusual? Could you have blacked out?"

"No, it was a night like any other at the facility, nothing weird, no one visited. If I'd have blacked out, wouldn't I have fallen or something?" He rubbed the back of his head. "I don't feel any knots or sore spots."

The more questions Cal asked, the more convinced he was that Johnny was telling the truth. Or Johnny thought what he was saying was the truth.

On the other side of the mirror from the guard and Cal, Deme stood beside Medea, listening and assessing for herself the truth of what the guard was saying. With only one item for evidence and a single witness, the case against Vladimir teetered on shaky ground.

Chief Warner excused himself, claiming he needed another cup of coffee to make it through the night.

"Do you think he's lying?" Medea asked, breaking the silence.

"You're the body language expert. You tell me." Deme's teeth clenched and she took a moment to unclench them before continuing, regretting her outburst. She was the newest member of the team and she wanted to be known as a team player in any investigation, not the jealous lover. "I think the guard believes he's telling the truth." Deme's words were cryptic. She didn't want to talk to the woman she'd caught kissing Cal. *If you can really read minds, read this, you stupid cow. I think you're an idiot and have no real body language or mind-reading talent.*

Deme stared at Cal through the mirror and waited for a response from Medea. After several minutes Deme shook her head. If the woman really was a mind reader, maybe she couldn't communicate with witches.

"Do you think whoever went after the evidence will go after the witness next?" Medea's voice echoed softly in the small room.

Deme shot a glance at the black-haired cop. "Why do you say that?"

Medea shrugged a beautiful, delicate shoulder. "Just curious. You would think they'd increase security."

The chief returned before Deme could form a response. But Medea's words had only echoed what Deme had been thinking, worrying her. She made a mental note to pose the question to Warner as soon as she could get him alone. Granted, she should be open with her entire team, but Deme didn't trust Medea any further than she could throw the sultry officer.

Cal concluded his interview and stood. "We'll get this sorted out," he said to the guard.

"Thanks. I can't afford to lose my job, much less go to jail."

Everything about the guard appeared to be on the level. But the gaps on the videos were too damning. Something had happened to the building and the guard allowing the theft of the evidence.

Warner nodded toward the man laying his head on the table in the interview room. "Did he say anything different?"

"No, sir." Deme sighed. "When you have a minute, I'd like to speak to you." She cast a glance at Medea and back to Warner. "Alone." There, that couldn't have been more obvious.

Medea's gaze captured Warner's, her blue eyes wide as she stared into his. "I have a matter to attend to. Excuse me." As she passed Deme, Medea leaned close and murmured, "By the way, Cal's a good kisser, isn't he?"

The punch in the gut made Deme suck in a quick breath and clench her fists by her sides.

As Medea left the room, she brushed against Cal who entered and closed the door behind him.

"That was a bust," he said.

Deme couldn't help noting the perfect timing of the two passing through the door at the same time. She fought to hold her temper and work the case, not fume over her relationship with Officer Black.

"I figured it would be." Warner scrubbed a hand through his shock of thick white hair. "All we have now between Vladimir and the Tribunal is one key witness."

"That's what I wanted to talk to you about." Deme paced the small room and turned. "Someone went to the trouble of stealing the knife. Don't you think he'll take the next step and kill the witness?"

Warner sighed. "I'd thought of that. We have tight security on the witness. Only I and the men who took the witness to the safe house know where it is. And they were instructed to park several blocks away from the house and walk in. They will stay with that person, and not return home or to the office until the Tribunal meets the day after tomorrow."

"Anyone else know how to get in touch with them?" Deme asked.

"They have a throw-away cell phone they are allowed to use once a day to check messages." Warner glanced at his watch. "If we need to get in touch, we can send them a text or leave a voice mail. The response will not be instantaneous, but at least no one can find them if they don't know where to look. "I'm headed home to bed for a few hours sleep. I suggest you get some too. Tomorrow should be interesting."

In the middle of a face-splitting yawn, Deme covered her mouth. "I could use some shut-eye. Didn't get much on the plane.

Warner blinked then his brows drew together. "That's right, you flew in today."

She snorted. "That was yesterday. It's already past three in the morning."

"Right. Go. Get some rest." The chief waved his hand. "I'm headed out, as well."

"Chief Warner." Deme shot forward. "Do you mind giving me a ride to my apartment?"

"Not at all." The older man's brows wrinkled. "But I thought you and Black rode together?"

"We did, and I'll take her home." Cal hooked her arm and herded her toward the exit. "No use going out of your way, when she's only a few blocks away from my place. Have a good night."

Deme bit hard on her tongue to keep from making a scene in front of her new boss, allowing Cal to lead her out of the building and into the night. Once on the sidewalk she faced Cal. "Did you ever consider the fact I might not *want* to ride with you?"

"Yes." His lips twitched in the hint of a smile.

Fighting the urge to wipe the growing grin off the man's face, Deme turned and strode for Cal's black SUV. "Fine, but you're not coming in."

"Agreed." He thumbed the key fob releasing the locks and

they both climbed in, settling into the bucket seats, securing their seatbelts.

Cal backed out of his parking space and eased out onto the road.

Deme looked away from the driver, her gaze panning the night, not looking for anything in particular, more avoiding focusing on the man she'd spent so many hours thinking about.

They entered the expressway leading toward Lake Michigan and their respective apartments, the silence lengthening painfully.

Deme stared out at the night, the street lights masking the sky above. She couldn't tell if the stars were shining or if it was cloudy.

Cal exited the expressway and slowed, maneuvering through streets with traffic lights. At one intersection the light blinked yellow then red. A figure of a slim teen stepped up to the curb, wearing a dark hoodie pulled up over his head.

Cal slowed to a stop.

Something about the way the figure stood with his head down captured Deme's attention.

"Kinda late to be standing on street corners." Cal glanced at the figure. "Wonder if his parents know where he is."

The boy looked up, his gaze going straight to Cal's.

Something about the boy's pale blue gaze made Deme's fingers curl and her nails bite into the arm rest.

"That guy reminds me of Medea." Deme shuddered. "He's giving me the creeps."

"I don't know why you're so bothered by Medea. She's just another member of the team."

"Yeah, whatever." Deme glanced back at the boy who hadn't moved since he'd stepped up to the curb. "Is he going to cross, or not?"

Cal chuckled. "Are you jealous?" He glanced at the boy again as he waited for the light to turn green.

"Hell, no." Though her response was quick and adamant, Deme wondered if Cal's words held too much truth. "Even if

I was the jealous type—which I'm not—it's more than that. I don't know what it is, but I don't like her."

Silence greeted her words. Deme ventured a glance at Cal.

He sat with his hands curled around the steering wheel, his gaze on the road in front of him. Even before the light turned green, his foot dropped to the accelerator and the vehicle shot forward.

They passed street after street, speeding through the city.

"Hey, you missed the turn." Deme turned in her seat as the streets flashed by. "You can take the next turn and double back."

At the next street corner Cal didn't slow, didn't even turn his head, just kept going straight, his eyes fixed forward.

Deme's chest tightened. The longer it took to get to her apartment, the longer she remained in a confined space with the man she thought she loved, but who had betrayed her trust by kissing another woman. Not that he'd made any formal commitment to Deme, but still…

She sat back and forced herself to calm. "Look, I'm tired and I'd like to get some sleep. Could you take me home, please?"

No response other than the steady increase of speed the closer they got to the lakefront road.

Deme leaned over the console and glanced at the speedometer and gasped. "Cal, you're exceeding the speed limit by thirty miles an hour. Slow down."

Her heart rate spiked as the SUV raced through a red light, nearly clipping another vehicle pulling into the intersection. She punched Cal's arm. "Cal. Stop the car."

He didn't and he wasn't responding to anything she said. It was as though he was somewhere else, not behind the wheel of his vehicle, frozen in position, unable to hear, see or respond to her shouts.

With the SUV more or less out of control, Deme was running out of sane options. She leaned over and slammed the shift into low.

The heavy vehicle lurched, slamming Deme's head against

the dash. Pain stabbed through her temple and her vision blurred.

The car slowed for a moment, the engine protesting, speed warring with RPMs.

Though they'd slowed, Cal's foot remained jammed against the accelerator, sending them charging toward the lake. At their current speed they'd hit the T of the road they were on and Riverside Drive in less than a minute. They'd either crash into oncoming traffic or speed across all four lanes and catapult into the icy cold waters of the lake.

Deme punched Cal in the arm. "Snap out of it, Cal," she shouted.

Twenty yards to the intersection Deme grabbed the steering wheel and pulled hard toward her. The tires squealed and the SUV leaned hard to the left, the rear end swinging around as the front careened toward a light pole.

Deme squeezed shut her eyes as they crashed into the pole. Airbags deployed, keeping her and Cal from flying through the windshield.

Her seatbelt retracted, the strap pressing into her shoulder, bruisingly tight. When the airbags deflated and the dust settled, Deme opened her eyes.

The engine had died on impact. Now they sat in eerie silence. Even the never completely quiet traffic seemed to pause for a long moment, as if the world was catching its breath.

Cal blinked, a spot of blood trickling from his forehead where a shard of windshield glass had found its way over the airbag. "What the hell happened?"

Deme sucked in a deep breath and coughed, powder tickling her dry throat. "You don't remember?"

"No. We were on the way home and now we're kissing a light pole?" He shook his head. "Damn, Deme, what the hell happened?"

"You zoned out."

"I what?" He stared at her as if she'd lost her mind.

Maybe she had, but Cal hadn't been himself prior to the crash. "You...blanked out, Cal."

His brows drew together. "Out cold?"

"No." Deme tugged against the seatbelt, punching at the release button. She didn't like what she'd seen in Cal's face when they'd been barreling down the street. "Your eyes were open. It was like you were paralyzed behind the wheel."

"How?"

"Good question." She pulled on the door lever and pushed the passenger door open and stepped onto the sidewalk, her body stiff, the bruise across her shoulder beginning to throb.

Cal climbed out of the driver's side and walked to the front of the vehicle, his gaze assessing. He lifted the crumpled hood and stared into the dark interior of the engine. "It looks worse on the outside than the inside. My car suffered more than the light pole. Any metal rubbing the tires on your side?"

Deme checked the tires and fenders. "All clear. Think it'll run?"

"We'll see." He climbed back into the vehicle and turned the key. The motor turned over and died. Cal turned the key again and held it longer.

The engine turned over, sputtered and finally settled into a steady rumble.

"Let's go, while it's still running."

"No way." Deme stood still, shaking her head.

"You can't walk home and the SUV will get us that far at the least."

"Oh, we're going and I'll be with you in the SUV. Difference is, I'm driving." She crooked her thumb. "Out."

Cal's mouth firmed, then relaxed. "Fair enough." He got out and rounded the vehicle, while Deme slipped into the driver's seat and slammed shut her door.

She familiarized with the instruments and levers, then shifted into Reverse, backing away from the light pole. When she shifted into Drive, the gears ground, but the SUV jerked forward spewing a light cloud of smoke from the engine.

Cal studied her. His gaze intense. "We should stop at the hospital and get you checked out."

Deme refused to face him, but she couldn't ignore him in her peripheral vision. She turned onto Lake Shore Drive and drove to the next block, where she hung a right, headed back toward her apartment. "I don't need a hospital. The airbag kept me from slamming into the windshield or dashboard."

Cal stared across the console at her. "With the force of the impact, you could still have a concussion."

"So could you. Are you going to see a doctor?" she challenged.

"I might."

"Yeah, and pigs will fly." But because they both might be suffering some at-the-moment-unseen effects of a head injury, Deme made the decision. "Just in case either one of us has a concussion, we're going to my place to sleep. That way we can watch out for each other."

"I thought you didn't want me there."

"I don't. But I'm not going to the hospital and I'm not calling the boss to ask him to give up his sleep to hold our hands through the night."

"Point taken."

The rest of the journey went by quickly with both lost in their own thoughts. As they pulled into the parking lot of the apartment complex, Deme's hands were cramped and her body ached all over.

Nothing else had happened, but the stress was no less intense. Whatever had triggered Cal's trance could occur again.

Deme not only wanted to watch him for a concussion, but also for unusual behavior.

As soon as they were inside her apartment with the door closed and locked, Deme handed Cal clean towels and pushed him toward the bathroom. "Clean all the powder off."

"What about you?" He winked. "Care to join me?"

"No, I'll wait out here. Take your time." The longer he stayed in the shower, the better.

When Cal disappeared behind the bathroom door and the sound of running water peppered the air, Deme grabbed her cell phone and dialed Selene.

"Deme?" Selene's voice was like syrup on gravel, all ruggedly soft and sleepy. "What's wrong?"

"I need your help."

"With what?"

"We're having some strange happenings at the station and elsewhere."

"What do you mean?"

"I think someone is using telepathy to control the minds of some of our guys on the force."

"Really?" Selene's voice grew stronger. "Where are you now?"

"At my apartment. Cal almost drove us into Lake Michigan."

"What?" The phone rattled and clattered. A few seconds later her sister came back on. "Sorry, I dropped my cell. I'll be there in a few minutes. Just give me time to dress."

"No, I think I have everything under control now. Cal seems to be alert and aware. At least he's responding to me now."

"I'm coming over."

"No. I just need to know what I could use or do to block whatever or whoever is controlling him. Is there such a thing?"

"Scent, perfume, candles," Selene said with authority. "Use a scent he can relate to, that he remembers. Do you have anything that might trigger memories? I could stop by with a few of my own candles, but they have to be something that sparks a particular memory, preferably one that relates to you."

Deme remembered a stash of candles she'd kept in the cupboard over the dryer. She'd used the same candles the night before she'd left for St. Croix when she and Cal had made love into the wee hours. She'd slept through her alarm and almost missed her plane.

Yeah, if Cal had any feelings left for her, maybe the candle would trigger his memories of that night.

The water stopped in the shower.

"I'll talk to you in the morning." Deme reached out to end the call.

"Deme, call me if you need anything. Forcing people to do your bidding is dangerous. Cal may not be himself right now."

"I'll keep an eye on him. Gotta go." Deme hit the end button and sprinted for the laundry room.

By the time Cal emerged from the shower, she had lit a candle and was carrying it through the living room.

Cal opened the bathroom door and stepped out, shirtless, his hair finger combed but dripping onto his shoulders. He'd slipped into his jeans but he was barefoot and sexier than Deme could handle. He crossed her bedroom and leaned against the doorframe.

Deme came to a halt, staring at him, her heart racing, her lips dry, fighting the urge to go to him and forget the kiss in the conference room.

His lips quirked up on the corners, a slight frown pulling his brows together, making that expression just as sexy as a wink and a smile. "Deme? Are you all right?"

Chapter Four

Deme gulped. "Sorry. Yes, yes. I'm fine. I must be tired."

"What's with the candle?" He straightened and closed the distance between them.

"Nothing. I thought it would make my apartment smell better. Since I've been gone for a month, it was a bit musty." Okay, now she was babbling.

The trouble with scented candles was that they brought back memories for Deme as well. Her body remembered everything about the last time that candle had burned.

"You lit that candle the night before you left for St. Croix, didn't you?" It wasn't so much a question as a statement. Cal closed his eyes and drew in a deep breath through his nose. "It reminds me of you naked."

Deme smiled, that Cal remembered that night made her insides burn. And that his most vivid memory was of her naked...only added to Deme's spiking desire. Her thighs clenched, her core tightening. The sudden rush of lust came on so fast her hand shook.

Cal removed the candle from her fingers, setting it on a table beside the door. "You had your hair down around your shoulders." He reached out and loosened the ponytail, removing the band holding it in place.

Her long thick hair brushed across her shoulders and cheeks. "That was a month ago."

"It was yesterday." He wound his fingers into the long tresses and tugged, forcing her head to tip back. Then he bent to slide his lips along the side of her neck where her pulse hammered against the skin.

Deme moaned. How could she resist him when he did that? She wove her hands into the raven-black hair at his nape, dragging him closer.

In a flurry of movement he ripped her shirt over her head and flung it to the floor.

She leaned close, her lips trailing across his chest, then she nipped one of his taut brown nipples, gently rolling it between her teeth. Deme ran her hands along his sides, skimming over tight skin, stretched over bunched muscles, finding their way into the waistband of his jeans. She slipped lower, cupping his ass, reveling in the knowledge he wasn't wearing underwear. A pair of pants was all that barred her from fully revealing his naked body.

Before she could reach for the buttons of his fly, he scooped her into his arms and crossed the distance to the couch in two easy strides, laying her out, not on the couch, but on the thick Persian rug in front of it.

Deme laughed. "I *do* have a bed."

"Too far." He dropped over her, his mouth searing a path from her neck to her breast, his hands slipping lower, fumbling with the button on her jeans.

"What makes you think I want you to make love to me?" she teased, counting the seconds, her breath lodged in her throat as she waited for him to free her of her clothing.

"The fact that you aren't telling me to leave." He sucked her nipple into his mouth and pulled hard.

She gasped, her back arching off the floor. "I could be too tired to tell you." The words rushed out, airy and slightly slurred. Who was she kidding? She wanted him inside her. Now.

"You talk too much." He nipped the tight little bud and slid down her torso, one kiss at a time.

"You're too slow." Deme pushed his hands aside, yanked the button free and ripped the zipper down.

Cal grabbed the jeans and tugged them over her thighs and off her legs, flinging them across the room.

He continued his path of kisses down to her flat belly. Cal rose up over her, nudged her knees apart and settled his big frame between her thighs, his cock bumping against the soft curls covering her sex.

Deme planted her heels in the carpet and pushed upward, urging him to take her, to ram that rod deep inside.

Instead he glided lower, spreading her legs wide, his fingers parting her folds to expose her clit.

He blew a warm stream of air over the sensitive flesh, then followed with a flick of his warm tongue.

Deme cried out, her hands grabbing for his hair.

When he tongued her again, she rose up, her bottom leaving the floor, her pussy throbbing, aching for him to fill her.

Cal swirled his tongue around her labia, then sucked the flesh into his mouth, tugging hard.

Tingles spread from her toes, up her thighs and into her center. "Now, Cal. Come inside me."

"Not yet." His whispered words breathed warm against her dampness. He slid a finger into her drenched channel, twirled it around, dragging it out and downward to her tight anus.

Her buttocks clenched in anticipation.

Cal pressed into her, his wet finger teasing the orifice while he slid his thumb into her vagina. At the same time, he released the suction and plied her clit with gentle strokes, over and over, raising her up to the highest precipice.

The tingling turned to spasms and her entire body shook with the force of her orgasm. Deme cried out, her body tensing, her heels pushing her upward, closer to that glorious tongue, those work-roughened fingers and ecstasy beyond anything she'd experienced.

When she thought she might die of pleasure, Cal climbed up her body and thrust deep inside her, filling her with his thick rock-hard cock.

He moved slowly at first, establishing a steady rhythm that increased in pressure and intensity with each thrust. Before long he was pounding into her, harder and faster, a thin sheen of perspiration shining across his face and chest enhancing his natural glow.

God, he was beautiful. Deme wrapped her legs around his waist.

When he stopped, she clenched, holding him inside her as his cock pulsed against her channel.

Basking in the beauty and the heat of their coupling, she almost cried when he started to slide out.

"Why?" She tried to keep him inside, by clamping her legs around him.

"I can't come inside you," Cal said through clenched teeth. "We're not wearing any protection."

"Oh." Deme's heels unlocked from around him and dropped to the floor.

Cal pulled free before he came, his cum dripping over her belly.

The warm liquid made her wish he could have stayed where he was. Would it be so bad to carry this man's child?

The thought intruded on its own, before she had a chance to really think it through. By the goddess, she wasn't in the market for a baby daddy and just because they had great sex together didn't make them a couple. Children were complicated when they were human. She could imagine the challenges of raising a witch child. What man would want the hassle?

When Cal's rigid body relaxed, he rose to his feet, gathered her in his arms and carried her into the bathroom, setting her feet on the cool porcelain of the bathtub.

Her knees buckled, still shaking from the intensity of their lovemaking. For a moment she clung to Cal, her naked breasts pressed to his chest, hunger burning, rising to consume her yet again.

Cal reached around Deme and turned the faucet handle to warm. Liquid sputtered from the shower head, then streamed over their bodies. At first cool, it steadily warmed until the jets of water were comfortable, lubricating and as intoxicating as satin sheets. His flaccid cock revived, nudging against Deme's belly.

When her leg slid around his calf and climbed up the back of his thigh, he couldn't resist. He scooped his hand over the backs of her thighs and lifted her, settling her legs around his waist, his cock pushing into her pussy, warm, wet and wickedly sensual.

Her channel squeezed around him, urging him closer, deeper.

Cal obliged, turning to settle Deme's back against the cool tiles of the shower wall. "We really should rest."

"Uh-huh." She leaned close and nibbled at the pulse pounding against the base of his throat, while settling her body over him, driving herself downward to take him more fully inside. "We will. Later." Her thighs tightened and she rose up, then sank down, setting the rhythm for him to follow.

He raised her arms, pinning her wrists together above her head. With his other hand, he grabbed her hip. "This is not the last time we will do this. Do you understand?" His gaze bored into hers. "I want you, Deme. I need you."

She sighed. With her hands locked above her head, she could only move her body. Deme thrust her chest forward, rubbing the tips of her nipples against his. "I want you too."

A rush of warmth and desire flooded Cal as he thrust into her, driving deep. Again and again his hips pumped, his hand steadying her to take his full, heavy length.

Her head dropped back against the tile, her eyes glazing as she cried out his name, "Cal."

One more thrust and he jerked out of her, spilling his seed in the spray of the slowly cooling shower.

Whatever had happened, whatever had made him black out, couldn't begin to do it again when he was with Deme. She completed him. He couldn't imagine loving anyone as much as he loved this beautiful red-haired witch.

He switched off the water and stepped out of the tub, taking Deme with him, letting her feet fall to the floor. With gentle strokes he dried her body with a soft towel. When they were dry, he led her to her bed and lay down beside her. "Now, we sleep." He sighed and pulled her into his arms, spooning her naked backside against his front, his arm draping over her breasts. This was how he'd envisioned her homecoming. Lying in bed, naked, making love. A smile slipped across his face as he fell into a deep, dreamless sleep.

Deme lay for long minutes, reveling in the warmth of Cal's arms. Her imaginings of her homecoming had been much like this. But a niggle of doubt remained in the back of her mind. Someone had taken control of Cal's mind to make him drive like a man possessed, straight for Lake Michigan.

She wondered who it could be and why he'd do such a thing.

When Cal's breathing settled into a steady, deep rhythm, Deme slid from his embrace and entered her hall closet. She pulled out a five-pound bag of gardening dirt she'd planned to use upon her return to start her herb garden.

At this time she needed more than herbs to get through this night. She needed power and protection.

Naked, she strode through the living room and back into the bedroom, knowing exactly what she had to do. Careful not to wake him, she poured a line of dirt on the floor around the bed, making a complete circle around Cal. Then she retrieved ivy from her bathroom and set it in the dirt. A quick trip back through the living room and laundry room netted the candle from earlier and three others.

One at a time she lit the candles, setting the first on the northern edge of the circle.

"Guardian of the North, protector of the earth that feeds us, I bid thee come. Welcome to the circle."

Deme lit the next one and settled it on the eastern edge.

"Guardian of the East, master of air that cools, and brings us life, I bid thee come. Welcome to the circle."

Moving to southern edge, Deme lit another candle and pressed it into the edge of the mound of dirt.

"Guardian of the South, keeper of fire that sparks flames in all of us, I bid thee come. Welcome to the circle."

The final candle completed the circle at the western edge. Deme lit the wick and drew in a deep breath.

"Guardian of the West, bearer of water that flows through us and nourishes our bodies in rebirth, I bid thee come. Welcome to the circle."

The flames brightened, the glow filling the room.

Deme raised her face to the ceiling, her arms rising beside her, palms up. "Goddess of the earth, wind, water, fire and spirit, seal this circle."

The flames intensified, almost blinding in their brilliance. Then they eased back to simple burning wicks.

"So mote it be," she whispered.

With the circle complete, Deme moved on to cast a protection spell.

"Goddess of power, vanquish this space of all evil, cleanse it and make it pure. Protect all those within from those who would do them harm. I call you now, attend me. This is my will. So mote it be."

The earthy scent of dirt filled Deme's senses. Calm invaded her body as she climbed into the bed beside Cal. Careful not to wake him, she pulled his arm around her like a blanket and nestled her face against his chest, inhaling the maleness of his skin.

Exhausted from her trip home and almost being killed by a possessed boyfriend, Deme lay for a few moments, her eyes wide, her ears pricked up for danger. As her body warmed, her eyelids drooped. Images of her sisters hovered around her in her mind. Reassured by their presence, Deme fell into a deep, troubled sleep.

In the midst of Deme's dreams a pair of ice-blue eyes peered out of the fog of slumber. A woman's curly tresses framed a face whose features Deme could not quite make out.

Deme strained to discover the owner. Her inky-black curls wiggled, undulating in waves as if each lock was alive.

Reaching through the mist, Deme tried to capture a strand to study it closer. As her fingers neared the woman's hair, a curl snaked out as if propelled by a gust of wind. When it hit Deme's hand, it burned like a vicious wasp sting.

Deme jerked back her hand, rubbing the injury to relieve the pain.

"Don't let her in. Don't be fooled." Selene's disembodied voice floated to her on the wisp of a wind."

"Who is she?"

"One to be watched, one who knows more than she should."

Deme jerked awake and sat up in the bed. "Who is she?"

Cal's eyes blinked open. "What?" he muttered sleepily. "Are you okay?" His hand slipped around Deme's middle, drawing her back down beside him. "Nightmare?"

"Yeah." Deme lay for a long time, well after Cal's breathing grew heavy.

Beside her in the dirt on the floor, her little ivy plant had spread new vines and leaves, completing the circle of dirt with a ring of green.

Deme sighed, thankful for her beloved earth. She lay for a long time, counting the hours until morning, when she could call Selene and find out just what was happening.

Chapter Five

Sunlight streamed through the open blinds, tickling Cal's eyelids, nudging him awake. He rolled to his back and stared at the unfamiliar ceiling. With a jerk, he sat up.

As soon as he saw the candle on the dresser, he remembered, he'd stayed what was left of the night in Deme's apartment, making love to her, not once, but twice.

The dent on the pillow beside him gave him the evidence he needed to know she'd slept with him.

But where was she now? He shoved away the sheet and swung his legs over the side into a pile of dirt and greenery.

"What the hell?" A ring of what looked like potting soil and ivy circled the bed. "Deme?"

"Good morning, sleepyhead." Deme popped her head inside the door. "I have the coffee on and bread in the toaster. As soon as you're up and moving we can eat and get to the office."

"What's with the dirt and vegetation?" He brushed the dirt off his foot.

"Oh, that. Just a protection circle."

"You think we needed protection?"

"Not so much me, but you." Her lips quirked upward on one side.

"Me?" Cal ran a hand through his hair and stood, naked and cool in the morning air.

"Yeah, you." Deme raised her eyebrows. "After a near-fatal car crash that you conveniently can't remember, I'd say you needed a bit of protection." She nodded at the dirt and ivy. "If you're worried about the mess, I'll let you sweep it up."

"No, it's okay. I guess." Cal shook his head, but no matter how hard he thought over the events of the night before he couldn't remember much. "I have a gap in my memory between the time we drove away from headquarters and when I woke up with my SUV wrapped around the light pole."

"Remember anything else?"

"Making love to you not once, but twice, here in this apartment. On the living room floor and in the shower, if I recall correctly." His gaze burned into hers.

Her cheeks reddened. "At least you didn't forget that." She retreated back to the kitchen, calling out over her shoulder. "Chief Warner wants us in his office in thirty minutes. Seems there's been an attempt on the witness's life and he wants us to get on it immediately."

Cal found his jeans and T-shirt neatly folded on the end of the bed. He slipped into his jeans and pulled them up over his thighs. "I don't need any breakfast. Let's go."

"You might not, but I do. It will only take a minute and who knows when we'll get to eat next?"

She had a point. But if the safe house had been compromised, how would their witness survive long enough to testify to the Tribunal about Vladimir's murderous crimes?

"You can bring it with you, if it makes you feel any better," Deme said.

Cal entered the compact apartment kitchen, quietly stepping up behind her. His hands snagged her hips and pulled her against his rising erection. "I'm glad you're home."

"Ummm." She leaned her back into him, letting her head fall back against his chest. "You're not off the hook yet, but you're getting close."

His hands slid from her hips up her sides to cup her breasts. "Thirty minutes, you say?"

"Sadly." Her butt ground against the ridge of his fly, tempting him to rip her pants down around her ankles and slam into her from behind.

The dishtowel she held in her hand fluttered to the floor.

When Deme bent to pick it up, Cal's fingers closed on the swells of her bottom.

"Like that?" she asked.

"You're doing crazy things to me," he admitted.

"I'd like you to be doing crazy things to me." Her fingers loosened the button on her fly and she slipped her jeans down around her ankles, sliding one foot completely out. "We have to hurry." Again she bent forward, her hands grasping the edges of the counter.

Cal parted her cheeks, sliding his finger down the line to her anus and farther to the entrance of her channel. "Wet, already?"

"You do that to me, damn you." She glanced over her shoulder. "Do you know what to do, or do I have to show you?" Her lips twitched, a challenging gleam encouraging him to make his move.

"Sassy, aren't you?" He slapped her bare bottom.

"So tough." She tsked her tongue and bent lower, the honey of her juices glistening in the overhead lights. "That didn't hurt. Maybe if you slapped a little harder?" She wiggled her naked bottom.

Passion surged. Cal ripped open his fly, shoved the jeans down his hips and plunged into her opening, his cock gliding through a wash of fluid.

Deme was as turned on as he was, which only made him want her more. Grasping her hips, he rammed into her over and over until the heat sizzled between them.

This woman knew how to make him hot. Cal bent over her, sliding his hands beneath her T-shirt to cup her breasts, pushing her bra up over the mounds so that he could tweak the peaked nipples.

Tension rose, his body stiffened and he plunged into her warm, moist center one more time before he pulled free and ran his hand along his shaft as he came.

Deme stepped back into her jeans and slid them up her legs, buttoning and zipping the fly. She reached beneath her shirt and adjusted her bra. She faced him, slipping her finger over the tip of his cock before rising to plant a kiss on his lips. "You owe me an orgasm."

"Tonight."

"Don't make promises you can't keep."

He knew she was right. If the witness was at risk, they might be on duty throughout the day and night. "Okay, how about next time?"

"Vague, but acceptable." She handed him the dishtowel. "Guess you'll be taking your coffee to go."

"Right." He headed for the bathroom, his cock still stiff and throbbing. Damn. The witch had him tied in knots. One minute accusing him of kissing Medea, the next minute offering him sex in the kitchen.

When he entered the living room, Deme was dressed and ready to leave, a foam coffee cup in one hand.

She handed him the cup. "I'm driving."

Cal didn't argue, but followed her to her car. His SUV stood beside her little sedan, the front bumper sporting a deep V. "Wow. I did that?"

"Between you trying to run us into Lake Michigan and me trying to stop you with a light pole, we did a number on your poor vehicle."

"I don't care as long as you're all right. The vehicle will get fixed or replaced." He frowned. "What I don't like is that I don't remember a thing about what happened."

"I don't like it, either. Someone is playing you."

Cal's hands tightened around his cup. "What do I have to do to keep it from happening again?"

"I'm not sure you can do anything."

"How can we break a trance like last night's?"

"Selene said to use scents. The candle seemed to work well with you."

"Because it reminded me of you." Cal shook his head. "We can't drive around with lit candles in the car."

Deme grinned. "I know." She fished a small spray bottle from her purse. "I have this, so maybe you won't try to kill us again."

"Perfume?" His brow wrinkled.

She sprayed a little in the air in front of him.

Cal sniffed. "Reminds me of you naked."

"I'm detecting a pattern, Officer Black."

Deme's teasing words warmed him and chilled him. He climbed into her sedan. If letting her do all the driving helped keep them out of harm's way, he didn't mind giving up control. For now. But the memory lapses had to stop. He had to find out who was causing them.

Deme kept her eyes on the road. After all the times they'd made love since arriving at her apartment in the early hours of the morning, she'd have thought she'd had enough.

But the way she felt about him left her panting whenever they were in the same room...or car.

When they arrived at headquarters, Warner emerged from his office, his jaw clenched. "Need you at the safe house, pronto."

"What's going on?" Deme asked.

Warner didn't slow, hurrying past them to the conference room. "One of the cops on duty let an intruder into the safe house and he tried to kill the other cop and the witness. Both survived. The officer who was shot is in the hospital, the witness escaped through a bedroom window."

"What the hell happened?" Cal followed the chief into the large room.

"That's what I'm trying to find out." Warner picked up a remote and hit a button. "Got computer geek Jonesy, on it. He's sending a feed of some of the surveillance cameras in the area around the safe house. Apparently everything was copasetic when Sergeant Masterson left the safe house to find some fast food. When he got back, he knocked on the door. When Simmons opened it, Masterson just stood there. Then someone came out from behind Masterson and pointed Masterson's Glock at Simmons, demanding to be let into the room where they were hiding the witness. Simmons shot at the intruder, but a little too late. He ducked, but took a round to the shoulder."

"The witness?"

"Got out through a rear window."

"Where is he now?"

"She—" Warner jerked his head toward his workspace "—is in my office. I need her out of here and fast, before someone figures out she's here."

Cal shook his head. "I know Masterson. He would never let someone take his weapon. The man is one of Chicago's finest."

"Masterson just stood there?" A cold lump formed in Deme's belly. Everything about what had happened to Masterson sounded much like what had occurred when Cal went blank, driving.

The chief nodded. "That's what I got out of Simmons before they gave him a hefty dose of painkillers."

Deme moved forward, her attention on the screen. "You say you have surveillance video on the place he went last night?"

"That's what Jones is about to send me, a clip during the time frame Masterson would have been at the Burger Bar." Chief Warner nodded toward the screen. "There it is now."

The black-and-white video blinked onto the screen, displaying fuzzy images of people passing by the front of a building. After several minutes Warner pointed. "There."

Deme's eyes narrowed. "The man in the sweatshirt and baseball cap?"

"That's Masterson."

Masterson passed by the camera, glanced up at the lens and

back to the door he then entered. In less than five minutes he exited carrying a white bag with Burger Bar written on it in bold red lettering.

"So, he bought burgers at the Burger Bar."

"Do they have a camera inside?"

"Afraid not."

A moment later a woman wearing a scarf around her head passed the camera lens. Most of her hair was covered, except a thick stray strand.

Deme blinked. Had the strand moved?

She glanced to her right at the chief and her left at Cal. Neither had noticed. Deme held her tongue, telling herself that she was desperate to find out what had happened, so desperate that she'd seen something that wasn't there. It could have been the wind, although wind didn't move hair quite that way.

"Whoever it was who jumped out from behind him had to have followed him from the restaurant."

"Do you suppose someone stopped him and injected him with drugs or something to make him freeze up like he did?" Cal grimaced. "Damn good thing Simmons was alert or he'd be dead."

"Where is Masterson now?" Deme asked.

"When the intruder realized the witness had escaped, he ran for the door, knocking into Masterson. The man fell to the ground and slowly came to. At least as far as Simmons could tell from his position on the floor of the living room. Masterson seemed groggy, but he managed to call for an ambulance."

"Have you questioned Masterson?"

"He went to the hospital with Simmons. I met them there. He said he didn't remember any of it."

"Damn." Deme fingered the pentagram hanging from the chain around her neck. "It's happening again."

"What's happening?" Cal asked.

"Think about it." Deme's eyes narrowed, gazing toward the video screen. "Masterson, a good cop, froze when he needed to be on his game. He lets another cop take a bullet and then lets the witness get away. And he can't remember doing it."

"She's right." Cal nodded toward Deme. "Last night I froze behind the wheel of my car and almost drove into Lake Michigan. I don't remember a thing."

Warner's brows furrowed. "Why didn't I hear about this sooner?"

"I didn't think it was connected." Cal paced the length of the conference room and back. "I thought I'd blacked out. Maybe had a seizure or something."

"It's all adding up, Chief." Deme stepped up beside Cal. "The guard in the evidence storage facility didn't remember a thing about what happened during the video surveillance blackout. From what video we had, he looked frozen, paralyzed."

"What are you saying?" Warner scratched his head. "Is someone drugging or hypnotizing them?" His gaze swung to Cal. "I've asked the hospital to perform a thorough drug screening on Masterson. We should get results soon."

"What about the witness?" Cal glanced toward the chief's office. "We can't leave her here."

"No, we can't," the chief said.

Deme agreed. The witness wasn't safe in the building, any more than in the safe house. "Whoever is doing this knew where the safe house was."

"Impossible." Warner crossed his arms over his chest. "The officers guarding the witness and I were the only ones who knew."

Deme didn't back down. "Apparently not."

Cal sighed. "The important thing is to find out who it is and stop him before someone is killed."

"Who said it has to be a man?" Deme asked.

Cal's lips twisted. "You have a point. Any suggestions?"

She nodded. "Someone in the department."

Warner's brows rose into the white strands hanging down over his forehead. "You think we have a mole on the force?"

"If the person who is drugging our people is an insider, it would explain why the guard wasn't worried about the person out of view of the camera in the evidence facility. He went so far as to smile at someone or something."

Cal picked up on her reasoning. "A good cop like Masterson wouldn't have let anyone past him. He would have been immediately on his guard if a stranger had stepped up to him. I'll bet he recognized the attacker or he would have at least struggled before he could have been drugged."

"What about Cal?" Warner tipped his head toward Deme's lover. "No one got close enough to jab a needle into him while he was driving. And he didn't freeze until you two were well on your way down the highway."

Deme frowned. Warner was right. Cal's situation didn't make sense like the others. Then she recalled the shadowy figure at the traffic light, right before Cal went into the trance and sped down the street out of control. "Did Simmons say what the intruder looked like?"

"He said he thought it was a guy with a slight build, like a young teen. He wore a dark sweatshirt with a hood pulled up over his head."

"That's the description of the guy we saw last night on the street corner, right before Cal went blank."

Chief Warner stared at Deme. "Which could rule out drugs."

Cal straightened his shoulders. "We need to get the witness somewhere safe. Somewhere out of HQ before anyone shows up and discovers she's here."

"What do you think this person is using to paralyze our men?" the chief directed his question to Deme.

Deme shook her head. "I don't know, but I'll ask around. There's bound to be a logical explanation."

"For now I'm assuming its some paranormal ability we haven't heard of yet." The chief glanced from Deme to Cal. "Be careful and don't get caught up in it."

Deme wanted to snort in the chief's face. How could they

be careful when they had no idea who or what it was or what shape or form it would come in? "We'll do our best."

Chief Warner jerked his head toward the door. "Now, get the witness and get out of here."

"Do we have a name for the witness?"

"Alexis Yelsov."

Deme shrugged. "Never heard of her."

The chief grinned. "Unless you're involved in the paranormal mafia, I didn't expect you to."

"Do you want us to let you know where we end up?" Cal asked.

"No. Whoever found the safe house in the first place might have somehow tapped into my mind and learned of its location. I can't even trust myself to know the location."

"How will we get in touch?"

"Stay on the lowdown until the Tribunal meeting tomorrow." The chief glanced from Deme to Cal. "Can you two handle it?"

Cal nodded. "Yes, sir."

Deme hoped he was right.

Chapter Six

Cal removed his Glock from his shoulder holster, dropped the magazine, pulled back the bolt and checked the barrel.

Deme stood beside him, staring at his hands as he worked the mechanisms.

"If anyone tries to take my weapon from me and I let him, shoot. Him preferably." He handed the Glock to Deme. "Shoot me, if you have to."

"I don't know how to fire a gun." She handed it back to him.

Cal's brows furrowed. "We'll have to change that." He slipped the weapon back into the holster. "For now, let's get our witness out of here. All we need to do is find a safe place to hide out for a night."

"I know of a place." Deme led the way to the chief's office.

"Someplace others won't think to look?"

She grinned. "You got it. And I'm calling in some backup to help protect our witness."

Cal frowned. "Are you thinking what I think you're thinking?"

Deme's brows rose. "Are you a mind reader like Medea, now?"

"No, but I can tell when you're cooking up trouble. Those green eyes go all smokey-like." Outside the door to the chief's office, he grabbed her arm and swung her around to face him. "Does this mean you've forgiven me for a kiss you say you witnessed, that I don't recall happening?"

Her eyes narrowed. "I'm considering it."

He pulled her into his arms and kissed her hard on the lips, pushing past her teeth to claim her tongue. When he came up for air, his heart pounded and his breathing came in short bursts. He wanted more than anything to take her home and make love to her for twenty-four hours straight. "Maybe that will help you speed up the consideration a little." He gave her what he hoped was his sexiest grin and pushed the boss's door open. Alexis Yelsov spun to face them, her deep green eyes wide, her fists clenching, making the dragon tattoos on her arms ripple. "Who the hell are you?" Her gaze darted toward the doorway. "Where's the chief?"

Cal straightened to his full six feet two inches, his dark eyes boring into the insolent gaze of the woman. "We're your new bodyguards. The chief will continue to work the case while we take you somewhere safe."

Alexis snorted. "Safe? Ha! Your own man nearly got me killed. At this rate I will not live long enough to testify in front of the Tribunal."

"We know of a place." Deme stepped forward, refusing to let Cal take the brunt of the witness's anger. "Deme Chattox." She stuck out her hand.

The woman ignored Deme, her gaze sliding over Cal like a dirty hand. "At least one of you might be interesting."

Cal's arm shot out, keeping Deme from taking a swing at Yelsov. "We're here to protect you. If we spend all our time protecting ourselves from you, that leaves *you* exposed."

Deme crossed her arms over her chest, leveling a glare at the woman. "What's it gonna be?"

For a long moment Yelsov held Deme's gaze. Finally she shrugged. "If we're going, let's get out of here now." Yelsov stepped around Deme, without touching her or Cal, and led the way through the door.

Deme shot a glance at Cal. "She touches you and I'll kill her."

"I love it when you talk tough, sweetheart."

"Too bad we need her testimony to convict Vladimir." Deme slammed her fist into her palm. She squared her shoulders and set off after the key witness to a killing by a murderous demon, thinking about murder herself.

The place Deme had in mind was located in one of the oldest neighborhoods in town. A neighborhood where people with a little spare spending money had renovated the homes that had been a part of Chicago history for a very long time. Homes that had survived the great fire. The house she took them to happened to belong to her and her sisters. The two-story cream-and-white colonial with its giant oak trees looked just as it had when the Chattox sisters had been little girls and their mother had been alive.

As soon as she stepped through the door, memories flooded Deme's mind and a knot formed in her throat. She hadn't been here in a long time. The memories were too poignant for her to bear. The property had been sold several times before the sisters had pooled their money and purchased it through an estate fund they'd established. Anyone looking for Deme would have to do a considerable amount of digging to link this house to the Chattox sisters now. Digging would take more than one night. And all they needed was to keep their witness alive through one more night, then that person could testify at the Tribunal hearing.

Deme parked at the rear of the house and handed the keys to Cal.

While she waited with the witness in the sedan, he entered the house, sweeping through each room before he returned to the back door and gave her the all clear sign.

Deme unlocked the car doors and stepped out, opening the rear door for Alexis.

The woman unfolded from the blanket she'd hidden beneath for the ride through the city. Once outside the car she crouched low and eased to the end of the sedan. After glancing right then left, she ran for the door, ducking inside. Unless someone had followed them and was lurking in the shadows nearby, Alexis had gone unnoticed.

Cal left the witness in the kitchen and returned to the car, retrieving the Chinese take-out they'd picked up on their way through town.

Deme grabbed her purse, her stomach grumbling. Already half past five, they'd spent a good portion of the afternoon zigzagging through the back streets to avoid being spotted on the main roads and to verify they hadn't been followed.

Once inside with the door securely locked, chains in place and curtains drawn, Cal handed Yelsov a box of noodles and a fork.

"Some last dinner," Alexis grumbled.

"Why do you think it's your last?" Deme asked.

"Vladimir doesn't tolerate traitors. I'm a marked woman." She popped the box open and dug her fork into the food.

"He's not going to kill you, if we can help it," Cal promised.

"Knowing Vladimir, he will send whomever it takes to accomplish his goal," she said between bites of food.

"Vladimir is in jail," Deme pointed out. "He's not sending anyone anywhere at this time."

"Whatever." The woman flipped her long blond hair. "I know his work. I've seen him sign a man's death warrant with just a snap of his fingers. He's got contacts everywhere. Some of the most vicious thugs in Chicago, willing to slice throats first and ask questions later."

"How do you know Vladimir?" Deme asked.

The woman shrugged. "I was his lover."

Deme's brows rose. "Why are you turning him in?"

Her lip curled in a snarl. "I wasn't his only lover." Alexis took the box into the living room and sprawled across the couch, switching on the television.

Deme and Cal sat at the small kitchenette table and opened the boxes containing Kung Pao chicken, rice and egg rolls.

The spices tickled Deme's nose as she dug in.

"So Vladimir had another lover?" Deme chewed on the information as she chewed on the chicken.

"Think the other lover is the one trying to kill our witness?" Cal glanced through the open doorway to the living room at the woman on the couch.

"Could be. The officer guarding Alexis described his attacker as slim and assumed he was a teen." Deme glanced up at Cal. "I'm more inclined to believe it was a woman, not a teen boy."

"And the dude in the hoodie on the corner before our wreck?"

Deme nodded.

"How is she doing it? How is she paralyzing us?"

"I venture to guess she's using some kind of magic." Deme glanced at the clock over the stove. "My sisters will be here soon and we'll set up a circle of protection around Alexis. If our attacker somehow finds us, we will be ready."

Cal patted his Glock, nestled beneath his jacket. "I'll be ready too."

A few minutes later cars pulled into the driveway and around to the back of the house. Deme's sisters climbed out, one at a time. Brigid rolled in on her Harley, wearing black leather from head to toe.

A swell of pride lifted the worry from Deme's shoulders. With the help of her sisters they would keep Alexis safe until she could appear before the Tribunal and put Vladimir Romanov away for good.

Selene, her sister affiliated with the spirit, carried the Book of Shadows. Gina, her sister whose calling led her to water, brought a bottle of the perfumed liquid. Aurai breezed through the doorway, a fluff of wind lifting her hair around her shoulders. "Hi, big sister." She kissed Deme's cheek and handed her a potted ivy plant. "Thought you could use a boost."

Deme hugged her little sister and clutched the little pot to her chest.

Brigid was the last through the doorway, carrying a black leather backpack. She set it on the kitchen table and fished five candles from within. "Got your message. Figured you could use some help."

Deme fought back a wash of tears threatening to spill from her eyes. "Thanks. I can." She told them of what had occurred so far.

Alexis remained in the living room, polishing off her noodles, her gaze sweeping over the sisters in the kitchen.

When Deme finished, she sighed.

Brigid clapped her hands together. "Let's get started."

Each sister took a candle and walked into the living room.

Alexis's eyes narrowed. "Witches, right?"

Brigid snorted. "Give the girl a prize."

The witness pulled her feet up beneath her on the couch. "You're not going to turn me into a toad, are you?"

Aurai laughed, the sound like tinkling wind chimes. "Of course not. We're going to cast a protection circle around you. It will help keep you safe."

"I don't know. Magic and me, we don't do so well together." Alexis held up her hand. "Vladimir liked to tie me up with invisible ropes when we were...you know."

"Did you tell him you didn't want to?"

"No." She shrugged. "I kinda liked it. I just didn't trust him to untie them when we were done. A couple times he forgot and left me there for hours."

Selene smiled. "We're not going to tie you up."

Brigid glared. "Unless you do something really stupid."

"Like?"

"Run."

Alexis frowned. "What if I don't feel safe?"

"You're better off in the circle than out of it," Gina hefted the canister of salt in one hand.

Deme touched Alexis's arm. "Seriously, if someone makes it through that door and threatens you, stay inside the circle. No matter what."

Alexis's gaze shot to the doors and windows. "I thought you said this house would be safe."

"It will be, with the five of us and Cal to make sure." Deme glanced at Cal. "Right?"

"Right." He stood back, away from the siblings. "I'm your first line of defense. The sisters are the next."

Alexis glanced at him. "Do you believe a circle will stop whoever made it past the last guards who were supposed to protect me?"

"Better than nothing." Deme signaled her sisters. "What have you got to lose?"

"My life," Alexis said, her tone flat, a frown denting her smooth forehead.

While Selene, Aurai, Deme and Brigid moved the coffee table and chairs up against the walls, Gina poured salt on the hardwood floors, forming a large circle, big enough to fit everyone inside, should they need to.

Once she'd emptied the canister, she collected her candle.

When each of Deme's sisters held a candle, Deme motioned toward Alexis. "We need you to come to the center of the circle. Bring a pillow and whatever else you want to get comfortable."

The witness glanced at the salt and the sisters and shook her head. "I don't know."

"You'll stand a better chance of survival if you do as we say." Deme glanced at Cal. "Tell her."

"I've seen what these sisters can do with their power. They're amazing. If they say this will help, take them up on it."

Alexis hugged a throw pillow to her chest. After a moment she eased off the couch, clutching her pillow, and stepped inside the circle of salt.

"See, didn't hurt, did it?" Aurai grinned.

"You haven't started your mumbo jumbo chants," Alexis noted.

Brigid rolled her eyes. "Let the bitch die. Mumbo jumbo, huh."

"Please." Deme caught Brigid's gaze and held it. "She needs our protection."

"Fine." Brigid glared at the witness. "But I don't have to like her."

"No, you don't." Deme lifted her candle and walked to the edge of the circle. "Protector of the earth that feeds us, I bid thee come. Welcome to the circle." The waxy wick on her candle flared to life and she set the candle against the circle of salt.

Aurai lit the next one and settled it on the edge, at a diagonal from Deme. "Master of air that cools, and brings us life, I bid thee come. Welcome to the circle." Like Deme's, her candle wick went from cool to flame in a fiery burst.

Brigid sighed and stepped up to the circle, pressing her candle into the edge between Deme and Aurai. "Keeper of fire that sparks flames in all of us, I bid thee come. Welcome to the circle." Her candle wick flamed.

Gina entered the circle, placing her candle near Deme. "Bearer of water that flows through us and nourishes our bodies in rebirth, I bid thee come. Welcome to the circle."

Selene, in her gossamer-light skirt, floated to the edge between Gina and Aurai and set her candle on the floor, touching the salt. "Guardian of spirit, fill us with hope, with truth and light. I bid thee come. Welcome to the circle." Her candle wick swelled to a steady flame. She raised her arms and the sisters completed the circle by a joining of hands.

The flames brightened, the glow filling the room.

As one, the sisters raised their faces to the ceiling and chanted, "Goddess of the earth, wind, water, fire and spirit, seal this circle."

The flames intensified, almost blinding in their brilliance.

Deme inhaled the fresh scent of earth after a light rain.

A light breeze lifted her hair and a sense of peace filled her heart as if someone stood beside her whispering sisters. As the breezed died down, the flames of the candles flickered and settled into simple burning wicks.

"So mote it be," Deme said, her sister's voices echoing.

"Well, that was entertaining." Alexis voice shook despite the sarcasm, and she held her throw pillow to her breasts like a shield. "Now, if only it will work. I've got a bad feeling about tonight."

Deme didn't want to agree with the woman, but she had to admit, she'd had the same feelings. The circle could only do so much. It would stop evil magic, and she wasn't certain it would stop bullets. Should Vladimir's henchmen find them, all hell would break loose and perhaps bringing her sisters in on this assignment would prove fatal.

A glance around the circle at Selene, Gina, Aurai and Brigid only drove it home how much she loved that they pulled together with times got tough. They'd proven it against the evil Chimera who'd stolen Aurai. Only through their persistence and Cal's help had they managed to kill the Chimera and save their beautiful baby sister.

"You know you don't have to be here," Deme said aloud.

Brigid frowned. "Now you tell us? Don't you think it's a little late for second thoughts?"

"It'll be getting dark soon and we don't know what Vladimir will have in store for us."

"We have Cal." Aurai smiled and waved at Cal. "Damn he's cute."

"I heard that." Cal's lips pressed together and he shook his head. "I am in the same room."

"Sorry," Aurai called out with a cheeky grin.

"And we have each other," Selene squeezed Deme's hand.

Deme's chest tightened. "I just don't want anyone to be hurt."

"We've been through worse," Aurai said.

"And almost died," Gina agreed.

"Trouble is, we don't know what we'll be facing." Deme glanced at the door, praying nothing and no one would find them that night.

"I say bring it on." Brigid dropped her sisters' hands and pumped her fists. "We'll kick some ass."

Deme smiled. "How can you argue with that?"

Cal chuckled. "You can't." He glanced out the window. Shadows lengthened in the living room. "It's getting dark."

"Only ten more hours until the Tribunal meets." Deme sank to the floor and sat cross-legged.

"Piece of cake." Gina dropped to the floor and pulled her feet up under her.

"Cake sounds good about now." Aurai sat and rested her chin on her knees. "Or a hamburger and fries."

"You can stop now." Alexis rolled her eyes. "It's not like any of us can leave the building to go out and get dinner. That's how the last guards almost got me killed."

"She's right. We only have ten hours to wait. It's not like we'll starve or anything."

"Speak for yourself." Aurai rubbed her stomach. "I slept past breakfast and almost missed my first class. Then I skipped lunch to study for a quiz. Got your text as I left the class."

"Poor Aurai." Brigid punched her sister's arm. "Trust me, you'll live."

Cal glanced out the window again, then moved to sit beside Deme, pulling her against him. "I'd feel a whole lot better if you and your sisters hadn't come."

"Wow, I'm not feeling the love." Brigid crossed her arms over her chest. "Deme says you were one of the guys who blacked out. How can you expect to protect the witness if you're out of it?"

His back stiffened. "Just because it happened once, doesn't mean it'll happen again."

Brigid balanced her hands on her hips. "Are you willing to risk Little Miss Evil-demon-lover's life?"

Cal hugged Deme tighter. "No. But I could have gotten someone else to pull guard duty with me."

Deme pushed out of Cal's embrace, her arms falling to her sides. "I don't think that would have helped." A chill slithered across her skin, raising gooseflesh. "Something tells me that whoever was paralyzing the guards was gender-specific."

Cal's brows rose. "Gender-specific?"

Her gaze met Cal's. "She's targeting *men*."

Chapter Seven

Cal leaned back and stared into Deme's eyes. "What do you mean?"

"I can't be certain, but you were the only one impacted when we were driving. I saw the same figure on the side of the road as you did. I didn't freeze."

"Maybe because you're a witch? Perhaps this woman doesn't have the power to freeze witches?"

Deme sighed. "That could be so, but what if I'm right?" She cupped Cal's cheek. "No offense, Cal, but you could be pretty useless as a protector in this situation."

Cal didn't like that Deme might be right. "I could have Warner send female officers."

"No, I think we can handle it. It's just one person. There are five of us Chattox sisters."

"We beat a Chimera," Gina offered.

"Yeah," Aurai's chin lifted. "What's a little female with the ability to paralyze men gonna do that can hurt five kick-ass Wiccans?"

"We don't know until she shows up." Deme pulled Cal's arm around her middle and leaned against him.

Her soft curves warmed him in the cooling air. Darkness settled over the city. As much as he wanted to remain holding Deme, he had to stand watch. He pressed a kiss to Deme's temple and stood.

Aurai's eyes closed as she nodded and her head jerked up, eyes popping wide, before she blinked sleepily. "Can we have a light in here?"

"No." Deme was adamant. "We don't want to draw attention to this house. It's been sitting empty for months. Turn the lights on and people will know it's occupied."

"I hate it when you're right." Aurai yawned, stretched and shook her head. "Gonna be a long night."

"You should be used to it. Isn't this the time of day you do most of your studying for school?"

"Yeah, but I usually have my music going and lights glaring."

"You can do this. We need to stay in the circle to provide the best protection we can with our combined strength."

"What if I have to pee?" Alexis asked.

"Hold it," Brigid retorted. "Good grief, you'd think we were having a slumber party. This is serious business."

"Brigid's right. A cop nearly died last night." Deme glanced at Cal.

"Yeah, hush, Aurai. We need to be alert. Cal and Deme need us." Gina squeezed her sister's hand. "I promise I'll get you the biggest, juiciest hamburger in the city tomorrow after we deliver our guest to the Tribunal."

"Argh." Aurai groaned. "You had to make it sound too good." Her ever-present grin resurfaced. "I'm fine, just bored."

Cal turned toward the front window and eased the blinds back to allow him to stare outside.

A streetlight glowed down on the street corner a couple houses down from the Chattox house. Shadows crept to the edge of the light, hiding anything that might be lurking in their depths.

One shadow undulated.

Cal tensed.

The room grew still as if waiting for something to happen.

"She's near," Selene's whisper pierced the silence more distinctly than a shout.

The soft sound shot straight to Cal's gut. "How do you know?"

"I can sense her aura," Selene closed her eyes and lifted her hands palm upward. "She's outside."

A knock sounded on the door.

Everyone jumped, including Cal. He'd been watching out the window and hadn't actually seen anyone walk up the sidewalk to the entranceway.

From his position at the window he couldn't see the person standing at the front entry.

He moved to the door and leaned against it. Unfortunately, it was solid wood and didn't have a peephole. He hesitated, unwilling to speak out and let the person on the other side know there were people inside.

A long moment went by and another knock rapped against the door. "Cal, it's me, Medea."

Relief washed over him. "Medea? What are you doing here?" he called through the door.

"Chief Warner sent me. I brought food for you and Deme."

"Oh, thank goodness. Food." Aurai waved at Cal. "Let her in."

Cal twisted the lock and had pulled the door open an inch when Deme shouted, "No."

Before he could slam the door closed, fingers and a delicate high-heeled shoe insinuated themselves into the gap. "Cal, what's wrong? It's me, Medea. Open the door the rest of the way, before I drop the food."

Cal stepped back and allowed Medea into the house. Without turning toward Deme, he could sense her displeasure. "How did you know where to find us?"

"Chief Warner told me." Medea stepped through the door and held out a white bag with Burger Bar written in bright red letters across the front. "Anyone hungry?"

Aurai raised her hand. "I am."

"No, you're not." Deme cast a narrow-eyed glare at Medea. "Chief Warner didn't know where we went."

Medea blinked, her ice-blue eyes widening. "Yes, he did. He had a tracking device attached to your car."

Cal's arm shot out and blocked Medea's further entry. "No, he didn't. He specifically said he didn't want to know where we went, so that no one could find out from him."

"You must be mistaken." Her pretty brows furrowed and she stared up into Cal's eyes.

"Cal!" Selene shouted. "Don't look into her eyes."

As soon as Selene said the words, Deme knew. The weird way Medea's hair curled around her face, the shadow of movement in the dark locks, the intensity of her icy stare.

Deme shot to her feet and would have stepped out of the circle had Brigid not barred her with a clothesline arm across her chest.

"Don't break the circle," Brigid said. She stood on the edge of the salt circle, her body stiff, a scowl aimed at the petite beauty standing before Cal.

"But she'll paralyze him." Deme had to get to Cal.

"He's a big boy, he can take care of himself."

"I'm okay," Cal called out. He turned toward Deme.

She sighed.

His eyes were tightly closed. "Why am I closing my eyes?" he asked.

Medea's lips curled upward. "They don't trust me." She slipped her hand along Cal's arm and up around his neck.

"They're right. I don't trust you, either." He grabbed her wrists and held them away from him. "How long do I need to keep my eyes closed?"

"You don't. Open them," Medea purred, straining to get her hands on him.

"Keep them closed as long as she's in the same room with you. She's a gorgon." Selene's eyes widened. "Wow, I've never seen one before, in real life, only read about them."

"A gorgon? What do you mean?" Aurai's brows wrinkled. "She's not ugly or disfigured."

"No, but her hair isn't hair, is it?" Selene stared at the woman.

"I don't know what you're talking about." Her efforts to twist her hands free increased. "Of course my hair is hair."

"Do any of you see otherwise?" Selene asked her sisters.

"I thought I saw strands moving," Deme offered.

"Exactly. She's a type of gorgon like Medusa."

Gina and Aurai gasped and closed their eyes. "Will she turn us into stone?"

"I've been staring into her eyes since she walked through the door and haven't turned to stone," Selene answered.

Deme's lip curled and she gazed boldly at Medea. "Doesn't your magic work on women?"

"You're crazy. Let go of me, Cal. I'll call the chief and he'll clear all of this up in no time. He sent me. These women are nuts." She pulled hard.

Cal refused to let go. "I know these women. I don't know much about you. But how convenient for you to show up about the time Vladimir was snagged. Too coincidental, if you ask me."

"And we don't believe in coincidence," Deme added. "Did Vladimir send you to do his dirty work?"

The light in Medea's eyes flared, the icy blue glowing a blinding white. "That bastard demon can rot in hell for all I care. He cheated on me." She jerked a hand free and pointed at Alexis. "With that woman."

Alexis backed away from the pointed finger. "I didn't know."

Selene blocked her, keeping her within the safety of the circle. "Careful, Alexis. Step outside the boundary of the circle and all bets off."

Cal fought blindly to get hold of Medea's free hand.

"You believe you're protected by nothing more than a flimsy

circle? You're a bigger fool than I was." Medea lunged for the Glock in Cal's shoulder holster.

"Cal, your gun," Deme shouted.

Too late, Medea had it out and pointed at Alexis. "The bitch has to die. No one goes behind my back and steals my man without paying the price."

"You can have him. He wasn't worth it," Alexis dropped to the floor, cowering behind her hands held up to her face.

"I don't want your sloppy seconds. But you can't have him either." Medea squeezed the trigger and the gun went off, kicking Medea's hand backward.

Deme shifted to block the bullet from hitting Alexis. Braced to take the blow, she was shocked when the circle caught the bullet and slowed its trajectory. With its forward momentum halted, the bullet fell, clattering against the solid wood flooring at Deme's feet.

Her heart hammered and her fingers shook as she stared at what could have been the bullet to end her life.

Medea growled, her lips curling back. "Damn you, witches. The woman needs to die."

"No one needs to die here. Give yourself up and we'll call it a day," Cal said. Still holding onto one wrist.

"I will not stand before the Tribunal accused of a crime when it wasn't me who committed it. Vladimir and this whore are the criminals."

"From my perspective," Deme said, "you've got a couple counts of attempted murder to answer for. That should get you a room without a view in the Tribunal holding cell for crazy and insane paranorms."

"No. That will not happen. If I'm locked up, it won't be for *attempted* murder." Medea jammed the gun to Cal's side. "Move and I shoot," she warned him.

Cal froze. "Don't add murder to your rap sheet, Medea."

"Shut up, and let go of my hand." She jammed the gun deeper into Cal's side.

Deme fought against Brigid's arm. "Let me at her."

"No, Deme. She's using Cal to get to Alexis."

"Let her have Alexis." Tears welled in Deme's eyes.

"Deme, you can't do that," Cal said. He opened his eyes, careful not to glance into Medea's blue-ice gaze. Instead he concentrated on Deme. "It's our job to protect the witness. Vladimir cannot be allowed to go free."

"You're going to let your man die for a woman who means nothing to you?" Medea laughed. "He's a very good kisser. I wouldn't let him go, if he were mine." The gorgon rubbed her body against Cal's. "Look at me, Calais Black."

Her dark hair whipped around his head and clamped onto his face, forcing him to turn toward her.

"No!" Deme grabbed the pillow from Alexis and flung it at Medea.

She raised her free hand, the one holding the gun, to block the pillow from hitting her in the face.

Cal grabbed the wrist of the hand holding the gun, spun around behind her and jerked her arm up the middle of her back. She fought, and the gun discharged, the bullet going wild, piercing the drywall ceiling, scattering dust on the furniture. Cal increased his hold until the Glock fell from Medea's fingers. "You have the right to remain silent—"

"You have the right to go to hell," she cried.

"I'm not the one who will be going to hell, Medea." He tugged a little harder.

Medea gasped.

"That's for kissing me without my permission, and getting me into trouble with the woman I love."

Deme's heart swelled and she almost stepped outside the circle for the third time that night.

"I know you want to go to him," Brigid's voice stopped her, "but the night isn't over and the Tribunal hasn't met to determine Vladimir's fate. He could have other things in store for the witness."

"I know." Deme stared across the floor at Cal and the

woman who'd caused all this trouble and almost gotten them killed.

Selene tugged her scarf from around her neck and handed it to Deme. "Here."

Deme wadded it and threw it across the room to Cal. After securing Medea's wrists with zip ties, he wrapped the scarf around her head, hiding her eyes.

"We can inform the chief in the morning. The less contact with him, the more likely we won't be discovered by anyone else."

"By the way, Medea, how did you find us?"

"You think you're so clever." She snorted. "Jonesy set me up with a tracking device. No magic needed. Just the magic of technology."

Cal shook his head, a grin spreading across his lips. "Lesson learned. Even gorgons use electronics."

"Would have gotten away with it," Medea grumbled, "if you hadn't called on every witch in the city."

"I didn't." Deme joined hands with her sisters. "I only called on family."

The Tribunal met the next morning. Cal and Deme had no trouble transporting Alexis and Medea to the location. Under heavy guard provided by the Chicago special investigations team, they delivered both…alive, despite Deme's urge to exterminate the mouthy gorgon.

Tired, hungry and ready to rip into anyone who stopped her from going home, Deme left the Tribunal and was backing out when Cal stepped up to her window.

"Forgetting something?"

She frowned and purposely glanced at her purse on the seat next to her. "No. I don't think so."

"Me." He rounded the front of her car and slipped into the passenger seat. "You really should lock your doors when you're driving around downtown."

Her lips curled into the hint of a smile, her insides hopping to the beat of her increased heartbeat. "To keep the riff-raff out?"

"That's right."

She pulled out of the parking garage in downtown Chicago and headed toward the section of town where they both lived. She couldn't assume they were back together. She'd accused him of making out with another woman.

Technically, he had.

But to clarify, he really hadn't been responsible. Medea had paralyzed him and wiped his memory clean, like she had with the evidence facility guard and Alexis's bodyguard, using some kind of Medusa Effect.

"Okay, so I forgive you," she said grudgingly. Admitting she was wrong had never been her strong suit. More than anything she wanted to start over. From the moment she'd entered the station upon returning from St. Croix.

"Where do you want me to drop you off?" She held her breath, praying to the goddess he would say her apartment.

"My place."

Her heart plummeted into her belly. "Oh."

The rest of the journey passed in silence.

Deme chewed her bottom lip, opening her mouth no less than five times to say something, but closing it before words could come out.

When she drove into his apartment parking lot and stopped, she sat staring at the steering wheel. Maybe this was his way of telling her it was over. Maybe he didn't want her in his life after she'd lost faith in him.

He opened the door and stepped out of the passenger seat onto the pavement. "Deme…"

She glanced up, daring to hope.

He hesitated, then said, "See you tomorrow. Get a good night's sleep." Cal closed the car door.

Deme sat behind the wheel as Cal walked away. If only they could start over.

She flung the door open and cried out, "Cal, wait." She caught up with him as he inserted his key into the lock.

Cal paused with his hand on the knob, and turned to face her as she ran toward him. "I thought you were tired."

"I am, but not too tired to tell you that I'm sorry I didn't believe you. It was just that she was so beautiful and I was looking forward to seeing you and…Oh, hell, I love you, damn it. Can we start over?"

He folded her into his arms. "Start over? From where?"

"From *hello, it's good to be back home.*"

"Oh, baby, let me show you how glad I am that you're home." He scooped her into his arms, shoved his door open and strode all the way across the apartment. He didn't stop until they were in his bedroom. He sat her on the edge of the bed."I missed you." She tugged at the hem of his T-shirt, dragging it up over his head.

"Not as much as I missed you." He started at the waistband of her jeans, flicking the button free and dragging the zipper downward. "So you think she was prettier than you?"

She sighed and lay back on the comforter. "Don't you?"

He leaned over her and pressed a kiss to her belly. "No." Cal pulled her jeans down her legs and let them drop to the floor. "Her hair was too dark and from what Selene was saying wasn't hair at all but snakes."

"A person can look past that to those intensely blue eyes." Deme feathered her hands through his hair.

"That can paralyze a man with one look." He pushed her shirt up over her torso, kissing his way to her bra-clad breasts. "I'm more into eyes the color of emeralds and hair like fiery copper that's softer than silk."

"Umm, waxing poetic on me?" she teased, tugging at his ears, wanting him to bring his lips within range of her own.

"I'm going a lot more than poetic on you." He reached beneath her and unclipped her bra. "I'm going all over you."

He parted her legs and stepped between them.

Deme sat up and unbuckled his belt, pulling it free of the

loops in a slow sensuous glide. "Aren't you a little overdressed to provide a proper welcome home to a girl?"

"You know it."

Her fingers wrapped around the button and pushed it through. When she reached for his zipper, he captured her hand. Deme glanced up and frowned. "What's wrong?"

"I just want you to know something before we go any further."

Her heartbeat kicked up a notch. "Don't keep me in suspense."

"I'm in this for the long haul. If you aren't there's no sense doing this now."

"I thought most men wanted a sex-only relationship with women? No strings attached."

"I'm not most men."

She smiled. "No, you're not." She nudged his hands aside and unzipped his jeans, pushing the edges open. "And I was just speaking out of hurt. I want you, Calais Black." His cock sprang free and she cupped it in her hands. "For a very long time." She caressed his length, sliding her fingers over his steely rod encased in velvety smooth skin. "A very long time." Her lips brushed the tip with a feather-light touch.

"That's good." His abs tensed on an indrawn breath, and he jerked the jeans the rest of the way down his legs, stepping free. He threaded his fingers through her hair, cupping the back of her neck. He bent to kiss her, bringing her to her feet. "I won't settle for less. Forever would be too soon to lose you."

"You don't have to worry. I'm all yours." She wrapped her arms around him and guided him to the bed.

He parted her legs and lay between them, his rod bumping against her entrance. "If you ever have to return to St. Croix, I'm going with you."

"I'm not going anywhere. I'm where I should be. With you. With my sisters nearby and in a place I feel needs me." She cupped his face between her palms. "Now shut up and make love to me before I cast a spell on you."

"You don't need spells and you don't have to ask this cop twice. You're the only witch for me." He thrust deep into her.

Deme sent a silent thanks to the goddess. She prayed that all homecomings could be so memorable—minus the Medusa, of course.

* * * * *

SEDUCING THE JACKAL

SERESSIA GLASS

Seressia Glass is an award-winning author of more than twenty contemporary and paranormal romance and urban fantasy stories. Her current series (Shadowchasers, Sons of Anubis) are steeped in Egyptian mythology. She lives north of Atlanta with her guitar-wielding husband and two attack poodles. When not writing, she spends her free time people-watching, belly dancing, and watching anime.

Seressia has always been a voracious reader and turned to writing at an early age, using her fantastical tales for extra credit in school. Her proudest writing moment remains winning the first Martin Luther King, Jr. holiday "Living the Dream" essay contest as a high school senior and getting to meet Coretta Scott King and read her essay to the King family. Since then, she's gone on to write a motley crew of characters and creatures including werewolves, djinn, demons, Egyptian deities and jackal shapeshifters with a few humans thrown into the mix. No matter who or what she's writing about, Seressia weaves in the universal themes of acceptance and being comfortable in one's own skin. Her stories have won numerous awards including an RT Reviewer's Choice Award, Emma Awards, and finalists in a variety of contests.

When not working on her next story, Seressia is an instructional designer for an international home improvement company, writing and developing training materials.

Chapter One

Silence drenched the dark street as if the creatures of the night were too afraid to make their calls. Probably because of the jackals and men that skulked through the shadows.

The silence didn't matter to Markus Grant. He and his brothers knew how to use the darkness and the silence to hunt, to survive. When they claimed their prize tonight, their future would be assured.

His right hand slashed the air in command to move forward. His men advanced, some in jackal form, some in their human shapes. The row of houses looked like plenty of others in this small community in the southern outskirts of Atlanta, with its maintained lawns and sidewalks fronting older, low-slung houses tucked beneath mature trees. Vegetation provided plenty of cover as the jackals raced toward their target, the house at the end of the street.

The only visible difference between it and the other houses was the number of large trees lining the high wooden fence framing the backyard. That and the lushness of the landscaping. The flowering azaleas and dogwoods seemed vibrant even at this late hour. A well-used four-door compact sedan sat in the driveway. Hardly the usual conveyance of an Isis witch.

Markus suppressed a growl. The Daughters of Isis used to collaborate with the Sons of Anubis to protect the funerary temples and complexes and prevent the dead from returning to the land of the living. Some of the dead didn't know the spells to make it through the Weighing of the Heart ceremony and on to the Field of Reeds. Some simply didn't want to go through the trials in the Underworld or were afraid that their souls would be fed to Ammit the Devourer. Still others lost their way or coveted what they'd left behind: life.

Regardless of the reason, some of the dead returned and in the journey back to the land of the living became darker, more evil: the Lost Ones.

When the dead rose from the sands as undead, the Sons of Anubis were called to action. The Daughters of Isis would empower them, weave spells to protect them and, after battle, heal them. When possible, they returned the Lost Ones to their graves and tombs so they wouldn't be forgotten. Otherwise they were destroyed and became as dust.

That was then, a glorious work lost in the sands of time. Now all the Isis witches seemed to do was find inventive ways to kill jackals. Markus bared his teeth. No more. Tonight the witches would learn the meaning of fear. Tonight a Daughter of Isis would become a prisoner of the Sons of Anubis.

At his signal men and jackals swept toward the corner house. The numbers were sheer insurance, nothing more. Most of the jackals were patrolling each quadrant of the city, sniffing out clutches of Lost Ones. The lone witch would know as soon as her wards fell but she obviously was either sloppy or overconfident, since she hadn't extended her wards below the fence line into the earth. Marcus led his men through the sliding glass door and into the darkened house. As planned, his men fanned out while he and two others entered the bedroom. The witch had just begun to stir from sleep as he slapped duct tape over her mouth. She kicked and thrashed, one blow connecting with his shoulder. It was the last punch she got in.

He grabbed her wrists as another jackal sedated her. "It's

for your own protection," he told her, staring into furious dark eyes. "No one needs to get hurt."

Fury gave way to fear then unconsciousness. With efficient movements, he bound her and tossed her over his shoulder, crushing guilt under his boot heel. She hardly weighed anything and her defensive skills were sorely lacking. Why had the local Isis witches allowed her to leave the safety of their circle? Had they ostracized her for a lack of magic? Was she not a Daughter of Isis after all?

No, he wouldn't think that. He couldn't think that. If that were true, all of this was for nothing, and more of his men would die.

Markus rejoined his men in the hallway. "The entire sunroom is a shrine to Isis, sir."

It was confirmation, not that they needed it. "Acknowledged. Load up what you can, in case we need it. Her keys are on the kitchen counter. Pack up her car quickly and get out quicker."

Markus carried his unconscious prize out of the house and over the back fence in less than two minutes. A quick dash through the wooded lot to the waiting van, and they were on their way.

Only when he had received word that the rest of his men were safely out did Markus allow himself to relax. So far, so good. The most dangerous part of the mission was complete.

"You think this will work?" asked Hector.

Markus knew his second in command didn't doubt the mission. No one questioned him in that regard; he'd proven his ability to lead centuries ago. Hector's blood brother was one of the afflicted, in the first stages of a debilitating illness that had cost the lives of four jackals so far. Markus swore there wouldn't be a fifth, and this witch would guarantee it.

"It will." Confidence loaded his words. "She's a Daughter of Isis. One of them cast the curse. She'll break it."

"What if she doesn't?"

"Then we'll use her as bait to trap another witch." He leaned forward on the jump seat. "One way or another, we'll end this curse. I don't care if we have to trap every Isis witch in the northern hemisphere to do it. We do whatever it takes."

He held up his fist. "For Sons and brothers."

Hector tapped it with his own. "For Sons and brothers."

Chapter Two

Consciousness rushed back with the subtlety of a freight train. The first thing Tia noticed was that her wrists were bound in front of her. Second, she wore only her thin cotton nightgown. Third, while she lay on a comfortable, richly appointed bed, the unadorned concrete walls and lack of windows made the room nothing more than a cell.

Kidnapped.

Tia fought to quell her panic, forcing the grogginess away so that she could think. She'd been taken from her home. Someone had to have had strong magic to break through her wards. She'd checked them thoroughly before going to bed. Not even another Daughter of Isis should have been able to unravel her protections without her knowledge. She hadn't even felt a warning until after the wards had been breached. By the time she'd roused from sleep, it had been too late.

"I know you're awake, witch."

The voice, cold and harsh, stabbed at any lingering hope. Did he call her a witch because he knew she was one, or was it an epithet of some sort? If he knew she was an Isis witch, he would have gagged her. Since he hadn't, it was a strong possibility her kidnapper had no idea who he'd taken.

A smile bent her lips. She'd make him regret that.

Tia struggled to an upright position on the mattress, twisting around until she could see the face of her captor. She could have tried using her Voice without facing him, but staring into another's eyes always strengthened the compulsion. Besides, her power reserves were low since she hadn't had time to replenish her magical energy. She didn't know if she had enough strength to put him under her control long enough to break free, but she'd try.

She expected her captor to be sitting but he stood instead, blocking the door. He was a slab of a man; dressed in old work boots and black jeans so well-worn they had a charcoal sheen to them and showed every bit of the muscles in his long legs. A gray T-shirt stretched across his wide chest, made even tighter by the defined copper-skinned arms folded across it. A close-cropped goatee called attention to a soft mouth, probably the only soft part of him. It balanced the dark cap of tight waves, and the amber-whiskey-colored eyes that glared at her from beneath strong brows and above an even stronger nose. Despite his size, his build wasn't that of a bodybuilder, more like that of an Olympic gymnast.

Presented with such a visual feast, her base magic stirred, but not enough to quell the renewed fear that stalked up her spine. She didn't need to see the sigil on his T-shirt or the gold Anubis-head pendant that hung on a thick chain around his neck to know who—or rather, what—her kidnapper was. She also knew that if she couldn't control him with her Voice, she had no other options.

Locking her gaze to his, she summoned her power. "Release me, dog."

The block of a man dropped his arms, his expression blank. He took a step forward, leaned over her...then burst out laughing. "You thought you could enslave and insult me in the same breath? I removed your gag just to see—or rather, hear—what you can do. Try again, witch."

Dammit! Like "witch" was an endearment, coming from

one of the Sons of Anubis. She knew her freedom hinged on her ability to use her power. Unfortunately, she hadn't had the time or the inclination to recharge her base magic.

Regret soured her stomach. What would her coven sisters think if they could see her now, as defenseless as they'd always thought? What about her grandmother?

Thinking about Aya, the high priestess of the coven, had Tia reaching deep inside to her magical core. She stared up at the jackal and put every bit of compulsion she could into her Voice. "Help me escape to safety."

Power filled the room. It rolled over the man. His eyes widened as the power of her Voice hit him. Again, he swayed toward her. Then he stepped back, shaking himself hard the way a dog dashed water from its coat. "You have magic, I'll give you that. But if you think you can control me, think again."

Tia cursed under her breath. If the jackal was immune to her compulsion, that meant he had magical strength in his own right. Still, he had kidnapped her, not killed her. Obviously, he wanted something from her. Something only a Daughter of Isis could provide. "Who are you and what do you want?"

"I am Markus Grant, and I lead the Sons of Anubis who have chosen to call this town home," he told her, his eyes glinting. "Those who still hold to our sacred duty to keep the Lost Ones where they belong, away from the land of the living."

Tia refrained from rolling her eyes. Pretty speech, even if it was a lie. She knew the Sons of Anubis had abandoned their "sacred duty" centuries ago, leaving a bloody trail of broken Daughters of Isis in their wake. Without the jackals' help, they hadn't been able to protect the funerary temples or much of anything else, and had to abandon their home, their land.

The news that a jackal clan not only lived in Atlanta, but also thrived enough to take on the Lost Ones, disturbed her. Her grandmother's warning slithered through her mind. Aya had told her to be extra vigilant when she left the protection of the coven, with good reason. Jackals tended to kill first and ask questions never. She'd thought she'd taken every precaution. Now she knew better. How long had the Sons of Anubis been in Atlanta? Had they somehow tracked her circle, followed them here?

She mustered what little defiance she had. "If you think I'm going to tell you where my sisters are, you're wrong."

"I don't care where the Daughters of Isis are holed up," he retorted. "At least, not at the moment. What I care about right now is you, Tia Jensen."

Air seized in her lungs, causing her voice to squeak past her lips. "How do you know my name?"

"I know more than your name. I know that you're a physical therapist with an exclusive client list. I know that you are affiliated with the Golden Lotus Circle of the Daughters of Isis, but you've been a solitary practitioner for the last four years."

Tia stared at the man before her, fighting to suppress her fear. It flooded her nerves, pushing her magic, the power of Voice, further away. He'd stalked her. This jackal had hunted her like a wolf chasing down a rabbit. "What do you want with me?"

"Your powers." His gaze raked the length of her, making her aware of the thin excuse for a nightgown that she wore. Her ears burned with embarrassment. The burn scalded her body in impotent rage as he half turned his back to her, as if implying that she wasn't much of a threat to him. Considering how easily he'd breached her wards and taken her from her own bed, he was right, and it made her even angrier. She tamped it down. Getting angry wouldn't help her escape, only hamper it. She needed to remain calm to keep her magic at the ready.

He gave her a sidelong glance. "I had hoped you'd be powerful enough to be of use to me, but if you're not…"

He didn't finish his statement, but he didn't have to. Tia knew exactly what the jackals did to those they found useless.

Shame stung her eyes. Her coven sisters had thought her useless when she'd failed to manifest greater power at the onset of puberty as the seventh Daughter of a seventh Daughter was supposed to do. Hurt by the rejection, she'd distanced herself from the other Daughters by going to college, staying in on-campus housing until she completed her studies, then putting a down payment on a modest house. She'd been making a solitary life for herself, but home was still in the circle with the other Daughters of Isis, even if they didn't think so.

"You say that you hunt the Lost Ones." She wasn't sure if she believed that, but she'd play along if it garnered her freedom. "Do you want my help fighting them?"

Again the laugh. "I've seen your defensive spells—or lack of them. I doubt your fighting skills are much better."

Anger flooded her. "Your pack of dogs broke through my wards and into my house in the dead of night like a navy SEAL team storming an enemy hideout. You drugged me, bound me and brought me here before I could blink. What can one Daughter of Isis do against a pack of jackals?"

"For one thing, not rely on magic to save her," he shot back. "Which you should have known, given how weak your magic is."

"I. Am. Not. Weak!"

Markus's eyes widened as the witch's power punched him, causing him to rock back on his heels. Not so weak after all. Obviously she needed her passions provoked in order to fully tap into her power. Something told him provoking her passions wouldn't be a problem.

He wasn't sure what he'd expected when weeks of reconnaissance had finally come to fruition, but this woman wasn't it. She appeared young, though that was hardly an indication of age for their long-lived races. He knew she still had a healthy student loan balance, and her driver's license stated she was mid-twenties. It was unusual for a witch so young to live outside of the safety of a coven, which was why he'd expected someone older, wiser, more of a challenge. Had she been thrown out of the Lotus Circle because she wasn't powerful enough?

No, he'd felt her power when she'd gotten angry. It was

there, waiting for her to tap into it. Maybe she was bait, living away from the protective circle of witches in order to trap the Sons of Anubis. His hand lifted, fingers wrapping around the gold Anubis-head talisman all adult jackals wore. Let the witches try. He and his jackals had survived and would continue to do so. No sacrifice would be too great.

He stared at the witch. If would be a shame if she was part of a trap. Women like her had always been a weakness to him—long-legged, thick in the thighs and full in the chest; eyes sloe, dark, fathomless and large in her copper-skinned face. Just the sort of woman he would pursue if he had the time or the inclination.

He had neither. Not with Lost Ones walking the night. Certainly not with someone targeting the Sons of Anubis. Not with two of his clan brothers so close to death just down the hall.

Markus fisted his hands. This Isis witch was a tool, a means to an end, nothing more. He couldn't think about his need, how long it had been since he'd enjoyed a woman. He had to think about his clan, their survival and their eternal fight against the undead. Not the need that spiked through him every time he felt her magic.

Angry with himself for being distracted, he bared his teeth at her. "For both our sakes, I hope you aren't weak. If you're weak, then you're of no use to me. And if you're no use to me…"

"Jackal, please." She rolled her eyes at him. "You know, threats tend to make people not inclined to help you. Just saying."

"You're right," he told her. Surprise lit her face, and he clenched his jaw against the sensual punch to the gut. "But what you don't seem to understand is that I'm not threatening you. I'm just letting you know what will happen if you don't do what I want. Just saying."

Her chin lifted. "What exactly do you want?"

He pulled a blade from the sheath strapped to his thigh.

She recoiled, hands coming up defensively.

"Relax. I'm not going to kill you."

He didn't say "yet," but she flinched as if he had.

Good. She didn't need to know that he'd only killed in defense of himself or his clan, or in his sacred duty to Anubis. What she did need to know was just how serious he was about keeping his clan safe.

Reaching over, he grabbed her wrists and slid the blade beneath the nylon tie that bound her. His fingertips tingled against her skin. She trembled as his thumb stroked over her pulse, but he didn't know if the reaction was due to his touch or the dagger. "Hold still."

A sharp jerk and he freed her. She immediately rubbed her wrists, staring up at him. "What now?"

"Come with me." He held a hand out to her just to see what she would do.

Continuing to chafe sensation back into her hands, she ignored his and stood on her own. "This way, I assume?" she asked, reaching for the knob.

Impressed despite himself, Markus rapped on the door. The witch stumbled back a step as a guard opened the door onto a long hallway decorated with depictions of Lord Anubis in his various funerary roles and the journey through Duat, the Underworld.

The witch stopped short. Her gaze roamed the walls, taking in each scene, every minute detail. "Amazing," she whispered as her hand came up to trace the closest brightly rendered image. "The details, the colors—it's beautiful!"

Markus allowed a swell of pride. "We tried to recreate the images as accurately as possible, even sourcing as many of the original pigments as we could." His fingers traced the graceful lines of a lotus flower. "We wanted a remembrance of what we'd lost. Luckily, our clan has never forgotten our past or our purpose."

He looked down at her, anger surging again. "Why don't I introduce you to the artist?"

Without waiting for an answer, he wrapped a hand around

her bicep and dragged her down the hall. Four other doors flanked the hall, but only two had guards stationed outside—the one they'd left and the one they approached, second from the end. The hall then veered sharply right, opening onto a large open room holding a pool table, a massive flat-panel TV, bar and other entertainments before ending at the stairs leading to the upper level.

He stopped at the second-to-last door, nodding to the jackal standing guard at the end of the hall. The guard opened the door, allowing Markus to shove Tia inside. She stiffened at his treatment, then gasped as she took in the contents of the room. Three strides in, she could see several cells. Jackals occupied two of them. One lay curled on a futon, his upper half human and the lower half misshapen jackal. The other, fully human, lay on his side, eyes wide and unblinking, minute twitches jerking his body. Markus could smell the sour notes of sickness choking the air and the acidic-ash burn of dark magic.

Tia cried out, rushing toward the closest cage. Markus snagged an arm around her waist, preventing her from reaching the bars. She frowned up at him, moisture shimmering on her lashes. "What's wrong with them? I know you can't take them to a hospital, but to keep them like this is beyond cruel—it's inhumane! Where is your healer?"

Her outraged horror pleased him as much as her tears surprised him. This particular Isis witch, at least, hadn't cast the spell that had felled his men. "They've been cursed, somehow," he told her, deliberately harsh. He didn't try to release her, and she didn't try to pull away. "If we knew how exactly, we'd know how to treat them. As for our healer, we no longer have one. She was one of the first to die."

"Die? You have to do something!" she exclaimed, tugging free of his hold to grip the bars of the closest cage. "They're suffering!"

"I did do something. I brought you here."

A myriad of emotions flew across her expressive face, shock prevalent. Her lips twisted as she turned away from the cage and looked up at him. "You've just doomed your brothers, jackal. I can't heal them."

A cold, hard knot formed deep in his gut. "You can't, or you won't?"

If she heard the menace in his tone, she paid it no mind. "I can't. I don't know how." She lowered her head, not enough to disguise the bitterness that filled her words. "Even if I knew how, I'm not strong enough. You should have shanghaied another Daughter."

Something turned over deep inside him. It took a moment for him to recognize it as compassion. He almost reached out to her—to pat her shoulder, to stroke her hair—he didn't know. Instead he forced his hand down, fisted it. He didn't want to feel compassion for the witch, his enemy. He didn't want to feel anything at all for her.

"You are a Daughter of Isis," he barked, bringing his military training to bear. "There was a time when your kind served with the Sons of Anubis, worked to drive the dead back into Duat. You gave us spells to protect us, spells to arm us and spells to heal us. It is—or was—the duty of every Isis witch. Though we are enemies now, it is still part of you, part of your nature. Part of your magic. You can do this!"

Chapter Three

Tia took the verbal kick in the ass for what it was, rediscovering her backbone with every word the jackal barked out. Straightening her shoulders, firming her chin, she wanted to believe as he believed, that she could reach down deep past the centuries of betrayal and hatred, and find the power that bound jackals and witches together.

You're out of your mind, a horrified voice inside her head said. *They're jackals. Jackals! You can't help them!*

It didn't matter that they were jackals. It didn't matter that their kind had killed and hunted her kind for centuries. It didn't even matter that they had kidnapped her. The two caged jackals were suffering. She had to try to help. The healer in her could do no less.

She knew her coven sisters wouldn't understand, much less agree. To them, the only good jackal was a dead or dying one. Then again, some of the Daughters had been around for centuries and had experience clashing with the jackals. Tia was young by the circle's standards, having been born in the New World and with no firsthand knowledge of fighting the Sons of Anubis.

"Okay." She gave a sharp nod. "The first thing we need to

do is make this place more conducive to healing. I don't suppose we can move them?"

He shook his head. "It took several of my men just to get them here. We caged them for their safety as well as ours. Does this mean you can help them?"

"I can try." She turned to face him. He really was a slab of a man, but in a very nice *hot damn* sort of way. It made her wonder what his jackal looked like. "I need to go home, get some stuff."

"No."

She bristled, even though she knew he wouldn't agree. "I'll come back."

He clearly didn't believe her. "The answer is still no."

"What you want me to do is a big deal," she spat. "I can't just wrinkle my nose and wish them back to health! Did any of your jackals train with your healer?"

"No."

"Do any of them possess any talent for healing or spell work?"

"No."

"Are there any female jackals who can help me perform the chants to Isis?"

He folded his arms, a stubborn expression crossing his features. "No."

She blew out a frustrated sigh and settled her hands on her hips. "Are you telling me no because it's the truth or because you don't want me to know? Because I gotta tell ya, if it's the second reason, you truly suck."

The left side of his lips kicked up in a smile as if he found her pissiness amusing. She wondered if he'd smile if she kneed him in the nuts. "There aren't any female jackals available to help."

Great. He was dooming her to failure before she even started. "Look. You want to save them, right? So do I, since that's the only way I'm getting out of here. So help me here. Do any of you at least know of the ancient hymns and prayers?"

He uncrossed his arms, just to cross them behind his back, military style. "We've kept up our prayers to Anubis, mostly for protection and guidance as we go into battle, prayers and blessings as we send the dead back to Duat, and thanksgiving when we return home safely."

Tia knew painfully little about the Sons of Anubis, but she didn't think their war prayers would work, or their fellows jackals would have healed already and she wouldn't be here. Still, she'd take anything she could get.

"Okay. Maybe those will help to invoke Anubis. Do you have the right incenses, the right altars to make prayers to Isis and Anubis? If someone here doesn't have a sistrum or know how to use it, I need to have my recordings. All of that stuff is at my house—you know, the sanctuary that you defiled and kidnapped me from?"

"Yes, the sanctuary that had an entire wall in your sunroom dedicated to Isis?" He again folded his arms across his chest. "I had my men gather up many of your things. We were respectful," he added when she opened her mouth to protest. "They have all been carefully arranged in the next room. And we have medical and spiritual supplies our healer left behind, in those cabinets against the wall. We can set up whatever you need."

The thought of these jackals manhandling her altar made her stomach churn. Her shoulders sagged. "Strangers, enemies, touching my personal stuff, my sacred things. I can't begin to use them until I purify them again."

He didn't offer an apology, not that she expected him to. Someone willing to kidnap a person wouldn't give a damn about her belongings. "Can you start without those?"

"Probably. I can at least try to find out what's wrong with them." She looked at him again. "If I do, will you let me go?"

"Of course."

The words flowed from those gorgeous full lips too easily. "I would have your word, sworn under the watchful eye of the god you hold dear, that you will let me go once I heal your men. In return, I will swear to Isis that I will do everything I can to break the sickness that taints them. Deal?"

Amber eyes bored into hers. She kept her gaze open, honest. She'd already shown that she was willing to help heal the afflicted men, but she wouldn't be able to focus completely on what she needed to do if she had to worry about whether or not Markus planned to keep her prisoner, or worse.

"Done."

"Okay." Breath rushed from her lungs in relief. She'd have to accept his word—if he had meant what he had said about doing his sacred duty with the Lost Ones, then swearing to his patron god was no small thing. She had to believe he would let her go.

"Tell me what happened to them." She knelt on the floor beside the cage with the fully human jackal. Glazed eyes stared unseeing as minute tremors shook his thin frame. She spread her fingers against the bars, reaching for her healing ability. "You said something about a curse?"

"Yes, they were cursed. By an Isis witch."

"Liar!"

The Isis witch leaped to her feet. "A Daughter of Isis would never attack a jackal warrior!"

"Of course not." He put his fists on his hips, goading her further because he needed to get the accusation out before it poisoned him. "Direct action has never been the way of an Isis witch. Your kind prefers stealth and tricks."

"You don't have the right to be angry, jackal," she spat. "We have done nothing to you but what we had to."

"The Daughters of Isis abandoned us!" he thundered. "You turned your backs on your own people, your own men and gave yourselves to the people of Greece and Rome! Left us to protect the temples while the Two Lands fell. We were there, fighting the undead and the curse of Ammit while you were being feted in Athens and Pompeii!"

"We escaped with our lives!" Tia shouted. "We had no

choice but to flee after your clan declared war on us by murdering our high priestess!"

He drew back, eyes wide, nostrils flaring, and for a moment, she thought he meant to strike her. "What. Did. You. Say?"

Her hands settled on her hips. "I. Did. Not. Stutter."

"The Sons of Anubis have never taken an innocent life!"

The door crashed open, men and jackals flying into the room. Tia flinched as they surrounded her, guns and teeth bared. Memories slammed into Marcus, memories of a time when the children of Isis had stood hip to hip with the children of Anubis, fighting with them instead of against them. He remembered his mentor, Sekhanu, with his mate, the Isis High Priestess Asharet, and how their love had united the witches and jackals. Just as he remembered how their deaths had separated both sides forever.

Hector stepped forward, placing himself between Markus and the furious witch. "Do you need us to remove the witch, my lord?"

Eagerness drenched his tone. Markus knew how much his second wanted blood, especially an Isis witch's blood. "No. She's already sworn to help us. She just learned the origins of the curse, and didn't take the news well."

"How can you be sure one of the Daughters caused this?" She gestured to the stricken men, ignoring the weapons pointed at her. "What proof do you have?"

"Your magic has a scent, unique to Isis witches," he told her. "As we can smell the Lost Ones even in the Great Western Desert, so we can smell magic cast by one of you. Our men reek of it."

"I don't believe you."

"Here." He grabbed her forearm, dragged her to the cell holding the half-shifted jackal. "Use your senses," he growled. "Feel the magic rising off him like a landfill stench then look me in the eye and tell me it isn't born of an Isis witch!"

She spread her fingers wide, her chin lowering. His hackles rose as he felt her call her power, but he kept his expression blank to all but anger. After a moment she gasped, stumbling back from the bars.

"Great Mother Isis." Dismay clogged her features. "It feels like the magical working of one of the Daughters' circles, but it's…wrong somehow." She shook her head. "It must be some sort of trick. It goes against all the tenets and aspects of Isis. How can you expect me to believe this was caused by the Daughters?"

"How can you expect me to believe that one of the Sons took the life of a high priestess of Isis on the temple steps?" The accusation angered him anew, rage reflected in the snarls of the men and jackals arranged around them. "What proof do you have?"

"That high priestess was my great-grandmother, Asharet," she said, her voice thrumming with emotion. "Her dying words were 'watch the jackals.' And there was a dead jackal beside her."

Markus crowded her. "That dead jackal was Sekhanu, my mentor and Asharet's mate. He would have no reason to slay the love of his life."

"The dead jackal was my great-grandfather?" she whispered, stricken. "I didn't know—grandmother never said. She doesn't like to speak of that time. She only told me that she'd received word that Asharet and many other Daughters were killed, the temple steps littered with the bodies of jackals. Aya gathered as many of the remaining priestesses as she could and headed south. Eventually they made their way out of Egypt."

He folded his arms, wanting to believe her, but finding it difficult to set aside centuries of distrust. Witches and jackals had fought each other over the stretch of time, until both sides had decided avoidance was the best policy. The dead needed to stay dead after all, and Isis witches were just as much a target of the Lost Ones as the jackals were.

"You should consider that Sekhanu died defending his mate from an outside threat, like another priestess making a power play. Rivalries happen."

She shook her head, more in disbelief than denial. "You can't ask me to set aside centuries of belief based on your say so. Both our versions of events are possible. When this is over, I want to learn more. I'm also going to talk to my grandmother. She doesn't like discussing that time for obvious reasons, but it certainly couldn't have been easy to believe that her father killed her mother, even then."

"Let's propose a truce," he offered. "Nothing can be settled tonight, and we have more important matters to face."

"Agreed." She turned back to the cells. "We need to light incense and begin the prayers to Isis and Anubis. If your jackals wouldn't mind, I need a couple of them here in human form. The others can relieve them when needed."

He gestured to his men. "Do as she says as she's healing our brothers," he ordered, picking two men to remain behind. "The rest can bring in supplies."

They left. Hector remained. "What is it?" Marcus asked, though he thought he knew.

"I just want her to know—" strain shot through his voice as he gestured to the half-man, half-jackal "—that's my blood brother, Alonso. He's only nineteen. He's never seen an Isis witch before now, and he's certainly never killed one. He didn't even join us in hunting the Lost Ones until earlier this year."

His expression twisted. "And yet, an Isis witch has doomed him to die, just because he's a jackal."

Tia didn't cower in the face of Hector's anger. "I understand being targeted because of what you are," she told him, her chin high. "After all, it's why I'm here, isn't it?"

Her features softened as she looked at the stricken jackals. "But I also understand that there is more to the Sons than what I've been told, just as there is more to the Daughters than what you think you know. All I can say is that I will do everything I can to heal your brother. When this is over, I will do my best to find out who is responsible for this curse. For right now, I need your help to help your brother. Can you do that?"

Markus couldn't hear the magical compulsion of an Isis

witch's Voice, but he felt the need to help Tia all the same. Hector did, too. He nodded, some of the tension seeping from his body. "What do you need me to do?"

"You have a blood bond with Alonso. We can use that bond to send healing, healthy energy to your brother, while I draw the negative out."

"You're sure?" Hope limned his voice.

"I'm not sure of anything right now," she retorted, then softened her words with a smile. "But we have a shared mission. We can only hope that Isis and Anubis will hear our prayers, recognize our intent and lend their strength to break this curse."

Markus watched Tia direct his jackals in setting up everything she required, bringing in water, bowls, music and an assortment of other things he couldn't figure out the use for. He was once again reminded of the Daughters of old, confident in their abilities and strong in their determination. Asharet had been much the same, holding her own with Sekhanu who had done the impossible and united the jackals into a cohesive group against their solitary natures. Hard men all, scoured fine by battle and the harshness of the Western Desert. Asharet had protected and defended them all with such devoted ferocity that Markus had been jealous, wanting an Isis witch mate as Sekhanu had, though he'd never found the right one. Now he wondered if someone else had been jealous of Asharet and Sekhanu, jealous enough to want to destroy them both.

"Markus."

He blinked away his memories to the past and focused on the here and now. The rich smell of incense wafted through the room, pulling him back once again to an older time. "You have *kyphi* incense?"

"Yes, mostly. A lot of the ancient ingredients and recipes are lost." She whispered a few words under her breath as she used a white ostrich plume to fan through both occupied cells the smoke of the incense pellets held in a small alabaster bowl.

"Frankincense is good too, but I figured the *kapet* was better since it's after nightfall."

Rashon, the second jackal, already seemed calmer, his breaths deeper, twitches less frequent. Guilt pricked Markus. He should have thought of procuring and lighting traditional incense to create a sacred space for the men. He was old enough to know better.

He looked to Tia, grateful that he'd made the decision to take her, though now he wondered if she would have come willingly had he asked her properly. She stared at him, her dark eyes luminous, her lips a full ripe blend of honey and raspberry. "What can I do?"

"You as a warrior lead the Sons of Anubis against the Lost Ones, but you are their spiritual head, as well," she explained. "I need you to invoke the presence of your patron god. Whatever prayers of protection you use before you go into battle should be a good beginning."

That he could do. He dropped to his knees between the cages, the remaining jackals in the room following suit. Stilling his mind, he began to recite the ancient prayer. "Lord Anubis, Anapa, Guardian of the Dead, He Who Sits upon the Mountain, hear the prayers of your humble servant."

He continued the prayers of thanksgiving, praise and protection, his words echoed by his men. Power gathered in the room as Tia mixed oils and herbs in a large bowl. As she worked, she began to sing. He recognized the song as a hymn to Isis, and somehow it melded with their chants to become something more powerful, more potent.

Markus couldn't take his eyes off Tia. Grace filled every movement she made, like a ballet of magic. Her magic called to him and his body responded. Need, unexpected and sharp, bit deep.

His voice faltered, but he blamed it on the sudden music flowing into the room. The recorded sounds of drums and sistrums were no less visceral than if musicians had been in the chamber. The beat threaded through the incense and sorcery, weaving the masculine and feminine halves into a powerful whole.

Blessed Anubis, he wanted her.

She lifted a large bowl in both hands. "Markus, please open the cell."

"No." Shaking his head for emphasis, he shoved his need down. "They become violent and try to escape. As far as we can tell, the curse seems to transmit through a bite. I can't risk more of my men."

Instead of arguing, she turned to the cage. "Alonso. Look at me, Alonso."

The stricken jackal slowly turned his head, moaning as if even that simple movement caused agony.

"Alonso. Anubis stands beside you, Isis holds you in her arms. We are here to aid you and break this curse, to lead you back whole and hearty to the sun. You will help us help you."

The cursed jackal struggled to work his jaw to form words. After an eternity he managed to push words out. "Yes, priestess."

A garbled sound tripped from Hector's throat. "He hasn't spoken in days. No matter how I begged, he wouldn't answer me. But he answered you."

Tia's eyes glowed with power—or perhaps, the power of her personality. "It means that your brother is strong and willing to fight. Markus, if you would please?"

Markus unlocked the cage then stepped through. Though Alonso's gaze never left Tia as she entered the cell, he made no move toward her. When she looked to Markus in question, he shut the cell door. "I won't have you say that I sent you in unprotected."

He took the large basin from her. "I'll hold this for you. Is this for what I think it is?"

"If you think we're going to give Alonso a sponge bath, then yes, you're right," she answered, kneeling beside the jackal's head. "We're anointing his body with this healing mixture as we offer prayers and blessings for him."

Markus blanched. When one of his men died in battle, it fell to him to prepare their bodies, assuming the role of a high priest of Anubis. "It's too much like a burial ritual."

"It's exactly like a burial ritual," she told him, "except Alonso is still alive. This purification ritual will go far in helping us keep him that way."

Markus didn't know if Tia actually knew what she was doing or grasped at any straw she could out of desperation. Considering that he'd grabbed her for a desperate cause, he'd grasp those same straws and they could burn or fly together.

"Okay. Let's get started."

Chapter Four

"Tia."

A growl of a voice, close to her right ear, pulled Tia slowly up through the intricate pattern of the spell weaving itself into the jackal's life force. "Hmm?"

"Tia." This time a hard hand to the shoulder, shaking her. "You need to stop."

She blinked, and the blurred image finally focused. Markus. He didn't look happy, not that she expected him to. She wasn't even close to pulling off a miracle for his men. "What?"

"You need to stop."

"Can't." Was that scratchy mewl of a sound her voice?

"Can." His hand slid from her shoulder to her forearm. She didn't feel the same tingle she had before, a sure indication of how depleted she was. "You've been at this for hours. Your voice is all but gone and so's your energy. No one will be helped if you pass out."

"Just a little more," she insisted. "I've never experienced a spell so intricate. It has a Daughter's touch, but there's much more to it, something I've never seen before. If I pick at it a little longer, I should be able to find the master thread."

"As much as I want you to continue, I don't want you

or my jackals hurt," he told her. "You can start again after you're rested."

The unexpected concern touched her. He had a point though. She needed food, rest—ugh, a shower—and some way to replenish her magical reserves. At this point, she'd do more harm than good by continuing. "'Kay."

Bracing her hands against the mattress, she attempted to push herself to her feet. Her arms shook with the effort and she couldn't unfold her legs enough to stand.

An arm snagged her about the waist, hauling her off the floor. Her body flew horizontal and she found herself cradled against a very hard and very warm body. Despite her fatigue, her nerve endings sang, sensing the vast resources of strength and power thrumming through the jackal. Her magic stirred, recognizing a perfect energy source. His power tasted potent, smooth as quality whiskey, and it made her wonder what the skin at his throat tasted like.

"Nice," she said without thinking. "Bet you make all the girl jackals howl."

Someone choked on a laugh. "Now I know you're exhausted." Markus's voice rumbled deep in his chest. "You're actually being nice to me."

Oh, yeah. That was probably not the smart thing to do, considering he'd kidnapped her and all. "We're under a truce, aren't we? I think it's okay to be nice to each other. I'll even give you a compliment. Did you know that you give good frown?" Especially with those tasty-looking lips.

Another smothered snort. "You've gone from exhausted to delirious," he rumbled, carrying her out of the cell and toward the door. He paused beside Hector. "Send the next shift in, and tell them to keep the incense and music going and notify me immediately if there's any change. See about some food, then take yourself off to bed."

"A bacon cheeseburger and cheese fries would be great," she piped up, her stomach yowling a protest at the mention of food. "Or pancakes, bacon, sausage and eggs if it's breakfast time."

Markus frowned down at her again. "What?" she asked, defensive. "I get horny when I heal someone. Sue me."

He stopped in his tracks. "You mean 'hungry,' right?"

"That's what I said." *Isn't it?*

"If you say so." He carried her back down the hall to the room in which she'd awakened. As they passed through a door at the rear of the room, she noticed her duffel bag atop the chest of drawers. Good. Besides a change of clothes, her go-bag carried a few necessary things that helped her replenish her energy. She wondered if Markus had rifled through it. Probably. He didn't seem the sort to leave anything to chance.

He took her into the surprisingly large bathroom and placed her atop the closed commode. A luxurious glassed-in shower dominated the space, its sand beige tiles interspersed with cobalt and turquoise squares imprinted with gold lotus flowers. So, not a cell at all. "This is your room, isn't it?"

"Yeah."

"Why no windows in the bedroom?"

"I live here to be available for the clan," he answered. "I catch sleep when I can, and having no windows makes that easier." He opened the glass door and reached for the water handle. "I'll start it for you."

"Thank you." Tia watched the muscles play over his back as he twisted the handle, sending water gushing into the enclosed space. The jackal was a fine specimen of a man with his wide shoulders, tight buns and powerful legs. Lethal grace and strength wrapped a keen mind and a fierce spirit, all very attractive qualities that called to her. Her magic stirred again, rumbling in harmony with her empty stomach. What would it be like, she wondered, to blend their magics together, to feel his body moving with hers?

"Tia?" Roughness filled his voice, though his tone sounded as if he'd called her name more than once.

She forced herself to raise her gaze from his body to his face. Mmm, his lips looked tasty, too. "Yes?"

"Are you okay?" Concern darkened his topaz gaze.

No, she wasn't. She'd always had a healthy sex drive, but being close to Markus was like adding gas to a fire. "I need," she explained, knowing it wasn't much of an explanation at all. She tried again. "I need to replenish. Untying the curse is more draining than I expected."

She didn't want to tell him that the quickest way for her to replenish was through sex. Each Daughter of Isis manifested different aspects of the goddess at the onset of puberty. Unfortunately for Tia, hers manifested primarily as sexual creative energy with a smaller gift of healing. While she'd been part of the coven she hadn't had sex, so her power had never been great. It was only after leaving for college that she'd had her sexual and magical awakening.

"Ah." His expression cleared. "The food should be here by the time you finish your shower. Then you can eat and rest while we gather more supplies. How long do you need?"

"More time than you probably want me to take, if all I can do is eat and rest."

The greater the magical work, the greater the amount of energy expended. Her coven, of course, could spread the energy toll over the circle, so no one witch was depleted. Since she didn't have her coven to rely on, she had to parse her magical work out carefully, saving any greater spell-casting for situations when she knew she'd be able to rejuvenate completely. Stuck in the jackal's den without her usual outlet, she ran the risk of draining her magic completely. She doubted Markus would give her the two days she needed to recuperate without sex.

Not that she could tell Markus that, of course. It wasn't as if he'd offer to help her out in that regard. Or would he?

"We'll figure something out. I know you're doing everything you can." He reached his hand into the spray, testing the temperature. "How do you like it?"

Damn. She gritted her teeth, biting back all the suggestive responses to his innocent question. Angry Markus she could withstand. This Markus, nice Markus, was too close to her type. Usually when she needed sex to recharge, she went for betas—men who had no problem with casual hookups and her lack of interest in long-term relationships. Men like Markus—gorgeous alpha males with fierce loyalty, intensity and protective streaks—those were the men she fantasized about alone in her bed.

She licked her lips. "A cold shower will work."

He turned to her then stopped, his smile slipping from his lips. His gaze dropped from her face to her chest and caught there. "I think…I think you're already cold."

Gods. Her nipples, already tight and sensitive against the thin material of her gown, peaked further beneath the heated weight of his gaze. "Actually, I'm burning up."

His nostrils flared as his gaze roamed her body again like a wandering hand. Desire coiled deep inside her, tightening her body as she matched his frank perusal. Tension built with the eddying steam in the suddenly small room. Tia's lips parted as she caught the sharp licorice liqueur edge of his need burning its way into her senses. Her own need rose in response, sharp, painful and necessary, slicking her core.

Desire met desire, magic met magic, obliterating her fatigue. Nothing mattered but getting a taste of him. She stretched out a hand, putting all her need into her Voice. "Markus."

Instantly he closed the distance between them, grabbing her hand before hauling her up and molding her to his body. Amber eyes glittered with barely banked hunger, then he crushed his mouth to hers.

Yes! Throwing her arms around his neck, Tia matched his wildness, giving herself over to the kiss and the dizzying sensations that buffeted her. A duel of lips and teeth and tongue curled her toes and left her moaning for more. The feel of the hard ridge of his cock pressing so sweetly between them made her breathless.

His hands palmed her ass, lifting her so that her pussy could ride the bulge in his jeans. She groaned again, rubbing against him, silently pleading for more.

A growl cut the air as Markus broke the kiss. Golden eyes dilated, canines peeking from lips curled in a snarl, breathing harsh over the sound of running water, he stared down at her. He was magnificent.

And pissed.

"Are you trying to put a spell on me?" he demanded, his hands scooping her up under her arms, his fingers biting into her shoulders as he held her off the floor.

She licked her lips, enjoying his taste and wanting more. "Spell you? No. Seduce you? Yes."

His breath hitched and he placed her back on her feet. "Why?"

Her turn to frown. "After that kiss, you have to ask me why? Look at you! I'm attracted to you in every sense of the word. My magic likes the taste of yours. My body likes the feel of yours. And if that kiss is anything to go by, the rest of it is going to be amazing."

"Tia." Warning, demand and desire lowered his voice to a bass rumble. He took a deep breath. "I'm not going to impregnate you."

"Who the hell said anything about getting pregnant?" she demanded, drawing back from him. "I'm on birth control and have condoms in my go-bag. I'm talking about sex, not babies!"

Relief, disappointment and curiosity all flew across his face. "You said you get horny when you heal someone. You also said you need to replenish. So this—" he waved a hand between them "—is a way to do that? Using sex to reenergize?"

"Yes." Hot and smart, damn him. "Each of the Daughters manifests a different aspect of Isis when she reaches puberty. I was expected to have more power than most because I'm the seventh Daughter of a seventh Daughter. I manifested healing early but had no more power than any other Daughter of Isis. Some would say less."

Understanding lit his eyes. "That's why you left your coven."

She nodded, her desire banked. "It wasn't until my sophomore year at college that I realized my second aspect is a more lustful facet of Isis. I tend to channel it as creative energy, fertile feminine energy that acts like a battery and can also serve as inspiration."

"And when the magical battery runs down, you need to recharge it. With sex."

Again she nodded. "That's pretty much it."

He remained silent, though his frown and his grip eased. Finally, he turned her toward the shower. "Go on, take your shower. I'll be back."

"Markus, what the hell?"

"Go." A gentle shove had her just outside the glass door. "I'll be back soon." He left.

Well, then. Stung, Tia discarded her sweaty nightgown and panties, made use of the commode, then toddled her way into the shower. A sigh seeped from her as the warm water sluiced over her sensitized skin. Somehow Markus had set the water to the perfect temperature. Damn him again. How could he be so considerate one moment, fry her senses with an amazing kiss the next and afterward turn around to leave as if his tail was on fire?

The rejection cut, dammit! Granted, it wasn't her best attempt at seduction, but she wasn't usually so...depleted. All right, needy. Tapping her magical reserves was a stupid move on her part, but she couldn't let those jackals continue to suffer. She'd given herself to unraveling the spell just as she'd ignored her empty stomach and exhausted muscles. The least Markus could do was help her gain some of her energy back.

A knock came on the outer door. "Tia?"

Markus. She ignored the little flip of excitement deep in her belly and concentrated on the irritation. She'd been so focused on his rejection she hadn't reached for the soap yet. "I'm not done."

"Good." The door closed, and a dark mass moved beyond

the shower glass, finally resolving itself into Markus. "Have you changed your mind?"

"About healing your men? Of course not."

"Thank you for that. But that's not what I meant."

"Oh, you mean have I changed my mind about you being an ass?"

Warm laughter filtered through the room, sending a delicious shiver up her spine. "I said I'd be back. Speaking of back, why don't I help you scrub yours?"

She wiped at the condensation opaquing the glass. Markus stood just on the other side of the door, perfectly naked and gloriously aroused. Holy mother goddess. "What if I said no?"

He bared his teeth. "Then I'd have to convince you."

It wouldn't take much to convince her, and she knew he knew it. Without another word, she stepped back, giving him room to enter.

Anticipation gripped Markus as he opened the thick glass door, stepping into the steam-filled shower. Magic, desire and appreciation sparked in Tia's eyes, and he couldn't help staring back at her. The thin cotton nightgown she'd worn had done little to conceal her curves, but seeing her lush skin bared to his gaze sharpened his need even more. The dark-tipped nipples that begged for his tongue jutted proudly from lush breasts that perfectly balanced the sweet flare of her hips and thighs. Just like a goddess.

He was one of the remaining few who remembered the days of witches and jackals working together for the purpose their gods had called them to, many living and dying together. He missed that, missed that collective power. He wanted that for himself. Gods, he wanted her.

"Why did you leave before?" she wondered.

"Because if I hadn't, it wouldn't have been about you," he told her. "I would have just taken and not given you anything in return."

Her eyes widened at his blunt statement. "And now?"

The huskiness of her voice sent anticipation spiking through his blood. He reached for the soap. "Now it can be about us. Turn around."

A slow smile curved her lips before she turned, offering her back. Markus soaped his hands then settled his palms on her shoulders. She released a bone-deep sigh, then relaxed. He took his time, working the knots from her shoulders, enjoying the feel of her lather-slicked skin, each ridge of her backbone, the curve of her buttocks.

Gods. He took a deep breath, bringing his will to bear to strengthen the tenuous hold on his control. The lust riding him wanted to immediately lift her so he could feast on her breasts, feel the heat and wetness of her pussy just before he filled her. Just before he fucked her blind.

He'd told the truth about why he'd left her. The need rode him so hard he would have lost control, something he could not allow. Too many people depended on him for him to let go. To feel that wildness for a woman he'd just met—for an Isis witch—was unusual, and hinted at magical influence. Even the few minutes apart from her, clearing his head and securing the compound, he'd felt the hunger for her, the balls-deep ache to take her.

Take her he would, the way he wanted and not the way lust demanded. He turned her back around, running the shea butter soap along her upper body. Her eyes slitted as he cupped her breasts, his thumbs skating over her hardened nipples. Hissing at the sensation, she tilted her head back, soaking her hair beneath the spray. The movement pushed her body against his, chest to chest. It was like brushing up against an electrified fence. His cock bumped against the curve of her belly, blindly seeking entry and he had to bite down hard on his lip to keep from lifting her and shoving inside. He'd been alive for millennia. He wasn't going to spurt like a teen just because a hot woman brushed up against him.

Gritting his teeth, he passed the soap to her, then reached for her hair, pulling off the elastic that held her ponytail, slipping it over his wrist. He loosened the plait then worked shampoo through the strands. She moaned, an earthy sound that tightened his balls, giving him no choice but to cover her mouth with his own. Much hotter than the first kiss because now those magic hands ran along his bare shoulders and arms and back, lathering his skin and setting him afire. Even with the shower pounding into them he could smell her magic and her arousal, blending in an intoxicating scent that called out to him.

"Markus?"

Her hands slipped down, soaping his buttocks. His hips thrust against her in response, and they both moaned aloud. "Yeah?"

"We need to hurry."

"No. It'll be worth the wait." He was hard enough to break rock, desperate to be inside her, but not desperate enough to go there without protection. He rinsed the lather from her hair then exchanged the ponytail holder for the soap, lathering his skin as she secured her hair. Dropping to one knee, he lifted her right foot, placed it on his raised thigh, and began lathering her leg in slow, sure circles. A tremor streaked through her thigh as his fingers stroked higher, but he denied them both the final satisfaction to tend to the other leg.

Her breathing deepened as his fingers rose toward her core once again. This time he didn't stop but stroked his fingers over the crisp hair covering her mound. Her hips slung forward in a silent plea for more. Looking up at her, he rinsed soap from his fingers, then pressed them into her.

Tia groaned aloud as Markus's fingers thrust inside her. She slapped her hands down on his shoulders as her hips bucked, taking his fingers deeper. He retreated then thrust again, his thumb circling her clit. Holding on for dear sweet life, she rode his hand, reaching out with her senses, her magic and her body for everything Markus offered. Pressure built inside her and she welcomed it, knowing release was sure to follow.

Markus rose, pressing her back against the tiled wall, his fingers setting a rapid rhythm that had her moaning his name repeatedly. "Come for me," he growled, slamming his mouth down on hers.

He flexed his fingers deep inside her. Orgasm slammed into her like a bolt of electricity. She cried out, the sound muffled by the bruising kiss. Her pussy clamped down on his fingers, squeezing out another arc of pleasure that left her collapsed against him, breathing heavily.

The absence of gushing water had her lifting her head. Markus had turned the shower off and carried her out of the shower. "Can you stand?"

She wasn't sure. It felt so good to be wrapped around him, her head on his shoulder. Satisfaction purred through her veins, but she needed—wanted—more. She slid down his body, the feel of his erection between them almost unhinging her knees.

He flexed his fingers, a wicked smile curving his lips. "Damn girl, you almost broke my fingers. I can't wait to get my dick inside you."

"Me neither." Unable to resist, she reached out to stroke him. His cock, hot and hard and ready in her hand, made her mouth water with anticipation. "You're beautiful," she whispered, stroking him again.

Groaning, Markus wrapped his fist around hers. He rocked his hips, pushing his cock back and forth through their joined hands several times before stopping. "Gods, we gotta stop," he ordered, his breath harsh. "When I come, I want to be balls-deep inside you, not spurting in your hand like a horny high school kid."

They toweled dry quickly, then he gathered her up again, smothering her with drugging kisses as he strode into the bedroom, tossed her onto the bed. Before she could say anything, he reached into her go-bag, dug around and came up with the carved rosewood box that held her supply of condoms. "Did a little search and seizure, huh?"

"Better safe than sorry, I always say." He joined her on the bed. "Are you sure about this?"

For an answer, she reached down, wrapped her hand around him. "You can't be having doubts with a rager like this?"

He released a shaky sigh. "Trying to do the right thing here. You had a go in the shower."

"That was for the magic," she said, rising up to kiss him. "This is for us."

He didn't argue further, thank Isis, just put the condom on. Once sheathed, he cupped her breasts in his hands. She arched into the stroke of his tongue, the pinch of his fingers, the nip of his teeth as the fire once again raced through her senses. Her hands gripped the covers, her legs moved restlessly, wanting him, needing him inside her. "No torture," she breathed. "You said we were on a truce."

"I'm the one being tortured." He huffed out a laugh. "But I'm all for ceasing hostilities."

"Then I think it's time to come to a resolution."

"Yes, ma'am." He brushed the head of his sheathed cock against her once, twice, then pushed inside.

"Markus." Her breath hitched at the oh-my-goddess fullness. Despite being wet for him, it was slow going as he stretched her.

"Just a little more." He blew out a breath as he finally settled balls deep. "Damn me, that's good."

He withdrew, taking his time, eyes sliding closed against the long, slow glide. Watching pleasure sweep across the harsh planes of his face had her hungering to give him more. Her nails dug into his shoulders at the mind-numbing pleasure as he pressed into her again. Wrapping her legs high around his waist, she was better able to take him, groaning as he slid deeper.

"Tia." He shuddered as he bottomed out. "Control…don't know how long I can take it easy."

Her nails dug harder into his shoulders. "Then don't. Let

go, lose control. Give me everything you've got." She reached up, bit his bottom lip.

Growling against her mouth, he thrust into her with furious intent. Once again her magic rose, reaching out for his power, riding the edge of the passion they generated. As his control shredded, his power rammed into hers, rich, sharp, overwhelming.

Markus shifted, hooking her legs with his arms. The angle drove him deeper and Tia cried out, caught in a cresting wave of ecstasy. His pace increased and he gave a guttural groan, driving into her with wild abandon.

Without warning she broke, shattering as the orgasm burst over her. Screaming her release, she threw her head back, her inner walls clamping down on him.

His eyes burning the color of molten gold, canines elongating and peeking between his full lips, he pounded into her. His thrusting rhythm grew jerky as his muscles bunched then shoved him over. Tia held on as he lifted his head and howled, his body stiffening as he came.

Power surged between them, white-hot arcs that lit the room. The surge fired her synapses, sending aftershocks zinging through her body. Unprepared for the onslaught, she gave herself over to it, trusting Markus to anchor her.

Chapter Five

A while later, Tia staggered out of the bathroom in a borrowed T-shirt to discover that their food had arrived. Heat crept up her cheeks as the perfect timing dawned on her. "I guess it was pretty obvious what we were doing and when we stopped, huh?"

Markus, now wearing a pair of black boxer-briefs that accentuated his sensual gifts, placed the tray of food in the center of the bed. "They have good hearing and didn't scent any blood," he told her, lifting the tray cover to reveal homemade oversized cheeseburgers and home fries. "Since they found me to be mostly in my right frame of mind, albeit slightly dazed, they didn't assume the worst."

With her magic recharged, hunger reasserted itself. She fell on the food with gusto, barely pausing for sips of sweet tea between bites of home fries. "Please tell whoever made this, thank you from the bottom of my heart!" she exclaimed, licking her fingers. "I think that's the best burger I've ever had in my entire life!"

Markus laughed again, activating her senses. "That appetite would do any jackal proud. I'll pass on the compliments."

Tia glanced up from her almost-empty plate, and forgot

about her food. Markus had stretched out along the foot of the bed, the epitome of masculine grace and power. She'd never seen abs like those up close and personal before. Honestly, she'd never had any man as gorgeous and full of prowess as Markus. It was obvious that he'd learned a thing or two over his long life.

He gave her a knowing smile. "That last bit of fries is going to get cold."

"Not likely." She scooped up the last crumb, then wiped her hands on the fingertip towel. Another myth about jackals burned to dust. They had structure, took care of each other, had the means to have a facility large enough to house them and build a luxury suite for their leader. Not a bare step above wild dogs as she'd been taught. "I was just thinking."

He stilled, caution filling his gaze. "About what?"

"Witches and jackals. Asharet and her mate."

"Sekhanu. Leader of the Sons of Anubis at that time."

"You knew them well?"

He nodded. "Since he and Asharet had no sons and I'd lost my father in a battle with the Lost Ones, Sekhanu adopted me. He groomed me to take his place, though we both figured that would be centuries later."

"What was he like?" She curled against the headboard, eager to learn more. "What was Asharet like?"

A smile lit his features. "She was amazing. Tiny by today's standards, but the power she wielded—both in magic and personality—drew everyone to her. Including Sekhanu."

Food forgotten, he stared into space. "As for Sekhanu, he was amazing, too. Jackals are solitary by nature, though family groups tend to stay together. Even though we were united in our calling to serve Anubis, most of our skirmishes were one family group against a clutch of the undead, or solitary hunters keeping the peace through wits. Sekhanu was the first to unite the jackals under a supreme commander, to help us see the benefits of organizing and making us a stronger, more cohesive unit. Meturare was high priest of the Cult of Anubis and remained our spiritual leader. Together they made us nearly invincible against the Lost Ones."

"What about Asharet? How did she and Sekhanu meet?"

"Asharet was already high priestess of the Daughters of Isis," he explained. "Usually she dealt with Meturare but Sekhanu wanted to form a closer alliance and make sure the witches were properly protected. He felt that if an enemy rose against the Sons for uniting, the Daughters would be vulnerable."

They had been, according to Tia's grandmother, Aya. They'd lost a third of their coven sisters the day they'd lost Asharet.

"I don't know if it was love at first sight," Markus went on. "Sekhanu never spoke of softer things like that, but he was taken with Asharet. She had power and beauty to go with it, balanced by a keen mind and a giving heart. Sekhanu always said she was his toughest challenge and his greatest conquest."

He packed up the remnants of their meal. "They showed us how jackals and witches could work together, to forge greater power and protections together. With them leading us, we were able to protect the land from the Lost Ones for five generations. And then the night of blood came."

"When Asharet and Sekhanu died."

A sharp nod. "An outbreak of Lost Ones rising in the desert near Saqqara had me away from home for several days. When I returned, the deed was done—the temples destroyed, our leader and priestess dead, our priest missing, our allies became our enemies. The undead we fought, they were different. Not mindless creatures intent on taking from the living but focused, thinking beings that attacked as if they'd been combat-trained."

"Do you think they were soldiers who retained some of their humanity?"

"Yes, and gained new abilities. I also believe the uprising was a deliberate ploy to remove a large number of Sons so that the temples—and Sekhanu and Asharet—were unprotected."

Guilt drenched his tone, and she reacted to it. "You couldn't have known what would happen. You did your duty as you've always done. Sekhanu and Asharet were powerful, you just said so. They wouldn't have fallen easily."

"No. But fall they did." He fisted his hands. "The least I could have done was die defending them."

Rising to her knees, she reached out and wrapped her fingers around his bicep needing to touch him, to offer some sort of solace. "What good would that have done, versus the good you've done since? Your clan has survived because of you. I think Asharet and Sekhanu would prefer this to your death."

He snorted, shaking off his sour mood. "Defended by an Isis witch. Who would have thought?"

He gathered their plates and tray and placed them on the dresser. "We have a common enemy, Tia. Someone powerful enough to command the Lost Ones and secretly betray both the Sons of Anubis and the Daughters of Isis. I have thought on this for years. Every jackal I have considered capable of that level of treachery I have discounted. I can only believe the threat came from an Isis witch."

Tia sank back down on the bed. She didn't want to believe that. How could she begin to consider that a distant coven sister had set off a chain of events that created a four-millennia-old blood feud? She knew her circle had a single-minded respect for power—her own supposed lack had been impetus for her to become a solitary practitioner. Still, she couldn't imagine anyone wanting to overthrow Aya, still a powerful high priestess. If Asharet was even more so, wouldn't that make her even less vulnerable? Surely if a Daughter of Isis was responsible for Asharet's death, Aya would have known and done something about it.

Tia rubbed her forehead with her palms in sudden fatigue and frustration. "I don't know anyone capable of that. I don't think Aya does, either."

"Think, Tia! Think of all the Daughters that you know. One of them has to know more about the night of blood. Someone,

one of the survivors, had to have seen something, or have suspicions of who would want Asharet destroyed!"

"I don't know, Marcus, all right? I don't know!"

They stared at each other for an electrified moment. Finally, Markus scrubbed a hand over his head. "I'm sorry. I've spent centuries on this mystery, coming close but never getting answers. The Lost Ones have gained in strength and numbers while the Sons of Anubis are threatened now more than ever. Even if I can't defeat the undead once and for all, it would end the conflict with the Daughters of Isis and return us to being the allies we once were."

Sincerity rang in every word he spoke and Tia found herself wavering, wanting to believe him, wanting to trust him. Wanting to do anything to erase the pain and weariness that tarnished his golden eyes.

"I'll talk to my grandmother," she offered. "I'll take your message to the Elder Sisters and the circle. If the threat is as great as you say, it would be stupid for our people to keep being at each other's throats."

His expression lightened. "I didn't think Isis witches like you existed anymore."

"I'm not all that special." Bitterness filled her mouth. "As far as my circle is concerned, I failed to live up to my promise or my potential. Nobody begged me to stay when I left. Even Grandmother Aya thought it was a good idea to go. The Elders might not let me speak to the full coven."

His touch to her shoulder surprised her. So did the compassion in his eyes. "Their loss is the jackals' gain. You promised to help my people and you have lived up to that potential. Maybe it was the will of the gods, you leaving your circle. After all, if you were still with your coven, you wouldn't be here now."

She arched a brow at him. "And that's supposed to be a good thing?"

At least he had the good grace to look chagrinned, even if

he didn't mean it. "For the record, I'm sorry I didn't offer you the choice to help us."

Her heart did another flip in her chest. "For the record, I don't know if I would have agreed to come with you or not," she confessed, something loosening inside her.

He smiled. "I would have taken you anyway. In this case especially, the ends justify the means. Still, it would have been gentlemanly to have offered."

It was so ridiculous she had to laugh, though her laughter quickly disintegrated into a jaw-cracking yawn. With a full belly and restored magic, sleep now asserted its hold. "Nice to know there's a gentleman inside there somewhere. I feel so much better now." She yawned again as she crawled beneath the covers.

"Talk about being gentlemanly." He shook his head in self-disgust. "You needed sleep."

"I needed the food and the sex more." She slid down deeper into the bed, her eyes sliding closed. Egyptian cotton sheets atop a mattress that molded to her body threatened to pull her under immediately. "But, yeah, it's catching up to me."

"Then get some rest. I'll come back in a few hours and we can start the healing rituals for Alonso and Rashon again."

"Come back?" she echoed, blinking at him. "Isn't this your room?"

"It is." He proved it by grabbing a pair of jeans out of a dresser drawer.

"Why don't you stay?" At his surprised glance, she held up her hands. "I promise not to kill you in your sleep."

"As if." He tossed the jeans onto the dresser. "Even if you did, you'd still have to get past the jackals guarding the hall, and we're all trained to grieve later, avenge now, no matter who falls. We have agreed to a truce, though, and after what we just shared, I'm inclined to trust you."

She snorted. "Gee, thanks."

"I should warn you, I am not a restless sleeper, but I don't usually share my bed."

"Same here." She yawned again, her jaw cracking with the force of it as she wiggled into a perfect spot. "Call me crazy—and everything about the last day or however long it's been has been the definition of crazy—but I think I'd feel better if you were here."

The surprise that lifted his dark brows was the last thing she saw before her eyes slid shut and she tumbled down deep into slumber.

Markus awoke to the best sensation a man could experience: a warm, wet mouth swallowing his cock. He fumbled for the lamp on the nightstand, tapped it on. "Tia, what are you doing?"

She rolled her eyes at him.

"I mean, I know what you're doing, but why are you doing it?" *Are you stupid, man? A beautiful woman is going down on you. Shut the hell up and enjoy it.*

She pulled off him with a wet popping sound that was the most erotic thing he'd ever heard. "It was poking me in the back. Since it so obviously needed attention, I decided to give it some."

"Blessed Anubis, woman." His hips rose as she swallowed him again. Lust and magic increased, a heady combination he could easily grow addicted to. Probably already was. If this was what being enchanted by an Isis witch meant, he'd gladly surrender to it.

Sex for pleasure's sake was foreign to him. Throughout the long years of their exile, the jackals' intimate habits had been focused on survival, and survival meant building their numbers. Every sensual act with the opposite sex was considered a sacred and deliberate thing, always begun with a prayer to Anubis.

This was...freeing. Wildness rose in him, the primal call of male to female. Curling his fingers into the sheets, he gave himself over to sensation. When Tia's fingers cupped his balls, he nearly whimpered but couldn't keep silent when her tongue traced over his sac. Buffeted by the need raging through him, he groaned aloud, helpless against the sensual magic she wove.

All too soon he could feel it, the urge to come surging up from his toes. No, gods damn it! Not yet. "Tia."

Relief and disappointment met as she pulled her sweet mouth away. "Yeah?"

He struggled for words as her fingers stroked him. "Condom. On me. Now."

Her throaty chuckle almost undid him. She crawled to the head of the bed, dropping a searing kiss on him before reaching for one of the foil packets on the nightstand. Thank Isis she had a whole box of them in her go-bag.

She straddled his thighs, dark eyes fixed on him as she tore the pouch open with her teeth. Fingers wrapping around his cock, she stroked him, strong, steady pulls with a twist over the head just the way he liked it but made better by her touch, her magic. His cock swelled anew, hard for her, hungry for her.

"Ride me," he demanded as she sheathed him. His fingers dug into her hips, muscles flexing as he lifted her. "Ride me."

She reached between them to guide his hardness to her opening, dragging his sheathed cock along her slit to coat it in her wetness. Keeping her gaze locked to his, she sank down even as he thrust up, fusing them together.

She threw her head back on a groan, the dusky copper of her nipples capturing his gaze. "Gods, that feels incredible. I can barely breathe." She squeezed him.

He let her go, digging his fingers into the sheets again in an effort to hold back, to wrestle for a shred of control. The fabric ripped as his nails elongated.

Her eyes rounded. "Are you shifting?"

"No." He mangled the word, his sharpened teeth getting in the way.

She smiled at him, a light sparking in her eyes. "My, what big teeth you have," she teased. "Like a big, bad wolf."

"Jackal," he ground out. "Desert dog. Not a wolf. Don't play."

Tia gave another throaty chuckle, obviously reveling in her sensual power. Tension coiled in Markus like an over-tightened wire, ready to snap with just the right touch. He needed release, needed to free himself of the pressure that threatened to consume him. She could do that for him.

"So I can't talk about the other big parts you have?" She rose, slowly sank back down on him, then did it again, inner muscles tightening around him and driving him sensually insane.

He growled as he clamped his clawed hands around her waist. "No talk. Fuck now." With that, he took the brakes off his control, driving up into her with rapid-fire strokes.

This! This was what Tia wanted, what she needed from him. Groaning with pleasure, she leaned over him, her nails sinking into his shoulders as she matched his frenetic pace.

He rolled his hips, igniting a wave of pure primal pleasure in her. She reached down, fingertips brushing over the spot where he speared her. His nostrils flared and he seemed to thicken inside her, his eyes burning with power. Riding his cock, she stroked her clit, driving pleasure even higher. She arched backward, his massive hands on her waist keeping her upright. She could feel his power, her power, rising between them, riding the crest of an ecstasy so sharp, so potent, she couldn't do anything but cry out, her body a rigid arc of pleasure.

A vision slipped through the haze of passion, Isis reviving the slain Osiris. Magic suffused the goddess, a white-gold glow that Tia could almost feel. She opened her hands, her body and her senses, reaching out for the offering.

Magic and orgasm struck each other like atoms, exploding behind her eyes in a massive burst of pleasure. She cried out again, her body burning, feeling as if her skin were too fragile to contain it. Then she could feel Marcus, feel his strength and his power wrap around her as he surged into her one final time, shouting as he came.

Chapter Six

A long while later, they quit the bed and dressed. Still trembling from the effects of her vision and her orgasm, Tia pulled a long white cotton sundresses from her bag. She smoothed the fabric down over her curves, then held her hands up. "I feel...different."

Markus zipped up his jeans then crossed to her. His nostrils flared as he scented her. "You smell different. There's more magic flowing through you than before. And your eyes—I can see swirls of power in your eyes."

Tia trembled as goose bumps broke out over her body. "Great Mother Isis, She who is the Throne, guide me," she whispered. "Show me your favor as you favored Anubis when you claimed him as your Son. Show me how to heal the jackal warriors."

She closed her eyes as warmth enveloped her, the presence of both gods filling the room. "Markus, we need to go."

She pulled open the door, stepping into the hallway. Jackals, drawn by the power surge, flooded the corridor.

"It's all right," Markus said, but Tia could hear uncertainty in his voice. The magic was a potent living thing, reaching

out, invigorating everything it passed. Even the depictions of
the gods on the walls seemed more vibrant, alive. "Let her
through."

They made their way to the holding room. Hector was already beside his brother while one of their few female jackals,
stood just outside Rashon's cage.

Markus snarled. "What are you doing here, Amarie? You
know full well I ordered all children and females to remain
sequestered until further notice.""Forgive me for disobeying
you, sir," she said, her words tumbling together. "They said he
was getting better and I wanted to see, but he's not, his fangs
are showing. I thought she cured..." her voice faded as she
stared at Tia. "Goddess."

"She's here with us," Tia said, placing her hand on Markus's
bicep. His anger at Amarie's disobedience dissipated. "She
hasn't abandoned us."

Markus followed her into the cage, dismay written on his
face to see that Rashon's condition had worsened.

A partial shift misshaped his face, fangs protruded from
his upper lips and a gray pallor dusted his sunken cheeks. The
odd scent of what could only be the Lost Ones mixed with
Daughters of Isis flooded her nose.

"Tia?" Markus asked.

Tia knelt beside the cot. Webs of dark magic surrounded
Rashon's body, digging deeper into the jackal's spirit. He was
fighting it though, fighting it with everything he had.

She reached out, touched a fingertip to a thick cord of the
strands. Several reached out, wrapping around her wrist, seeking her veins. She could feel the pulse of Isis magic coated and
twisted with the decay of the Lost Ones. The two should have
repelled each other but didn't. How was it possible?

"What are you doing?" Markus hissed. "I can smell the
curse on you now."

"It's trying to infect me, but it can't," she assured him.
"It's a blend of the undead and Isis magic, twined together

into something new. It's fast-spreading and insidious, like the kudzu vines that overtake everything nearby."

"Can you stop it?"

"We can stop it," she corrected. "I didn't sense the undead power before, but I recognize it now. I can stop the part of the curse that has twisted Isis's gift, and you can stop the undead magic."

"Tell me what to do."

She smiled up at him, grateful for his presence, his strength and his courage. "Put your hands on me. Our magics will connect again. We'll draw the curse out and split the two components apart, then destroy them. When I ask, you'll have to force Rashon into his jackal shape to burn off the last vestiges of the curse."

Markus knelt behind her, his knees flanking hers, his heat and bulk comforting and already familiar and needed. He settled his hands on her shoulders. At once, her magic reached out for his, found it and clasped it to her.

A shudder passed through the gathered jackals. "Blessed Anubis," someone whispered. "That power...it's amazing."

Tia agreed. She'd never felt power as pure and full and capable as this. This gloriousness must have been what had drawn Sekhanu and Asharet together, and had ultimately cost their lives. To always be able to feel this vital, this connected—who wouldn't want it?

"I can see it now." Markus's voice cut through her thoughts. "It's everywhere, just like that damned vine. Let's uproot this crap."

Pushing out negative thoughts, Tia combined their magics then reached out with both hands, grabbing fistfuls of the cursed strands that strangled Rashon's life force. The jackal cried out as she pulled, but Markus reached out with his own power, lending the younger man his strength and force of will.

Extricating the curse was just like weeding, with the curse the invasive vine and the jackal's body the fertile soil. Years of tending her own garden gave her the insight and plan of attack. Markus's magic buttressed hers, giving her the energy she needed.

Still the curse was as tenacious as any weed, refusing to give up easily. It took even more effort to unravel the twisted magic into its separate parts. The undead energy took solid form as they pulled it free of Rashon's weakened form. Several jackals shifted and attacked, shredding the undead mist into nothingness with claws and teeth. She drew the Isis magic into herself, using the golden glow of the goddess's favor to purify it.

"I think it's all gone," Tia said after a while, lifting her hands free of the ill jackal. "You can force him into his jackal form now."

Markus moved until they knelt hip to hip beside the cot. Tia rested a hand on his shoulder, lending some of her magic to him. Not that he needed it. Markus splayed his right hand across Rashon's chest, covering his heart. He spoke to Rashon in the old tongue, command ringing in his voice. Soft golden light suffused the young jackal's body, warming as his body magically changed shape. When the glow faded, an oversized dun-colored jackal lay on the cot.

Amarie gripped the bars. "Is he...?"

"Sleeping," Markus answered. "He's sleeping."

Tia felt a minute tremor pass through Markus. "Rashon's no longer contagious and could do well with a warm soak in a healing bath and rest in a comfortable bed," she told him. "Is there a place here he could sleep?"

"Yes." He gestured to the burly male jackal beside Amarie. The large man entered the cage and scooped up the sleeping jackal with surprising gentleness. "I'm coming with you," the female jackal said, tears glistening in her eyes. She quickly followed the others out.

"Priestess!" Hector called from the other cell. "Come quick."

Tia hurried over to the other cell. Alonso had apparently worsened, as well. Hector had his brother's clawed hand in a death grip. "He's fighting for every breath. I don't know how much longer he's going to last." He looked up at them with red-rimmed eyes. "Please save him."

Markus turned to Tia, hoping for a second miracle. They couldn't afford the loss of another jackal. Their numbers had dwindled over the centuries, especially after separating into smaller groups in a clandestine diaspora. He wasn't a man who begged, but he would demand. She had to save Alonso because nothing else was allowed.

They knelt beside the cot as they had beside Rashon's. "The curse has burrowed deeper," Tia told him. "It's beginning to choke the life from his cells."

"No." He would not allow Alonso to die. "What do we do?"

"What we were born to do, Son of Anubis." She covered his hands with her own. Magic drenched the room like a sudden summer shower, carried by the power of her Voice. "You protect the living from the Lost Ones. Alonso is one of the living. Death should not have command of him. Put death in its place and I will call on Isis to give him the energy of life."

Trusting Tia, Markus shifted his hands into claws. The curse covered Alonso like a mass of black snakes, writhing and burrowing. Calling his power, Markus sunk his claws into the seething mass. Alonso howled, his misshapen body jerking.

Hector leaned over his brother, a growl rolling from deep in his chest. "You're hurting him."

"The curse has invaded every part of his body," Tia explained, her voice equally soft and ringing with power. "It's not going to give up without a fight, but neither will we. No fight can be won without pain, but when we win, his pain will cease. After all, we have the gods on our side."

Her obvious faith overrode any doubts Hector had. He nodded at her, then pressed his forehead to his brother's, closing his eyes in silent prayer. Tia began chanting a prayer of life, then nodded to Markus to continue.

Once again Markus reached for the curse coiling around

every cell in Alonso's body. The coils were tenacious, requiring all of his strength to pull free. Handful by handful, he dragged the curse out of the young jackal, cursing and praying under his breath. Reaching for his will and his magic, Markus shifted even more of his body, felt the deep, low thrum of Anubis magic, the magic of his clan. Felt Tia on the periphery, offering the gift of Isis.

Strand by strand Markus pulled the curse apart, sending the undead portion to his jackals to shred and the corrupted Isis witch magic to Tia to purify. He didn't think about the ache in his shoulders, the headache blossoming between his eyes, or how much time had passed. All he could think of was ridding Alonso of the curse, of Tia bolstering him with her power. He wondered if Sekhanu and Asharet had faced a trial such as this while he'd been out fighting in other parts of the Two Lands. If they had, they'd never had the chance to share the details with him. Would they be proud of their descendant, of how they'd set aside their distrust to save the jackals? He had a feeling they would be.

"Markus." Tia's soft voice broke into his thoughts. "The curse is gone. Shift Alonso to his jackal form to heal."

A healthy glow limned the young jackal's features, his breathing deep and even. As before, Markus splayed his hand across Alonso's chest and spoke the ancient command Sekhanu had taught him to send subordinate jackals into their animal forms. His shift took longer than Rashon's, but soon enough, a sable-colored jackal lay on the cot.

Markus sat back on his haunches, hope, exhaustion and euphoria spinning in his gut. "It's gone, right? I don't sense any traces of the curse nearby."

She tilted her head, the swirls of power in her eyes fading. "It should be completely gone. If you and your clan anoint yourself with the potions we used yesterday—was it yesterday?—before your fights with the Lost Ones, and use the ritual cleansing afterward, you should have no more troubles."

Using his shoulder for leverage, she pushed herself to her

feet. "I can write down everything you need, but since you'll need blessings from a Daughter of Isis, it'll just be easier for me to make batches of it at my house."

Her words punched a hole in his euphoria. Right. She'd healed the jackals as she'd promised, and now it was time for him to live up to his end of the bargain.

"Of course." He rose to his feet, irked when she grabbed his elbow to help him. He pulled away. "I'm fine."

"You expended a lot of energy," she reminded him. "You probably should shift to recuperate, too."

He brushed her concern aside. "As alpha, I've got larger reserves than that. I suppose you need to recuperate the usual way?"

The glow left her eyes. "No. I don't have any large magical works on my plate after this. A few days' rest and I should be fine...."

She swayed, and he scooped her up in his arms, holding her high against his chest. If the limpness of her body was any indication, breaking the curse for Rashon and Alonso had taken more power than she'd let on. Brave, foolish witch.

"How's Alonso?" Markus asked Hector.

Hector ran his hand over his brother's fur. "Sleeping peacefully for the first time in days, thank the gods."

"Good. Get him out of here and into a real bed, okay? The last thing he should see when he wakes up are these damned bars."

"You bet." Hector looked up, eyes shining. "How's our healer?"

Markus dropped his gaze to Tia, barely refraining from lowering his head to brush his lips across her temples. "She's not our healer," he retorted, his voice harsher than called for. "In fact, I'm going to honor our agreement and take her back home today."

"Take her back?" Hector repeated. "Why?"

Markus didn't feel like explaining something that wouldn't

sound rational, so he ignored Hector's question. "Any activity around her house?"

Hector bared his teeth. "The men report that no one's been there in the two days that she's been with us. If that's the concern the Daughters of Isis show to one of their own, one who happens to be the granddaughter of their high priestess, then Tia would be better off with us!"

Markus gritted his teeth to keep from agreeing with his second. "She's not staying here."

"Why not? We need her more than they do."

Just like Markus needed her more than his fellow jackals did. He didn't share that with Hector, however. "I made a deal with her, and I'm going to keep it. I swore on the gods that she'd go home after she healed our people. She's done that, and now it's time to send her back to her life. We are the Sons of Anubis. We hold to our duty and our honor when all else falls to dust."

Honor and duty were all that had kept him alive—kept them all alive—through the centuries. It wouldn't fill the emptiness in his bed or his soul, but it was all that he had. He would hold on to it with all his might.

Chapter Seven

Sensing that Tia hovered on the verge of regaining consciousness, Markus shifted back to his human form. Dressing quickly and quietly, he sat down on the far corner at the foot of the bed and waited for her to wake up.

She stirred, stretching her limbs and rubbing the sleep from her eyes. He watched her stiffen as she realized where she was. "Bastard could have said goodbye!"

He chuffed out a laugh. "You mean me?"

Startled, she sat up, turning to face him. "You're still here—and here is my place."

He nodded, taking in her sleep-tousled appearance. She looked good, warm, perfect for tucking up next to on a cold night. Or a hot night. Or any night, for that matter. "I thought you'd feel better getting back to your own space. Since you haven't had a chance to rebuild your wards, I decided to watch over you until you woke up."

"I appreciate that." She smoothed a hand over her hair. "How long was I down for?"

"Roughly three hours. How do you feel?"

"Like I need the bathroom." She gave him a sidelong glance. "Will you still be here when I come out?"

"Yeah."

While waiting for her to reemerge, he perused her room again. It was the exact opposite of his: Light and airy; the colors of sun, sand and sea. Warm and modern, just like the woman who lived here.

He ran his hand across the spot Tia had occupied. Something had tugged at him as he'd tucked her into her own bed and climbed in beside her, and he was pretty sure it wasn't the remnants of her wards. Snuggling up next to her even in jackal form had been...soothing. He'd felt relaxed, at ease, and not because his men were stationed outside. Waking next to her, breathing in her scent and her life essence, had filled him with a peace he hadn't felt in centuries.

"Now I feel ordinary." She reentered the room, spreading her hands. "It was so amazing, feeling Isis so close, so loving. I could even feel Anubis, through you. Now I'm back to plain old ordinary me."

He stared at her, his gaze lingering on her lovely curves. "You'll never be ordinary, Tia."

Sadness rimmed her smile. "That's the problem, isn't it? I'm a Daughter of Isis." A sigh lifted her shoulders. "You brought me back home just as stealthily as you took me. Guess that tells me all I need to know. Our truce is over and I'm back to being the enemy."

Regret settled like a lead weight in his gut. "Tia." He bit back the words he wanted to say but couldn't. "You're not our enemy, Tia. You healed Rashon and Alonso. Both are doing fine and my clan has joy again. The Sons of Anubis owe you a great debt."

"You don't owe me anything, Markus," she said softly. "Despite how we started, I'm glad I was able to help. Discovering something about my history and my power in the process was pure bonus."

Her gaze pierced him. "So what happens next?"

"I programmed my number into your phone. Call me when there's word from the Daughters or if you have a need."

"I have a need now."

"Oh, yeah. You expended a lot of magic yesterday. Of course you need to replenish."

She walked over to stand in front of him. "No. This isn't about replenishing my magic."

Something in her tone made him pause. "What is it about then, Tia?"

"It's about you and me." She met his gaze for a long moment before looking away. "I need you."

The soft words cut through him, sounding an echo. He'd done his duty for thousands of years, growing and protecting his clan. Relaxing his vigilance, being selfish, for even a moment, could have deadly consequences. Here now, with this woman, with this Isis witch, he wanted to be selfish. He wanted something for himself.

He wanted her.

Something inside him, something buried deep, stirred, struggling to claw itself to the surface. Whatever it was, he would not set it free. Not now. Not ever. He had a duty to his clan that superseded all else.

She stepped forward, cupped his cheek. "Markus. The magic we made—I've never felt anything like that before. Ever. But besides all that, we are good together. Forget about witches and jackals and the Lost Ones. Think about you and me, a man and a woman. Let's just pretend for a little while that that's all there is."

"Don't you think I want to?" He surged to his feet, curling his hands into fists. "Thousands of years of doing my duty, of making sure my race survives, that our clans thrive. Even sex was about increasing our numbers, not about giving and receiving pleasure. If I relax my guard, if I focus on anything other than my duty to my people, I put my people in danger."

"So what—that's it? You spend so much of your time making sure your people stay alive that you don't have time to get a life?" She settled her hands on her hips. "Look, I know we didn't have the best of beginnings. If there's anyone who should be saying 'good riddance,' it's me."

She thrust a hand through her hair with a sigh. "Maybe I'm crazy. Maybe I've got some sort of Stockholm syndrome or something. Or maybe I'm just addicted to your magic cock. Don't know, don't care. What I do know is that I want more of you, whatever I can get for as long as I can get it. I want to feel you on me, in me, wrapped around me. I want—"

Markus snatched her up against him, crushing her tight in a bruising kiss. She threw her arms around his neck, kissing him back with hungry intent. Growling, he grabbed her skirt, hiking it up her thighs so he could cup her ass. She responded by locking her gorgeous legs around his waist. Tongues dueled, breathing harshened, need rose as she pulled his shirt off over his head.

With lengthening claws, he grabbed two handfuls of her dress and ripped. "Tell me that wasn't a ritual robe," he muttered against her lips.

"No. Just a dress." She nipped at the tendons along his neck.

"Good gods, woman." Without ceremony, he tossed her back on the bed. Keeping his gaze locked to hers, he quickly shed the rest of his clothing. Careful not to scratch her, he wrapped his fingers around her white cotton panties and jerked. The material shredded around his claws. He tossed them over his shoulder, then dropped atop her, bracing his weight on his forearms.

He nipped his way down her throat, lingering over her collarbone before dipping into the hollow between her breasts. Her scent rose to infiltrate his senses, as sweet and spicy as the finest incense. His mouth watered as he dragged his tongue along her skin, feasting on her breasts. Every day, every hour, every gods-damned minute, he could spend tasting her, and it still wouldn't be enough.

"Open for me, beautiful one," he urged, kissing and nipping his way down the soft curve of her belly. "Let me have more of you."

Her legs fell apart for him, revealing the dark rose pink of her core. He dipped his tongue inside her, a long, slow lick that had her mewling. He swirled his tongue through her folds, circling her clit, needing her taste, needing her pleasure with a bone-deep hunger. *More.*

Tia thrust her hands into Markus's hair as he raided her senses with lips and teeth and tongue. Wanting him as she did, needing him as she did, it wasn't long before she felt the sweet tidal wave of pleasure sweeping through her blood. It smashed through her pitiful defenses and swept her into a maelstrom of orgasm.

She cried out, then cried out again as he surged up her body and lanced into her in one thick thrust. She saw the wide golden glow of his eyes just before he lowered his head and kissed her into oblivion. This was all about wild, primitive, sweat and sex and sensation.

She wanted to claim him. The urge burned within her as she clutched his shoulders, as he powered into her over and over again. Each thrust, each retreat seemed to say *mine*, *mine*, *mine*, and she echoed the sentiment. She wanted to give him everything, even without knowing if he would accept it.

Her teeth dug into his shoulder as passion broke her apart yet again. He shuddered, groaning, then pulled out of her. Still reeling from her second orgasm, Tia barely registered Markus turning her, pushing her to her knees.

He skimmed a shaky hand down her back. "Tia," he whispered, her name rough and broken-sounding on his lips. "Tia."

"I'm here." She scrunched her eyes shut against an unexpected flood of tears that surged over her bared emotions. "Take it," she demanded, pushing back against him. "Take it now."

He fit his still-hard cock against her swollen labia, then slowly glided inside her. Her name, a mixture of prayer and plea, fell from his lips again. Slowly he withdrew and just as slowly returned, as if wanting to commit every minute sensation of penetration to memory.

The frenzied coupling had broken her apart; this slow, intent glide of flesh in flesh threatened to completely undo her. She knew that this time was for him, him to savor and enjoy and commit to memory. Arms and legs shook as her nerve endings sang, as body, magic, mind and heart reached for him.

"Markus." She called his name on a sob as she fell off the precipice again, her muscles tightening around him. Only then did he increase his pace to a steady rhythmic thumping, burying himself to the root each time he rocked into her. His fingers dug into her hips as he stiffened against her, a deep, guttural moan escaping him as he finally came.

Her legs buckled. He tightened an arm around her waist, guiding her down with his chest pressed to her back. Holding her close, he pressed his forehead against her back, chest heaving as he struggled to regain his breath. She wondered if he was as shaken as she was. She'd changed—he'd changed her, and she wasn't sure how she'd manage if she couldn't see him again.

It was a long while later before she turned over to face him. Shadows lurked in his amber eyes, shadows she hadn't seen before. Her fingers brushed along his jaw. "Tell me what you're thinking."

His lips twisted in a rueful take on a smile. "Impossible things."

"Please tell me."

He focused on her. "Why?"

"Because I hope it's what I'm thinking, what I'm feeling. I don't want to be alone in this."

The sigh he released seemed to take all his strength with it. He pressed his forehead against hers and sighed again. "I'm losing my mind. Or you've bespelled me. There's no way I should be thinking of wanting to take you back with me."

Her heart leaped, then sank as his words registered. "Because I'm a witch."

"Because you're an Isis witch." He rubbed his cheek against hers. "We've been enemies for millennia."

"Before that we were allies," she reminded him. "And I did heal your clan brothers. I'd like to think that you and I, at least, can bury our differences."

"Yes." He nuzzled her throat. "I know. But whoever stands beside me will lead the jackals with me. Can you align yourself with the Sons of Anubis, Tia? Can you give up the Daughters to be with me?"

"I don't know," she hedged. "I don't know if I'm talking about forever or a year or a week. All I know is I want to try. Surely that's something."

He didn't budge, damn him. "Will they let you be with me, Tia? What if they refuse to condone us? Can you turn away from the Daughters of Isis?"

"They're my family, Markus," she whispered past a tight throat.

"A family that cast you out."

"I know." Tears pricked her eyes. "But they're still my family. I can't turn my back on them. My grandmother is still there, and I—I want to go back someday."

He quit her bed to get dressed, and she dug her fingers into the sheet to keep from reaching for him. She'd made her case; she wouldn't beg.

Once dressed, he turned to face her. "I've got to go."

"I know. Jackals to drill, Lost Ones to hunt, all that." She slid from the bed, reaching for her gold silk robe draped over the nearby chair. She followed him through the kitchen to the back door. Obviously he didn't want anyone to witness a jackal leave an Isis witch's house.

Bitter regret rose in her throat, harsh and acidic. Trying for nonchalance, she shrugged her shoulders. "Oh, well. Maybe the one good thing that comes out of this is peace between jackals and witches. If so, I'll count that as a win."

"So will I."

"Yeah, well." She wrapped her arms across her belly. "Once

there's some distance between us, I'm sure we'll both get back to normal pretty quickly."

"Normal. Yeah." He turned to her, golden eyes dark. "Tia—"

"Don't. Just don't, okay?" She took a deep breath, then kissed him on the cheek. "Have a good life, Markus, Son of Anubis."

With a hand to his chest, she gently pushed him out the door, then closed it.

Chapter Eight

After a long hot shower and an equally long hot cry, Tia dressed and braced herself to check her phone. A handful of messages from her grandmother, and two texts from a client greeted her as she reset the Smartphone. She deleted them, thankful that she'd only missed one appointment in the time she'd spent with the jackals. Promising her client a free session as an apology would work. She hoped. At that moment though, she couldn't think about work. She could only think about jackals and witches.

She wasn't going to give up. Markus would come around to her point of view, realize that what they had together was way better than being apart. If she could get the Daughters to agree to a truce, one huge obstacle would be gone. She didn't know if being with Markus would fail or fly, but she was certain failing would be better than not trying at all.

Her hand trembled as she placed the call to her grandmother. "Tia! Where have you been? I could sense you expending a great amount of magical energy, but couldn't pinpoint where you were."

"I had an emergency." She paused, taking a steadying breath. "With the Sons of Anubis."

"Oh." Silence on the other end.

"Oh?" She'd never known her grandmother to be at a loss for words, not once in all the time she'd known her. "Is that all you can say? You've taught me all of our spells, all of our rituals and prayers, but you've never once told me the story of Asharet and Sekhanu. Your parents."

"I know." A sigh crossed the line. "Believe it or not, I had my reasons, Tia. Now, I think, it's finally time you know them. We need to talk."

"Yes, we do." Tia cleared her throat. "Grandmother, do you remember who told you about Asharet's death?"

"Tia." Centuries-old pain filled her grandmother's voice. "Do we really have to go into this now?"

"Please, Nana, it's important. How did you get the news?"

"One of mother's priestesses ran to our house, covered in dirt and blood. Amansuanan, I think. She said that jackals attacked the temple, killing my mother, our high priestess. I might have been twelve at the time, about to enter service myself. I gathered the remaining priestesses and fled."

"What happened to Amansuanan? I don't think I've ever met her."

"No, you wouldn't have. We lost her centuries ago, shortly after we crossed the sea. Why do you ask this?"

"Because Markus said he returned from a campaign to find Asharet and Sekhanu dead together, as if defending each other and the temple of Isis. He seemed to think witches were the cause. Just as he thinks the Daughters are behind the curse afflicting his people."

"Does he now?" Aya asked, acid creeping into her tone. "Can't say that I'm surprised."

Belatedly Tia wondered if her grandmother had been involved with Markus sometime during the last four thousand years. Ew. Surely he would have said something. "He's not the only one, Nana," she said, keeping her voice free of accusation. "When I examined the jackals, I could feel Isis magic. It had been twisted, perverted by Lost Ones."

"Lost Ones?" Aya's voice sharpened. "Isis magic tainted with the undead? Mother of Horus!"

"It's something to be worried about, isn't it?" Tia asked. "If the Lost Ones have gained in strength and power, the Daughters of Isis could be their next target. Markus asked me to ask you to agree to a meeting to discuss a permanent truce and a new alliance against a common enemy, the Lost Ones."

"This jackal presumes much."

"What the jackals want makes sense," Tia answered. The Daughters, especially the Elders, were fixated on ritual and propriety. Tia understood that following a strict path had kept them safe, but there had to be some value in becoming friendly with the enemy of your enemy. "Don't you think, after four thousand years of hating each other, our two groups can learn to get along? We have to be stronger together than we are alone. Wasn't that the will of the gods in the first place?"

"My, my. Look what happens when we send a Daughter out into the world."

Tia swore she could hear a smile in her grandmother's tone.

"I'll gather the Elder Sisters. Come visit me. We'll go to circle together."

"I'll be over as soon as I reset my wards. Will the Elders let me speak?"

"You are the seventh Daughter of the seventh Daughter of the High Priestess," Aya reminded her with all the hauteur of one confident in her own power. "Be here at sunset. It will be good to have you in ritual again."

"Okay, Nana. Thank you." Tia disconnected the call. She paused before scrolling through her contacts and finding Markus's number. The idea of talking to him sent butterflies tap dancing in her belly. Would he reconsider being with her? Would he want to go with her to the grove where the Daughters of Isis gathered? What if he only grunted when she shared the news—or worse yet, sent her to voice mail?

In the end, her courage failed her. She sent him a text about meeting the Elder Sisters later that evening, pocketed the phone, then set about restoring the wards on her home, extending the protective barrier several feet beneath the house. Unfortunately she hadn't started soon enough.

Unfamiliar magic raised goose-bumps on her arms as the air before her wavered then ripped, revealing the swirling gray-black clouds of a magic portal. Several desiccated creatures crawled through the opening. Screaming, Tia threw handfuls of consecrated salts and incense at the undead. Those hit imploded, but more came, swamping her. Despite kicking and hurling curses, they managed to drag her to the portal, then beyond.

Gods. Markus gripped the steering wheel hard enough for the material to whine in protest. He could still feel Tia pervading his senses like that damned curse, still feel the imprint of her hand on his chest. How long would he have to endure her essence stealing across his mind and his magic without hungering for her? Somehow he didn't think his immortal soul would last that long.

He wanted her. She wanted him. It should have been easy from there, but it wasn't. Even in the time of Sekhanu and his Isis priestess, the alliance between jackals and witches hadn't been effortless. It was easy to look into the past with a gold-dusted view. He'd put Sekhanu and Asharet on impossibly high pedestals. Maybe the golden age of their people was more tarnished than he cared to remember. If history had taught him anything, it was that the pairing of a jackal and a witch would always be doomed.

Even if he and Tia weren't doomed, being together wouldn't work. He had a good four thousand years of experience over her. Though he'd adapted to survive, he remained old-fashioned in many ways. He'd want to bond with her, live together, love and fight together. He'd want children with her, but had no idea if she wanted kids. Hell, he had no idea what her favorite color was.

They'd had an intense couple of days together. A magical

connection. Incredible sex. What would happen when they tried to go back to normal? Even their normal wasn't like anyone else's—she was a Daughter of Isis, newly come into her power, destined to follow in her grandmother's footsteps as high priestess. He was the leader of the Sons of Anubis, warriors sworn to fight the undead. One day he would lose, one night he wouldn't come home. He wouldn't want to wish that on Tia.

Still he wanted her. Wanted her with a soul-deep need. Imagining her being with another, rejuvenating her magic using someone else's body, made him want to kill.

Markus rolled his shoulders in the too-small van. He needed sky. He needed to hop his bike, open the throttle and ride full-tilt into a fight, the more targets the better. Maybe if he got bloodied and bruised from taking out twenty or thirty Lost Ones would he finally be able to ignore the pain in his chest.

"Sir." The jackal beside him cleared his throat, then tried again. "Sir, I have to ask."

"Ask what?"

"Did the priestess bewitch you?"

The steering wheel groaned beneath his grip. "No. Tia didn't use her Voice on me. Why?"

Again, the jackal looked behind him, as if getting encouragement from his clan mates in the back of the van. "You've been growling nonstop since we left."

Markus slammed on the brakes, causing the van to skid to the roadside. Throwing the vehicle into Park, he turned in his seat and pierced the others with a baleful stare. "And just what do you think that means?"

"We think that means that you want to keep the priestess."

"She's a Daughter of Isis."

"She doesn't act like one," the young jackal pointed out. "She didn't have to be nice to us while she healed Rashon and Alonso, but she was. She told us everything would be all right, and we believed her. And it came to pass. Our brothers are back with us."

The young jackal shook his head. "I have never questioned my faith or my duty. I am what I am, and that's proof enough. Seeing you and the priestess joined in magic, I actually felt as if Anubis and Isis were with us in that room. I want to feel that again. We all want to feel that again."

Markus snarled. Tia was his! Not for a month, or a year. He would have her by side side as his mate for the rest of his life. Even if that meant sharing her with the witches.

His phone beeped. He checked the display, his heart thumping as he saw the text from Tia. "She's already spoken with the High Priestess Aya of the Daughters of Isis," he told his men. "She's meeting with them later tonight."

The men didn't cheer, but he could feel their cautious hope. Acid churned in his gut. He wanted to believe that the Daughters were receptive to a truce, but it would take a gargantuan effort to convince some of the Elders that the jackals weren't to blame.

A sudden urgency gripped him as his chest began to burn. Tia. He'd left men near her place, wanting to ensure her protection until she could reestablish her wards. Now, every instinct screamed at him to turn the van around, return to her and see for himself that she was safe.

On cue, his phone beeped. He tapped his earpiece. "Go."

"Lost Ones," the jackal on the other end replied. "Coming from the priestess's house. She's not answering the door."

"Break the damn thing in!"

For the first time in centuries, true fear blossomed in his gut. The Lost Ones had targeted Tia because she'd helped the Sons of Anubis. She could not pay for that assistance with her life. He had to save her, had to get her back—even if that meant laying waste to the entire city.

"She's not here," the jackal finally answered. "She took out several of the undead, but they must have dragged her through a portal. I'm sorry, sir."

Throwing the van into gear, Markus spun the wheel, turning the bulky vehicle around. "Return to base."

The jackals beside him held up another phone. "I've got base on the line, sir. It's Hector."

He snatched the phone. "Hector."

"I heard. Mobilizing now."

"I want all jackals on the ground in ten. Any whiff of portal activity, any scent of Duat, send it to me. Track Tia's phone in case she has it with her. Send me the coordinates as soon as you have them locked."

"Yes, sir."

Markus disconnected, then howled in rage. If the Lost Ones hurt Tia, he wouldn't rest until he'd destroyed every last one, even if he had to go into Duat itself to finish the job.

Chapter Nine

A twisting, reality-bending scream of a ride later, and the portal spit Tia back onto solid ground. She scrambled across low grass on her hands and knees to put some distance between herself and the Lost Ones, her mind grappling with the knowledge that she'd just been transported through a slice of the Underworld. Her body struggled to shake off the effects of inter-dimensional travel. More nauseating than the most extreme amusement park ride, the journey was one she never wanted to repeat.

She wiped her mouth with the edge of her shirt then climbed to her feet. Lost Ones crowded around her, hemming her in and blocking her view, her escape. Bile rose again as she fought down her terror. Though she'd been trained to defend against them her entire life, she'd never seen a Lost One in person. The reality was far worse than anything she could have imagined, worse than the fascinating yet macabre beauty of mummies she'd seen in museums.

These…things stank of death and decay and evil, their movements like the bare *skritch-skritch* of insects moving through dead leaves. They were dried-out imitations of people, leatherlike skin pulled back from pointed teeth and fingernails, rotted fabric hanging by threads.

She turned away from the horrifying sight, only to notice the familiar surroundings. Shock raced through her as she took in the ring of hardy palm trees ranged around a large circle of golden sand with a large golden ankh embedded in the center. This was the sacred space of the Daughters of Isis. This was home.

"No," she whispered, her vision blurring. "Please, Mother Isis, no."

"Do you really think she'll help you now, when I can smell the stink of jackal all over you?" a harsh female voice asked. "Never did I think I'd live to see the day when a Daughter of Isis again became a jackal's chew toy."

Tia turned with a gasp. Dread gave way to small relief as she realized the woman was not her grandmother. The woman was stunning in a cruelly pretty way, her dark hair falling in a straight sheet. She dressed in the ancient attire of an Isis priestess, the long white gown belted and collared with gold. Where the Daughters of Isis wore the symbol of life the proper way, this pseudo priestess wore the ankh inverted.

Relief gave way to anger. Tia balled her fists, furious that this witch had made her think, even for a moment, that Aya had betrayed the Daughters of Isis. "Look who's talking, whoever you are," she said, lifting her chin in defiance. "You smell like the undead and you look like a low-rent version of a Daughter of Isis. You profane your calling by siding with these undead, and for what? Did the high priestess throw you out of the temple?"

Anger contorted the woman's features. "I should have been the most high priestess of Isis instead of Asharet! I should have led the alliance with Sekhanu. That power and glory should have been mine!"

"So pitting the Sons and Daughters against each other for four thousand years was all because you were jealous?" Tia asked, incredulous. "That seems so...small."

"You dare?" the woman screeched.

"You damn right I dare!" Tia shot back, ignoring the way the Lost Ones rustled like dried leaves around her. "You killed my grandmother's parents out of spite for what they had!"

"Enough! Grab her!"

Lost Ones reached out with their bony hands, holding Tia fast with superhuman strength. The witch gripped Tia's jaw, fingernails digging deep into her skin. "Behold the seventh Daughter of a seventh Daughter, descended from the great Asharet. So full of promise at your birth, so fully a disappointment now. I had thought to break Aya's spirit by leaving your broken body in her precious circle, but I doubt you will be worth the effort. You are far too weak to matter."

Tia's anger erupted into white-hot fury. "I am not weak!"

Growling her rage, Tia head-butted the rebel witch, forehead connecting with nose. The pain that erupted was matched by the satisfaction of hearing the other woman scream and stumble back. She struggled against the undead holding her fast, managing to wrench her right arm free. "Let go of me!"

Fury gave way to surprise as the Lost Ones immediately released her. The rebel witch shrieked through blood-drenched fingers cupping her broken nose. Her free hand reached for a wicked-looking dagger at her waist. "I will not let you take control of my Lost Ones! You're going to pay for this!"

The undead advanced on her. Tia backed away, frantically looking for a weapon. Her gaze fell onto the circle, the shimmering haze of power there. "Mother Isis, live in me!"

Magic flooded the circle, then shot upward in a shaft of gilded light. Tia stretched out a hand as light coalesced into a golden staff. She grabbed it, the weight of power almost knocking her to her knees. Grunting with effort, she managed to spin it around in time to block the other witch's downward stab.

The collision of power knocked them both back several steps. Calling on her flag corps training, Tia spun the staff overhead then swept it down in a wide circle. Every undead creature she made contact with disintegrated. They backed off, and she whirled to face the other woman, ready to pummel her into the ground.

"Hold."

Power rolled over them, immobilizing the Lost Ones in midstep. The rebel witch froze in midstrike, her face a mask of fury. Tia, still brimming with the sacred circle's magic, lowered her staff and turned to see her grandmother leading a column of Daughters and Elder Sisters down the stone path from the compound to the circle's sacred space. Aya, carrying the gilded staff of leadership and resplendent in her ceremonial robes and headdress as the embodiment of Isis, fairly crackled with power as she took in the scene.

"Daughters to the circle," Aya ordered. "Defend our sacred space!"

The priestesses quickly moved onto the circular patch of consecrated sand. Power rose as they joined hands and began to chant.

"She's the one, grandmother," Tia called out, pointing one end of the staff at the renegade witch. "She's the one responsible for Asharet and Sekhanu's deaths. She's controlling the Lost Ones!"

"Amansuanan. Behold our sister, long-thought dead to us." Aya stepped between them. "How far you have fallen."

"Don't condescend to me, girl," the priestess spat blood as she regained control of herself. The remaining undead stirred like dust disturbed by a stagnant breeze. "I should have been high priestess after Asharet. Instead, the Daughters chose a child barely out of swaddling to lead them. That spot belongs to me."

"Leading the Daughters was never your path, Amansuanan," Aya told her. "My mother knew you had neither the heart nor the mind for it. And your betrayal proved her right."

Hatred contorted the other woman's features. "If I cannot lead the Daughters, I will destroy them!"

Tiny hairs stood up along Tia's arms as Amansuanan threw her hand out. Reality tore again, and more of the undead skittered into existence. Dozens headed for the Daughters in the circle, the remainder turning to defend Amansuanan.

"Grandmother!" Tia swung her staff, driving back the Lost Ones who would have attacked Aya, clearing a swath of ground.

"Deal with the Lost Ones. I will attend to our lost sister."

"By myself?" Tia asked, surprised.

"You were doing fine before I got here," her grandmother said, her power making her staff glow. "Start swinging, head or heart. I'll deal with the traitor."

Tia started swinging. Undead burst like dried piñatas as the staff contacted their desiccated flesh, blows to the heart or severing the head. Bile rose in her throat, but she tamped it down and twirled the staff, ignoring the lactic acid burn in her biceps. The more undead she felled, more took their place. In the midst of fighting for her life, she wished for Markus and the Sons of Anubis. The Daughters hadn't been in a battle like this in decades at least. The Sons had probably fought Lost Ones before breakfast.

Fatigue or carelessness, she wasn't sure, but somehow she tripped over a severed limb. She fell hard, the luminous staff vanishing as it left her hand. Lost Ones swarmed closer. Fear hammered in her chest as she realized her odds of survival had dropped into single digits.

Howling split the air. A massive dark shadow blotted the light above her then landed beside her, causing the ground to tremble. A scream boiled up her throat before she realized that it wasn't a shadow at all, but a half-man, half-jackal giant holding a wickedly curved sword in one claw. "Holy Anubis."

No, not Anubis. Markus, resplendent and awe inspiring in his glossy black Anubis form, had brought his jackals to the fight. Snarling, he swung his sword in a deadly dance, dusting more than a dozen Lost Ones with an economy of swings.

He was absolutely magnificent, standing protectively between her and the undead. Seeing his raw masculine energy in action caused the primitive feminine part of her mind to send a bolt of lust shooting through her. Gods, how she wanted him!

A flood of sleek dark shapes spilled down the steep incline, leaping onto the Lost Ones. Markus helped her to her feet, careful of his strength. Sounds of battle faded as she looked up into his fathomless amber eyes. "Markus, I—"

"Who hurt you?"

"What?"

His voice rumbled low like two massive stones grinding together. "You're bleeding. Who did this?"

She touched her forehead, looked at the blood on her fingertips. "Oh. I head-butted the wicked witch."

Pointed ears twitched, and she wondered if he wanted to smile. It was hard to tell with the muzzle and the bared teeth.

One of the Daughters screamed. "Jackals!"

Crap. Buoyed by the presence of the jackals, Tia cut a swath through the mass of Lost Ones to the circle of witches. Power rose over them like a dome, sending out bolts of magical energy that pierced the undead in puffs of dust. Jackals darted through the remaining creatures, making short work of the enemy. Now, however, the Daughters in the circle focused on the jackals, fear evident on their faces.

"Attack the jackals!" One of the witches, Cassandra, pointed her staff toward a small knot of jackals that had placed themselves between the Daughters and the undead.

"Don't you dare throw a spell at the jackals," Tia yelled at them, spreading her arms as she stood between the Daughters and the Sons. "They're here to help!"

"You expect us to believe that?"

"You see a former Daughter at the head of an undead army and you still want to doubt the jackals? Are you really that blinded by hatred?"

"Maybe you're working with them," the witch said. "Who knows what happened over the past two days you've been with them?"

Tia froze. "Aya is the only one who knows that. Did you

listen to my conversation with my grandmother? Is that how Amansuanan knew to abduct me from my house?"

The circle of power wavered as the Daughters close to Cassandra dropped their hands. "So what if I did?" Cassandra asked, defiant and accusing. "Aya's faith in you is misplaced, but she wouldn't listen to me. And now you consort with jackals. Look at how they flock to you!"

Tia knew the jackals stood at her back. She felt Markus just behind her, the comforting wall of his magical and physical strength wrapping about her. "Yes, take a good long look, all of you. Look at how the jackals came to our aid, not knowing how they'd be received. Look at how they placed themselves between you and the undead. Look at their actions, though a Daughter of Isis cursed a number of their people. Look, and know how honorable they have been. I'm proud to stand with them."

The rest of the Daughters stepped away from Cassandra. Markus strode forward until he stood at Tia's shoulder. In his Anubis form, Markus was beyond impressive, well over eight feet tall, the black of his hide gleaming in the dim light. His pointed ears flattened as he roared a challenge.

Realizing she no longer had support, Cassandra turned tail and ran, heading toward Amansuanan. The renegade witch, scraped and bloodied from her bout with Aya, opened a portal to escape and ran through, Cassandra and the last few Lost Ones following.

The portal slammed closed. Silence fell, thick and immediate. Whether by accident or design, Daughters stood on one side of the circle while the Sons ranged along the other. Each camp stared at the other with equal expressions of mistrust.

Tia turned to Markus, still in his Anubis form. "You came for me."

He nodded. "Of course."

"How did you find me? How did you even know to look?"

"I left two of my men to watch over you. When they reported that you'd been taken, we used the GPS in your phone to find you."

Of course he'd hacked her phone. She wouldn't have expected less. "Thank you. Thank you for showing up when you did."

Aya took that moment to join Tia and Markus in the center of the two camps. Though she was a grandmother and four millennia old, bathed in power she seemed no more than forty. "Tonight we have seen the true face of our enemy," she said, her voice ringing in the quiet. "There is no doubt that the threat is very real and very personal for all of us."

She looked at each one of the Daughters. "We have lost Cassandra, just as we lost Amansuanan centuries ago. I would not have us lose another of our sisters because of our misplaced distrust of the Sons of Anubis. It is time for us to set aside centuries of animosity and discord and return to our heritage, our calling, of working together."

A murmur rose over the throng. Markus folded his arms across his chest. "The Sons of Anubis will hold to our heritage and to our calling. We will work with the Daughters of Isis—through Tia."

Though Markus towered over all of them, Aya stared at him with equanimity. "Our sister Tia has proven that jackals and witches can cast magic together for the greater good. We would do well to follow in her steps. So let it be done."

A tense silence followed, then the Elder Sisters spoke as one. "So let it be done."

Aya turned to Tia, her eyes glowing with her power. "It will take some time for us to forget our version of the past. I will count on you to help the Daughters cross this bridge."

"Yes, High Priestess," Tia answered.

"Tia belongs to us," Markus declared as he stepped forward. He looped an arm around her shoulders, dragging her close.

Aya didn't seem surprised by the declaration, but Tia sure was. "What?"

Markus-Anubis stared at Aya. "I claim her for my clan and for myself."

"And if the Daughters say you cannot have her?" The high priestess returned his glare with power-filled eyes. "She will lead this circle one day. She belongs to the Daughters of Isis."

Markus growled in warning. "She is ours. We won't give her up without a fight."

"I'm not a trophy to be passed around," Tia protested even as her heart sang. Markus's claim was what she had wanted to hear, just not the way she had wanted to hear it. "I decide my own way."

"I know you're not a trophy." He looked down at her with unfathomable eyes. "You are a woman, a good heart, a gentle soul, a fierce spirit. You are a Daughter of Isis, and we would not ask you to give that up when that is what saved us."

He gathered her hands in his own. "You stood before your sisters and defended us and our honor. To the Children of Anubis you are a blessing and a gift, and it will be hard for us not to put you on a pedestal like a trophy."

"What about you?" she asked, her voice soft. "You said you claimed me for yourself as well as the clan. What am I to you?"

"You want to know what you are to me?" A golden glow surrounded him, then he stood before her in his natural form. "You are the fulfillment of a wish I didn't dare make. A need I denied I had. A hunger I thought would never be sated. Everything I could ever ask for."

He pulled her close. "I don't know the future, so I can't say where we'll be a year, a decade, or a century from now. What I do know is that I have never felt so great a rage or fear as when you fell among those Lost Ones. I think my heart actually seized."

"I'm sorry you were worried," she whispered, awed by the emotion she heard in his voice.

"I don't know if this is love, Tia," he told her. "I haven't had the luxury of experiencing that emotion. But I'm willing to find out. I'm willing to learn, if you're willing to teach me. Say you'll give us the chance. Say you'll be with me."

Warmth filled Tia's chest, a sense of rightness and purpose that was undeniable. "Yes, Markus. I'll be with you." She grinned. "I might even be able to teach you a thing or two about love and other matters."

He tightened his grip, though some of the tension left his expression. "If you say something about an old dog and learning new tricks, I'll be forced to bring you home and take you to bed until you beg for forgiveness."

She twined her arms about his neck. "We should do that anyway."

A soft cough snagged their attention. Tia stepped back, acutely aware of their audience. Aya gave her a knowing smile as she placed her hands atop theirs. "Blessed of Isis, blessed of Anubis. Joined together, a blessing for Sons and Daughters. So let it be done."

Jackals and witches raised their voices together. "For Sons and Daughters. So let it be done!"

* * * * *

SOME LIKE IT WICKED

LAUREN HAWKEYE

A firm believer in the power of a woman's innate sexuality, **Lauren Hawkeye** originally intended to obtain a doctorate in sexology and become a sex therapist. Instead she was thrown headfirst into an accounting position—her worst nightmare. In need of an outlet, the English minor returned to words in her spare time, and her new love was born.

Inspired by authors ranging from the incredible Megan Hart to Canadian legends Margaret Atwood and Robertson Davies, Lauren likes to explore the female journey, often with a new discovery of that aforementioned sexuality along the way. Though she has only been writing for a year and a half, she has been very lucky thus far, and hopes that her luck will hold!

Visit Lauren at her website at www.laurenhawkeye.com.

Prologue

Aria's irritation was a tangible thing as she entered Belladonna, the apothecary that she owned and ran with her twin sister Lorelai. The heat of the paper cups in her hands scalded her skin as the bell hanging above the door jingled merrily.

"What's wrong?" Her sister's voice was immediately colored with concern.

Though Aria was certain that not all twins were like Lorelai and herself, the fact remained that they had always been acutely attuned to one another's moods and thoughts. And no matter how much Aria wasn't in the mood to talk about it, today was no different.

She tried to school her face into nonchalance as she set the cup of Lorelai's orange blossom tea and her own triple-shot latte on the counter. From the expression on her sister's face, she suspected that the effect wasn't quite what she'd hoped for.

"I don't want to talk about it." Denying that she was upset was useless around the woman with whom she'd shared a womb. Lorelai might have been sweeter and softer than Aria, but she could be ruthless when she wanted something. "It's nothing new, anyway."

Hoping to change the subject, Aria nodded to the dried

chamomile and lavender, the fresh sprigs of rosemary and spearmint. "Are you making more salve?" Wandering to the back room where they prepared their concoctions, Aria inhaled the aroma into her lungs, hoping the familiar scents would relax her a bit.

With the herbal smell, she caught an edge of something else—that burnt sugar smell of magic.

Turning, she raised an eyebrow at her sister. Though Belladonna did indeed provide magical services to those who knew to ask, they never added anything extra to the stock on their shelves.

"Mr. Garrison was in. His arthritis has been bothering him with all of the rain we've been having. He asked if there was anything else I could add to the salve to help."

Aria watched as, flushed, Lorelai spooned the warm salve from the pot into a small tin. Though humans wouldn't have been able to see it, Aria saw the faint blue glow emanating from her sister's fingers as she added one final charge of magic to the salve.

"There." Nodding, Lorelai set the tin aside to cool, then turned back to Aria. "Now. What's going on?"

"I already told you, I don't want to talk about it. Don't be nosy." Crossing her arms defensively over her chest, Aria tried to glower at her sister. Lorelai simply tapped her foot on the floor with impatience.

"I'm waiting."

"Fine." Scowling, Aria raked a hand through the sleek strands of her glossy chestnut hair. It swung back around her chin as if she'd never touched it.

Wondering how to phrase it, she opened her mouth, then closed it again. Wetting her mouth with another sip of coffee, she finally blurted it out.

"I haven't had sex in almost a year."

Lorelai's expression didn't change as Aria spoke, but Aria thought she caught the faintest flicker in her sister's eyes.

"I see," Lorelai spoke slowly, as if she didn't really see at all. "Uh… I'm sorry?"

Aria couldn't help but quirk the corners of her lips up in a smirk. "I'm just setting the stage here. Anyway, you know I have a hard time with the men in town." Her smirk faded as she thought further.

Surely there was one man out there—just one—who wouldn't be scared of her. It wasn't as if she was a gorgon, or anything. And any idiot with half a brain knew that a witch was probably a safer bet than a human, bound by the three-fold rule—any harm done would be revisited upon herself times three.

And there had been one man—one vampire, to be exact. But Declan Steele, her vampire lover, was long gone, and it was her own damn fault.

She shook her head to clear it of the thought. The past was the past. She just needed a man with enough balls to get her naked, scratch this itch and let her go back to normal life.

"Continue." Aria was pleased to hear the frost that had entered her sister's tone, irritation on her behalf. Still, she knew that Lorelai didn't understand, not fully. They were twins, they made no secret of their magical heritage and they were co-owners of Belladonna, but Lorelai didn't have quite the same troubles with the locals as Aria did.

Her sister was sweet of nature where Aria was fiery. Lorelai liked to please people, and Aria could not have cared less. Her sister even had the golden good looks of an angel, while Aria frequently changed her hair color and style. She also preferred torn denim, red lipstick and her ancient leather jacket to her twin's floaty skirts and cardigans.

In other words, she scared the hell out of most people and Lorelai didn't. And Aria didn't care, except when it came to sex and men.

"There was a new guy working the espresso machine. Super tall, blond, just a bit of scruff. You know who I'm talking about?"

Lorelai nodded enthusiastically, hitching herself up to sit beside her sister on the counter. "I do. Oh, I do."

"Yeah. So." Aria drained her coffee and hesitated. This part stung. "He was into me. I *know* he was into me. He asked me what I was doing later. *Then* he asked my name."

"Uh-oh." Lorelai bumped her shoulder against her sister's, and Aria felt the warmth from the touch streak down her arm. It helped…a bit.

"Yeah. I can see the wheels turning. Ding ding ding, he's flirting with the scary Prescott twin. The *witch*." Aria crunched the paper cup in her palm, wishing she was doing it on the idiot's head. "And this is the worst part. He ran away."

"He what?" Lorelai turned and looked directly at Aria, disbelief painted over her face.

"You heard me. He ran away. Scurried into the back without another word." Normally Aria tried to laugh these situations off, but this one had been the straw that broke the camel's back.

She was hurt. Not because she wanted that guy, specifically, but because she wanted some damn companionship. If it came in the form of some hot, sweaty sex, then so much the better.

She was lonely, damn it. And that was something that she wasn't going to admit, even to Lorelai.

She saw the sympathy registering on her sister's face. She really didn't want to hear it. Lorelai knew better than to give platitudes about how it would all get better, but she still tried to soothe her sister's hurt.

Aria wanted to hold on to her irritation, illogical as it was.

"Anyway, I just came to bring you your tea, not to cry on your shoulder." Swinging her legs, Aria lowered herself down off the counter. "If you leave the tins out to cool, I'll set them out on the shelf in the morning."

"Aria…" Aria held a hand up, her emerald-green eyes sparking at her sister as Lorelai spoke.

"Please, Lori. Not now." Her sister knew her well enough not to take offense at her curt tone. "I'm going to head to Harry's for a few drinks, I think, then head home. Alone, most likely, but at least I'll have had some beer to soothe the pain."

Before Lorelai could protest any further, Aria waved her goodbyes and pushed out of the glass door of Belladonna. Yes, she'd head to Harry's Bar and Grill, have a burger and some beer. And if she headed home alone afterward, she figured she'd rather keep her own company than be stuck with someone as spineless as the idiot from the coffee shop.

Lorelai watched Aria leave with a pang in her heart. She knew that Aria thought she didn't understand, but she knew what her sister was feeling better than she'd like to admit.

Lorelai had wanted to be a teacher—specifically, a kindergarten or elementary school teacher. But the way in which parents held their children tight when either she or Aria was around had told her early on that, unless she wanted to move somewhere else and hide her magic, she'd better settle for another career choice.

And while she tended to scare men off less than her outgoing sister, it didn't mean that any of them stayed around. When push came to shove, no one wanted to marry a witch, no one wanted to have children with one.

Her desire for true love couldn't be solved with a spell. But, she reflected as she locked the front door of Belladonna and turned the sign around, her independent sister's desire for some temporary companionship could be.

"A lust spell." Cocking her head to one side, Lorelai thought for a moment, letting her intentions come to her. After the picture was clear in her head, she began to gather her supplies— a fat red candle, jasmine oil, dried strawberries and vervain.

She wouldn't try to draw love to her sister, because that would be attempting the impossible. Nor could she create lust where there was none. But men—lots of them—had a healthy amount of that emotion when it came to Aria. It was simply a matter of removing barriers—both Aria's and the man's.

This spell would make the attraction burn hot and bright between Aria and the next man that she saw and was attracted to.

Mixing the herbs and the oil together in a small wooden bowl, Lorelai furrowed her brow and, after a brief surge of energy crackled through the air, lit the red candle with her magic. She paused for a moment as she thought of how angry Aria would be if she found out, but she shook it off.

Her sister deserved to get what she wanted, just once. And maybe it would give her enough confidence that next time, she wouldn't need a spell.

Nodding, Lorelai cast her circle and began to chant the words that came flowing to the front of her mind.

"Do what ye will, and it harm none."

Chapter One

"Are you sure you want to do this?"

Declan Steele shook his head, forcing himself out of the near trance he'd been in as he stared across the parking lot of Harry's Bar and Grill. It had been years since he'd been back to Salem's Hollow, and he wasn't entirely sure why he was back now.

He didn't speak as his lover handed him the ebony cane that he now had to use to walk. But he did study Adam's face, the golden skin, the expressive eyes, wondering how he'd been lucky enough to wind up with someone so patient.

"I can't explain it." Declan frowned as he felt something prickle his cold skin—the merest whisper of something that didn't belong on the breeze. His first taste of blood had come from a human with the ability to see things she shouldn't have. Since then he'd often had premonitions that couldn't be explained.

One of those had been dogging his heels for the last week, telling him to come back to the town he'd never thought he'd visit again.

"I suppose the question should be, are *you* okay with this?" Declan narrowed his eyes, watching his lover carefully. He had been with the werewolf for nearly two years, knew him as well as he knew anyone.

Adam knew—had always known—that a piece of Declan's heart still belonged to someone else. To a woman.

To a witch.

Adam smiled, and Declan saw the strength that had attracted him in the first place. He'd always been drawn to those with cores of steel, those like Adam.

Like Aria.

"I'm not threatened by the little witch." Adam raked fingers through his coal dark hair, smiling the sexy grin that made heat tighten in Declan's gut. "You know me better than that."

This was true, Declan realized, as he weighed the options for the final time. The supernatural creatures in the world had much more open ideas about sex and love than humans did. In the years since he'd turned, he'd been with men, with women, with other vampires, with werewolves. Adam felt the same, as had the woman who had once held his heart in her hands. But Declan had spent enough time among humans in the last few years, doing research for his report for the Council, that some of their uniquely human thoughts and feelings still clung to his skin like a mist.

"I don't think I've been drawn back here just because of Aria," Declan began, and as he spoke, he felt a tug in the direction of the bar. She was in there, he would have bet his long life on it. "Regardless, you have to know I still have feelings for her."

Lots of feelings, ranging from throttling her pretty neck to thrusting between her creamy thighs.

Adam grinned at Declan, and Declan saw the whiteness of the wolf's teeth flash in the artificial light of the parking lot.

"I'm looking forward to exploring those feelings. All of them." Reaching out, Adam squeezed the fingers that Declan had clenched on his cane. There was more than just heat between them—there was caring, love.

Just as there had been with Aria, once.

Urgency worked its way into Declan's gut as he searched the outside of the building, his eyesight keen as a hawk's.

There was something else at play here, something besides Aria. Something that had drawn him here, and that the universe hadn't seen fit to give him any clarity on yet.

But in the meantime, he might as well confront the little witch who had thrown him out of her life. The very air of the town seemed to pulse with her scent, and until he at least saw her, spoke with her, he wouldn't be able to focus on much else.

Decision made, he jerked his chin in the direction of the bar. Adam's eyes followed the movement.

"Let's go."

A pint glass of beer later, Aria was feeling a bit mellower. Who needed men, anyway? She had a credit card. She could buy a vibrator.

It would just be easier that way.

Lifting her glass to her lips, she drained the dregs of her drink and slid from her bar stool. She liked Harry's, with its rickety tables, no nonsense menu and ancient jukebox that sat on the edge of a tiny dance floor underlain with horsehair. Harry never gave her any of the nonsense that so many people in the town did, but neither did he hit her up for magic.

"Thanks." Nodding at the man in question, she slid a twenty-dollar bill across the bar. Her burger and beer wouldn't come to more than ten, but she liked to leave a good tip when it was due.

She was shrugging back into her leather jacket when she felt tingles begin to dance across her skin. Casually—warily—she raised her head to look around the room.

She only felt that sensation when another supernatural being was around, and in the small town of Salem's Hollow, Pennsylvania, she didn't often come across one.

Her gaze was drawn across the room, to the tall, intimidating-looking man who stood just inside the door of the bar.

There was no surprise on his face as the blaze of his bright blue eyes burned into her.

"Oh, hell no." Aria prided herself on being tough and in control at all times. But as she looked into the eyes of Declan Steele, the man—the vampire—who had broken her heart, as she registered the heat that immediately crackled through her veins beneath his stare, she fought the urge to flee.

"Breathe, you idiot." Shaking like a wet puppy, Aria noted the smirk that played around the corners of Declan's eyes as she spoke and cursed herself internally. Damn vampires and their enhanced hearing, anyway.

Once she'd anticipated that he would hear things, see things about her that others wouldn't. She'd fallen out of practice.

"Aria."

Her breath caught in her throat as Declan began to move across the bar toward her. The music of the jukebox, the chatter of the other people around her all faded as, for one long, heart-throbbing moment the world around her ceased to exist. The air between them pulsed with a heat so tangible that it very nearly hurt her to look away.

She forced herself. Heat had never been a problem for them. It had been everything else.

"Declan. When did you get back to town?" Somewhat calmer, Aria took a deep breath and looked back at her former lover. He was as tall, dark and dangerous as ever, his licorice-black hair looking as though he'd just run his fingers through it, his eyes deep and blue. He was pale, as were all of his kind, but she noted the rosy flush on his cheeks that told her he had recently fed.

Jealousy was a blade in her belly as her hand lifted to the curve of her neck, the skin where he had once sipped from her.

Following the motion with his eyes, Declan cocked his head, taking her in.

"It's good to see you, Aria."

Instantly defensive, she crossed her arms over her chest and scowled.

"That's…nice." Her words were harsh, but truthfully, she didn't know what else to say. Seeing him—a man who knew her better than she knew herself—was like a balm to her lonely soul.

Yes, he got to know you and then left. Even the snarky inner voice in her head couldn't erase what Aria hated admitting even to herself.

You told him to go.

It was water under the bridge.

"Well, I was just leaving." It wasn't until she stepped back that Aria noticed that Declan was leaning on a cane. Her lips parted with surprise, and her eyes darted rapidly back up to his face.

"What the hell happened to you?" The cane didn't diminish from the danger that Declan had always exuded. If anything, he made the polished stick of black wood look like a weapon capable of doing great harm, just by being in his hand.

But there wasn't much that could permanently cripple a vampire.

"Silver. Nerve damage." Something dark flitted across Declan's face, but was gone just as quickly.

Aria hissed in a breath. She knew that silver was like kryptonite for vampires. When they'd been together, she'd made a point never to wear it.

She wanted to ask where he'd come into such brutal contact with it, and saw that he was expecting her to.

She swallowed the question. Five minutes in the man's company and she wanted to pick up where they'd left off. Another five minutes and she'd be rubbing against him like an animal in heat.

"After I left, I worked for the Capitol for a while." Declan's words were flat, yet Aria saw a flash of anger in his eyes. The Capitol was the governing body for the supernatural creatures of the world. They left the creatures alone for the most part.

Unless they wanted something. Knowing about Declan's

precognition, it wasn't hard to guess what they'd decided he'd be useful for.

"Let's just say it was an occupational hazard." His voice was wry, and took Aria straight into the past. He'd always been self-deprecating, and on his big, bad self she'd found it sexy as hell.

She still did. She'd had lovers since he'd left—human and supernatural, male and female. But none had ever made her passion burn as bright as the vampire had.

Declan made no attempt to hide his own blatant interest as his eyes slowly traveled up her body and then down. Her nipples puckered under his stare, and she felt heat gathering low in her belly.

"That's a shame." Damn it, her voice was breathless. What was *wrong* with her? She'd been feeling sexually deprived lately, sure, but this man had broken her heart.

Her traitorous hormones didn't seem to care. They were flooding into her veins, reminding her of every reason she'd always found Declan so sexy.

Her lips were dry, and she licked her tongue over them for moisture.

Declan's eyes followed the gesture, and she saw his expression darken.

"I wondered." His voice was everything she remembered—dark, rich like chocolate. It sent shivers skating over her skin. "I wondered if it had all been a dream, what we felt for each other."

Aria shuddered out a breath. She wanted him—no matter that he'd once left her, she still wanted him with an intensity that was frightening.

"The key word is *felt*." Her voice was raw, and it physically hurt to step back, away from him. "Past tense. We were no good."

"We were young." Declan followed her, the thud of his cane sounding before his footfall. "But I never forgot you. Part of the reason I came back was you."

"No." Panic warred with delight in Aria's gut.

"Let's not overthink it." With the hand not holding the cane, Declan reached out to touch Aria's cheek, trailing his knuckles over her skin. A blaze of sensation followed in the wake of his touch. "Maybe this is what we both need."

Aria closed her eyes, savoring his touch. Her body wanted nothing more than to shove Declan down on the top of Harry's bar and have her wicked way with him.

What would it hurt, after all? She could scratch this itch with someone who knew her well enough to please her.

Only the palpitations of her heart reminded her that she might not survive him leaving a second time.

"No, Declan."

The vampire's eyes narrowed as, drawing her strength about her like a cloak, she pulled away from his touch. No matter what she felt in that moment, she couldn't. "I value my sanity more than that."

"Don't you feel it, too?" His voice was as rich and delicious as she remembered it.

Aria still knew him well enough to see that Declan was warring with the same overwhelming need that was swamping her.

"I do." She couldn't lie—he would see right through it. "That was never the problem."

"Goodbye, Declan." These were words she'd never had a chance to say before. She couldn't tell if she was relieved or devastated when she finally managed to turn away from him.

Despite all that had happened, she knew him. He was too stubborn, too proud to come back to Salem's Hollow just for her. So why was he here?

Turning to walk around Declan, Aria found her nose meeting the hard wall of a solid male chest.

"Ow!" Shoving back against the offensive obstruction, Aria scowled up, even as she felt the tingling on her skin intensify.

"Apologies, little one." The barest hint of a smile played across the lips of the man who had caught her wrists in his hands.

Aria felt her breath catch. Damn it, was the universe trying to torment her today? First Declan, now this gorgeous creature, whose fingers were hot around her wrists.

Nearly as tall as Declan, his skin was a golden brown that gleamed under the pale lights of the bar. His hair was the color of bittersweet chocolate, and his eyes only a fraction lighter.

She could tell that he was something more than human, but she couldn't say what—though she ruled vampire out of the equation.

He wasn't nearly pale enough. Also, she could see puncture marks on the cords of his neck, ones that she'd often had herself after a night with Declan.

Holy hell. What were the chances?

Aria backed up a step, looking from Declan to the other man and back again. Declan's expression told her that he was waiting for her reaction.

"Aria, this is Adam Patel." With the hand not clutching his cane, Declan reached out to run a hand over Adam's biceps in much the same way as he had touched Aria's cheek only moments earlier. "Adam is a werewolf."

"And a guy who needs a drink." Adam smiled at Declan, and the intimate curve of his lips, the puncture marks on his neck, the flush on Declan's cheeks told it all to Aria. "Let me buy you a drink, little one, to apologize for almost breaking your nose."

"No, thank you." So Declan had a new love. Well, that was fine. She certainly hadn't been a saint in the years since they'd parted.

But she was unsettled by the heat that crackled between them still…the heat that pulsed among all three of them.

Never again. She couldn't feel hurt like she had when Declan had gone again. She didn't think she'd be able to survive.

"I'm going now."

"Stubborn as always." This was Declan, but his voice held exasperation instead of amusement. From the corner of her eyes Aria saw the two men exchange a glance.

"This is the one?" Adam's voice was quiet, but he didn't seem to be trying to hide his words.

"She always has been." Declan spoke in barely more than a whisper, and Aria wondered if she'd heard right.

Rubbing her hands over her face with embarrassment, Aria wondered if there was a graceful way to exit a situation like this.

"Don't leave yet." Though Adam was a stranger to her, something in his expression as he smiled down at her pulled at her in a way similar—and yet kinda different—from the way she felt when Declan looked at her. "I'd love to spend time with the woman Declan speaks so highly of."

That was enough. Aria's nerves snapped.

"Why on earth would you want to spend time with your lover's ex?" She wasn't bitter, not exactly, but she was certainly perplexed. She'd thought—hoped—for a brief moment when Declan had said he'd come for her. Hoped that there was some way to erase the past and find her happy ending.

He had found someone new. It was his right. But since she knew he couldn't have come back just for her, it seemed like a slap for him to come to her, to tease out these feelings that she'd thought were long buried.

It angered her to have them brought to the surface. Turning to Declan, she drilled her finger into his chest.

"You have a lot of nerve, coming in here to proposition me when your lover is barely out of earshot." Declan blinked as if she'd managed to catch him off guard, and she felt the same surge of satisfaction that she once had when she'd managed to do the same.

"I wasn't trying to proposition you." His voice was mildly amused, and as Declan exchanged yet another glance with Adam, Aria felt her cheeks begin to burn with mortification.

Had she read the entire thing wrong? Was she burning up for him while he felt nothing?

Heart in her throat, she took a step toward the door. Her upper arm was caught in the cool grip of a vampire's hand,

and then she found herself hauled against the unyielding chest of the same.

"Something told me to come here this week. I think you know me well enough to know that I wouldn't have come if the tug came just from you."

She'd already known that, but hearing it from his lips stung. She glared.

"I had to see you, because I knew if I didn't, I wouldn't be able to get you out of my mind. But I find that I like where your mind's gone." The words were dark, hot.

Aria saw the intent in his eyes. She felt like she could protest, but didn't have to work very hard to quiet it.

She wanted the kiss. She wanted it bad.

When Declan's lips met hers for the first time in three years, she felt as though she'd had the wind knocked out of her. He blew cool air between her lips, giving her his breath, before he deepened the soft brush of lips and claimed her mouth with a possessive nip on her lower lip.

Aria moaned as Declan's tongue traced the seam of her lips, then slid inside to dance with her own. She stiffened, fighting it, before her body took over and she wrapped her arms around his chest as his fist tangled in her hair, tugging gently.

Then, as quickly as it had started, the kiss ended. Declan released her and stepped back, leaving Aria panting and needy.

"I think we all might get along." Declan's words were thick. With heavy lids and swollen lips, she looked up at him, then at Adam, who stood nearby, watching them with hunger evident on his face.

"You mean…" He couldn't. It wasn't unheard of in the supernatural community to have more than one partner at once. But when they'd been together, they'd been so consumed by one another that it hadn't been a consideration.

No. No way. This was the worst idea on the face of the planet.

But…she was burning, badly. The idea of having not just

Declan, but both men sent power surging through Aria's veins, crackling into magical energy in her fingertips.

If Adam was there too, then how hard could she fall for Declan again? His new lover's presence would be a constant reminder to keep her guard up.

She was so hot, the ache between her thighs growing so that the thought was enough to convince her. She would enjoy her time with them, enjoy the mind-blowing sex that she knew Declan was more than capable of.

Then she'd go back to her normal life, the way she always did. It hardly seemed fair, but that was just the way things had to be.

"All right." She was sure that she was imagining the flash of triumph that she saw in Declan's eyes.

No matter what he said, she couldn't believe that he'd come back here just for her. No doubt running into one another was just a coincidence that he'd taken advantage of.

Well, she was going to take advantage right back. Here was a man—men, actually—who weren't afraid of her. She didn't have to hide any part of herself, and that was something rare.

Smiling slowly, sensually, Aria licked her lips and looked first at the familiar face of Declan, then at Adam, the face she didn't yet know by heart.

"Where are you staying?"

Chapter Two

Declan felt his fangs prickling through his gums as soon as Aria acquiesced. As it always had, the submission borne from her strength was a heady rush.

But he also got a jolt of energy as she spoke, and he knew that her decision had clicked something new into the future. Hard as he tried to reach for it, he still couldn't see what it was.

"We're staying in the motel across the road." Declan looked at his lover, saw anticipation on Adam's face. It made shivers dance up and down Declan's spine.

He was about to be with the only two people who had been able to reach past the feelings that had been frozen so many years ago, when he'd turned. The very thought made his cock hard.

But as they stepped outside the bar, and the noises of the jukebox and the chatter of the inebriated faded into the night air, another blast of energy pushed against him, this one strong enough to shove him back a full step.

"What the fuck?" Declan's injured leg dragged on the ground as he righted himself, instantly shoving Aria behind him as he pulled the hidden sword from his cane.

"Declan!" Aria's voice was a growl as she shoved back

at him. In his peripheral vision he saw blue light crackling from her fingers, knew he'd startled her enough to activate her magic.

From behind them Adam growled, and though he didn't shift, Declan saw the other man's hair stand up on end.

"What is it, Dec?" Adam sniffed the air and looked puzzled. "I'm not getting anything."

Aria looked between the two men, suspicion painted over her face.

"I don't know." After a long moment, Declan straightened and let his muscles relax. Adrenaline still pumped through his cold flesh—he didn't understand what had just happened.

"I've never felt anything like that before. It was the jolt that happens when I get a premonition, but it was...stronger." Way stronger, he though with a trickle of unease. Almost sentient.

And now it was gone.

"Dec?" Aria eyed him warily. He wondered if she knew she'd fallen into the old habit of shortening his name.

"Whatever it was, it's gone now." Declan caught Adam's eye and understanding passed between them. They would discuss what had happened later, and in the meantime they would be wary.

But the danger seemed to have passed, and with it Aria's resolve. He could see the need to flee skittering over her skin.

"Aria." He deliberately layered his voice with the dominance that she'd once responded to.

"Don't pull that shit with me, Declan." She looked at him sharply, her features twisted into an irritated scowl.

"I'm not doing anything besides being myself, Aria." He softened his voice, aware of Adam standing on Aria's other side. She seemed to become of aware of it too, and shivered. "And a moment ago you wanted me, wanted us. Are you backing down?"

He watched as her spine stiffened, as he'd known it would when he dared her. He saw the pulse that beat beneath the line of her jaw increase. He struggled to keep himself in control, when the sight mesmerized him, fragile butterfly wings beating beneath translucent skin.

He remembered what she tasted like. He wanted to taste her again.

"I'm not backing down from anything." Her voice would have seemed controlled to most, but Declan heard the slight breathiness of arousal. "Let's go."

With a saucy swish of her hips, Aria sashayed across the dull gray parking lot, her ass swinging in a way that had Declan's throat going dry, though he'd fed off Adam only hours before.

"The Capitol?" Adam asked in voice that had gone half wolf at the sight of Aria's swaying hips. His words were tight with both need and concern.

"I don't know what they would want with me here." A phantom pain ran through Declan's injured leg at the very thought of the governing body. To leave the Capitol was death, but he'd been free of them for over a year.

He looked after Aria. He and Adam should simply leave, before anything became more complicated. But he couldn't escape the nagging feeling that he was where he was supposed to be.

Aria looked back over her shoulder then, her green eyes bright in the moonlight. She cast a wicked smile at Declan and Adam, and Declan's fangs descended the rest of the way through his gums.

"Coming, boys?" Her voice was a growl, the come-and-get me tone that had always driven him crazy.

He wanted her. He needed her. And he didn't have to look at Adam to know that his lover felt the same way.

Striding across the parking lot, his cane scraping on the asphalt, he grabbed Aria by her shoulders and pulled her in for a hot, hard kiss. He heard her sharp intake of breath, watched her eyes go cloudy.

"You're the one who's going to be coming, little witch." He

couldn't help but grin at the snarl that passed over her face. She'd always been such a fascinating bundle of contradictions. "Let's go."

Aria's heart pounded a wicked tattoo against her rib cage as Declan swiped his key card through the reader on the motel room door. As the door swung open, he gestured for her to enter ahead of the men.

She did, her sharp eyes taking in the room and noting several details despite her nerves.

If she channeled her magic, she could see the lingering remnants of two separate threads of energy in the room—the deep blue of Declan, and a golden yellow that she thought was Adam.

The streams of energy were concentrated over the king-size bed, and threaded through with tendrils of crimson.

Crimson energy was highly sexual.

She didn't need to guess what had happened here.

"You said she always overthinks things, Declan." Closing her eyes, Aria heard the door to the room close with a click. Adam's voice was as yet unfamiliar to her, but she was attracted to it regardless, its husky rasp reminding her of the burn of whiskey in the throat. "I think she's doing it right now."

"We'd better make her stop it then." Cool hands—Declan's hands—pressed flat overtop of Aria's belly, pushing her back against a wall of rigid heat.

"If she changes her mind, I just might die," Adam said roughly.

Arching back into Adam's heat, Aria slit open her eyes to look at Declan. If she'd had any doubts about his desire for her, she no longer did. His fangs were fully extended, something that only happened when he was hungry or aroused.

She knew he was well fed.

"I don't want to think." Aria gasped as Adam's hands stroked up from their grip on her hips to cup her breasts.

She pressed back against him and felt the hard ridge of his erection in the small of her back.

"Adam, take her coat off for her." Declan leaned his cane against the wall beside the bed.

Aria shifted restlessly as Adam's hands left her breasts to peel the leather down her shoulders. He then gripped the hem of her T-shirt in his large hands and lifted it up and over her head, leaving her torso naked but for her bra.

"You're still wearing too many clothes." Declan's words were muffled a bit because of his distended fangs, but she still heard him and tensed with anticipation. Adam pulled at the fabric of her bra until her breasts popped free, pushed upward by the garment caught beneath them. He caught their sensitive tips in his fingers, rolling her nipples slowly as Declan pulled at the button and zipper at the top of her jeans, shoving the material to the floor.

"Still no panties." Dropping to his knees before her, the movement somewhat stiff because of his injured leg, Declan grinned up at Aria, who was arching into Adam's caress. "It's good to see that some things never change."

"Hopefully your skill at this hasn't." Her voice was tart, but inside she was shaking. Declan's words were teasing, but his touch…Adam's touch…made her feel special. Cherished, even.

Behind her Aria heard Adam chuckle as she challenged Declan.

"You're going to eat your words, sweetheart." Aria's heart melted a bit as Declan used the words he once had. She refused to let it show on her face.

"We'll see." Aria gasped as Adam slid one hand down her torso, over her rib cage and to the heated, naked space between her legs. It had been so long since she'd felt any touch but her own there that her knees buckled.

"Easy." Declan caught her by the backs of her thighs, then ran his lips over the seam where her belly met her leg.

"Oh!" Aria couldn't swallow the cry as, with sure fingers, Adam parted her labia. His other hand continued to play with her breasts, moving between one and then the other, teasing the nipples until they had hardened to the point of pain.

"I'm dying to taste you again." Declan flicked his tongue over the curve of her belly, then over Adam's fingers before sliding through her heated folds.

Aria jolted at the touch. With Adam pressed against her from behind, she had nowhere to go.

"Still so responsive." Not bothering to tease, Declan suckled her clit into his mouth, his tongue swirling and his fangs grazing the sides.

A rush of liquid heat surged between Aria's thighs. For one vague moment she felt as though she should be embarrassed, but then she remembered how Declan had always loved her taste, likening it to sweet honey.

Inhaling deeply, she pushed her hips forward, wanting more of his delicious touch.

"That's my girl." Wrapping his lips around the tight bud, Declan began to suck, causing Aria's entire world to rapidly become focused on the burning space between her legs.

Every muscle in her body tightened as she waited for the inevitable. Declan had always been able to make her come faster than she could even do for herself.

"I want you wrecked tonight, baby." Drawing her to the edge of the orgasm, Declan stopped sucking to thrust his tongue into her slick folds. She shuddered, crying out as a hot, hard burst of pleasure shot through her body. She ground back against Adam as she came and felt the slickness of his arousal against her spine.

"Aah." Aria found herself lost for words as sensation washed over her. She sagged back against Adam, trembling. In front of her, Declan rose to his feet, weaving his arms around her waist.

Surrounded by two hard male bodies, Aria felt an emotion that she couldn't quite put a name to click into place.

She liked it.

"Off." Impatiently she worked her hands in between her body and Declan's and tugged at his belt. "Too many clothes."

Reaching behind, she ran her palm over Adam's hip. He rocked forward, pressing his erection into her bottom.

"Patience, little one." Adam chuckled as he spoke, his hands tracing lightly over her spine. Aria bit her lip. If any other man had called her that, she would have been extremely irritated. In this situation, though, it seemed strangely right.

She barely knew the man, but she'd been born a witch, and she couldn't deny the energy that was flying hot and fast around the room.

Closing her eyes, she decided to just let it take her where it would.

"More." She reached behind her back to undo the clasp of her bra. Adam's fingers nudged her aside, undoing the hooks and sliding the garment down her shoulders slowly, his touch sure.

"As the lady wishes." Stepping back so that she could see his full length, Declan left Aria in the cradle of Adam's arms and lifted his shirt up and over his head.

"Damn." Aria whispered the word and saw the resultant tug upward of Declan's lips. She didn't care that he'd heard.

She was too busy looking at the hard ridges and planes of muscle that made up his torso. She'd deliberately buried the memory of his gorgeous body deep in her mind after he'd left, but now she drank in the sight.

Declan raised an eyebrow at her as his hands came to rest on his belt buckle, and Aria nodded, her mouth dry.

"More." Declan undid the buckle of his belt, then pulled down the zipper of his worn jeans, the noise of the zipper a harsh metallic rasp in the air.

Behind her Aria could feel Adam's muscles tighten, just as her own were, as Declan slid his jeans and briefs down over his lean hips. He stood naked in front of them, the impressive length of his erection pointing toward the ceiling.

"So hot." Aria was momentarily disconcerted at Adam's words when she realized that he was speaking of Declan. But she found she wasn't jealous. And her body yearned to be between the two of them, on the bed, and the need overcame the strangeness of the situation.

Clearly both Adam and Declan still wanted her, even though they obviously lusted for each other as well.

"Your turn." Declan reached for Aria—she noticed that he only stumbled a bit when the distance was short and his cane wasn't present. Sitting himself on the edge of the bed, he pulled Aria down onto his lap, facing forward and waiting for Adam to disrobe.

The werewolf obliged with a cheeky grin. Aria had met shifters before, but never a wolf—they didn't tend to congregate in Salem's Hollow. Fascinated, she watched as Adam quickly divested himself of his clothing. He was shorter than Declan, not as lean, but every bit as ripped. His caramel-colored skin gleamed in the warm light of the solitary lamp, emphasizing the lines of his muscles.

"You okay like that, Dec?" Adam gestured to Declan's leg and Aria, horrified at the thought that she might be hurting him, tried to stand. Declan banded his arms tightly around her middle, holding her in place as he nuzzled his face into her hair.

"I'm much better than okay," he said hoarsely. Aria squirmed on his lap as his hands slid over her breasts, her belly and down to clasp her hips. When his fangs grazed the skin of her neck, right in the place where he had once loved to taste her, she arched her back and moaned.

She found herself a little bit disappointed that he didn't bite.

"Declan. Adam. Please." Aria didn't know how much more teasing she could take. It had been so long, and she wanted them both so much. She reached out for Adam's cock, which was thick and long and already damp at the tip. "No more teasing. I want it fast. I want it now."

Before either man could argue, Aria bent at the waist and sucked the tip of Adam's cock between her lips. His groan rent the air as she ran her tongue beneath the crown, then nipped with her teeth. His taste was warmer than Declan's, more redolent of musk, and she found that she wanted more.

"Declan." She writhed on the vampire's lap. He anticipated her need. Lifting her hips momentarily, he pressed his length to Aria's wet slit and slid inside, moving slowly so that she could feel every inch stretching her flesh.

"Goddess, that's good." Aria spoke around Adam's erection. With the pleasure of Declan inside of her came a sharp bite of pain on flesh that had been so long unused, but she liked it.

"Aria." Declan's voice was husky as he clasped her hips in strong hands and urged her to rock back and forth. The movements caused her mouth to slide up and down the length of Adam's shaft, and she held her breath as he slid deep down into her throat.

"Declan. She's so beautiful." Adam's voice washed over Aria as she let the pleasure take her over. Looking up through the tangle of her lashes, she saw the werewolf's head thrown back in need, the cords of his muscled neck standing out in sharp relief.

He was the beautiful one, him and Declan both. If Aria hadn't felt secure in her own skin she might have been insecure in that moment.

With two gorgeous alpha males looking at her like she was a goddess, though, she thought that that would be a bit ridiculous.

"Lie down, Dec." Adam's voice was thick with desire as, with a great groan, he pulled his cock free of Aria's mouth. Aria wasn't sure what he planned to do, but as Declan lay back on the bed, his feet still flat on the floor, she began to have an idea.

Her nerves began to hum with anticipation.

"Brace yourself." Aria's pulse quickened as Adam placed his hands gently on her shoulders and eased her back until she lay flat on top of Declan, his cock still embedded inside of her. The new position changed the angle at which Declan penetrated her, and she gasped as the head of his cock hit a sensitive area deep inside.

"Aah…" When Adam clasped his cock in his hand and began to brush it through Aria's slippery folds and lower, she couldn't stop the flinch, despite her arousal.

"I'm not sure how I feel about that." She couldn't form a more delicate way to put it. "I don't know if I want you…there."

Beneath her, she felt Declan vibrate with laughter. The movement caused an interesting friction where their bodies were joined, and she propped herself up, her elbows on Declan's chest, as she looked up at Adam with wide eyes.

The grin he gave her was wicked and unapologetic.

"I don't intend to put my cock *there*." Adam's voice was full of wicked intent. Aria frowned as he prowled over her. Where on earth else would it go?

"Holy goddess!"

Adam ran his cock along the exposed length of Declan's before pressing the slick head against Aria's opening. One thrust of his hips and the tip of his member had worked its way inside of her, pressed tightly together with Declan's erection, and filling Aria so tightly that the pleasure and pain mixed and she saw stars.

"Oh. I don't…I don't think…" Adam began to withdraw, and Aria whimpered. It wasn't an entirely comfortable sensation, but the razor sharp slash of pain was edged with dark pleasure.

"Go slowly, Adam." Declan wrapped his arms around Aria's waist from beneath her. He traced fingers over the plump undersides of her breasts as Adam again began to work his way inside of Aria, not stopping until both he and Declan were sheathed to the hilt.

For a long minute all that Aria could do was struggle to accept the physical sensations that were rioting through her body. Heat crackled through her veins when Declan lowered one hand from her breast to strum over her clit, his touch slow and sure.

"Yes." She barely recognized her own voice, escaping from between her lips before she had time to think about what she was saying. "Yes. This is what I want."

A groan escaped both men as Adam pressed his hips forward. At the same time, Declan thrust upward. Neither man could move very much, but the tiny slide of the cocks inside of her made tight coils of need spiral deep in Aria's gut.

"Fuck." From beneath her Declan brushed a damp kiss over Aria's shoulder. "You're so tight. So good. I don't know how long I'm going to last."

"That makes two of us." Sweat beaded Adam's brow as Aria bowed at the pleasure of another small thrust inside of her tight heat.

The two men timed their small movements, moving into her at the same moment, pushing until Aria felt certain that she would explode. Then they would recede, just enough for her to catch her breath.

Her need coiled ever more tightly. She needed something, just something more to explode.

As her body tightened, Adam slid his hands down to her opening. Pulling the skin of her labia taut, he nodded at Declan, who increased his pressure and pace on Aria's clit. In less time than it took to her inhale, the pleasure crashed over her, an out-of-control blaze that made her scream.

Though her haze she felt Declan's fangs scraping over the tender skin in the spot where her neck met her shoulder. She knew what he wanted, but even through her need she wasn't sure she could give it to him.

"Drink from me, Dec." Adam bent lower, causing a second series of ripples to riot through Aria as he offered his neck to Declan.

Aria was trapped in the middle of the dense, dark bliss as Declan sank his fangs into Adam's neck and began to suckle. Adam groaned, stiffened, then pushed all the way inside of Aria's heat. The smell of musk scented the air as Adam came, and rich red blood dripped down onto Aria's shoulder as the movement pulled Declan's fangs from Adam's skin.

Declan slowly laved his tongue over the spilled drops. The rasp of his lips on her sensitive skin made her shudder, and the small movement sent Declan over the edge. She felt him shoot inside of her, and a final shudder racked her body.

Though she knew that it wouldn't last, Aria allowed herself to be held, to be pulled tightly against hard male flesh as they all collapsed in a spent heat on the bed.

It felt so good, felt so right that she didn't want to think about what was to come.

She just wanted to bask in the bliss, and worry about returning to the reality of her own life later.

Hours later, Aria awoke feeling as if a brittle cold had seeped into her bones and was there to stay.

It wiped away the sweet glow from her encounter with Adam and Declan in an instant, turning the delicious warmth into shards of ice. Sitting up abruptly, she raked her fingers through her hair and looked around, her heart pounding wildly. She could see the energy in the room, Adam's aura, Declan's, the crimson haze of sex.

Something else was there too, but try as she might, she couldn't see it.

Magic crackled in her fingers as she crawled to her knees, careful not to disturb the men who lay on either side of her, one cold as ice, one hot like a flame. Declan, she knew, slept like...well...the dead. Adam, she had no idea, but his animalistic snores told her that he was deeply asleep.

Crawling to the edge of the bed, she pulled the sword from Declan's cane, a backup to her sometimes unreliable magic.

The sensation that she wasn't alone, that something was watching her faded as quickly as it had come. Before Aria could blink, she knew, somehow, that she was once again alone.

Adrenaline coursed through her body as she looked down

at the slumbering men. Her belly did a slow roll as she studied the lean lines of Declan's face, a face she knew so well and yet seemed new to her all over again.

What had happened between the three of them had been more than sex. She couldn't deny it. But she couldn't think when she was around Declan and, more than that, the energy that had woken her had left her shaken. It had left an oily residue in the air, one that she could all but smell.

The energy hadn't appeared to her until Declan had reappeared in her life. It was tied to him, but she was shaken enough by the tender, steamy encounter that she needed to clear her head before she questioned the men.

Warily Aria shifted on the bed. Declan, she knew, was well able to take care of himself—he'd been a soldier, a warrior, many times over his long years. Adam, she wasn't sure about, but his rigid bearing spoke of military training.

Still, she wasn't comfortable leaving them, vulnerable to the dark energy as they slumbered.

She closed her eyes and drew her desire to her mind's eye. Unlike her sister, Aria rarely used words spoken aloud to channel her magic, preferring instead to rely solely on intention and will.

She pictured Declan and Adam sleeping soundly, so deeply that they did not wake as she slid from the bed, dressed and left the motel. They wouldn't wake unless a malevolent energy made its presence known.

The surge of power in her fingertips, and the resultant blue light, told her when she had tapped into the stream of power.

Waiting a moment to make sure that the spell took hold, Aria then performed the actions she had envisioned. Once she was dressed she raked her fingers through her now messy bob of chestnut hair and turned to indulge in one final look at the two men.

She could see the energy trails of both, swirling together in a sensuous dance. Hers was there too, because sex entwined spirits.

The fact that she could physically see her energy twined in the rope that bound the two men was something she needed to think about. She wasn't upset, exactly, that Declan had found Adam—the supernatural were sexual creatures, and needed the comfort of skin-to—skin contact. And she'd long ago accepted her part in their breakup.

He might have left her, but she'd pushed him until he did.

But if he left her again, could she survive? Could she turn away now that she'd experienced the tenderness of the man she'd once loved, and another man as well?

She needed to think. And she needed to do it alone.

Chapter Three

The chill of the fall air outside the cocoon of the motel room added to the desolation that Aria felt. Shoving her hands into the pockets of her leather coat, she strode down the sidewalk to her motorcycle, which was still parked in the now-empty lots of Harry's.

As she pulled her helmet from the storage beneath the seat, something that felt like a million tiny needles showered over her skin. She stiffened, waiting to see if the now-familiar sensation passed.

It didn't. Inhaling deeply, she discovered the scent of something otherworldly on the air, something that wasn't werewolf, vampire or magic.

The blow struck from behind, causing pain to explode through her skull as, caught off guard, she fell to the sidewalk. The concrete kissed her skin, and she could smell blood—her blood—hanging on the air.

"Stop!" She didn't have a chance to picture what she wanted as, out of the corner of her eyes, she saw a blur of gray rushing at her again. Throwing up her arms, she managed to catch the blow there and save her face.

Rolling away quickly, she sprang to her feet and whirled to face her attacker.

Her mouth fell open when she saw that it was. She didn't know what it was. It had the form of a person, but was misty and gray. It didn't look like a solid entity, though it had certainly felt like one when it had hit her.

"What do you want?" Aria tried to distract the thing as she pictured the gray thing disappearing, and the sensation of safety surrounding her.

Her magic sparked fitfully, and Aria knew it was because she couldn't focus.

The gray thing didn't respond, just swung back and forth fretfully...stalking her, Aria realized. There was something off about the being.

There was no sense of sentience. It was as if this creature was no more than a shadowy zombie, programmed to do only one thing.

"What do you want?" Aria repeated herself, and there was still no reply—there wasn't even a sense that the creature had heard her, let alone acknowledged her.

This was her chance. Drawing everything that she had into her will, she pictured the scene again, and this time the heat of her magic streamed blue light from her fingers.

The gray mass charged at her again, swinging its ghostly fists as she lifted her hands and willed the streaks of blue light to make the creature disappear. With a great roar and the stench of burning flesh it did, fading away to little more than remnants of smoke.

As her heart pounded in her chest, Aria scrambled backward, still crouched at the ready, the light of magic still streaming from her fingers.

"What the fuck just happened?"

Aria groaned. From behind her she heard the crash of the motel room door slamming open, and recognized Declan's voice.

Casting a new spell had clearly broken her previous one. The men were awake, and they were not impressed.

"Aria." Declan was at her side before she could blink, and his arms were around her, pulling her tightly. Her heart skipped a beat. This—this touching without lust—this made her want all kinds of things that she couldn't have.

She batted his arms away, then crossed her own over her chest.

"Are you all right?"

Aria could see the wolf in Adam as he crouched, sniffing the air. He growled, the sound more animal than human, and a shiver skated over her skin.

"I'm fine." Her magic was still giving off feeble, last-minute sparks from her fingers. She saw Declan glower at it, then at her, and she knew that she'd been caught.

"What the hell did you think you were doing?" Declan was nothing if not alpha, and his male pride was quite clearly wounded at the thought that she had run out on the pair of them.

"Leaving." Her words were defensive. *Like you left me before*, her brain silently added, a knee-jerk reaction before she could stop it. From the way Declan's pale brow furrowed, she knew that he'd made the connection.

"I don't recognize the smell." Clearly frustrated, Adam rose to his feet, scrubbing his strong hands over sleepy-looking eyes. "It stinks of dying flowers, and it's not something I've scented before."

Dying flowers. Aria frowned, not sure what to think of that.

"It looked like a person, but…not." Suddenly weary, she fisted her hands in her hair and tugged lightly. "I don't think it was fully…I mean…it was like it was attacking on instinct. I don't think it had any thoughts of its own."

Declan caught her chin in his hand, and his vampire vision scrutinized the skin of her face, which was thankfully unmarked.

Her elbows, knees and forearms were another story.

"Why were you leaving?" Avoiding his stare, Aria looked over his shoulder to where Adam stood. Her eyes moved to the bite marks that marred his neck, and she felt as though her heart was being squeezed by a giant fist.

Aria shrugged off Declan's touch, shaking like an angry bird, though she was more unnerved by the tender touch than angry. She didn't answer, didn't know how to express what she was feeling.

"I'm going back to Belladonna. I want to make sure that Lori's okay." Aria didn't make it five steps when she found herself scooped off her feet and dangled ass over teakettle, her stomach pressed into Declan's shoulder.

Rather than kick and scream, which she knew from experience that he'd enjoy, she growled, the sound full of the wrath of woman.

"Save it, sweetie." Adam fell in beside them, protecting Aria's exposed side as, together, the two men broke into a supernaturally fast run down the street, Aria bouncing over Declan's shoulder the entire time.

"We told you why we were back here. We've had a taste of you now, and we're sure as hell not letting go."

Wrathfully, Aria stared at the fantastic view of Declan's ass, which was at eye level. Declan had done what she couldn't— had acknowledged the intensity of what had happened between the three of them.

But she wasn't the only reason Declan was back. And until he told her more, she would hold her heart close.

"What the hell?" Aria heard her sister's exclamation as she was carried upside down into the closed shop, accompanied by a werewolf and a vampire.

Still, Aria didn't miss the quick flicker of glee that sparked in Lorelai's eyes as she no doubt saw the sexual red energy threads binding the three.

"It's a long story," she began, glowering at Declan as he slid her down his body.

She tried to ignore the lust that ignited as she felt the skin-to-skin contact.

"I'd love to hear this, too." Adam crossed his arms, looking just as irritated as Declan, and Aria blinked in surprise.

She'd been so lonely, how on earth had she wound up with two pissed-off alpha males in her company? She was so not in the mood to deal with even one right at the moment. She was edgy and emotional, and she couldn't quite quell the nausea from her race down the street at vampire speed.

"It's a story I'm happy to share with my *sister*, after the two of you leave." Aria pointed at the door, and neither man moved so much as a whisper. Frustrated, she cast a look at Lorelai, who was staring at Adam in disbelief.

"Do you really have to hog both of them?" Aria was darkly amused to see Adam shift uncomfortably beneath Lorelai's frank perusal. "Obviously I'd never go after Declan, but this one? Hello."

"Lori!" Her twin wasn't often so frank, but then, these two were fine specimens of manhood.

"And I didn't have a choice. They're sort of…a package deal."

Lori furrowed her brow

"Oh." Understanding seemed to dawn, and Aria felt her cheeks flush scarlet under her twin's frank perusal. "Well, that worked better than I had intended."

Lorelai's eyes widened as the words fell from her lips. Knowing her twin as she did, Aria narrowed her eyes, honing in on what her sister wasn't saying.

"What did you do?" Her words were a whisper, but one she knew that the two men would pick up on.

Whatever it was, she knew that she did *not* want them to hear it.

"Could you two please go somewhere else?" She thought of the shadowy gray figure and felt her pulse speed up. She wanted them to go so that she could talk to her sister, but she was a little bit afraid of being left alone.

It seemed to be the story of her life.

She thought that they would refuse, but Declan instead inclined his head to one side, his version, she knew, of an enthusiastic nod.

"We'll be right outside." She only hoped that that was enough distance to put a damper on Declan's vampire hearing.

As soon as the men left, she whirled on her sister, her finger pointing accusingly.

"I smell roses. I smell strawberries and jasmine. A lust spell, Lori? Am I really so scary that my own sister thinks I can't get a date?" Anger trembled through her, as did disappointment. She would forgive Lorelai, she knew that already, because her sister never acted with anything but the best intentions.

But now she understood why the two men were so focused on her. They were being compelled by a spell. None of it was real.

Trying to fight through a crushing depression, she looked her sister square in the face. Lorelai was eyeing her warily.

"I only wanted to make you happy."

Aria heaved a sigh and tucked a strand of hair behind her ear.

"I know." She was more disappointed than she wanted to be, knowing that the two men—especially Declan—weren't acting of their own accord. "I'm pissed, but let's talk about it later. "

"Why are you all scratched up?" Seeming grateful for the distraction, Lorelai reached out and ran tentative fingers over her sister's cuts. The worst of them were still tacky with blood.

"Have you ever come across any mention of a gray, shadowlike creature in any of the books?" In the back room of the apothecary the twins kept all the volumes of their family's history, the diaries, the *Books of Shadows*.

"What kind of gray shadow?" Lorelai had paled at the words, and Aria knew with a sinking sensation in her gut that she wasn't going to like what she heard next.

"It looked like a person. But it was more of a mist…and it

wasn't sentient. I'm sure of it." Aria resisted the urge to press her fingers to her temples as Lorelai uttered a curse.

"One of Gran's diaries mentioned the exact same thing." Lorelai tugged on the length of her ponytail, the golden curls springing back as soon as she released them. "I don't remember which one, though. Let me look."

"It's from the spell, isn't it?" They'd never been able to keep secrets from one another.

Lorelai shook her head stubbornly.

"It can't be. We've both cast thousands of spells and nothing like this has ever happened." Lorelai looked as though she might cry when she looked at the blood on Aria's arm.

"I think it might be, Lori." She couldn't sugarcoat it, not even to save her sister's feelings. Her intuition was telling her that this creature was cued into her specifically, and she had a sinking certainty that it was an unwitting result of the lust spell.

"Let me go look through Gran's diaries." Lorelai set her chin, as if she knew that her sister would argue. "If I made this mess, then I need to clean it up."

"No." Aria's voice was firm, and she made sure that it was loud enough that Declan would be able to hear her outside. "I don't want this thing anywhere near you."

"It would be best for you to go upstairs, Lorelai." Declan was in the room so quickly that Aria blinked, startled. Once upon a time she'd been used to the speed with which he moved, but it had been so long. "Go to bed. We'll talk again in the morning."

"Do you think she'll be safe up there?" Aria asked.

Lorelai grumbled and insisted on at least dragging the box of Gran's diaries out of the back room. She placed a stack of them on the counter for Aria and the men to flip through.

"We'll be able to hear her." They'd also be able to reach her in time, Aria knew, if anything happened. Or at least, Declan would—she didn't know about Adam.

The werewolf entered the shop as Lorelai passed through

the door to the stairwell which led upstairs to the apartment that the twins shared. He paused to lock the door behind him, and to draw the blinds over the glass.

In his hand he held a coffee cup from McDonald's, the only fast food joint in the small town.

"I thought you might need a boost." He handed the steaming cup to Aria. The heat seeped through the thin cardboard to singe her fingers.

She was floored by the thoughtfulness of the gesture.

The reserves that she had built over the years began to melt.

"Did Lorelai have any insight into your assailant?" Declan raised an eyebrow at her, and she squirmed under the intensity of his stare.

She wanted him again, damn it. She wanted them both, even though she'd just had them.

She couldn't have them. They didn't know what they were doing.

"She remembered a mention of something similar in one of my Gran's old books." Aria gestured nervously to the pile that Lorelai had left on the table. Aria recognized the look in Declan's eyes.

He wanted her, too.

She didn't know if she had the strength to resist him.

"Did she have any idea of why?" One look at Declan's face as he crossed the small space between them told her that he already had a pretty good idea of the answer, and she wondered how much he had overheard with his vampire hearing.

She couldn't, just couldn't, admit that her twin had cast a spell to get her laid.

"It's to do with a spell." Aria kept her tone deliberately vague. She was distracted as Declan stalked the remaining distance between them, then lifted her onto the counter.

With one quick movement he'd unsnapped her jeans and his own and was pressing his cock against her entrance. She was already hot and wet, and all of her common sense fled as, without any warning, he seated himself inside of her.

"Declan!" Aria's voice echoed off the walls of the shop as she clung to his shoulders and looked over his shoulder at Adam. After what had transpired between them, she knew it was ridiculous to feel embarrassed that the werewolf was watching.

"Don't stop on my account." Though the werewolf continued to chew on his late dinner, he watched with avid interest as Declan caught Aria around the waist and began to thrust, hot and fast.

"I just can't get enough of you." Declan's fangs extended as he set a merciless pace. Aria's fingers slid from his shoulders to claw at the counter, trying to find something, anything, to grab on to. "I never could."

Though her heart quickened with guilt, she was too far gone into the pleasure to do more than moan as Declan brought her to a quick, brutal climax with the press of his thumb on her clit. She felt him flood inside of her himself, his tongue swiping over the tips of his fangs as he came.

Panting, Aria winced as Declan slid from between her legs. What the hell had that been?

She blinked in amazement as Adam filled the space Declan had vacated. He pushed inside her more slowly than Declan had, his passage eased by the vampire's pleasure.

"Declan." With wild eyes Aria looked at the man who had once meant so much to her. He was zipping his jeans, but possession sparkled in his eyes.

Mine, he seemed to be saying. *You're both mine.*

Aria barely had a moment to catch her breath before Adam began to move, seating himself inside of her again and again with long, hard strokes.

She came before he could even move his hand between her legs, her flesh so sensitive by that point that every little move was painful and still full of pleasure.

As her flesh clenched around his cock, Adam thrust one last time and grunted, his heat filling the depths of her belly.

Aria's elbow knocked one of her Gran's diaries off the counter as Adam withdrew from her heat. Flustered, she slid from the counter, straightening her hair, her clothing as she bent to retrieve it.

"Holy goddess." It had fallen open to the page with a pencil drawing of the shadowy figure.

Her Gran had always taught her that there were no coincidences in the world. This page was important.

With trembling fingers, she held it out so that the two men could see.

Declan looked at her, his face expressionless.

"There are no coincidences." His words were low, but she realized at once that he was repeating something she'd often said to him.

"No, there are not." She turned the book back to face her, reading aloud.

At times a spell will multiply by three, despite the practitioner's intentions. When this occurs, there needs to be darkness to balance the light, a payment for the pleasure. In my experience, this took the form of a man, a demon of sorts who nevertheless had no mind to call his own. His purpose was to track the one who benefitted from the spell, to eliminate him or her. To erase one is to erase the other. Though this shadowy figure seems to threaten, he is, at the bottom, simply the universe's way of again balancing the scales.

"Shit." Aria could think of nothing else to say.

"Indeed." This was all that Declan said in reply.

"Should we...I don't know. Should we go hunt it down?" She'd be damned if she was going to let some shadowy byproduct of a spell haunt her. With a pang she realized that killing it would mean that the spell would be broken—Adam and Declan would realize that they didn't actually want her.

They would leave.

It was the right thing to do. Apart from the fact that she

couldn't live with a demon stalking her every move, she couldn't live her life as a lie.

Although neither of them had told her why they were really here. And she couldn't bring herself to ask.

Swallowing thickly against the flood of emotions that the realization brought out, Aria looked up when Adam stepped in front of her.

The werewolf sniffed the air and nodded.

"I don't think we'll have to go hunting. I think it's going to find us."

Chapter Four

Declan studied Aria in his peripheral vision as the three of them made their way down the street to the town's only all-night, non fast food diner. He'd thrown her off-balance when he'd placed her on the counter and touched her, but he'd meant to do just that.

It wouldn't be long before she realized that her sister was wrong, that a demon birthed from a spell wasn't what was hunting them. He wouldn't be at all surprised, in fact, if she'd already figured it out.

But he knew her better than she thought, even after all these years. If she discovered why he had really left her, that he'd sacrificed his freedom to save her, she'd rip out his hair strand by strand.

He'd always loved her violent side.

He'd have to tell her eventually, he knew. And she'd never forgive him for the decision he'd made. Because when the Capitol had come to him three years earlier, when they'd told him they required his precognition services, they hadn't given him a choice. If he refused, those he loved—namely Aria— would die.

If she'd known, she would have insisted on coming with

him. And the Capitol would have sucked her dry, feeding on her magic until only a brittle shell remained.

So he'd left. And now, because his senses had pulled him back toward her, he had placed her in danger once again.

This time was different, though. This time he wouldn't leave.

Sitting in between a vampire and a werewolf did nothing to diminish Aria's lust.

The last thing she'd expected after they'd found her Gran's diary was to be dragged to Stella's, a diner she'd come to since she was a child. But Adam hadn't been able to track the scent of the demon.

"I can smell it, all around, but it doesn't lead anywhere." His frustration was apparent and made Aria long to stroke her fingers through his hair. "And I need a decent meal if we're going to be facing down a demon."

Aria hadn't wanted to leave Lorelai alone, but Declan had pointed out that the demon was attuned to Aria and no one else.

"It's going to come after you. Lorelai will be safer away from you."

Aria knew better than to argue with him. Declan was alpha to the core and would never dream of leaving her in danger, and she could already tell that Adam was cut from the same cloth. So here she was, picking at a plate of French fries while Declan sipped from his flask on one side of her, and Adam ate everything on the menu on the other.

"How are you holding up?" A faint residue of scarlet painted Declan's lips as he sipped from his metal flask. His eyes watched her every move. "You're not eating."

"I don't normally eat a meal at four in the morning." Her tone was waspish and she knew it. Willing herself to calm down, she managed a tight smile. "I'm fine. I'm more irritated than anything."

Her nerves were humming because of the overbearing presence of a vampire and a werewolf. The reappearance of Declan in her life had aroused all of the longing she'd once had, and though it might have just been the result of their sexual encounter, Aria didn't care for the idea of being without Adam, either.

And she was terrified that none of it was real. It wouldn't be a sudden surge of knowledge for them, but she knew that they would wonder why they had taken up with her.

"In all of this drama, we haven't had a chance to talk to you about why we came for you, Aria." Screwing the cap back on to his flask, Declan reached across the table and caught her hand in his. He looked at Adam as he did, and though the werewolf was busy inhaling what appeared to be his third steak sandwich, he nodded in agreement and understanding.

"You didn't come for me." The words were out of her mouth before she thought them through, and though she cringed inwardly, she pressed on. "You weren't disappointed to see me again, but I wasn't the reason you came here."

"True." Declan spoke slowly, and Aria felt her heart sink as he confirmed what she had said.

"Why?" Dropping all pretenses of spunk, she rested her cheek on her hand, suddenly weary. "Why not just leave things as they were. We were doing all right."

"Adam and I met not long after you and I parted ways." Declan began, reaching for Aria's hand,

She pulled away.

"I always knew that there was a piece of his heart that I could never have," Adam added, shoving his empty plate away and fixing his eyes on Aria's face. "Because it belonged to a woman he'd once known. He was determined to get back to her someday, once he'd fulfilled what the Capitol wanted from him."

Aria felt her thoughts stutter as she turned that knowledge around in her head.

"Wait a minute." She saw Declan's eyes fixed on her face, saw the truth in them. Fury began to rise inside of her. "You told me you left because vampires needed to roam."

"I left because the Capitol would have killed you if I'd refused their demands." Declan's voice was steady and full of strength. Aria ground her teeth to keep from shouting obscenities. "And you can hate me for it. But I would rather have broken your heart and still have you alive than the alternative."

Aria's mind whirled.

"It wasn't your choice." Hot, angry tears clawed their way through her throat. "I would have chosen to fight at your side."

"They wouldn't have allowed it." Declan said flatly, slamming his palm flat on the table. "They didn't allow anything. Complete obedience or death. Though they told me they'd let me go someday—told Adam the same thing—I began to see that they never would."

"Declan's precognition was too valuable to them," Adam's voice was full of suppressed rage. "And so were my connections to the wolf packs. But it's how we met, how we decided to escape. If we died trying, well, we figured we were better off."

Aria's mind whirled as she tried to take in the influx of information.

"But why come here?" Turning, she looked Declan square in the face. "If you left to ensure my safety, that seems like a waste of effort."

The men looked at each other, and Aria found herself wanting to smack their heads together. It was as if they had their own nonverbal language.

"I had one of my premonitions," Declan's voice was low and determined. "And it drew me—us—here."

Hope was a wild thing curling inside of Aria's chest. Could it really be?

"So…in theory, we destroy this spell creature, and we can… can…" she couldn't spit out the words.

Declan's face was set and serious.

"I think there's more than a spell creature, Aria."

Aria frowned and looked from Declan to the werewolf, who had finished his steak and was now guzzling what appeared to be a pint glass of orange juice.

Realization clicked. "You think the Capitol has found you.

That they tracked you down after you escaped." Panic rose in a dark cloud, and she tried to stand. "Lori!"

Two large, masculine hands gripped her, one hot, one cold, pulling her back down to the table. Two pairs of hard eyes—soldiers' eyes—stared at her.

"Lori will be safer if we're not there." Adam spoke flatly. "And you'll be safer if we are."

They were talking in circles, and Aria had had enough. She'd had one hell of a day, her emotions were a mess and a demon was stalking her.

"Spit it out already." She slammed her hands on the laminated tabletop. The movement jolted her glass, and cold water sloshed over the side, wetting her hand.

Declan raised an eyebrow at her. She glowered back.

"We're not leaving you. Not until the Capitol has fallen." Aria's mouth fell open as she looked from one alpha male to the other. Anger rose, hot and fast, as she realized that they had planned this all out for her, just as Declan had made life-shattering decisions for her three years ago.

Fury painted her vision red.

Standing, she hissed when Declan laid a hand on her wrist.

"Touch me again, and I'll give you a hex that will make your cock fall off." Though she was certain that he would follow her, she climbed right over him and out of the booth, stomping her way to the washroom that was located at the back of the restaurant.

She slammed the door shut behind the small, single stall room and leaned back against it, her heart pounding a rapid tattoo in her chest.

"This sucks." Aria had never been one to cry, not if she could help it. But this—there was nothing she could do about this.

Declan had tried to save her with his leaving, but she couldn't get past the fact that he'd made the decision for her. A decision that wasn't the one she would have made herself.

She knew her lover, and suspected Adam wouldn't leave Salem's Hollow—wouldn't leave her—until she was safe.

She'd be damned if she was going to tie them to her like that when they already had each other, though if she was honest with herself, she wanted them both, wanted them willingly back in her life.

Sometimes Fate was a bitch.

Once she could breathe again, she crossed to the cracked porcelain sink. The pipes groaned and the water spurted out, tainting the air with the scent of minerals. Rinsing her face, she ground her teeth and understood what she had to do.

Closing her eyes, Aria inhaled deeply and pictured the creature she had seen earlier, the gray, ethereal shape. She focused her intentions, and at the same time channeled her energy into her fingertips.

She wasn't afraid of a shadow creature. Wasn't afraid of the Capitol. They were the organization that ruled over the supernatural creatures of the world, true enough, but she refused to believe that they couldn't be beaten.

Especially not with rage filling her blood.

"Come and get me, asshole." Aria's voice echoed off the walls as she invited the creature to her. "If I can't handle a little shadow demon, I don't deserve to call myself witch."

It took a moment before the whoosh of energy came, before she registered the out-of—place scent.

Decaying roses.

Her muscles tensed as she raised her head but saw nothing in the mirror. She didn't trust her eyes—she could sense the demon.

She whirled, pressing her back to the sink. The thing hovered just inside the door, the size of a large man. She again sensed the lack of awareness from the creature.

Something wasn't right. If the Capitol had sent something to get Declan back, or to hurt her in his place, surely they would have sent something more than this. This demon was dark, but it was as if it had been cued for one purpose only—

to kill her and restore the balance altered by Lorelai's spell. As it slid slowly, threateningly toward her, she tried to channel her magic.

Focus, she told herself. She would take care of this, of what she was suddenly sure was indeed a by-product of Lorelai's spell, and deal with whatever shit the Capitol threw down after.

She'd accepted the need for balance, even if it meant giving up Adam and Declan. But she wasn't the one who was going to die to accomplish it.

As she'd done outside the motel, she pictured the demon disappearing. A few sparks danced from her fingers in the direction of the creature, but the stream of power that she was trying to reach for eluded her.

Tendrils of fear began to wind their way around her muscles as her bravado disappeared and she realized that she might very well be in trouble.

"Fuck this." Taking a precious moment to close her eyes against the threat, Aria tried to pull her magic toward her again. A short burst exploded from her fingers, slamming the creature back against the bathroom door, but it wasn't deterred and just kept coming.

Blast, slam. Blast, slam. Aria could feel her energy draining, and it became harder to channel even the small bursts of magic.

She tried again to pull her power to her, and with her heart in her throat realized that she was drained. She had nothing left.

The creature reached for her, its arms outstretched, and Aria feinted to the side to avoid its grasp. Her foot looped behind her ankle, and she fell hard onto the tiles of the floor, jarring her spine painfully.

She shrieked as the demon turned and bent, those fingers inches away from brushing her skin.

The door exploded open, half of the door frame coming with it. A massive silvery wolf leaped into the small room, its muscles bunching with power. It flew at the demon, jaws open wide, lethal-looking teeth glinting in the neon light.

Declan was in the room a fraction of a second later. Aria was in shock as he drew a dangerous-looking blade from the hilt of his cane. His movements graceful despite his injury, he swiped the blade through the air once, twice.

As the possibility of losing him again slapped her hard in the face, Aria was faced with a hard truth.

I still love him.

Before the demon's shadowy head separated from its body beneath Declan's blade, Aria felt power blast through her. Raising her hands, she sent a wall of her magic careening toward the demon. It slammed into the creature—through it—and the thing floated upward before bursting into eerie amethyst flame.

The rest of its form quickly followed suit, tingeing the air with the smell of flowers.

Declan was at Aria's side, lifting her into his arms before she could even process what had happened. With his arms wrapped tightly around her waist, he kissed her over and over again.

Something was wrong with that, but her mind was too full of Declan, and she couldn't think what.

"Thank you." She managed to mutter when her lips were finally free. "I...I was running out of steam." It galled her that she hadn't been able to handle the demon on her own, but she had her life, so she wasn't about to complain.

"If you hadn't run away from us..." Declan's words were a growl. Remembering why she had run, Aria looked away from the probing blue beam of the vampire's eyes.

A silvery wolf rubbed its furry head beneath her hand as they all turned to watch the lavender remnants of the demon dance on the air.

"Aria." Declan buried his face in her air. Shaken, Aria leaned into him, savoring the sensation of his solid body beneath her fingers. "Please. Let us stay. All of us, together."

Joy leaped through her. It was tinged with fire. Fire...heat...

her warm feelings faded as an inferno of pain swept through her body.

Movement in the corner of the room caught her eye and she jerked, turning to see a great purple serpent, its teeth sinking into the tender flesh of her leg. Her magic sparked fitfully in her fingers, but she'd used it all vanquishing the shadow creature.

"Dec...Adam..." She could feel toxins moving through her as the snake, the symbol of the Capitol, a symbol that was familiar to every supernatural child even if the workings of the mysterious group were not, worked through her body. She watched, as if from outside of her body, as the werewolf howled with rage and slammed the snake into the ground. As she fell, the last thing she saw was Declan, his own throat bared to the fangs of the snake, as he slashed his sword at the beast.

The snake, with an impossibly human look on his evil face, lowered his teeth to Declan's neck.

"No!" The scream came from Aria, and yet not. Her body became stiff as a board as something she had never felt and couldn't describe slammed through her, taking over her body, suffusing her with heat.

"Love is the strongest magic of all." The voice that came from her throat was hers, but sounded as if a hundred of her were speaking at once. The heat of magic pushed through her entire body, but it was more than she'd ever felt before, ripping through her flesh, a wash of crimson that began a wall of flame. She screamed, her eyes rolling back in her head as the flame—her energy—incinerated the snake whole.

She collapsed to the ground as the snake disintegrated, then disappeared as if it had never been there at all.

Minutes passed. Or maybe it was hours. Finally Aria felt the touch of a cool hand on her cheek, looked up to find Declan staring at her with amazement.

"What the hell was that?"

"I don't know." She turned to see the last moments of Adam's shift, the silver pelt disappearing from view and leaving golden skin for her to eye.

Lots of naked golden skin.

She should have been exhausted. Confused. Terrified.

Instead she felt like a goddess, full of power and life. And a pleasant hum worked along her skin when she saw that Adam had a massive erection.

"Goddess." She inhaled sharply as she saw it.

Adam grinned. "Fighting gets wolves excited."

She choked on a protest when he fisted his cock in his own hand and stroked once, up and down.

Aria cast a nervous glance over her shoulder at the splintered door frame. Neither Adam nor Declan seemed at all bothered by the idea that someone could walk in on them at any moment.

"Declan worked his vampire mojo to clear the restaurant." Aria jolted at the searing heat of Adam's skin as he pressed up behind her. His cock jutted into the small of her back, and she couldn't hold back a moan.

"Guys, this hardly seems like the time…" Her words were lost as Declan dipped his head to suckle her breast into his mouth through the thin cotton of her T-shirt. Her back arched and she cried out at the sensation.

Something wasn't right about this…the thought was hovering just below the surface…

It surfaced.

"You were serious? That if the threat from the Capitol was gone, you would still want me?" Aria's body tensed as she blurted out the question. Both men halted their movements, and Aria looked up to see a hint of confusion on Declan's face.

"Haven't we already said so?" His hands were cool against the skin of her stomach as he tugged her shirt up and off her head, then pulled her bra down below her breasts.

His fingers began to strum her nipples, and Aria had a hard time following the conversation.

"The Capitol will never stop coming, Aria." Adam made short work of her jeans, shoving them down her hips until they fell to the floor, binding her ankles. Placing his hand flat on her back, he pressed gently until she was leaning forward a bit at the waist.

She shuddered at the feel of four hands on her skin.

"But I'll never leave you again. *We'll* never leave you." Declan scraped his fangs over her neck, a mark of possession, and Aria felt her last reserves crumble. She wasn't sure how she felt about Adam in the long term yet, but she liked him and was attracted to him. Relationships had been built on less, so she was willing to give it a try. "But I won't take the decision away from you again. I need to hear you say it, Aria. Will you be with us?"

Adam rubbed his fingers through her wetness, then slid the liquid through the division of her ass cheeks.

"What…" Aria's body tensed as Adam's finger pressed against the pucker of flesh. She felt like she could protest, but the dark pleasure she felt as he worked a damp finger into that forbidden tightness excited her unbearably.

"Aria." Abandoning her breasts, Declan undid his own jeans. Bracing his injured leg, he lifted her easily with his vampire strength, pressing his own erection to her damp cleft and filling her in one thrust.

"Goddess!" The angle allowed him to seat himself deeply inside of her, and Aria saw stars. She twined her arms and legs around Declan, clinging tightly as he began to move, forcing Adam's finger to work in and out of her as well, relaxing the tight ring of muscle.

"More." Aria's arousal soared fast and hot, like the flames of a fire. She tilted her pelvis forward, pressing into Declan's cock, but she still wanted—needed—more.

"Answer us."

Aria inhaled sharply as she felt Adam withdraw his finger, then work the head of his massive erection between her lower cheeks. She arched her back, silently begging for more, but the werewolf held himself still. "Damn it, Aria, you owe Declan an answer, at least."

Aria closed her eyes and tried to focus on the question. Adam's free hand splayed over her stomach, stroking the skin there in a feathering motion, and she squirmed and sighed with delight.

This—this felt so right. Now that the spell had been broken, she had everything she wanted within arms' reach.

"Please." Neither men gave her what she wanted, and she huffed with exasperation. She knew what she would do—there was no other choice for her. But she also knew that it would not be easy—this relationship would be full of strange dynamics, and having to keep not just one, but two alpha males in line would surely test her patience.

"Yes." As soon as she spoke Adam began to press forward, entering the impossibly tight channel with painstaking slowness. "Oh. Oh."

Adam groaned as slowly, finally he hilted inside of her. Aria felt impossibly full, to the point of pain, and yet nothing had ever felt more right than the two of them with her.

"Yes?" Declan pulled back to look into Aria's face, and she met his brilliant blue stare with her own emerald green one. If she looked over her shoulder, she knew that Adam's golden eyes would glow with the same intensity.

She smiled at the man who had never relinquished his hold on her heart. It was a wild risk, but it was one she was willing to take.

"Yes. Yes, I'll try.

* * * * *

A sneaky peek at next month...

NOCTURNE™

BEYOND DARKNESS...BEYOND DESIRE

My wish list for next month's titles...

In stores from 21st March 2014:

❑ The Wolf Siren – Karen Whiddon

❑ Immortal Cowboy – Alexis Morgan

In stores from 4th April 2014:

❑ Demon Heart – Doranna Durgin,
Jessa Slade, Vivi Anna, Zoey Williams
& Georgia Tribell

Available at WHSmith, Tesco, Asda, Eason, Amazon and Apple

Just can't wait?

Visit us Online You can buy our books online a month before they hit the shops! **www.millsandboon.co.uk**

0314/89

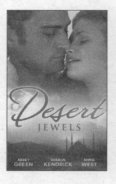
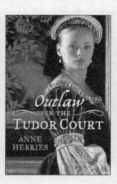
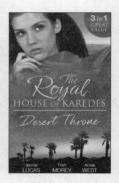

Join the Mills & Boon Book Club

Subscribe to **Nocturne**™ today for 3, 6 or 12 months and you could **save over £50!**

We'll also treat you to these fabulous extras:

- **FREE L'Occitane gift set worth £10**
- **FREE home delivery**
- **Rewards scheme, exclusive offers…and much more!**

Subscribe now and save over £50
www.millsandboon.co.uk/subscribeme

The World of Mills & Boon®

There's a Mills & Boon® series that's perfect for you. We publish ten series and, with new titles every month, you never have to wait long for your favourite to come along.

By Request

Relive the romance with the best of the best
12 stories every month

Cherish™

Experience the ultimate rush of falling in love
12 new stories every month

Desire™

Passionate and dramatic love stories
6 new stories every month

nocturne™

An exhilarating underworld of dark desires
Up to 3 new stories every month

Discover more romance at

www.millsandboon.co.uk

- ❤ WIN great prizes in our exclusive competitions
- ❤ BUY new titles before they hit the shops
- ❤ BROWSE new books and REVIEW your favourites
- ❤ SAVE on new books with the Mills & Boon® Bookclub™
- ❤ DISCOVER new authors

PLUS, to chat about your favourite reads, get the latest news and find special offers:

- 📘 Find us on facebook.com/millsandboon
- 🐦 Follow us on twitter.com/millsandboonuk
- ❤ Sign up to our newsletter at millsandboon.co.uk